ALLAN M. GRANDGENETT

Galilee Rising

Two Brothers, Two Ships, One Reckoning: A Military Sci-Fi Space Opera

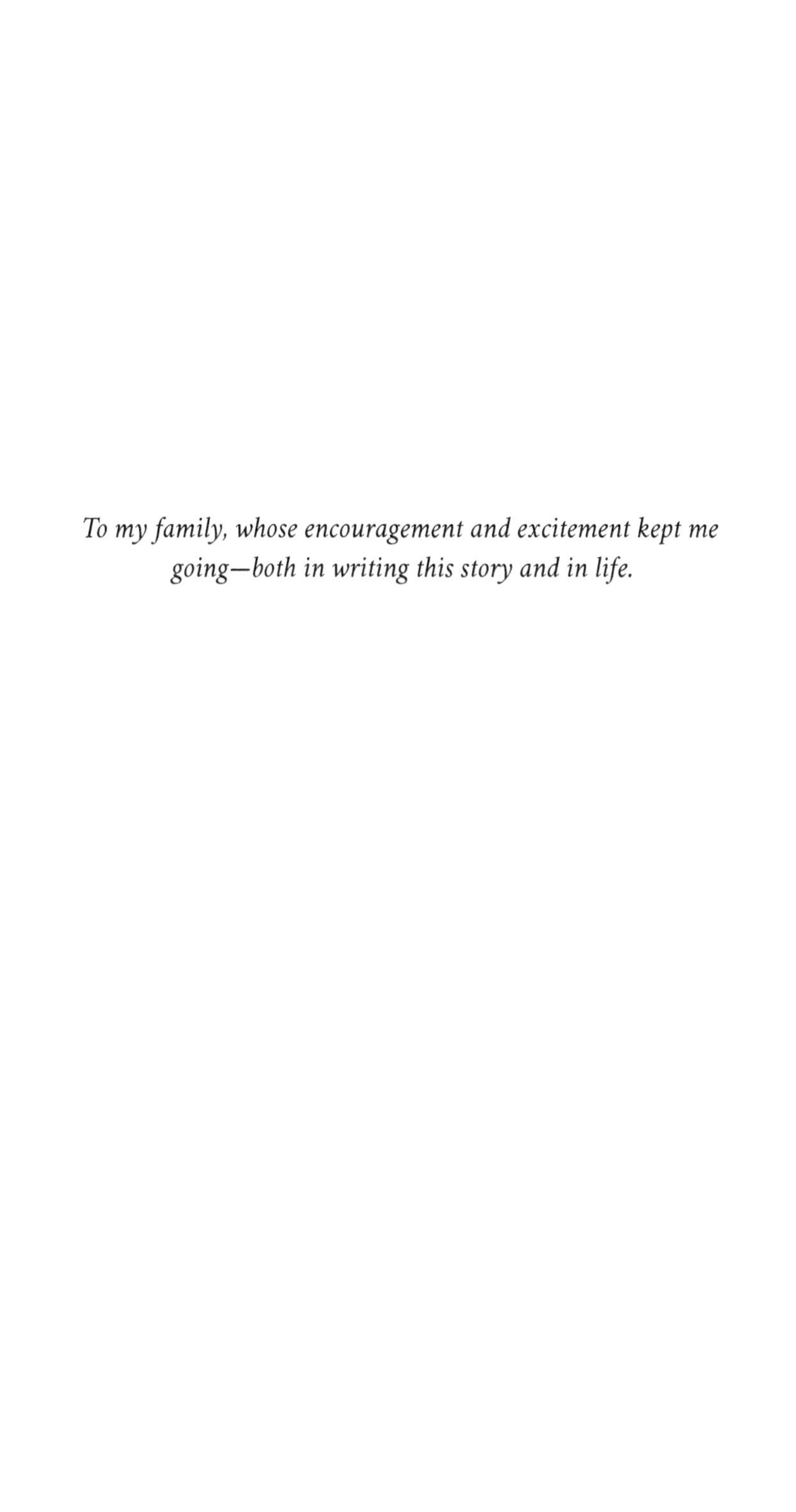

*To my family, whose encouragement and excitement kept me
going—both in writing this story and in life.*

Contents

Acknowledgments	iv
Chapter 1	1
Chapter 2	10
Chapter 3	15
Chapter 4	22
Chapter 5	26
Chapter 6	31
Chapter 7	35
Chapter 8	39
Chapter 9	44
Chapter 10	50
Chapter 11	56
Chapter 12	59
Chapter 13	64
Chapter 14	67
Chapter 15	74
Chapter 16	80
Chapter 17	90
Chapter 18	94
Chapter 19	103
Chapter 20	106
Chapter 21	112
Chapter 22	117
Chapter 23	125

Chapter 24 130
Chapter 25 140
Chapter 26 144
Chapter 27 148
Chapter 28 151
Chapter 29 155
Chapter 30 159
Chapter 31 164
Chapter 32 171
Chapter 33 179
Chapter 34 184
Chapter 35 187
Chapter 36 190
Chapter 37 195
Chapter 38 199
Chapter 39 202
Chapter 40 209
Chapter 41 213
Chapter 42 219
Chapter 43 221
Chapter 44 227
Chapter 45 233
Chapter 46 239
Chapter 47 248
Chapter 48 251
Chapter 49 255
Chapter 50 262
Chapter 51 272
Chapter 52 276
Chapter 53 279
Chapter 54 285

Chapter 55	288
Chapter 56	296
Chapter 57	315
Chapter 58	319
Chapter 59	321
Chapter 60	325
Chapter 61	330
Chapter 62	335
Chapter 63	339
Epilogue	343
A Note from the Author	346
Sneak Peek: Valley of Shadow	348
About the Author	372

Acknowledgments

I would like to extend a special thanks to Devin C., Jessica C., and Michael H. for their generous support, excellent feedback, and for seeing what I could not. Thanks to your encouragement and keen insights, this story has become a reflection of my true vision.

Chapter 1

The quiet hum of the Galilee was the sound of home. It was a deep, resonant thrum that vibrated through the metal deck plates and settled into the bones of every person aboard. For most, it was just background noise, but for the family that lived and worked within its quarter kilometer-long frame, it was the ship's voice—a constant, reassuring whisper that all was well.

On the bridge, the silence was occasionally broken by a soft chime or the click of a console button. The expansive forward viewscreen showed a starfield that seemed to drift by at a leisurely pace, a stark contrast to the faster-that-light speed the ship was actually traveling. In the command chair, Captain Isaac—a man whose salt-and-pepper hair and crinkled eyes spoke of both wisdom and a good sense of humor—reviewed a datapad. He wore the Galilee's gray coverall uniform and a small, content smile on his face as he watched his family at work.

Nearby, his wife, Rebecca, known to everyone as Becky, was a picture of calm focus. Her fingers danced across a holographic star chart, a constellation of data points and intersecting vectors glowing in the air before her. "A straight line is the most efficient path," she said, her tone a gentle counterpoint to the thrum of the ship. "But it's not always the safest. Sometimes you need to add a detour to avoid a certain type of celestial body, or, in this case, certain unsavory types of people. The trick is to find a route that's just as fast, but also safe."

Her son, Joshua, Josh for short, leaned in, his young face earnest and his brow furrowed in concentration. He was learning to read the cosmic map the way others read a book. He was tall for his age, with his father's broad shoulders and his mother's dark, focused eyes. In the same gray coveralls, he could be mistaken for his father at a distance. "Like taking a shortcut through the back alleys of some city," he said, and his mother smiled.

"Precisely," she replied, her eyes twinkling. "Never trust the straight path. It's often the one with the most trouble."

Down in the engineering section, the sound was different. Here, the hum was louder, a deeper growl of power conduits and drone generators. It smelled of ozone, hot metal, and something a little more earthy and comforting—maybe a faint, nostalgic hint of brewing coffee. Eli, the ship's grizzled engineer, was kneeling over a glowing power relay, a multi-tool in his hand. He was a man with more gray hair on his face than on his head and a perpetual frown that never quite reached his kind eyes.

"She's a stubborn auld lass, this one," Eli grumbled in a thick Irish accent. "Just needed a wee bit o' coaxin' t' get 'er back online."

The ship's chief of security, Judah, a lean man with a fastidious nature was standing nearby in his spotless and creased uniform, a confused expression on his face. "What was that, Eli? Something about power?"

Noah, Josh's twin brother, who was watching intently, his hands tucked behind his back, chimed in smoothly, "He said she just needed a bit of coaxing to get back online." He had his father's kind eyes and his mother's sharp intellect, but his passion was the machinery of the ship itself. He loved how the systems worked, how one thing connected to another to make the great vessel fly. "Is there a better way to fix it?" Noah asked, ever the inquisitive one.

Eli let out a short, rusty laugh. "A better way? Ah, now, there's always a better way, lad. But a good mechanic knows how to make do wi' what he's got, so he does. That's the difference between a textbook engineer an' a real one." He gave the conduit a final twist, and the hum deepened, a perfect, steady tone. He stood up and dusted off his grease-stained hands. "Now, how about we get that coffee goin' before that auld witch gives us any more trouble, eh?"

In the galley, a small but sturdy coffee maker gurgled and hissed, its scent a warm, welcoming presence that drifted through the utilitarian space. This wasn't a sterile commercial ship; it was a home. A collection of family photos was magnetized to the bulkhead above the mess table. One showed Isaac and Becky, younger and smiling in front of a half-built Galilee. This ship was their dream come true. Another photo showed the twin boys as toddlers, laughing as they "flew" a toy spaceship through the mess hall. These little touches were everywhere, personal islands in a sea of functional steel.

The crew, a tight-knit dozen, moved about their duties with a practiced ease, their conversations a mix of ship business and friendly banter. The ship's quartermaster, Simon, was checking off a manifest with the supply clerk, Tabitha. They were an extended family, bound by a shared life and a shared vessel. The Galilee, or "Gally" as the crew affectionately dubbed her, wasn't just a place they worked; it was a place they belonged. It was a fortress against the cold, indifferent expanse of space, and it was a home.

The mess hall was alive with the clatter of cutlery and the low murmur of conversation, a stark contrast to the vast, empty space outside. The air still held the lingering aroma of the night's meal, a rich stew served with crusty bread. In the galley, the cook, Lazarus, a short, round man with a seemingly perpetual tomato stain on his standard issued gray coveralls, whistled to himself as he worked his way through a pile of dirty dishes. He was a meticulous man who believed that good food and a clean kitchen were the keys to a happy crew. He listened with one ear to the card game taking place at the central table.

Isaac, Becky, Eli, Judah, and Simon were gathered around the table, a deck of cards spread out between them. But the game, a simple version of five-card draw, had long since lost its focus. The pile of credits in the center was small, and their minds were elsewhere, drifting to the dark space outside the ship's hull.

"It's just the fringes of the sector that get me," Judah said, picking up his cards but not looking at them. "The law just doesn't seem to reach out this far. We had a run-in with a couple of sector patrol ships two days ago, and they were more concerned with our cargo manifest than our safety."

"The patrols are stretched thin, Judah," Isaac replied. "They have to prioritize. And to be fair, we are a good distance from the main trade lanes. It's a risk we've always known was a part of this route. Higher risk, but higher reward."

Becky nodded, "The route is sound. We've accounted for every known asteroid field and gravity well. It's a long way from the core systems, but it's a path we've traveled before."

"Aye, but ye ken, Cap'n, that's not the worry of the crew," Eli grumbled, his Irish brogue thick with concern. He shuffled the cards in his hand, a frustrated look on his face. "It's the other ships, so it is. The ones what ain't on the maps."

A heavy silence fell over the table. The conversation had arrived at the unspoken fear that had been lingering in the back of everyone's mind. The danger of running cargo on the fringe wasn't just celestial or logistical; it was human.

"Pirates," Simon whispered. He laid his cards face down on the table. "We're a sitting duck out here. The Galilee is a freighter, not a gunship. She's too slow to run, and we've got nothing to fight with. What happens if they come for us?"

Isaac leaned forward, his hands clasped on the table. He was still calm, but a seriousness had entered his eyes. "A fair question, Simon. We have procedures. We're not helpless. We're trained in basic anti-piracy maneuvers from our days in the academy. We'll lock down all the access points and vent the atmosphere. If they board, we'll make Gally too inhospitable for them to stay"

"And if they blow a hole in the hull to get in?" Judah pressed, his tone skeptical.

"They'll risk damaging the loot they're trying to take," Becky interjected, "They want the haul intact. They're scavengers, not destroyers. They'll hail us first, attempt to take us peacefully. And our best defense is to be ready to comply. We give them what they want, and we walk away with our lives."

Lazarus, the cook, stopped scrubbing a pot and looked up

from the galley. He'd heard the whole conversation, and his usually cheerful demeanor had a hint of anxiety in it.

"Pirate attacks are rare," Isaac continued, his tone gaining a stronger, more reassuring note. "They're a high-risk, low-percentage gamble. The odds are always in our favor. The vast majority of our runs go off without a hitch."

"I just want this haul to be over, Captain," Simon said, voicing what was on everyone's mind. He stood up, running a hand through his hair. "I'm heading to my bunk."

The others followed suit, the card game forgotten. As they dispersed, the easy camaraderie was gone, replaced by a quiet, professional tension. Isaac and Becky lingered for a moment, their hands touching across the table. They exchanged a look, one that said they shared the crew's concerns but had to remain strong for them. The Galilee was quiet again, but the hum of the ship now felt a little less like the sound of home and a little more like the sound of a countdown.

The ship was silent now. The crew was in their bunks, and even the mess hall was quiet, the last traces of Lazarus's cooking long gone. In their shared quarters, the twin boys, Noah and Josh, lay in their bunks, staring at the ceiling. Sleep wasn't coming.

"My stomach's rattling the whole deck," Josh whispered, a hand pressed to his gut. "I think the stew's already gone and went."

Noah chuckled softly from his own bunk. "That's not your stomach, that's just Gally singing to you."

"Yeah, singing for a snack. Come on," Josh urged. "The galley's not far."

They slipped out of their room and into the ship's passageways. These were thick and utilitarian, with conduits and maintenance access panels running along the curved walls. They moved with a practiced ease, their bare feet silent on the metal deck, navigating the ship's internal map by instinct.

As they passed the security office, a light was still on. "Old Judah's probably still organizing his 'strategic defense plan,'" Noah whispered, mimicking the man's serious tone. "He's got more data about potential pirates than he has about our own crew."

"Well, that's because the crew doesn't need to be tracked," Josh said with a grin. "He's just being careful. Someone has to be. Unlike Lazarus, who I'm sure is still trying to figure out how to get the stew stains off his uniform. You think he even knows what a sponge is?"

"Only when he's trying to sop up the coffee he spilled," Noah retorted, and both boys had to stifle their laughter as they continued down the tube.

Their path took them through one of the large access hubs, a spherical junction point where several of the ship's internal tubes intersected. It was an enormous, echoing space that felt more like a grand cathedral than part of a spaceship. From here, they could look out through a transparent bulkhead and see the massive, trusswork lattice frame of the Galilee filled with thousands of neatly slotted cargo containers, their hulls reflecting the light from a distant star. It was a constant reminder of the ship's true purpose: a home for their family, but also a vessel of commerce.

They reached the galley, its automated lights clicking on softly as they entered. Josh went to the pantry and pulled out a loaf of bread and a jar of some kind of processed, shelf-stable meat spread. Noah, ever the pragmatist, found a carton of rehydrated cheese and a half-empty bag of chocolate wafers. They cobbled together a sandwich that would likely make their mother gag with its questionable mix of processed food and sugar, but to their nineteen your old palates, it was a masterpiece.

Sitting at the mess hall table, their snack forgotten for a moment, they fell into a more serious conversation.

"Dad says I can take the Conn on the next run." Josh said, his voice full of quiet pride. "The thought of a ship that big… being able to command it, to navigate the stars. It's an incredible feeling."

Noah took a thoughtful bite of his sandwich. "I don't know if I'd want to be a captain. All that paperwork. And the meetings. I like being with Eli, you know? He gets it. The ship… she talks to him. Tells him what she needs. I like being able to listen to her."

"You always did have a better ear for the noises," Josh replied, but the comment was affectionate, not sarcastic. "You hear the ship, and I listen to the stars. I guess we're a good team."

"Yeah," Noah said, a rare note of wistfulness. "A good team."

Their snack finished, they began the walk back to their quarters. As they passed Isaac and Becky's private cabin, they stopped. The door was sealed shut, but they could hear muffled voices from within. They couldn't make out the words, but the tone was unmistakable. It was low and serious, not the usual casual conversation of a married couple. There was a quiet desperation to it that sent a shiver down their spines.

Without a word, they exchanged a look—a look that said they had both heard it, too. They crept quietly back to their room, the joyful bravado of their midnight snack run now replaced by a quiet, shared sense of unease. The ship's hum, which had always been a lullaby, now sounded more like a warning.

Chapter 2

The rhythm of life aboard the Galilee was a familiar, comforting metronome. The days blended into one another, marked only by the turn of navigational watches and the cycle of work and rest. On the bridge, the quiet thrum of the great freighter was a deep, steady heartbeat. Captain Isaac watched as Becky worked with Josh, a small, contented smile on his face.

"The celestial bodies are all aligned for a clean burn," Navigator Becky said, a finger tracing a line on the star chart floating before her. "We'll be able to bypass the last of the asteroid clusters in this sector and shave half a day off our ETA."

Josh, his eyes scanning the data, nodded. "A straight line," he said, recalling her earlier lesson.

Becky's lips quirked into a small smile. "Not entirely. The path of least resistance is often the one that leads to the most trouble. We're on a slight curve that will keep us out of the main trade lanes and away from any unwanted attention."

Down in the engineering section, the air was warmer and the ship's sound was a more visceral growl. Noah and Eli were deep in the guts of the ship's power distribution systems. Eli's grimy multi-tool vibrated as he worked on a conduit.

"Ya see, lad," Eli's thick accent was an almost musical presence in the space, "she's like a woman, she is. A bit of a mystery, but once ye get to know her, she'll tell ye exactly what she needs."

Noah, his face and uniform streaked with grease, was running a diagnostic on a secondary power relay. "The Gally's running perfectly on the output, Eli. No anomalies."

"Aye," Eli grumbled, "but the best engineers don't wait for a problem. They listen for the whispers. The little things that tell ye somethin's not right before it's gone and put the whole ship in a bind."

A soft chime from a nearby console broke the silence. A proximity alert. A deep-space vessel had just entered the Galilee's sensor range. The Captain's voice, calm and professional, came over the internal comms. "Bridge to engineering, we have a contact. Just a routine check-in. Continue your work."

The small, red dot on the tactical map was a few hours away at their current speed. The ship was approaching from behind them and was closing at a slow, deliberate pace. It was a standard-class freighter, according to the automatic ID signal. Nothing unusual. Just another ship trying to make a living in the cold expanse.

"Looks like they're on a similar heading to ours," the Navigator noted, her hands moving over the console. "Could be a competitor, or just another freighter trying to get to the same port as us. Standard procedure is to ignore them."

But Isaac's brow was furrowed. He had a sixth sense about these things, a gut feeling that had kept him alive for decades. "The profile is a little off," he mused. "It's small for a long-haul freighter. And the power signature... It's reading a little hot.

Like the engine's been modified." He shook his head. "Could be a new model. Nothing to worry about. Just… keep an eye on her."

The minutes bled into hours. The strange ship held its course, slowly gaining on them. As it drew to within fifty kilometers, a prominent, distinctive flash of scarlet paint decorated its forward hull. Its power signature was now registering at a concerning level.

"Captain," Judah was firm on the comms, "the ID signal is still reporting a standard freighter, but that thing is built for speed. It's a bit of a wolf in sheep's clothing."

The moment the ship closed to within fifty kilometers, an unencrypted comm signal crackled to life on the bridge. The voice was smooth and polite. "This is the freighter *Babylon*. We've been tracking you for a while and just wanted to reach out. It's a big, lonely universe out here, and it's nice to meet other friendly traders. We'd be happy to trade a bit of cargo, or perhaps just sit down for a meal."

"This is the Galilee," the Captain replied calmly and even. "We're on a tight schedule. Thank you for the offer, but we'll have to decline."

A brief, tense pause. Then the voice returned, its tone shifting to one of urgency. "Captain, I'm sorry to trouble you, but we've had a system malfunction. Our life support is on the fritz, and we're not sure how much time we have. We just need a couple of engineers to take a look at our system and see if they can help us get back online."

Isaac's hand hovered over the comms button. His gut screamed at him that this was a lie, but his heart told him that a good man didn't leave a fellow traveler stranded in the void. He made a decision he knew he might regret.

"Captain," Judah's call came over the internal comm, a note of warning in it. "This is a trap. I don't like it."

Isaac looked at Becky, who had already pulled up a full sensor scan of the other ship. Its engines were quiet, but the power signature was still high. They were powered up and ready to go. Was the Babylon a freighter in distress; or was she predator lying in wait?

"I know," Isaac said softly to his wife. Then, "This is Captain Isaac of the Galilee. We will rendezvous with you. Stand by to dock."

He turned to Judah, his face grim. "Lock down all non-essential access points and prepare a secure boarding route. Take whatever measures you need to ensure the crew's safety. Just do not engage unless they do."

Judah nodded, his face a hard mask. He spoke a quick command into his comm unit. "All access ports to the engineering sections, supply bays, and crew quarters are sealed. Perimeter security is now active." He turned and left the bridge without another word. Simon, the Quartermaster, who was standing nearby, gave him a confused look. Judah ignored it and stepped into his office. Inside the small, tidy space, Judah unlocked a secure locker and pulled out a laser pistol, the only one on the ship. He strapped on a shoulder holster over his coveralls, secured the gun, then slipped on his duty jacket to conceal it.

Down in the engineering bay, the metal door sealed with a solid, final *hiss*. Noah watched the pressure gauge on the bulkhead door and the flashing red light. "We're sealed in, Eli. Judah must be on high alert."

"Aye, the poor soul," Eli muttered, more to himself than to the boy. "He's a good man, but a bit too jumpy for my taste."

He simply returned to his work, the low thrum of the ship now a little louder and a little more urgent.

On the bridge, the silence was tense and absolute. The crew focused on their readouts, their hands moving with the practiced efficiency of a routine docking, but their minds were screaming with unease. The two ships, now a mere few kilometers apart, fell into a perfect station-keeping formation, a silent, tense ballet. The Babylon was a black silhouette against the distant stars, its scarlet flash of paint exuded an aura of menace now . A small docking shuttle launched from its hull, a tiny insect moving across the vastness of space.

On the bridge, the crew watched in tense silence. There had been no visual communication, no faces on the screen—just the smooth, unsettling voice of the captain and the automated readouts of the shuttle's approach. Judah's hand twitched, ready to grab for the hidden grip of his weapon.

The shuttle, moving with a practiced grace, approached the starboard airlock, one of the "ears" on the Galilee's wedge-shaped command section. The robotic docking clamps extended, a silent hiss of hydraulics as they engaged. A small light turned from red to green on the viewscreen, confirming the link. The shuttle was now a part of their ship.

Captain Isaac held his breath, his eyes fixed on the display. He could feel the tension radiating off his crew. This was it. The moment of truth.

A final, soft hiss echoed throughout the bridge as the inner airlock door sealed. The sound was an eerie punctuation mark in the silence—the sound of a line crossed, of a home invaded.

Chapter 3

The docking clamps of the Babylon's shuttle engaged with a jarring thud, a sound that resonated through the Galilee's quarter-kilometer-long trusswork. On the starboard side of the wedge-shaped crew and command section, The Captain and the Navigator stood a few tense feet from the airlock, a pair of figures dwarfed by the massive framework of their ship. Their hands were clasped, their expressions a mixture of grim resolve and silent prayer. This wasn't the way it was supposed to go. They were supposed to be safe. They had always been safe.

A hiss of compressed air announced the shuttle's airlock opening. A tall, dark-haired man stepped onto the small gangway, a custom-tailored coat of rich, dark material hanging perfectly on his broad frame. Three hard-faced crewmen followed him. As he drew closer, the low light of the Galilee caught his face—a face that was both handsome and intimidating, framed by a well trimmed beard and a smirk that seemed to hold a world of secrets. This was not a man in need of rescue. This was Captain Cain.

"Captain Isaac, is it?" Cain spoke in a low, pleasant baritone, a cultured instrument that didn't match the predatory gleam in his eyes. "A pleasure to make your acquaintance. My apologies for the theatrics, but a man in my line of work can't be too careful." He gestured with a gloved hand. "My crew will see to the securing of the ship while we… discuss your manifest. The market for medical supplies is quite lucrative at the moment."

Cain gave a short nod, and his crewmen fanned out, their movements practiced, their weapons held at the ready. With Cain leading the way, they began the walk through the curving passageway that led from the airlock to the bridge, which sat at the front of the pod. Joshua, who had been ordered to remain on the bridge, watched the security feed, his heart a frantic drum against his ribs.

"A fine vessel you have here," Cain said. "The Galilee… a beautiful name. Biblical, is it not?" He didn't wait for an answer. "I find names are important. They say so much about a person's character, their hopes, their… faith." He paused, turning to face Isaac with an unnerving calm. "Tell me, Captain. Did your faith tell you I was a man in need of help?"

Isaac's gut twisted. "A man in trouble is a man in need of help, no matter the circumstances," he replied, firmly despite the tremble in his hands.

Cain simply chuckled. "A noble sentiment. Unfortunately, in this sector, nobility often leads to ruin."

Below decks, the low, steady thrum of the engine room had always been a source of comfort for Noah. It was a language he understood, a heartbeat he could feel in his bones. He and Eli were deep in the guts of the ship, in the maintenance tubes that ran the length of the trusswork, far from the crew section.

"Ah, the docking sequence is a bit rough, eh?" Eli's Irish

brogue a comforting presence in the metallic symphony of the engine room. "Bet yer old man didn't get a proper greeting. Still, a man's gotta help another in distress. Even if it feels a bit… off."

The words hung in the air for a moment, and then the muffled sounds of footsteps and voices echoed through the ship. The comms panel on the bulkhead chimed, and Judah's call, low and urgent, came through. "This is Judah to all crew. I've just activated the intercom for ship-wide announcements. Something is not right. Remain where you are and do not engage. Stay quiet." A second later, the intercom buzzed with the live feed from the bridge, picking up the pirates' conversation as they walked.

Back on the bridge, the air was thick with tension. Judah had appeared as if from nowhere, his face a mask of grim determination. He moved with a quiet efficiency that spoke of years of training and a deep-seated cynicism that Isaac had never fully appreciated.

"The manifest, if you please," Cain said, his tone still pleasant, but his patience wearing thin.

Isaac moved to the navigation console. "There seems to be an issue," he said, his hands moving slowly over the controls. "The encryption is… refusing to disengage."

Becky picked up the cue instantly. "It happens sometimes on these older systems. The software is a bit persnickety. It might take a moment to… reboot the subsystem."

Cain's smirk widened, a flicker of cold amusement in his eyes. He leaned against the console, his movements as fluid and graceful as a predator toying with its prey. "My dear woman," he said, his voice dropping. "I find it's best to be honest with me. It saves so much trouble." He nodded to one of his lieutenants, a hard-faced woman with a single braid that fell down her back.

The woman didn't hesitate. She stepped forward and backhanded Becky across the face. Becky reeled from the blow, her head snapping to the side, and her temple struck the hard edge of the console. She fell to the floor in a silent heap.

A searing rage ripped through Judah. He drew his hidden laser pistol with a speed that startled even Cain. A red flash of energy lanced across the bridge, striking the woman in the chest and sending her flying backward, a smoking hole in her uniform. At the same moment, two of the other pirates reacted, their shots hitting Judah in the chest and shoulder. He crumpled to the floor, his weapon clattering beside him.

Cain didn't even flinch. He tsk-tsked at the sight of the smoking body of his lieutenant and the bleeding Judah. "Such a terrible turn of events. So unnecessary," he said, his words calm, as if he were discussing the weather. "We simply can't let it happen again."

With that, he drew his own pistol. With the calm of swatting a fly, he raised his arm and shot Isaac between the eyes. Isaac fell backward, dead before he hit the deck.

The sound of the shot, a sharp, final crack, was a physical blow to Joshua. A scream of pure, raw grief and rage tore from his throat. He ran, bolting to Judah's body, his eyes fixed on the fallen pistol. He grabbed the weapon, his hand trembling as he pointed it at the nearest pirate. He fired blindly, the shot grazing the pirate's arm. The pirate yelped in surprise and pain, but his comrade was faster. A single, brutal punch connected with Joshua's jaw, and he was knocked out cold. The last thing he saw was Cain, standing over his father, the pistol still smoking in his hand.

Meanwhile, in the engineering bay, Eli and Noah had heard everything over the open intercom. The sounds of the fight, the sharp crack of the laser blasts, Becky's muffled cry, and Isaac's final, heart-wrenching thud as he hit the deck. The sound of Joshua's scream of pure, unadulterated pain was the most devastating sound of all.

Noah's legs gave out, and he slid to the floor, his knees hitting the cold metal with a clatter. His face, streaked with grease, was now a mask of silent, numb agony. He curled into a ball, his hands over his ears, as if he could un-hear the horrors that had just transpired. He didn't sob or scream. He simply became an unmoving, silent statue of despair. Eli knelt beside him, his large hand a reassuring weight on the boy's shoulder.

"They're taking the ship, lad," Eli murmured, a sob catching in his throat. "They're takin' our home. And… and they've got yer family."

Noah's heart felt as though it had shattered into a million pieces. The silence on the comms, the absence of his father's steady tone, his mother's calm instructions—it was all too much. He knew, with a terrible certainty that settled deep in his bones, that his parents and his brother were dead.

"We have to do something!" Noah whispered, a desperate plea, his words a faint, broken whisper.

"And we will," Eli said resolutely, his eyes blazing with a fierce, protective light. "But not yet. Right now, we wait. We wait and we listen. The Gally…she's still breathing. And so are we."

The silence that followed was broken only by the mournful

hiss of a pressure valve and the distant echo of shouting. The Galilee had fallen, but in the heart of its machine, two souls remained, waiting for the time they could begin to rebuild.

The world returned to Joshua in a fog of pain. His jaw ached, and a dull, throbbing headache made his vision swim. He was on the floor, his face pressed against the cold metal deck of the bridge. He heard the muffled sounds of his parents' bodies being moved, the rustle of fabric, and the creak of equipment. He was unable to get up or even move, but his hearing was hyper-attuned.

"We've secured as much valuable cargo as we can. There isn't much worth taking, Captain," a pirate said from nearby. "and we've rounded up the rest of the crew."

"Very well." Cain replied, his tone as pleasant as ever. "Bring them to the starboard airlock. We'll jettison them. It's a clean way to deal with things. No mess."

"What about the boy?" another pirate asked.

Cain was closer now. "He's a fool, but not without spirit," he said, the words meant more for himself than for his crew. "There's fire in him. Bring him to the shuttle. He'll make an interesting project."

A new pain, sharper and more potent than the one in his jaw, pierced Joshua's heart. He lay there, helpless and broken, listening to the muffled sounds of his crew being herded into the airlock on the opposite side of the ship. He heard the hiss of the outer airlock door opening, a sound that meant only one thing: the crew was being jettisoned into the cold, unforgiving vacuum of space. He heard his mother's body being moved again, and a voice muttering, "She hit her head on the console. Nasty cut." The words were a final, brutal blow, confirming his worst fears about her fate. The silence that followed was absolute, a void filled with the echoes of his lost family and crew. He was the only one left. He was alone.

The pirates returned to the bridge to collect Joshua. They lifted him from the floor and dragged his unresisting body from the bridge, a silent witness to the murder of his family. As they dragged him away, a final line from Cain, devoid of any sympathy, echoed through the abandoned bridge. "A pity. I had hoped for more."

Chapter 4

The air was thick with a silence that felt heavier than any gravity. For days, Noah and Eli had stayed in the cramped, dark confines of the maintenance tubes, a tomb within a tomb. Now, they emerged, blinking in the dim, emergency-lit corridors of the Galilee. The pirates had reeked havoc on the ship, tearing her apart searching for booty. It was a violation. The ship's familiar hum, the low thrum of a sleeping giant, was gone, replaced by an oppressive quiet. Their footsteps echoed unnervingly on the deck plates as they moved through the heart of what was once their home.

Noah walked like a ghost, his shoulders hunched, his eyes fixed on the floor. He didn't speak or look at Eli; he just followed. Every shadow seemed to hold a memory—his father laughing on the bridge, his mother's calm voice giving commands, Josh's easy grin as he studied the nav charts. The ship was empty, but it was crowded with ghosts. Eli moved with purpose, his face a mask of grizzled determination. He was the anchor, and Noah was the drifting boat.

They eventually made their way to the galley, and the simple act of turning on the lights felt like an act of defiance. Eli rummaged through the cabinets until he found what he was looking for: a small, dented bag of coffee. He measured out the grounds, the familiar, rich scent filling the cold air. The coffee machine hissed and sputtered to life, a small, stubborn sound in the ship's vast emptiness. Eli poured two mugs, placing one in Noah's hands. Noah stared into the dark liquid, his reflection staring back at him like a stranger.

"Alright, lad," Eli's Irish accent was a rough comfort. "We've got to fix her."

Noah just shook his head, unable to form words.

"We can't just sit here," Eli continued low and steady. "Your Da' would have wanted us to finish the job. We've still got some cargo." He took a sip of his coffee, his eyes never leaving Noah's. "We'll get ol' Gally back to port. That's it. One job, then we'll see what's what."

A flicker of something—not hope, but focus—entered Noah's eyes. A single, manageable task. He nodded slowly, and for the first time in days, he felt a pull other than his grief.

Their first meal together was a grim affair. Eli managed to find a canister of nutrient paste, which they ate in silence. Cooking felt like a sacrilege, a reminder of the family dinners they would never have again. Eli cooked for both of them from then on, a quiet, simple kindness that spoke volumes. The scent of whatever simple food Eli could prepare slowly began to replace the metallic tang of dried blood and dust.

The work was slow and meticulous. Over the next month, they worked on the Galilee, a day-by-day effort to bring her back from the dead. Eli's thick fingers and Noah's nimble ones worked together without a word. They started in the engine room, and it was here that they found the first signs of professional sabotage. Wires weren't just cut; they were cleanly snipped with a high-grade laser cutter. Fuel lines had been carefully depressurized and drained. It was clear the pirates wanted to make sure she was dead in the water.

"See that, lad?" Eli pointed to a charred junction box. "They didn't just smash it. They bypassed the safety, then overloaded the circuit. That's not random destruction; that's someone who knows what they're doing. They wanted us stranded. Maybe to collect us later, or just to prove a point."

Noah's face tightened. The calculated malice behind the act was somehow worse than mindless violence.

As they worked, Eli began to teach Noah. "This is a quark capacitor. Don't go messin' with it unless you've got a death wish. But this here, this is the main power bus. Easy enough to get a current flowin' again." He'd explain the inner workings of the ship, pointing out subtle design flaws and clever fixes he'd made over the years. Noah listened, his mind, once consumed by images of the massacre, now filled with schematics and repair manuals. The ship was no longer a tomb but a puzzle to be solved.

The work wasn't easy. There were days when a system they'd repaired would fail again, sending them into a frustrated despair. There were nights when Noah would wake up from a nightmare, and Eli would be there with a calming word. Slowly, the grief that had consumed Noah was replaced by a new, focused energy. With every weld, every repaired circuit, and every system that came back online, they weren't just fixing the Galilee; they were fixing themselves.

The final repair was the primary navigation console. They had repaired the comms array and patched a small hull breach in the cargo bay. Now they just needed to get the nav system back online. The two of them worked late into the night, their gray coveralls stained, torn and threadbare. The clank of wrenches against metal echoed through the ship. The welding torch flared to life in the darkened corridors. The rhythmic thrum of air compressors filled the air. Finally, after a month of back-breaking labor, Eli flipped the final switch. The red glow of the main console flickered to life, and as it stabilized, the ship's familiar hum returned, a sound of stubborn, unbreakable will. Gally was alive again.

Chapter 5

The transition from the bridge of the Galilee to the cold, grating floor of the pirate shuttle was a blur of pain and terror. He wasn't fully conscious, but the images were seared into his mind: his father's look of shock just as Cain fired, the muzzle flash of the laser pistol, the sudden, impossible stillness of his mother's body as it crumpled to the deck. He remembered the crimson stain spreading on the white plating, the way his brother's name had died on his lips, swallowed by the rising tide of unconsciousness. Now, the sounds were different: the low, guttural thrum of a larger engine, the chatter of rough voices, the clang of metal against metal. He lay on his side, the air thick with a greasy, unfamiliar smell. He knew, with a certainty that chilled him to the bone, that the silent shapes he had seen on the deck were gone forever. He was a prisoner, a survivor adrift in a sea of his own loss.

His body ached with a dull, persistent throb, a stark contrast to the sharp stabs of grief that still pierced through the haze. Eventually, rough hands hauled him to his feet. The world swam for a moment before settling into a grim reality. He was in a cavernous hold, filled with a mishmash of stolen cargo and surly-looking individuals who eyed him with undisguised contempt.

His days bled into a monotonous cycle of hard labor. He hauled crates heavier than he was, scrubbed grime from decks that never seemed to get clean, and ran errands for pirates who barked orders and shoved him aside like he was less than nothing. The Babylon was a chaotic, brutal place. Its interior was a patchwork of bolted-on additions and jury-rigged repairs, a stark contrast to the Galilee's clean, familiar lines. The air was thick with the smells of stale rations, unwashed bodies, and the ever-present metallic tang of the ship's aged systems. It felt ancient and predatory.

The crew saw him a weakling who had been foolish enough to resist. They hazed him constantly, petty acts of cruelty that chipped away at his physical comfort but did little to touch the core of his simmering rage. Food was often just out of reach, tools went missing when he needed them most, and laughter followed him like a shadow after every stumble.

Leading the charge in his torment was Baruch. The pirate he'd managed to wound on the Galilee seemed to relish Josh's suffering. Baruch was a hulking brute, his shaved head a landscape of crude tattoos that seemed to writhe with his movements. A thick metal ring pierced one earlobe, and a jagged scar bisected the milky white of his blind eye. His powerful build spoke of a life lived through violence, and his every glare held a simmering resentment. He would "accidentally" step on Josh's hands as they worked, his heavy boots grinding down with deliberate force. He'd snatch Josh's meager rations, his one good eye glinting with malicious pleasure as he devoured them. Once, he'd cornered Josh in a narrow passageway and shoved him hard against the cold metal wall, the impact stealing his breath. Baruch had leaned in close, the stench of stale breath and something fouler filling Josh's nostrils. "I still have the scar you left on my arm, whelp," he growled, his threat a low rumble. "You'll pay for that, piece by miserable piece."

Captain Cain was a phantom presence during these moments. Josh would sometimes catch a glimpse of him observing from a shadowy corner or a raised platform, his expression unreadable. Cain never intervened, allowing the pecking order of his crew to play out. Josh understood. He was nothing here, a piece of salvage taken from a wreck. He would have to earn his place, or perhaps, simply endure until an opportunity arose.

One particularly grueling shift involved unloading heavy plasma coils. Baruch was "supervising," his one good eye fixed on Josh with a cruel smirk. As Josh struggled with an especially cumbersome coil, his muscles screaming in protest, Baruch deliberately kicked a support strut out of place. The coil shifted, its weight slamming against Josh's leg, sending a jolt of white-hot pain through him. He cried out, stumbling, and the heavy object crashed to the deck with a deafening thud.

"Clumsy fool!" Baruch's roar echoing through the hold. Other pirates turned to stare, snickering at Josh's misfortune. Baruch swaggered closer, jabbing a thick finger into Josh's chest. "You're nothing but a liability."

The humiliation stung more than the physical pain. A red haze began to creep into Josh's vision. He was tired of the pain, tired of the fear, tired of being treated like vermin. As Baruch turned away, basking in the amusement of the other pirates, something snapped within Josh. An idea, sharp and cold, took root in his mind.

Later that cycle, during the ship's clumsy attempt at meal distribution – a lumpy, nutrient-paste served in dented metal bowls – Josh put his plan into action. He'd noticed earlier that Baruch always added an extra jolt of industrial-grade lubricant to his bowl, a disgusting habit that the other pirates tolerated with grim amusement. While Baruch was distracted, boasting loudly about Josh's earlier mishap, Josh swiftly swapped the lubricant dispenser with a near-identical container of industrial-strength bonding agent he'd "borrowed" from a nearby maintenance station.

The moment Baruch squeezed a generous portion of the thick, viscous fluid into his nutrient paste, a hush fell over the small gathering of pirates. They knew what was happening even before Baruch took a large, unsuspecting mouthful. A look of confusion flickered across Baruch's face as the sticky substance coated his tongue and palate. He tried to spit it out, but the bonding agent was already at work, gluing his mouth firmly shut.

A wave of laughter erupted from the watching pirates. Baruch, his face contorted in a silent roar of outrage and panic, flailed his arms wildly. He pointed a shaking finger at Josh, his one good eye blazing with fury and mortification. The sight of the hulking brute rendered speechless and utterly ridiculous was too much for the crew, and the laughter intensified.

Blind with rage, Baruch lunged at Josh, his large hands reaching out to crush him. Just as Baruch's fist was about to connect, a command cut through the chaos, sharp and commanding.

"Enough!"

Captain Cain stepped out of the shadows, his presence

instantly silencing the raucous laughter. His gaze, cold and assessing, swept over the scene. He looked from the sputtering, wide-eyed Baruch to the small, defiant figure of Josh, his face bruised but his eyes holding a flicker of grim satisfaction.

"Baruch," Cain said with a threat in his eyes. "Your lack of control is…disappointing." He then turned to Josh. "And you, boy. Your ingenuity is noted. But insubordination will not be tolerated."

Without another word, Cain gestured to two hulking pirates. "Discipline them both. Baruch, twenty cycles in the isolation chamber. The boy… fifteen."

The pirates roughly seized both Josh and Baruch. Baruch struggled, a muffled scream of protest escaping his glued lips, but he was easily subdued. Josh offered no resistance. He was dragged to a dimly lit section of the hold. He was strapped to a cold metal frame, and he braced himself for the pain. It came in waves, a searing, all-encompassing agony that left him gasping for breath. He clenched his jaw, refusing to cry out, focusing on the image of Baruch's humiliated face.

When it was over, the restraints were released, and Josh's legs buckled beneath him. He collapsed onto the hard deck, every nerve in his body screaming. He lay there for a long moment, the rough metal cold against his burning skin, his breath coming in ragged gasps. Dimly, he felt strong arms lift him. The world swam in and out of focus. He was being carried somewhere, the rhythmic jostling a dull counterpoint to the throbbing pain. The last thing he saw before darkness claimed him was the sterile white of what he vaguely recognized as a medical suite. Then, blessed oblivion.

Chapter 6

The Galilee's bridge was a ghost ship of memories. The control consoles, with their silent, blinking lights, felt alien to Noah and Eli. Every inch of the deck was a painful reminder of what they had lost. The silence of the command pod was broken only by the breeze of the life support systems and their nervous breathing.

"Well," Eli said. "At least we've got power. Now we just need to get the old girl movin'." He clapped Noah on the shoulder, a familiar gesture that felt awkward in this somber space. "I suppose you were payin' attention during your navigation lessons with your ma?"

Noah gave a small, humorless smile and nodded. Between the two of them, Josh had been taken to navigation as if it were second nature, but Noah had enough lessons to get the fundamentals down. His gaze fixed on the main console. He moved forward, his fingers hovering over the controls. The memories came in a crushing wave, the sight of his father, Isaac, at the captain's chair; his mother, Becky, leaning over the navigation board, her face illuminated by its glow. The fear and rage from the day of the attack came flooding back, and he froze, his hand shaking.

Eli saw it. He gently put a hand on Noah's shoulder and

guided him to a chair, pushing him down. "We're not here to remember the bad, lad," he said, his thick Irish accent softening. "We're here to make somethin' good again. This is how we honor them. We get this ship movin', and we finish their work."

Nodding, Noah took a shaky breath. "The flight manual," he rasped, the words catching in his throat. He pulled a thick digital handbook up on a screen. Together, they fumbled through the intricate procedures. They were engineers, not bridge crew, and the process was a clumsy dance of trial and error. They read the pre-flight checklist aloud, their voices alternating between frustration and relief. "Main thruster ignition sequence… check." "Auxiliary power… check." Eli's grumbled translations of the technical jargon brought a moment of levity to the grim task.

It took them two long, excruciating weeks, but they did it. With a final, triumphant click, the main engines roared to life. The familiar, deep-seated vibrations coursed through the ship and into their bones. A smile, real and unburdened, broke across Noah's face. He looked at Eli, who was beaming with pride. They were on their way.

For three peaceful days, the Galilee glided through the blackness of space. The ship had settled back into its familiar rhythm, and so had they. In the small, galley mess, Eli poured two steaming mugs of coffee. The rich aroma filled the air, a scent of home and comfort that Noah hadn't realized he'd been missing. They sat at a small table, the same one where they used to have family dinners.

"To us, and to Gally," Eli said, raising his mug. "May she always fly true."

"To Gally," Noah echoed.

They sipped their coffee in a silence that was no longer heavy with grief but filled with a quiet sense of accomplishment. They had faced the unimaginable and emerged victorious. It was a small, rebellious celebration, a defiant act of normalcy. For a few brief moments, the trauma faded, and they were just two men, a surrogate father and son, on a long journey, enjoying a well-earned rest.

Their relief was short-lived. A series of klaxons shrieked, and a cascade of red alerts flashed across every console. The deep hum of the main drive vanished, replaced by a jarring, ominous silence. The Galilee didn't stop, of course. In the vacuum of space, it simply ceased to accelerate, continuing its trajectory as a dead hulk, subject to the subtle gravity wells and solar winds that could send them off-course into a perilous part of the sector.

They raced back to the bridge. Arriving at the engineering systems console, Eli's hands flew over the controls, but the problem wasn't electrical. The sabotage, so cleverly hidden, had finally reared its head. He pulled up a schematic of the main drive and stared at a cascade of diagnostic readouts, his face contorting in confusion and then a slow, burning rage. "The blaggards," he muttered. "The sneakin' wee buggers!" His bark rose with each word, until he was shouting. "They didn't just want to kill us! They wanted to leave us floatin'! A derelict! A monument to their evil! For the love of Moses, I'll go mad from it!"

His rage was a tidal wave. He began pacing, kicking at a loose panel. "I worked my fingers to the bone, I did! I was happier than a pig in muck puttin' her back together! Now look at her! It's a grand misfortune, a right savage turn of events!" He grabbed a torque wrench and flung it against a bulkhead. "Weeks! Weeks of work! All for nottin'!"

Noah, who had never seen the old engineer so unhinged, watched in stunned silence. Eli's rage, so sudden and complete, was an almost comical display. He was a small, angry tornado of frustration. And then, a sound escaped Noah's throat. A single, choked-off laugh. It quickly built into a full-body, uncontrollable fit of giggles. The more Eli raged, the more Noah laughed, the sheer absurdity of the moment breaking through weeks of bottled-up grief.

Eli froze mid-rant, utterly bewildered. The sight of the stoic, serious boy laughing was a shock to his system. A slow grin spread across his face, and he, too, broke into a loud, booming laugh. The two of them stood on the silent bridge, two survivors in a broken ship, laughing until tears streamed down their faces.

When their laughter finally died down, a heavy, comfortable silence fell between them. Noah, still wiping his eyes, looked at Eli with a newfound maturity. "Don't worry, Eli," he said resolutely. "We've fixed Gally once. We can fix her again."

Eli's face crumpled. He rushed forward, pulled Noah into a tight, brief hug, and then just as quickly let go. He ruffled Noah's hair, a familiar gesture that, in this moment, held a world of emotion. He turned back to the control panel, a single tear tracing a path down his grizzled cheek. "Aye," he said, his voice thick with emotion, "we will indeed, lad. We will indeed."

Chapter 7

The first thing Josh registered was the absence of pain. The searing ache that had consumed him after being strapped to the cold metal frame was gone, replaced by a dull, throbbing awareness. He opened his eyes to a world of sterile white and a low, rhythmic drone. He lay in a medical bay, a small, clean space filled with the scent of antiseptic and something faintly metallic. A tall, thin man with wire-rimmed spectacles and a severe crew cut bent over a console. He looked up, his face breaking into a weary smile.

"Ah, you are avake," the man said, his lilt carrying a soft, melodic accent that Josh couldn't quite place. "Good. You gave us a little fright, you did." He gestured to a readout on the screen. "Your vitalz are solid now. Only exhaustion und a little shock, really. I am Doctor Samuel." He made a quick adjustment to a monitor, his back to Josh, his tone shifting to one of clinical detachment. "Now you rest. Your body must recover."

Dr. Samuel was the one spot of quiet kindness Josh had found aboard the Babylon. He was efficient and professional, but beneath his detached demeanor, Josh could sense a genuine concern. Dr. Samuel tended to him with a gentle hand, bringing him warm broths, a thick, earthy brew that tasted of comfort and home. As Josh's body slowly mended, he watched the doctor. He noticed the weary lines around his eyes, the subtle tremor in his hands, and the way he seemed to flinch when the ship's comms crackled with a new order. He seemed like a man running from something, a man who had seen too much.

A day later, the doors to the medical bay hissed open, and Captain Cain stepped inside. Josh quickly squeezed his eyes shut and held his breath, feigning sleep. The tension in the room was palpable.

"How is he, Doctor?" Cain's timbre was low and calm, but it held an edge that made the hairs on Josh's arms stand up.

"Healing, Captain," Samuel replied. "It vas a most severe punishment, but he is young, with much strength."

Cain nodded slowly. "He is. He has a spark," Cain said, "A rebellious one, but a spark nonetheless. I've found that those who bend but do not break are the most useful. He will need to be stronger. Both his will and his body."

Josh's mind raced with a mixture of fury and confusion. He wanted to leap from the bed and scream at Cain, to demand why he had killed his parents, why he had taken him. But he also wondered why this man, a ruthless pirate captain, was showing any concern at all. He felt a twisted sense of obligation for the "lesser" punishment, even as his hatred for the man solidified.

Cain gestured to a datapad on the doctor's desk. "I've put a rush on the new med supplies. I want them delivered to the Dead Sea along with the next resupply run. The boys are restless, and I want everything we need for our next endeavor."

"Understood, Captain," Samuel said, his voice flat.

When Cain finally left, the silence in the room was deafening. Josh's mind was reeling. A new destination, the Dead Sea, and some new mission? He now knew a small piece of Cain's plan, a piece of information he could hold onto.

After two days of rest, Josh was released back to work. The change in his circumstances was subtle but undeniable. He was no longer assigned to the lowest, most grueling tasks. Instead, he was working alongside other pirates, moving crates in the vast cargo holds. The hazing was gone. He still received hateful glares, particularly from Baruch, who now avoided him, but the crew's contempt had been replaced by a grudging respect. They no longer saw him as a helpless whelp, but as someone who had stood up to Baruch and survived the captain's fury. His food was also better. The lumpy paste was still there, but now his portions were bigger, and a piece of nutrient-rich protein or a small, sweet fruit was occasionally included.

Josh felt a cold knot of resolve tighten in his gut. This was Cain's way of rewarding him. He was no longer just a slave; he was an asset, a pet to be groomed and used. He accepted the small mercies with a grim determination, knowing they were not a sign of kindness, but a means to an end.

Later that day, while moving a heavy crate of circuit boards, his foot slipped on a greasy patch of deck plating. The crate tilted, its flimsy lock giving way. The crate slammed to the deck, spilling its contents in a cascade of shattered electronics. A nearby pirate scoffed, but he didn't move to help.

Josh's heart sank. He had worked so hard to prove himself, and now this. As he was trying to clean up the mess, a comms officer approached him.

"You've been summoned to the Captain's cabin, boy," he said with a smirk. "And don't be late."

Josh felt a knot of dread twist in his stomach. He was sure it was for the broken crate, and the last punishment had nearly killed him. He walked the long, winding corridors to Cain's cabin, a cold sense of foreboding settling over him. He was a prisoner again, about to face the man who had stolen everything from him. What could Cain possibly want?

Chapter 8

The smell of ozone hung in the air of the small staging room as Noah wrestled with the bulky life-support pack of his spacesuit. It was an unfamiliar weight on his shoulders, an awkward shell that felt more like a cage than a protector.

"Right then, lad," Eli said, as he checked a seal on his own suit. "First things first. You can always come back in if you've a mind to. I won't judge a soul for that." He looked at Noah, his gaze soft but firm. "This is nothing to be taken lightly. It's a grand misfortune if a thing goes wrong out there."

Noah nodded, swallowing the lump in his throat. Eli moved over to him, expertly checking the pressure seals on his gauntlets and helmet. He tapped the comms unit on the side of Noah's helmet. "Can you hear me now?"

"Loud and clear," Noah replied, his side-tone tinny in his own ears.

"Good. Don't be making any big moves, don't be touching a thing you don't know, and don't let go of your tools. Got it?" Eli grinned. "It's a lonely place out there. Gravity is the only thing keeping your feet on the ground. Out there, your tether's your mother."

With the final checks complete, they made their way down a short passage to the airlock. They cycled through, stepping out into the tractor tug bay on the Galilee's "chin." The bay was a cavernous space, a workshop open to the stars, but for now, it was sealed off from the vacuum by two massive, closed "garage" doors. The tug itself was squat and functional, with manipulator arms and a cargo bed piled high with tools and parts.

They strapped themselves into the tug's pilot seats, the harnesses clicking into place. Noah's heart hammered against his ribs.

"Ready, Captain?" Eli asked with a mischievous look.

"Ready, Eli."

Eli tapped a button on the console. A deep, grinding sound resonated through the deck as one of the two garage doors began to split apart, its immense panels retracting into the hull. The barrier between them and the universe dissolved, and the vast, coldness of space rushed in. The breathtaking, silent view of a million stars was both terrifying and beautiful.

Noah powered up the tug, and with a soft whine, they detached from the ship. He piloted them away from the command pod, the massive, 250 meter long trusswork of the Galilee stretching out before them, a geometric silhouette against the distant stars.

The journey was slow and deliberate. As they traveled toward the engineering section at the aft of the ship, the sheer scale of the Galilee became awe-inspiring. They navigated the gridwork, following a thicker maintenance conduit that served as their guide. When they finally reached their destination, the tug's headlights illuminated the aft of the engineering cube. The drive's massive nozzle was a dark, silent pit of failure.

Eli tethered them to a maintenance rail, and they went to

work. The problem was a damaged power regulator in the main drive's fusion manifold. The repair was intricate and demanded extreme care. The first moment of drama came when Noah was trying to attach a diagnostic sensor. The tiny, specialized tool slipped from his clumsy, gloved fingers. It spun end over end, a tiny glint of light against the infinite black.

"My tool!" Noah yelled, his heart in his throat.

"Stay put!" Eli commanded, with urgency. He fired a small burst from his suit's micro-thrusters, propelling himself toward the spinning object. He snagged it with a gloved hand a moment before it could drift past the point of no return. "Rule number one, lad," Eli said, as he floated back, "hold on to your bloody tools." The close call left Noah's heart pounding.

They resumed their work, painstakingly following Eli's verbal checklist. Step 1: Disconnect the primary power conduits. Step 2: Vent the residual plasma from the manifold. Step 3: Use the orbital welder to seal the regulator. The work was slow, methodical, and tense.

Just as they were finishing the welding, a proximity alarm blared on their comms. "What in the blazes?" Eli muttered. Suddenly, a massive automated cargo arm on a nearby strut activated, its immense claws moving with a low, hydraulic groan toward their location. It was part of the ship's automatic cargo loading system, coming to secure a container that had been left in a non-standard position before the attack.

"Get out of the way, now!" Eli bellowed.

Noah's panicked instincts kicked in. He pushed off the hull with all his might until his tether snatched him to a halt. The cargo arm swiped past him, its massive claws missing him by mere centimeters. The proximity alert went silent as the arm's claw clamped down on the container, which then shuddered slightly as it locked into place.

Shaken but unharmed, Noah pulled himself back in and they finished the last steps of the repair. Step 4: Re-connect the primary power conduits. Step 5: Perform a systems integrity check. The final checklist item was complete. After an anxious moment of waiting, a single green light on the fusion manifold glowed to life. The repair was a success.

They quickly packed their tools and supplies back onto the tug. Eli sealed the cargo bed, and they set a course for the docking bay. The return trip felt faster, filled with a new energy. Back in the safety of the bay, Noah expertly piloted the tug into its berth. They detached, the harnesses unbuckling with a soft click, and headed for the airlock. Once inside the staging room, they carefully helped each other out of their bulky suits, folding the material and storing their equipment with a renewed sense of purpose.

With their gear stowed, they walked to the bridge. The air was thick with a nervous tension that transcended the silence. The moment of truth had arrived. Noah's hand rested over the main drive activation control, his heart pounding a rhythm against his ribs. He felt the weight of everything—the weeks of agonizing work, the memory of his parents, the vast, cold space outside the viewport. He took a breath and slammed his hand down on the activation.

The familiar, deep hum filled the ship, stronger and more reassuring than ever. The navigation screen confirmed it— they were accelerating again, on their proper course.

Noah leaned back, a slow smirk spreading across his face. He put his feet up on the console, a gesture he had seen his father do a thousand times. The view out the bridge windows was a tapestry of stars, and he felt a quiet sense of ownership and pride.

Behind him, Eli stood with his arms crossed over his chest, a mirror of Noah's satisfied expression. He wasn't watching the stars. He was watching the boy who was becoming a captain, and a proud smirk of his own was fixed firmly on his face.

Chapter 9

The journey to Cain's cabin felt far longer than the winding corridors actually were. Each step was a beat of a drum against Josh's ribs. He stopped before the polished steel door and took a ragged breath. The last time he had faced Cain, he had nearly died. This time, he walked toward a fate he couldn't predict, but he was certain it would be just as painful. The door hissed open, and he stepped inside.

The room was not what he expected. It was a captain's cabin, yes, but it was nothing like his father's. There were no family photos or comforting personal items. The walls were lined with large, tactical charts of star sectors and ship-to-ship engagement plans. A massive, mahogany desk dominated the space, a single datapad resting at its center. The air was clean, faintly smelling of polished metal and something herbal that reminded him of home.

Captain Cain sat behind the desk, a figure of calm authority. He wore a crisp, dark tunic with a high collar, his hands clasped before him. The only hint of the man's brutality was the long, wicked-looking pistol resting on the desk, a silent, deadly promise.

Cain didn't look up from the datapad. "Close the door, Mr.

Joshua," he said, his tone proper and professional.

Josh did as he was told, the hiss of the door sealing behind him sounding like a final exhalation. He stood before the desk, his hands hanging at his sides.

Finally, Cain looked up. His eyes, the color of a stormy sea, were sharp and assessing. He looked at Josh for a long moment, not with malice, but with a detached curiosity that was far more unsettling.

"Do you know why I have summoned you, Mr. Joshua?" Cain asked.

Josh's heart hammered against his ribs. He thought of the cracked crate of circuit boards, the cascade of shattered electronics. "Captain, sir," he stammered, "I believe it is about the crate. I… I slipped. It was an accident. I will work to pay for the damages."

A ghost of a smile touched Cain's lips. "The crate?" he said, a low chuckle in his chest. "Do you think I concern myself with such trivial matters? With a few broken toys?"

Josh's mind went blank. If it wasn't the crate, what was it? He wracked his brain, but came up with nothing. He stood silent.

Cain leaned back in his chair, the leather creaking softly. He reached for a small kettle on a warming plate beside his desk. A plume of steam rose from its spout as he poured hot water over a filter in a mug. The scent of green tea, a scent Josh had always hated, filled the room. Cain did not offer him a cup.

"Most people," Cain said, his tone conversational, as if he were discussing the weather, "are predictable. They are driven by hunger, greed, or fear. They run. They break. But you… you are different. When we boarded the Galilee, I saw it."

Josh's body went rigid. The word was a punch to the gut. The memories came flooding back: the smoke, the sounds of fighting, the sight of his father falling, the frantic moment of grabbing the pistol Judah had dropped as he was gunned down defending his mother. He eyed the pistol on Cain's desk.

"You picked up a fallen man's weapon after I had just killed your father. You even wounded one of my men, Baruch, I believe. A rather impressive feat, considering the circumstances." Cain said, now sipping his tea.

Josh's breath hitched. In the chaos and grief, he had tried to bury the memory of that moment. He stared at the Captain, a cold fury rising inside him, eclipsing his fear. Josh couldn't hold back. He spat the words out, his fists clenched with a rage that had been building for weeks. "You killed my family! I wanted to kill you! I wanted to kill you all!"

He stood there, panting, his jaw clenched, waiting for the killing shot. He was certain this was it. The same gun, the same villain that killed his father would kill him too. He had sealed his fate with his own words. But Cain didn't move. He simply stared at Joshua, a slow, predatory smile spreading across his face. He looked… pleased.

"Honesty," Cain said, purred. "A rare and valuable commodity. And courage. A boy with a spark of fire." He took another sip of his tea, his gaze never leaving Joshua. The unspoken question hung in the air: Do you still?

"Why were you on that bridge in the first place, Mr. Joshua?" Cain asked, his tone shifting back to the calm curiosity that had defined the beginning of the interview.

Josh, taken aback by Cain's lack of a violent reaction, felt the anger drain away, replaced by confusion and the raw, lingering grief. He was emotionally disarmed. "My mother… she was teaching me navigation," he said, the words barely a whisper. "I was learning to run the ship."

Cain's eyebrows rose slightly in genuine interest. He put his tea cup down and leaned forward. "Navigation" The Galilee was a simple cargo vessel. *How much had this young man learned? How sharp were his skills?"*

"My mother was an expert, sir," Josh said, finding a small measure of confidence. "She didn't just teach me the charts. She taught me about cosmic currents, gravitational pulls, and how to use them to our advantage."

Cain stood up and walked around the desk, stopping at the wall lined with tactical charts. He gestured to a detailed star map of a dense asteroid field. The chart showed a web of interlocking gravitational shadows and dangerous nebulae. "Let's test that, shall we? Consider this your final exam."

Cain tapped the chart with a long, elegant finger. "Your ship, a lumbering transport like the Galilee, is here, at the edge of this field," he said, indicating a point on the map. "You're being pursued by a patrol ship—faster, heavily armed, and closing on your position. A straight line is suicide. How do you escape?"

Josh's heart was a confused mess. Fear and hatred battled with a strange, undeniable spark of excitement. He stepped closer, his eyes scanning the star map, the puzzle taking over. He thought of his mother's gentle voice, of the countless hours on the bridge. *"A straight line is the most efficient path,"* she had said, *"But it's not always the safest. Sometimes you need to add a detour to avoid a certain type of celestial body, or, in this case, certain unsavory types of people. The trick is to find a route that's just as fast, but also safe."*

He saw it. The solution. He traced a winding, looping path through the asteroid field, avoiding the main gravitational anomalies but hugging their edges, using their pull to sling-shot the ship forward. He also pointed out a small, almost invisible nebula that would block the patrol ship's sensors. The route wasn't a straight line, but by using the natural forces of the field, it was just as fast, maybe even faster.

Cain watched him, his face a mask of stone. When Josh finished, a slow, cold smile spread across the Captain's face. He clapped him on the shoulder, a brutal, possessive gesture. "Impressive, Mr. Joshua. Most impressive."

He led Josh back to the desk, and this time, he gestured to the leather chair opposite him. The gun was noticeably absent. Josh sat down, his body still rigid with a mix of fear and something he couldn't name.

Cain returned to his own chair, his tone changing, becoming more like a commanding officer discussing strategy with a trusted subordinate. "The deckhand you wounded. Baruch. You also glued his mouth shut."

Josh's stomach dropped. He didn't answer, his eyes fixed on Cain's.

"Your vengeance was… poetic. Devious," Cain said, a note of something…was it admiration in his tone? "He was not just humiliated; he was silenced. I've found that fear can be a powerful tool, but true terror comes from the loss of control." He leaned forward, his elbows on the desk, his hands clasped. "The discipline I gave you was harsh, but his was far worse."

Cain's face became serious, all traces of the paternal mentor gone. "You've made a dangerous enemy, Mr. Joshua. Baruch is not a man who forgets, and I cannot be there to watch over you all the time. Your place on this ship will not be a lowly deckhand for much longer. That much, I can promise you. Whether it is because of your potential as a navigator, or because you end up dead at Baruch's hands, remains to be seen."

The silence hung between them, a heavy, unspoken understanding. Cain had seen the rage, but he had also seen the promise. He had found a tool, a weapon, and now he would mold it.

Chapter 10

The deep hum of the Galilee's drive was the only sound on the bridge, a steady thrum that felt more like a heartbeat than a machine. Noah was in his father's captain's chair, feet propped up on the console. Eli was at a different station, head buried in a datapad, his brow furrowed in concentration. The Galilee was running well, a testament to their hard work. In a couple of days, they would be at Jericho.

"What exactly do we do when we get there?" Noah asked, the silence suddenly broken by the weight of their uncertainty.

Eli looked up from his datapad, his thick Irish accent coloring his words. "Now there's a good question. I've been so busy making sure the bloody thing doesn't fall apart that I didn't even think about the rest."

They shared a moment of quiet realization. They were so consumed with surviving that they hadn't considered the next step. A plan began to form. They would have to figure out how to navigate the complexities of their new roles. Over the next day, the two fell into a new rhythm of work.

Noah settled in front of a console, pulling up the old navigation logs. The process was slow and methodical. He charted the ship's last approach to Jericho, noting the orbital paths and the designated cargo transfer points. He then reviewed the comm logs, listening to his father's calm, professional cadence as he spoke to Orbital Traffic Control. He practiced the cadence in his mind, trying to imagine himself sounding that confident.

Meanwhile, Eli scoured the digital checklists from the ship's past Loadmasters. The tasks were not so foreign to him, as engineer he had been required to assist the Loadmasters many times over the years but the specifics of the codes and procedures for labeling, securing and releasing cargo were details he hadn't needed to know before. He was a mechanical man, a fixer of things, but this was a different kind of puzzle, and it was a bit intimidating. He grumbled good-naturedly to himself as he worked through each step.

Later, the two of them descended into Isaac's study, a space Noah had rarely entered before. The captain's office was a sanctuary of organized chaos, a place of worn leather chairs and the lingering smell of old books. They spent hours sifting through the shipping records, a treasure hunt for data that would tell them what containers to offload and who the customers were. The task was tedious, but it was also a concrete step forward, a small assertion of control over their new lives.

When they finally returned to the bridge, the silence was different. No longer a comfortable hum, it was now filled with tense anticipation. The orbital marker for Jericho was a small dot on the main viewer, growing steadily larger. Noah was in the captain's chair, his feet now firmly on the deck. His finger hovered over the transmit switch for the comms, a single button that felt as heavy as a planet.

"Are we ready to do this?" he asked, the words barely a whisper.

Eli, watching him from his station, leaned forward with a wry grin. "Ready? Lad, we've rebuilt this whole heap o' flyin' scrap metal and sailed it halfway across the sector, we did. Talking to some fella in a box is the easy bit. Now, stop gawking at the button and tell him we're here before they start charging us a waitin' fee." He winked. "Sure, you'll be grand. Just don't forget to thank them kindly for the air."

Noah took a deep breath, his finger trembling just above the comms switch. He glanced at Eli, who gave him an encouraging nod. "Sure, you'll be grand," the old engineer muttered again.

Noah closed his eyes for a second, picturing the words he had practiced a dozen times from the comm logs. He pressed the transmit button.

"Jericho… uh… Jericho Orbital Traffic Control, this is… this is *Gally*—I mean, the freighter Galilee, a-and we're requesting approach instructions. Uh, over."

He released the button, feeling his cheeks burn. *Gally?* What was he thinking using their personal nickname for the Galilee over an official channel? He squeezed his eyes shut, berating himself for the clumsy introduction.

The speaker crackled to life. A calm, professional female voice, with just a hint of an amused sigh, replied. "Freighter *Galilee*, say again your designation? I have no traffic for a *Gally* on my board. Please state your registration and flight plan."

Noah's spine went rigid. He'd forgotten to give their registration number. And they didn't have a flight plan on file, not anymore. He pressed the button again.

"Jericho OTC, this is freighter *Galilee*, designation FN-387. We… We are several weeks late. Our, uh, our prior flight plan was, uh, was interrupted. We sustained some… some damage, and casualties, from a pirate encounter. We're requesting to come to dock."

Silence. The brief, stark statement hung in the air, transforming the slightly comical moment into something grave. The controller's intonation, when she responded, was stripped of all humor.

"FN-387, understood. We've been notified. Standby."

Noah released the button, the tension in the cabin so thick it could be cut with a knife. He looked at Eli. The old engineer's face was grim. Several minutes passed, each one stretching into an eternity. Noah watched the planet swell on the viewscreen, its swirling storms and glittering orbital structures a beautiful but daunting sight.

Finally, the comms returned to life.

"Freighter FN-387, you are cleared for autonav approach to orbital dock number seven. We have Longshoremen teams waiting for you at your transfer point. The Port Authority has also been notified and will be boarding you to take your statement. Be prepared to provide copies of your ship's logs. Thank you."

Noah let out a long, silent breath he hadn't realized he was holding. He pressed the transmit button one last time. "Uh, thank you, ma'am." He sheepishly released the button and looked at Eli, a wide, relieved grin spreading across his face. He quickly engaged the ship's navigation system, the ship's computers taking over the piloting as the Galilee smoothly began its descent into the orbital lanes.

The Galilee moved with a grace that belied its massive size, a slow, majestic descent toward the geometric sprawl of Dock Seven. It was a chaotic symphony of commerce: huge stacks of cargo containers were stacked like children's blocks, some in neat rows, others in haphazard piles. Cranes with long, spindly arms glided over the stacks, and smaller tugs and forklifts shuttled goods between the piles, operated by longshoremen in bulky space suits. It was all a dizzying, beautiful mess, a far cry from the serene emptiness of space.

"Freighter FN-387," the controller's broadcast came over the speaker. "Your parking is dock seven, berth twelve, change frequency now, contact Dock Control."

Noah dutifully flipped the switches and pressed the transmit button again. "Jericho Dock Control, this is freighter FN-387, requesting to dock at Berth Twelve."

A gruff male answered with the gravelly impatience of someone who had a thousand jobs to do. "FN-387, you're cleared for Berth Twelve. But your approach is a bit…wobbly. I've got your vectors on my screen; match 'em. And for goodness sake, watch out for the traffic. We've got a thousand tons of fertilizer being moved at your ten o'clock."

Noah's face reddened, but he quickly went to work, his fingers flying across the controls. He and Eli worked together, a clumsy dance of corrections and small bursts from the maneuvering thrusters. It was a painstaking process, but with Dock Control's gruff guidance, they finally nudged the ship into its designated spot.

"Position locked," Noah said, letting out a heavy sigh of relief.

"Good, welcome to Dock Seven Galilee" the controller on the comms grunted. "Now let's get this show on the road.

Your cargo manifest is on file; we're ready to start unloading."

Noah quickly shifted to a different console, the console for the Galilee's cargo arm. Eli, meanwhile, was already in the small docking bay, suiting up for an EVA. He grabbed a small tug and piloted it out of the ship, a nimble, quick moving speck against the massive framework of the Galilee.

The unloading was a silent ballet. Noah expertly released a container from its cell, a smooth, controlled push into the blackness of space. Eli, in his small tug, would deftly collect it with the tug's manipulator arms, and then repeat the process with a second and a third container. Once he had a small train of three or four, he would maneuver them toward the massive Dock Seven, where the platform's enormous cranes would reach out and pluck them from the void, bringing them into the organized chaos of the docks.

The process went off without a hitch. Off loading cargo had always been an "all hands" duty and this was a dance both of them knew well, a routine they had performed many times. Noah's hands moved with practiced ease, and Eli's movements in the tug were fluid and precise. It was a welcome relief from the uncertainty of the last few weeks, a moment of confident, peaceful purpose. They were no longer lost souls simply surviving; they were two working men, doing what they knew how to do.

Chapter 11

The punishment for the broken crate wasn't what Josh expected. A grim-faced comms officer led him not to a holding cell, but to the ship's navigation station. He handed Josh a professional datapad. "Captain's orders. You're to report to Mr. Ithamar. You're his new apprentice."

He reported to Ithamar, an Indian man with a nervous, busy energy. Ithamar had a habit of muttering to himself and a bewildered expression when someone spoke to him. At first, he seemed frustrated by the imposition. "An apprentice? A boy? What good is this one for?" he muttered, his thick accent making the words a soft, almost musical jumble. "So much paperwork. So much to explain."

But as the days stretched into weeks, Josh proved himself. He didn't just understand the basic charts; he had a deeper grasp of cosmic currents and gravitational pulls, the very things his mother had taught him. One afternoon, Ithamar, lost in his muttering, asked, "The currents… they shift near the K-11 sector… where does the nebula's shadow fall?" He was genuinely surprised when Josh, without a moment's hesitation, answered precisely. The old navigator looked at Josh with newfound respect. "Ah, Mr. Joshua," he said, a weary smile on his face, "You are a quiet one, yes, but you have a good mind."

One day, on Ithamar's watch, he and Josh were on the bridge, the only two in the control room besides the pilot and systems operator. The air was calm, filled with the drone of the ship's engines. Then, a ping on the long-range sensors shattered the peace. An icon appeared on the main viewscreen: a small gold six-point star symbol indicating a law enforcement patrol ship, at a distance, and so far, unaware of their presence.

Ithamar's eyes went wide. He began to punch commands into his console, muttering to himself, "The Jericho Passage… we can make the jump… we will lose them there…"

Before he could finish, Cain's voice, a low rumble from behind them, cut through the air. "Stand down, Mr. Ithamar. Step away from the console."

Ithamar, startled, looked over his shoulder. Cain stood by the main hatch, a calm, commanding presence. He didn't look at the patrol ship icon on the screen. He only looked at Josh. "Mr. Joshua," he said with all the coldness of the void outside. "Plot our escape."

Ithamar was visibly agitated. He sputtered, "Captain, sir, I have a route planned! It is a good plan! It is safe!"

"I am not interested in your plan, Mr. Ithamar," Cain replied, his gaze still fixed on Josh. "Stand down. Now."

Ithamar swallowed hard, his hands trembling. He shuffled back, muttering to himself as he retreated into the shadows of the bridge. The full weight of the situation settled on Josh. Cain was not simply trusting him with a task; he was putting the entire crew at risk to test his new tool.

Josh's mind raced, recalling a lesson from his mother about using gravitational forces to their advantage. The situation was not too dissimilar from the test Cain had given him in his office. He quickly formulated a plan. He punched the commands into the console, the display lighting up as he traced a new route. There was a gravity well they could use to draw the Babylon into a nearby nebula. They would ride the gravitational pull to accelerate away without increasing engine power, keeping the Babylon off the patrol's sensors until they were in the nebula. Once inside, the clutter and radiation would provide more than enough cover for them to slip away undetected.

He finished and looked at Cain, who simply nodded. "Execute," he ordered.

The pilot adjusted their course, and the ship lurched slightly as they entered the gravity well. Slowly, like a serpent she slid down the invisible pathway allowing the natural forces to guide her course drawn in by the gravitational pull. As they headed toward the nebula, the Babylon's engine output remained low. The patrol ship passed by, utterly unaware.

Ithamar, his shoulders slumped in relief, let out a long, shuddering breath. "My goodness," he muttered, "That was… a brilliant plan, Mr. Joshua."

But Cain was not relieved. That slow, predatory smile spread across his face again as he looked at Josh. It was in that moment that Josh understood with chilling clarity: his new life was a different kind of prison. His skills, nurtured by his mother and father, once a source of connection to home, were now a tool to be used by the man who had murdered his family. The question lingered in his mind, cold and terrifying: What would the Captain have done if his plan hadn't worked?

Chapter 12

The gruff timbre of Dock Control crackled over the comms. "FN-387, Port Authority shuttle, designated PA-7, is on approach to your port airlock. They'll be docking in approximately three minutes."

Noah's stomach twisted into a knot. He glanced at Eli, who had just entered the bridge after his long shift. The old engineer's face, still a bit flushed from his exertions, was now grim.

"It's about bloody time," Eli grumbled, not looking at Noah. "This ain't goin' to be easy, lad."

"I know," Noah said, quietly. He felt the familiar dread creeping back in, a cold, unwelcome guest. The brief, peaceful interlude of purposeful work was over. The Galilee gave a small shudder as the shuttle's magnetic grapples locked on. A second later, the airlock doors opened.

The two officers who entered were a study in contrasts. The uniformed man was a big, broad-shouldered officer with a neatly trimmed beard and a no-nonsense demeanor. His partner was a lean, hawk-faced man in a rumpled suit that looked a size too small. He wore an expression that suggested he'd already seen it all, twice.

The uniformed officer, whose name tag read Gideon, spoke

first. "Captain Noah, I presume? Officer Gideon, Port Authority. This is my partner, Agent Abner." He nodded toward the man in the suit, who simply grunted in return. "We're here to take your statement and collect evidence related to the pirate attack."

Their manner was professional and detached, their faces unreadable. It was just another day at the office for them, but for Noah and Eli, it was the raw, open wound of their lives. Gideon and Abner moved through the ship with an unsettling efficiency, making copies of every log and scan. They meticulously documented the damage and the crime scene, even taking scans of the empty bridge where Isaac and Becky had fallen. Abner's handheld device emitted a low whine as he swept it over the scuff marks on the deck and the still-visible char marks on the chairs.

After a thorough sweep of the ship, Abner turned to Noah. "Alright, kid. We need to do this properly. One at a time. Gideon will take your statement in here. I'll take Mr. Eli to the galley."

Noah's eyes darted to Eli, a wave of panic washing over him. He wasn't ready to do this alone. Eli met his gaze and gave a subtle shake of his head, a silent message: *I'm with you, lad.* The two were separated, and the interviews began.

In the galley:

Abner didn't bother with small talk. He simply pulled up a chair across from Eli and activated a recording device. "Now Eli, let's start with the approach. Can you describe the events leading up to the attack?"

"It was a small freighter," Eli said, his thick accent growing even more pronounced with the stress. "The Babylon. Her

Cap'n said twas a life support malfunction he did, but the engineering data… its engines were overpowered. No honest freight hauler needs da kinda output. Our Cap'n, Cap'n Isaac, bless his 'eart, he wanted to help."

"Your Captain, Isaac. What was his judgment? Did he have reservations?"

"Reservations?" Eli scoffed. "He knew it felt wrong he did, but he was a good man. Couldn't leave a soul stranded, could 'ee."

On the bridge:

Gideon was calm, almost gentle, as he started the interview. "Noah, we've reviewed the security logs. You were in engineering when the attack happened. Can you tell me what you heard over the comms?"

Noah spoke in a brittle, toneless whisper.. "Everything. The… the fighting. My parents…" His voice broke, and he swallowed hard. "I heard them."

"And your brother, Joshua. The logs show he was on the bridge."

"Yes. He was learning navigation from my mom. I… I heard him yell… and then it went silent." Noah's hands balled into fists on the console.

In the galley:

"And your hideout? You and Noah. No one saw you?" Abner's tone was all business, emotionless.

"The maintenance tubes. We knew 'em like the back o' our hands. They're a maze, they are. And we stayed put until we was sure the blaggards were gone."

"And you never saw Joshua, Noah's brother again?"

"No. We figured… we figured they got 'im."

On the bridge:

"You and Eli were the only survivors. After the pirates left, what was your first action?" Gideon asked.

"We… we came out of the tubes. I went to the bridge, and I saw… saw my dad. And my mom. I saw what they did to them. We had to fix the ship. We had to get it moving again. It was all we had left." The pain in his voice was raw and unfiltered.

The interrogation continued for what felt like an eternity, the same questions asked in different ways, forcing them to relive every painful moment. When Abner finally brought Eli back to the bridge, Noah felt an immense wave of relief just from seeing his face.

"Alright," Gideon said, snapping his datapad shut. "We have what we need for now. The logs will be reviewed, and your statements will be cross-referenced with all known pirate activity in the sector. We'll be in touch if we have any updates."

Noah stepped forward, his heart pounding. "You're going to get them, right? The pirates? Captain Cain. I want to help you. Whatever it takes, I'll do it."

Gideon looked at him with tired eyes, a practiced, almost apologetic half-smile on his face. "Kid, we've heard it all before. We'll do what we can. We'll let you know if we make any progress."

With that, the officers turned and walked out. The airlock hissed shut behind them. The silence on the bridge felt deeper and more profound than it had before. Eli put a hand on Noah's shoulder.

"They're not gonna do anything, are they?" Noah asked, his voice shaking. "They just gave us lip service."

Eli just looked at him, the old man's expression a mix of sorrow and grim determination. "I don't know, lad. I don't know."

Chapter 13

The months that followed were a blur of training, and the lines between hatred and survival began to blur for Josh. He was no longer just a navigator, but a student of war. Baruch's hatred remained a constant shadow, a promise of violence lurking around every corner. One day, while retrieving supplies from a dark, cramped service corridor, Josh found his way blocked. A huge shadow detached itself from the gloom. Baruch stepped into the dim light, his face contorted in a mask of rage. "You think you're better than me now, boy?" he growled. "This job… it's for real pirates, not for pampered pups."

Josh's heart hammered against his ribs. He had nowhere to run. Baruch lunged, his massive fist a blur of motion. With pure instinct, Josh dodged, his foot slipping on a greasy patch of deck plating. Baruch stumbled, his momentum carrying him into the wall with a sickening thud. Josh scrambled past him, sprinting away, leaving the cursing pirate behind. "This isn't over, whelp!" Baruch bellowed after him. "Watch your back!"

The incident, and the promise of more violence to come, weighed on his mind. He didn't have to wait long. A week later, a comms officer came for him, not to take him to the bridge, but to the ship's training deck. The space was a grimy, walled-off room filled with equipment for drills and maintenance.

Cain was waiting for him in the sparring ring, a cold, knowing look in his eyes. In place of his usual high uniform and high collared coat, he wore a fighter's gi. He didn't mention Baruch's attempted assault. "Mr. Joshua," Cain said, his tone that of a school master. "I've decided to test your fortitude. A tool is only as useful as its strength. Let us see yours."

Josh hesitated. Was this a trick? A cruel game to toy with him? He held his hands up in a placating gesture. "Captain, I… I don't know how to fight."

"You'll learn," Cain replied, his tone brooking no argument. He gestured for Josh to assume a fighting stance, then took a simple one himself. "Strike me, Mr. Joshua. Try."

Josh was frozen. To strike the man who had murdered his family? He wanted to, desperately, but he was terrified. He threw a halfhearted, clumsy jab, pulling back the moment it left his shoulder. Cain dodged it with ease, not even a hair out of place. He watched Josh, a strange, expectant look on his face. "Again, Mr. Joshua. With purpose."

Then, a memory flashed in Josh's mind: his father, falling to the deck. His mother's dying gaze. The rage, a cold, pure fury, rose in his chest, eclipsing his fear. He wasn't a scared boy anymore; he was a vengeful son. He lunged forward, a primal cry tearing from his throat, his fists a whirlwind of aggressive, clumsy blows.

Cain moved with an effortless grace, his movements like a fluid dance. He easily evaded Josh's frantic strikes, countering with a series of quick, targeted blows that sent Josh sprawling to the deck. He was battered and bruised, his nose bloody and his lip split, but his spirit refused to break. He climbed to his feet each time, his body battered, but his resolve unshaken.

"Enough," Cain said, with a strange note of satisfaction. He had seen what he wanted to see. He gestured toward a silent, imposing figure who had been watching from the shadows—the ship's Master-at-Arms.

"Your mind is a tool, Mr. Joshua, but a tool without a strong handle is useless," Cain said. "You will begin training with our Master-at-Arms. This is Master Jair. He will teach you how to fight."

Josh, battered but defiant, rose from the deck one last time, his eyes fixed on the Master-at-Arms. His hatred for Cain now held a chilling new truth: to survive, he had to become more like the man he despised.

Chapter 14

The rec room was quiet, its silence punctuated only by the soft clink of a coffee mug against a saucer. Noah and Eli sat at a small table near a viewport, watching the ant-like activity on Dock Seven. The relentless, organized chaos of the cranes and tugs shuttling containers back and forth was a strange, soothing sight. The coffee was hot and strong, and the familiar smell filled the small room, a comfort against the cold, hollow feeling that the Port Authority officers had left behind.

"Well," Eli said. "That's done, then. The government's been told their part." He took a slow sip of his coffee. "Doesn't feel like it's enough, does it?"

Noah shook his head. "It felt like… like they were just ticking a box. Like we were a footnote." His gaze was fixed on a forklift shuffling a stack of containers. "We have to meet with the agent next. The Import/Export agent. Mom and Dad always used the same one here. That's why we'd come here to Jericho. The agent must be good, right?"

"Right," Eli grumbled, putting his mug down. "Another official. Another person who's going to look at us like we're out of place."

"I found the paperwork in Dad's office," Noah said, pulling

up a datapad. "The insurance forms, the manifest… everything." He scrolled through the documents, the numbers and clauses a blur. "We're so late. It's going to cost us a lot. But… What about the insurance? Will it cover what we lost?"

"That's the question, isn't it?" Eli sighed. "That agent… they're the key. They'll tell us what we're owed, what we can claim. They'll be either our friend or the other kind."

"The agent's name is Leah. Mom talked about an old friend by that name for time to time. If I've met her, I don't remember. If it's the same person, I hope she'll remember us." Noah looked up from the datapad, his gaze drifting from the busy dock back to Eli's tired face. The sense of purpose from a few hours ago was fading, replaced by a deep, gnawing uncertainty. "And after that? After we figure out how much money we have?"

Eli ran a hand over his grizzled jaw. "That's the question that's been nagging at me like a hungry dog, lad. The big one. The 'what now?'" He paused, looking at the boy across from him. "We can't answer that until we know what we've got to work with. We can't decide where we're going until we know where we are."

Noah nodded, the stress from the past weeks catching up to him. He took a long, final gulp of coffee, the bitter taste a perfect match for the lingering questions in his mind. The next meeting would determine everything.

The trip from the Galilee to the Dock's habitable facility was a short one, the small shuttle pod zipping across the black void like a bee. On his datapad, Noah reread the last message from the Import/Export agent. The text had been brief, just a few lines of condolences, followed by an overly-enthusiastic message about their arrival. It was a strange mixture of grief and cheerfulness, and it left Noah and Eli feeling even more on edge.

"She seems… excited," Noah muttered, tucking the datapad away as the shuttle docked.

"Some folks just don't know how to act," Eli said gruffly, his words clipped. "Just remember why we're here."

They stepped off the shuttle and into the clean, sterile corridor of the hab facility. The air hung thick with the scent of recycled air and old paper. They followed the directional signs to the office of the Import/Export agent, their steps heavy on the polished floor.

They found the agent's office door and hesitated for a moment. They had just stepped inside the reception area when a woman came bursting through the inner door, a blur of motion and color.

"Noah! Eli!" she cried, a rich Southern accent dripping from her voice. "Oh, praise be, you're here!"

Before either of them could react, she had wrapped them in a massive, exuberant, and tear-filled hug. The sheer force of it knocked the wind out of Noah, and he and Eli stood stiffly, caught completely off-footed by the greeting.

Her name was indeed Leah, and her appearance was as loud as her voice. It was hard to tell her age, but her bouffant, curly red hair seemed to defy gravity, and it was framed by a pair of enormous, thick-lensed glasses that made her eyes look impossibly large. She was rail-thin, but her energy was hyperactive, like a librarian on fast-forward.

She released them, now almost frantic an emotional torrent. "I just can't believe you're here! Becky… oh, my dear Becky… I was just so heartbroken! I knew you two were with her, and

I just… oh, let's not talk about it! Come! Come in, you two, you look like you need to sit down!"

She swiftly ushered them into her office, a whirlwind of motion. She pointed them to two plush chairs, then dashed behind her desk and pulled out a small, gleaming espresso machine. She handed each of them a tiny cup filled with rich, dark espresso and several packets of sugar.

"Go on, you'll need it," she said, her tone dropping to a conspiratorial whisper before bouncing back up. "My Becky… She was my college roommate, you know. Oh, we used to get into so much trouble. And we stayed in touch, we did! She'd tell me all about you Noah and Joshua, what you were up to, your little adventures on that old ship of yours. When I heard the news… oh, I just couldn't believe it. I cried for days! I'm just so, so glad you two are here."

She sat back in her chair behind the desk, her expression a mix of profound sadness and boundless joy. The men were still processing the espresso and the shocking hug, their initial plans to conduct a stoic business meeting completely derailed.

Noah, the first to recover, cleared his throat and set down his empty espresso cup. He squared his shoulders, a look of new-found determination on his face. He pulled the datapad from his bag and slid it across the desk. "Ms. Leah, we appreciate everything. Truly. But we have to talk business. We're late, and the cargo was damaged, some was stolen. We understand we lost some revenue because of it."

Leah's frantic energy seemed to calm for a moment, her face shifting into one of sharp, professional focus. "Yes, Noah, of course. We will get right to it." She tapped a few commands on her console. "Now, listen to me, and listen good. You and Eli… you've been through the wringer. But let me tell you, you are some of the luckiest people alive. We got some cancellations, yes. And a few folks demanded price reductions. But I've been able to smooth out the ruffled feathers, and I've only had to reduce payments by a minimal amount." Her eyes lit up with pride. "At the end of the day, we didn't turn a huge profit on this run, but we turned *a* profit."

Noah slid the ship's insurance policy and a copy of the Port Authority report across the desk. "We also have the ship's insurance policy. The PA gave us a copy of the report they filed. We were hoping we could file a claim and get a settlement to make up the difference."

As she spoke, she glanced at her desk and then back at Noah, a slight, almost imperceptible shift in her focus. "All these years, you'd think I'd have found a good man by now to share a cup of coffee with. But a woman's work is never done, is it?"

Eli, who had been quietly sipping his espresso, choked on his drink and went a shade of crimson that even his Irish heritage hadn't prepared him for. He hadn't been paying attention to the conversation, but the comment about coffee and a man had hit him out of the blue. He recovered quickly, a blush still staining his cheeks. "Ah, now, is that a fact? A beautiful lady like yerself still on the market?" he said with a playful wink. He puffed out his chest a little, a twinkle of charm in his eye. Noah, still focused on business, was completely oblivious.

Leah smiled at Eli, her expression one of pure amusement. She turned back to her console. "Alright, gents. I'm calling the agency right now. I'll make sure they know how this works. I'll handle the negotiations for a settlement. You two have been through enough." She looked from Noah to Eli, her expression once again changing to one of professional concern. "Now for the big question… What do you do now? Do you sell the Galilee? Settle down? What's the plan?"

There was a heavy silence. Noah looked at Eli, a sincere and slightly desperate look in his eyes. He thought of the pictures hanging on the wall above the mess table on Gally. Especially the one showing Isaac and Becky, younger and smiling in front of a half-built Galilee. This ship was their dream come true, they had scrimped and saved every credit to build her. She wasn't just a cargoship, she was meant to be a place to live free and a home to raise a family among the stars. He couldn't give that up, he was part of the dream and he wanted it to continue. He wasn't a boy asking a question; he was a man asking for a partnership. "I want to keep her," he said, his inflection full of emotion. "Gally, she's home. She's family. It's what we have left of them. It's their legacy… and Josh's…and mine."

Eli looked at Noah, his initial bewilderment from Leah's antics replaced by a profound pride. He saw the boy he had helped raise taking on the mantle of his father. A slow, heartfelt grin spread across his face. "Aye, lad," he said, quiet but firm. "We keep ol' Gally."

Leah burst into tears of sheer joy. She leaped from her chair, a blur of red hair and frantic energy. "That's exactly what I hoped you would say!" she cried. She paused, and her enormous eyes, welled with tears and magnified by her glasses, fixed on Noah. "And listen to me, honey. From now on, you will call me Aunt Leah. You hear? It's what my Becky would have wanted."

Noah's face, so focused on being an adult just moments before, softened. A genuine smile, the first truly relaxed one in weeks, spread across his face. He felt a wave of relief wash over him, as if a weight he didn't know he was carrying had just been lifted. He nodded, the word feeling both strange and profoundly right. "Yes, ma'am. Aunt Leah."

Leah turned, a whirlwind of motion, her sadness completely replaced by a new mission. She rushed to her console. "Now don't you two worry your heads about a thing! I'm way ahead of you! I've already secured you a contract for your next run! A full manifest of medical supplies and luxury goods for the colony on Gethsemane! And I've already put in the orders for the provisions you'll need to get there!"

She stopped, breathing heavily, her face flushed with excitement. "Now, getting her fully repaired, and hiring a new crew… it's going to be tight. But if we can get that insurance settlement we're hoping for… oh, it's absolutely doable! This is going to be the start of something wonderful!"

The pair looked at each other, their initial plan to "figure things out" having been completely blown to pieces by this whirlwind of a woman. A new path had been laid out for them, a hopeful future in the midst of their grief. Noah and Eli felt a shared sense of hope. The Galilee was home, and they were going to keep it that way.

Chapter 15

The training deck of the Babylon was a stark, utilitarian space. Josh stood awkwardly in the center, his body aching from the last beating he'd endured. Across from him stood the Master-at-Arms, a man Cain had simply named Master Jair. Small and wiry, he was all coiled energy, his posture a study in stillness. He wore a simple, dark tunic and trousers. Before the training began, he carefully removed the sheathed dagger from his hip and the pistol from his waistband, placing them on a rack at the edge of the deck. His dark eyes held a calm intensity that was more unnerving than Baruch's rage.

Master Jair bowed curtly, a single, fluid motion. He then gestured with a precise hand to the open space between them. Josh shuffled his feet, unsure of what was expected of him. Master Jair's gaze narrowed slightly, the silent pressure increasing.

Then, a command, surprisingly deep for such a small man, cut through the silence. The words were clipped, direct, and final.

"Attack."

Josh flinched. "Attack? Now?"

Master Jair simply repeated himself, his impatience was clear. "Now."

Nervously, Josh lunged forward with a clumsy, uncoordinated punch. Master Jair sidestepped with effortless grace. In a lightning-fast blur of movement, he swept Josh's leg. The deck rushed up to meet him. Josh hit the ground with a grunt, the wind knocked from his lungs. He lay there, dazed, and saw Master Jair standing over him, impassive.

"Again."

Josh scrambled to his feet, his heart hammering against his ribs. He tried a different approach, a wild, clumsy kick. Master Jair blocked it with his forearm, the impact jarring Josh's leg. He then used Josh's momentum, spinning him around and delivering a sharp, controlled strike to his back, sending him sprawling once more.

"Slower. Think," Master Jair said.

Josh pushed himself up, every muscle in his body protesting. He faced Master Jair again, his fists clenched, a flicker of something new—of desperate resolve—igniting in his eyes.

The lesson had begun, and it was a brutal awakening.

Days bled into weeks, each one a relentless cycle of physical punishment and agonizing repetition on the training deck. Josh's life became a stark contrast of two separate disciplines: the intellectual pursuits of his navigation training with Ithamar and the brutal, visceral lessons with Master Jair.

He learned to fight with his body first. Master Jair drilled him in basic hand-to-hand combat, a grueling process of throws, blocks, and strikes. The older man was a human machine, every movement economical and purposeful. Josh was constantly bruised, his muscles sore, but with each fall, he got up faster. He learned to anticipate a feint, to brace for an impact, and to use an opponent's momentum against them.

Then came the weapons. The knife was a natural extension of Master Jair's movements, a fluid, deadly ballet. Josh's hands, clumsy at first, slowly began to find the rhythm of the blade. He learned to parry a thrust, to close the distance for a strike, and to see an opening in his opponent's guard. The swords were heavy and awkward at first, a jarring weight in his hands, but Jair's relentless repetition molded his stances, strengthened his grip, and ingrained in him the discipline of the cut and the thrust. Finally, the pistol became another tool in his arsenal. Jair taught him to control his breathing, to trust his aim, and to understand the weight of a ranged weapon.

Cain would occasionally appear, a silent observer from the edge of the training deck. He never spoke, never offered a word of advice or encouragement. He would simply stand there, leaning against the bulkhead, his green tea cup in his hand, a thin wisp of steam rising to join the ship's quiet rumble. His presence was a constant reminder of why Josh was here and who he was learning these deadly skills for.

One afternoon, in yet another hand-to-hand session, something clicked. Master Jair lunged with a speed that had always left Josh sprawling on the deck. But this time, Josh was ready. He moved with an instinct born of countless hours of pain and repetition. He parried the strike, pivoted, and countered with a clean, sharp blow to Master Jair's body. The sound was a solid *thump*.

For the first time, a flicker of surprise crossed Master Jair's face, a brief widening of the eyes before his expression hardened again. He returned the blow with a swiftness and power that left no room for defense. The master's fist struck

Josh's nose with a sickening crack. Josh went down, hitting the deck with a finality that shook the air out of his lungs. He lay there for a moment, the warm, sticky liquid of his own blood running down his face.

He propped himself up on his elbows, wincing. But instead of despair, a fierce grin stretched across his face, even as he tasted the blood. He had landed a hit.

"Good," a voice said, a voice that was not Master Jair's.

Josh looked up to see Cain standing over him now, his cold eyes holding a hint of sinister approval. He took a slow sip of his tea.

"See Dr. Samuel," Cain ordered. "Then report to the bridge for your navigation watch."

With that, he turned and strode from the training deck, leaving Josh with the sting of his bloody nose and a renewed sense of purpose. He was still a tool, but he was a tool becoming sharper, and a tool in his own right, not just Cain's.

The Babylon's infirmary smelled of antiseptic and ozone, a sterile contrast to the grimy corridors outside. Josh stepped inside, the pain from his broken nose a throbbing drumbeat in his head. Dr. Samuel looked up from his desk, his thin, reclusive frame hunched over a microscope. Wire-frame spectacles sat low on his nose.

"Ah, the Captain's new pet," Samuel said. He motioned for Josh to sit on the examination bed. "A broken nose, yes? It is of no surprise. Master Jair is… thorough."

Josh sat, wincing as Samuel's surprisingly strong hands prodded his nose. "He is," Josh said, his tone muffled.

"You are stronger than you look," Samuel mused, taking a vial of clear liquid from a cabinet. "Or perhaps just more stubborn, no? I have zeen many men break under his tutelage. You have a fire in you. Do not let it extinguish." He dabbed the liquid onto a swab, and a moment later, Josh felt a cool, numbing sensation spread across his face.

As Samuel worked, straightening the cartilage with a few sharp, practiced movements, Josh found his moment. He had been listening for an opportunity, and the doctor's rare quiet kindness was it.

"Sir," Josh began, trying to keep it casual, "I was looking at the nav charts. It seems we're heading toward the Dead Sea. Have you been their? What's it like?"

Samuel paused, his fingers still on Josh's nose. His eyes, magnified by the lenses, met Josh's with a flash of suspicion that quickly softened. He went back to work, his movements slow and deliberate.

"Da. Busy like a hive of hornets with no queen." He chuckled, a dry sound. "It is the last refuge for those who 'ave nowhere to go. A place of no laws, no rulers. Only profit und… survival. A den of thieves and scoundrels. Und of those who were once scoundrels, und now wish to be zomething else,. he added, his lips barely moved as he spoke.

The words painted a vivid picture for Josh, confirming his suspicions. It was an outlaw port, an entire city of pirates and opportunists.

"And the Captain has dealings there?" Josh pressed, trying to sound naive and innocent.

Samuel glanced at the door, a nervous energy coming over him. "Enough questions. Curiosity is a dangerous commodity on dis ship. It will get you in much more trouble than a broken nose. Remember, in such a place, you are nothing. Only the tools you possess vill speak for you." He taped a small splint to Josh's nose, a final act of care.

"There. It is fixed," Samuel said, stepping back and straightening his spectacles. He looked at Josh, a silent message passing between them—a recognition of shared secrets. "Now go, go. The Captain has ordered you to the bridge. Do not be late."

Josh slid off the bed, his nose no longer throbbing, but his mind now racing. He had part of his answers at least. The Dead Sea was a lawless, chaotic world, and in that chaos could lay opportunity. The skills he was now acquiring, the very tools Cain was forging for himself, were his only chance at freedom.

Chapter 16

The air in the Galilee's engineering space was thick with the scent of metal and machine oil. Eli stood over a massive conduit, its metallic casing still scarred from the recent attack. Two men in nondescript coveralls and hard hats knelt beside him, their toolboxes open.

"We bypassed it on the run to port," Eli explained, a note of exasperation in his thick Irish accent. "We cobbled together a workaround, but she needs a proper fix. It's the primary power conduit, so the new one has to be perfect. The diagnostics are showing a wee bit of energy bleed, but that's what we expected. Just get her done right, lads."

He gave the men a curt nod and headed for the lift, leaving them to their work. The steady, purposeful drone of the ship's generators was a comforting sound. As the lift ascended, Eli felt the familiar vibrations of the deck plates beneath his feet. He could hear the low thrum of the ship's systems and, as he got closer to the bridge, the rising tension in the air.

He stepped out of the lift and paused just before entering the bridge, his sharp ears catching the terse exchange between Noah and a large, bull-shouldered man. Eli's eyes narrowed as he watched the scene unfold.

"Container 2B-delta is in cell 33-gamma," Noah said,

his tone clipped with frustration. "The manifest says it's supposed to be in cell 27-delta. And it's not secured to the main truss."

The supervisor, a hulking man, leaned against a tactical console, a half-smile on his face as he watched his crew on the video feed. "My guys know what they're doing, kid. They'll get it where it needs to go."

Noah's jaw tightened. "They've already sealed it. And look at the utility conduits." He pointed a trembling finger at the display on his console. "This feed for the cryogenic unit on container 6F-alpha is connected to a primary power line. It should be on an auxiliary."

"It's fine, kid," the supervisor said dismissively. "We're on schedule. Your ship's old, these dated computers don't always read right."

Eli's face hardened. He saw what was happening: the man was dismissing Noah, treating him like a child. He knew exactly what he had to do. He strode onto the bridge, his posture straight and formal. He walked directly to Noah, stood at a respectful distance, and snapped to attention like a man reporting for duty.

"Captain," Eli said, his tone uncharacteristically crisp and formal. "Reporting as requested, Sir."

Noah blinked, caught completely off-guard by the formality.

"The two-man repair crew is on the job, Sir," Eli continued, his gaze locked on Noah's face. "They're making good time in the engine room. They're running a full diagnostic on the power conduit and will have the work completed well before the scheduled departure."

The supervisor straightened up a little, his eyes narrowing

at Eli's unblinking deference. He took in Eli's grizzled face and the confidence in his posture.

"That's good, Eli," Noah said hesitantly at first, then gaining a new-found authority. He instinctively shifted into the role Eli had cast him in. "Report for duty as soon as they're finished. You'll be working directly with me, running diagnostics from the bridge."

"Aye, Sir," Eli said with a sharp nod. He paused, looking out at the cargo feed on the main screen. "Is there anything else, Captain? Since I'm free until the repair team wraps up, perhaps I could assist you with the loading? It looks like a complex job."

Noah glanced at the supervisor. A slow grin spread across Noah's face as he pointed to the screens, his confidence growing.

"As a matter of fact, Eli, there is. Come over here and take a look at this," Noah commanded. He then pointed out the issues on the cargo console. "They've placed container two-B-delta in the wrong cell. They've also connected several cryogenic units to the wrong utility lines."

Eli leaned in, his face a mask of profound interest. He made a show of rubbing his chin, his eyes wide. "Well, will ya look at that, now! The officer's a genius, isn't he? Caught it all on the first pass!" He turned to the supervisor, a playful twinkle in his eyes that didn't quite reach them. "It's what happens when a young man spends his whole life on a freighter. He's got more experience than most of us old salts."

He leaned closer to the supervisor and dropped his voice to a conspiratorial whisper, but it was loud enough for Noah to hear. "I tell ya, a mistake like this could cost a fortune. I'd be real worried about the liability if I were you. Damaged goods, lost cargo… it all falls on the longshoremen.

The supervisor's smile vanished. He stared at Noah, a newfound respect replacing the previous condescension. He cleared his throat and turned to the intercom, his cadence now hard and efficient. "Team A, report to cells 27-delta and 33-gamma! Team B, you've got a utility line issue on 6F-alpha. Fix it now!"

Eli simply nodded, a faint smirk on his lips as he returned his attention to Noah.

"Is there anything else, Captain?" he asked, once again in a respectful, formal tone.

Noah, standing a little taller now, a new sense of purpose in his eyes, looked at Eli and returned the grin. "No, Eli. You're dismissed."

The morning dawned on Dock Seven, a symphony of industrial sounds and the relentless dance of tugs and cranes moving containers. On the bridge of the Galilee, Noah and Eli stood with the longshoremen's supervisor, watching the video feed with a shared look of exasperation. The supervisor's team was clearly struggling. Their movements were sluggish, their coordination poor, and the progress was agonizingly slow. Eli had once again taken up his role as the grizzled first mate, standing a half-step behind Noah, his presence a silent endorsement of the young man's authority.

A sharp squawk from the comms panel cut through the ambient noise. "Freighter FN-387," the transmission from Dock Control announced, all business. "You have a shuttle requesting to dock at your port-side airlock. Do you grant permission?"

Noah's brow furrowed in confusion. "A shuttle? Identify

passengers and craft, please, Dock Control. We're not expecting anyone."

There was a moment of static, followed by a low chuckle from the controller. "The crazy lady said to tell you it's Aunt Leah."

Noah's head snapped up. He and Eli exchanged a look of profound surprise, followed by a shared, resigned sigh. They both knew that when Leah decided something was important, nothing would stand in her way.

"Permission granted," Noah said, a faint smile on his face. He nodded to the supervisor, who simply shrugged, and then he and Eli headed for the lift, the familiar hum of the Galilee's systems now a warm, reassuring presence.

They stood at the end of the airlock corridor, the massive metallic door hissing as it pressurized and then slid open. The shuttle's airlock extended to meet the Galilee's, the seals clicking into place. A moment later, the inner door of the shuttle opened.

Noah and Eli were prepared for Leah's signature whirlwind of motion. They were not, however, prepared for what emerged first. It was a massive, terrifying robot, nearly two-and-a-half meters tall. Its frame was painted a construction-orange, its bulky, vaguely human-shaped torso fixed with a series of work lights and micro-thrusters designed for a zero-g environment. In place of feet, it had treads like a tank, and its broad shoulders held arms that looked less like limbs and more like a collection of giant, articulated tools. Currently, however, the tools were configured into human-like hands, which it held at its side. Its spherical head had two optical sensors for eyes and a third on the back of its head. A cartoonish smile, the work of a talented graffiti artist, was painted in red where a mouth should be.

The robot rolled forward with a low thrumming of its treads, its massive form a hulking presence in the small corridor. It stopped abruptly just a few inches from Noah, who stood frozen, his eyes wide with a mixture of awe and fear. He and Eli were too surprised to move.

A sharp, commanding female voice, with a crisp Australian accent, cut through the tense silence. "Jabez, make a hole, mate!"

The massive orange robot rumbled to life, its treads grinding as it rolled to the side of the corridor, revealing the source of the voice. She was a tiny woman, barely 1.5 meters tall. Her long, dark hair was pulled back into a severely tight braided ponytail, and she wore loose-fitting coveralls, scuffed combat boots, and black fingerless work gloves. Her pockets and belt were a jangling assortment of tools. Her expression was all business, stern and no-nonsense. She moved to stand next to Jabez, her hands planted firmly on her hips, looking like a miniature foreman next to her imposing partner.

Leah then burst through the airlock door. She was a riot of color, wearing a hot pink pantsuit and a full-length leopard-print coat. High heels clacked on the metal floor as she entered, a suitcase tucked under each arm and another in each hand.

"Well, don't just stand there with your mouths open!" Leah cried, dropping the last of the suitcases with a final clatter. "I told you I'd get you a crew, and I meant it!"

She placed a hand on Jabez's massive orange chassis. "This, my dear fellows, is Jabez. He is a modified 'Job' series material handling and heavy lifter bot with auxiliary ship maintenance functions. I was lucky to find him. He's over 100 years old, a rare antique, but a workhorse, a real treasure. I got him on a 'lease to own' program. Per the contract, he will be the sole property of the Galilee after a year of payments. He will assume the role of your Assistant Loadmaster and Assistant Engineer."

Noah and Eli stared at the immense robot, impressed despite their shock. It was a serious piece of equipment.

Leah then turned to the small, stern-faced woman. "And this is Deborah. She is your new Chief Loadmaster. She served in the Zion Marines as a Loadmaster on amphibious assault vehicles and she's also a trained combat medic!"

Deborah stepped forward, her expression unreadable. She shook hands with both Noah and Eli, her grip firm and brief, but offered no words.

"Aunt Leah, this is incredible," Noah said, still taking it all in. "But we're still short a Navigator."

Leah's enormous eyes, magnified by her glasses, gleamed with mischief. "Oh, honey, didn't I tell you?" she said with a coy smile. She made an over-dramatic curtsy and a bow, sending the leopard-print coat swirling around her. "I've spent years navigating freighters like your Galilee. Your sweet mother and I were college roommates, and we both studied Navigation together. After a while, I settled down, hoping for bigger money and, well," she said, glancing pointedly at Eli, "a man to share a cup of coffee with. But I'm tired of the office. It's time to get back out among the stars again."

Once again, Noah and Eli were stunned, but after a moment both broke into wide grins. "Well, welcome to the Galilee, or just Gally as we like to caller her!" Noah said, with a beaming smile. "Guess we'll have to print you all some uniforms, they come in any color you want as long as you want gray!"

The brief, joyous moment of relief was broken by Deborah. "Alright, let's not dilly-dally. Let's just crack on with it." she interjected flatly. Without waiting for permission, she turned on her heel and strode back down the corridor, her combat boots thumping on the deck plates. A sudden wave of purpose washed over Noah. Someone had to man the bridge. It was his job. He nodded to Eli and took off for the lift, leaving the engineer with Leah and a small mountain of luggage.

He arrived on the bridge to find the video feed of the loading operation alive with a new, aggressive energy. Despite her small size, Deborah was a force of nature. She was a tiny, relentless drill sergeant, barking commands into a handheld comms unit. She directed Jabez with crisp, efficient hand signals, the huge orange robot a graceful extension of her will. The longshoremen, who had been struggling just moments before, now moved with a purpose, their haphazard work replaced by a precise, efficient ballet.

Meanwhile, back in the airlock, Eli had turned on the full Irish charm. "Well now, you can't be haulin' all that yourself, darlin'," he said, a warm grin on his face. With surprising strength, he grabbed all four of Leah's suitcases. "A gentleman must see a lady to her quarters."

Leah's mouth fell open, her enormous eyes wide with surprise and pleasure. "Oh, Eli," she said, her timbre dropping to a theatrical whisper. "Why, I do believe you've just made my day."

Hours later, the last of the cargo was aboard and sealed, and the longshoremen were gone. The entire crew—Leah, Deborah, Jabez, Eli, and Noah—were on the bridge. The air was thick with the scent of recycled air and something new: the buzz of a team working in unison. Leah, now dressed in the sensible, gray uniform coveralls, sat at the navigation station, her fingers dancing over the controls, a look of pure excitement on her face. Eli stood at the helm, his hands resting on the steering yokes. Deborah, her expression as stern as ever, manned the communications station. Jabez stood silently behind her, an orange, mechanical sentinel. Noah sat in the captain's chair, the worn leather a familiar and comforting presence. It was a silent, organic thing, but it was clear to everyone. He was in command.

Deborah's pronouncement was crisp and efficient. "All cargo aboard, sorted and secured Captain. All moorings detached."

Eli responded. "Thrusters and main drive are green, Captain."

Leah's eyes sparkling. "Course to Gethsemane is plotted and locked in, honey."

Noah took a deep breath. "Contact Dock Control for departure clearance."

Deborah nodded. "Dock Control, this is Freighter FN-387 requesting departure clearance."

"Freighter FN-387, you are cleared for departure. Proceed to jump point Alpha-Six," the controller's voice crackled back.

"Freighter FN-387 copies," Deborah responded, a perfect echo of the controller's professional tone. "Cleared for departure. Proceeding to point Alpha-Six."

Noah looked at his new crew, a quiet smile on his face. This was it. The start of something new. He leaned forward and gave the order. "Right fifteen degrees, ahead slow."

Eli's hands moved on the controls, and the Galilee's

thrusters fired with a low, powerful rumble. The stars began to slide past the viewport, and the old ship, a home and a legacy, was finally on her way.

Once they were clear of the dock, and the flight path was stable, the tension on the bridge seemed to release all at once. Leah, with a happy sigh, handed Noah a steaming mug. The familiar, comforting scent of coffee filled the air. Eli, Deborah, and Leah all took a mug for themselves. They were on their way, a new team and a new purpose.

Chapter 17

The bridge of the Babylon was an oddly quiet place. The low vibration of the engines and the rhythmic ping of the long-range sensor were the only sounds as Josh stepped out of the turbolift. The new shift was already moving to their stations. They were a motley crew of bruised knuckles, scarred faces, and tattooed arms, their tattered uniforms a testament to their trade. Yet, they executed their duties with a chilling professionalism, their movements precise and efficient. It was a testament to Captain Cain's brutal discipline.

He headed for the small galley unit in the corner, its worn finish a stark contrast to the sleek command chairs. He poured himself a cup from a steaming carafe. The black tea was thin and bitter, tasting more of recycled water than tea, but he drank it anyway, the liquid warmth a small moment of peace.

With his cup in hand, he moved to the navigation station. Ithamar was muttering to himself, his fingers flying across the holographic controls, a constant state of nervous energy. His busy eyes immediately fixed on the splint and swelling on Josh's nose.

"Ah… that is, a… a new look for you, yes? Is it… comfortable?" Ithamar asked.

Josh managed a small, pained smile. "It's fine, Ithamar. A training accident."

Ithamar's eyes widened slightly, and he looked from Josh to the Captain's chair, where Cain was seated, his attention seemingly consumed by a datapad. "A… a training accident, you say? With Master Jair, I assume? He is… spirited in his methods."

"Something like that," Josh replied, "Anything to report?"

The question pulled Ithamar back to his routine. He took a deep breath, his professional demeanor returning. "All clear. No contacts in our cone. No debris fields. We are on the… on the green line… to Dead Sea. Everything… everything is on the line." He looked around the bridge, as if for confirmation. "We are… on schedule."

He gave a final, nervous nod and shuffled past Josh, a small sigh of relief escaping him as he headed for the turbolift. The bridge fell silent again, the low, steady thrum of the ship filling the air. Josh settled into the navigation chair.

In the Captain's chair, Cain remained motionless, a dark, imposing figure of absolute control. He was a silent anchor in a world of turmoil, a reminder of the paradox Josh now inhabited. A pirate ship run with the cold efficiency of a corporation.

The quiet of the bridge was broken by the hiss of the turbolift doors. The First Mate, Dathan, a burly, scarred man with a neatly tied ponytail, and the Tactical Officer, Delilah, a hawk-faced woman with a flinty gaze, stepped onto the deck. They moved with an aggressive confidence, their bodies held in a tense competition as they strode past the crew. Their uniforms were stained and patched, but their movements were purposeful, their posture ramrod straight.

Without a word, the pair crossed the deck and stopped by the large, circular plotting table. At the center of the table, a blue-hued star chart pulsed into life. They leaned in, their heads bowed close to Cain's, who had risen from his chair and now stood at the head of the table.

Josh appeared to busy himself at his station, his eyes glued to the nav charts, his fingers lightly dancing across the controls. But he was eavesdropping, his ears straining to catch every word of their hushed conversation.

"Target is confirmed, Captain," Dathan reported, with a poorly disguised note of smug pride. "The Gomorrah. She's two days out from Dead Sea, just as you planned. We can confirm she's carrying a full cargo of refined stimulants, a very profitable haul." He glanced at Delilah, a slight smirk on his lips. "The men are ready for the take. They're itching for a payday."

Cain gave a thin, approving smile, his eyes flicking between the two officers. "And how are we going to deliver Captain Korach his final judgment, Mr. Dathan? Ms. Delilah?" he said, growling dangerously.

Delilah's gaze hardened. "My weapons are ready, Captain," she said. "Her defenses are a known quantity. We can make short work of the Gomorrah's bridge, leaving the rest to your strike team. We're a well-oiled machine. My fighter crews are prepped for launch. On my mark, they will punch a hole through his defenses. He won't have time to beg."

Josh's heart hammered against his ribs. Fighters? He had not known the ship carried a complement of those.

"Weapons status is good," she continued, looking down her nose at Dathan. "The fighters will be the key. The first wave will punch a hole through his defenses, then the boarders will do the rest."

Cain simply nodded. He was a spectator at a gladiator match, and they were competing for his approval. He gave neither a direct word of praise, but his silence was more effective than any compliment.

"We will proceed as planned," Cain said, a quiet command that held the finality of a death sentence.

With the briefing concluded, the two officers gave a curt nod—to Cain, but not to each other—and strode from the bridge. The turbolift doors hissed shut behind them. Cain watched them go, then turned, walking over to the galley to pour himself a cup of green tea. He did not look at Josh, did not acknowledge his presence. He was a man with a plan, and the final piece was falling into place.

Left with the captain and the quiet, professional crew, Josh's mind reeled. He was a pirate now. He was a part of this. The reality of it was shocking, terrifying, and in a way, exciting. This was not a subtle game of deception like with the Galilee. This was a planned, direct assault. He was a witness to a crime in the making, and there was nothing he could do to stop it. He wanted no part of the murder and piracy. But what would Cain expect of him? What would he do when the time came?

The question gnawed at him, a cold and hollow pit in his stomach. He looked down at his tea, the comforting warmth he had sought now gone. It was cold and bitter, a perfect mirror of his new reality.

Chapter 18

Gally breathed with a quiet contentment, her old systems a comforting presence as the crew settled into their mid-watch routine.

"Tell me again, honey," Leah drawled, her lilt a soft Southern melody. "You really have to go outside to check the thrusters?"

Eli, perched on a stool at the engineering console, let out an endearing grunt. "A man needs to feel the hum of the drive, Leah. Can't trust these newfangled sensors to give ya the full picture. The vibrations, the heat signatures… it's a language, ya see. A language a good engineer speaks with his hands."

"I just can't imagine floating around out there in a space suit," Leah said, a shiver running through her. "All that… nothingness."

"It's not so bad," Noah chimed in, a soft smile on his face. He sat in his father's chair, the worn leather a familiar presence. He knew he was still new to this role, and the title of "Captain" still felt foreign. But he accepted it for simplicity's sake. "It's peaceful, in a way. You feel… small. But the stars… they're incredible."

Deborah, who had been quietly monitoring the comms, snorted without looking up. "Unnecessary risk and a waste of time. Sensors are more reliable. You should trust the data, Captain." The clipped Australian accent made her words sound like an order.

"Deb's right," Noah conceded with a grin. "But sometimes, you just gotta trust your gut."

A low whirring sound from the back of the bridge broke the rhythm of their conversation. Everyone's eyes went to Jabez, the huge orange robot who stood silently at the rear of the command center. He hadn't moved or made a sound since they left port. He was a sentinel, a silent, imposing presence.

Then, a voice.

"Observation: Preventative Maintenance. I have found it is more cost-effective to replace the organic components than to listen to them."

The voice was not what anyone expected. It was surprisingly chipper, with a synthesized, almost melodic lilt. It sounded nothing like the hulking, industrial robot who spoke it. The entire crew froze, their mugs halfway to their lips. Noah and Eli exchanged a look of pure shock. They had no idea the robot could vocalize, and was that sarcasm?

Leah was the first to react. She let out a shriek of surprise that was quickly followed by a fit of giggles. "Jabez! You can talk?" she squealed, her Southern accent elongating the words, clutching her stomach in laughter.

Eli let out a belly laugh that was more of a wheeze. "Well, bless my soul!" he roared, his thick brogue a joyous rumble. "The bloody thing talks!"

Even Deborah, usually stoic, cracked a small smile before returning to her work. "The bloke's a 'bot of a few words," she said, without looking up. "Just as a bloke should be. More efficient that way."

The laughter was a breath of fresh air on the bridge, a moment of pure, unadulterated joy. But just as it began to subside, an alert tone chimed from Leah's console. She leaned forward, her face a mask of focus, the mirth evaporating instantly.

"What is it, Aunt Leah?" Noah asked, suddenly serious. The relaxed atmosphere was gone, replaced by a sudden, cold sense of dread. The last time a distress signal appeared on their sensors, it was a lie, a trap to lure his parents and crew to their deaths.

"I'm picking up a weak transponder signal," she said, her fingers flying over the console. "It's a freighter, a cargo vessel. Looks like it has a life support malfunction."

A phantom chill ran down Noah's spine. His mind replayed the memory of the transponder signal from the Babylon. Life support malfunction, they'd said, a simple plea for help. His father, Isaac, had debated the risk, knowing they were in a dangerous sector. But compassion and duty had won out, and his parents had extended a lifeline, only to be met with a cold-blooded attack. The memory was a physical weight on his shoulders. He didn't want to make that mistake again. He wanted to turn away and run.

Eli saw the fear flash across Noah's face. He walked over to Noah's chair and put a heavy hand on his shoulder. "Your Da and your Ma made their choice, lad. And it was the right one. They weren't fools, they were good people. Now, it's your turn to make yours."

Noah looked up at Eli. He saw the genuine, unwavering support in his mentor's eyes. He thought of his father and mother, their unwavering commitment to helping others. It was the legacy they had left him. This wasn't a trap; it was a choice. A choice to be better than the monsters who had taken everything from him.

He took a deep breath and looked at Leah, at Deborah, at Eli, at the quiet strength of Jabez. They weren't a family, not yet, but they were a crew, bound together in this moment by a choice—a choice that was entirely his own.

"Aunt Leah, uh, plot a course," Noah said, his voice a little too loud. "Maximum velocity."

Leah looked up, her expression a mix of concern and loyalty. "Where to?"

Deborah leaned forward, her Australian accent sharp, her tone cutting through the bridge's tension like a wire. "*Maximum velocity*, Captain? This maybe a threat Are you sure you want to charge in blindly?"

Noah paused. Deborah was the most rational one here, and her advice was sound. If it was a trap, speeding in was a fatal mistake. *But what if it wasn't?* He could almost hear his father, Isaac, weighing the odds, and his mother, Rebecca, arguing for the lives they could save. Caution meant delaying aid, and delay meant death if the distress was real. It was a terrible risk, but the memory of his parents' commitment settled the agonizing debate.

He held up a hand. "Deb, you make a good point. We proceed at three-quarters maximum velocity—a compromise between haste and caution."

Deb nodded, "If the distress signal is legitimate, there may be injured personnel. I'll prep the aid station and assume the life support failure is real."

Noah met her gaze, his trepidation still visible but hardening into resolve. "To the signal," he replied. "We are running a risk. I know. But we're going to help them."

The Galilee arrived two hours later. Drifting in the star-dusted blackness was a freighter, dark and silent, its name painted in a faded scrawl on the hull: Horeb. It was a wreck. The massive latticework of its cargo frame was mangled, a jagged tear running down one side. Several cargo cells were empty, and the seals on others were broken, the contents gone. Scorch marks from energy weapons scarred its hull, a clear signature of a pirate attack.

"Oh, my word," Leah whispered over the comms, her tone tight with worry. "Poor souls."

Noah looked at the wreckage. He was standing in the Galilee's airlock, his suit sealed, the helmet secured. Beside him, Eli and Deborah were in their suits, and Jabez with them, his massive orange form looking more imposing than ever.

"Crew, check in," Noah called over the comms.

"I'm here, Captain," was Deborah's clipped acknowledgment.

"Ready as I'll ever be, lad," Eli's brogue crackled.

"Communication function nominal. " Jabez's new chipper vocalization added in.

"I'm all set, honey," Leah said. "Just waiting on y'all to make the connection."

The Galilee's airlock hissed open, and the four of them stepped out into the absolute silence of space, their suit thrusters firing with quiet precision. They propelled themselves toward the Horeb's forward pod, the docking collar undamaged.

"All right," Noah said. "Here's the plan. Deb and Jabez, you take the cargo bays. We're looking for anything—survivors first and foremost, but also salvage. Tools, parts, cargo… anything you can secure. Eli and I will head for the bridge to see if we can recover the logs. Leah, you hold down the fort."

"I'm a worryin' woman, so don't be dawdling, you hear?" Leah came through, a mix of concern and sternness.

"We will," Noah promised. They landed on the Horeb's hull, and Noah and Eli made their way to the airlock of the forward pod while Deborah and Jabez jetted off towards the immense, open-space cargo frame.

Inside the derelict freighter, the only light came from their suits and Jabez's powerful floodlights. A few scattered emergency beacons flickered weakly, casting a red, ominous glow. The silence was absolute, broken only by the low breeze of their life support systems.

Noah and Eli made their way to the bridge. Their suit lights swept over the chaotic scene. Consoles were smashed, and scorch marks were everywhere. They found no survivors.

"Looks like a battle took place here," Eli said with a low growl. "I've seen it before. A scuffle, and then… they're gone."

Noah's suit light swept across the main console. He found a small emergency power unit, still functional, and quickly hooked it in. The console screens flickered to life, showing the ship's last log entries.

Noah started skimming through them, his hands trembling. The entries were a record of the last moments of the Horeb's crew. The distress call, the pirates' response, the boarding… it was all there, a sickening replay of the last day of his parents' lives. He scrolled to the final entries, to the bridge logs, and found the video files. His heart hammered in his chest.

"Let's see what happened here," Noah muttered to himself. He clicked on the final bridge tape.

The screen flickered to life, showing the captain of the Horeb, a man with a graying beard, standing defiantly before a tall, dark-haired man with a roguish smirk. It was Cain. The pirate was speaking, a chilling calm in his voice, but the audio was garbled. The captain of the Horeb spat in Cain's face, and the pirate's smile vanished. The video showed Cain raising a pistol, and with a single, cold-blooded shot, executing the captain.

A choked sob escaped Noah, and a wave of pure, unfiltered rage surged through him, making his vision swim. He slammed his fist down on the console. The entire console vibrated with the force of the impact.

"That bloody pirate," he hissed, trembling with fury. "It's him. It's always him."

Eli put a hand on Noah's shoulder, his own anger simmering just below the surface. "Easy, lad," he whispered. "Calm yourself. We've got him now. We'll find him, and we'll make him pay."

"I'll kill him!" Noah snarled, his rage spilling over. He looked at the face on the screen, at the pirate's cold, dead eyes. "I'll make him pay for everything he took from me."

Just then, a call broke through their tense comms. "Captain, Eli," Deborah said, a note of excitement seemed to leak through the static. "We're in the main cargo area. Jabez and I have found something you'll want to see."

Noah and Eli jetted back through the airlock, moving through the cold vacuum toward the main cargo frame. They found Deborah and Jabez hovering next to one of the standardized containers. Their suit lights, along with Jabez's powerful floodlights, illuminated the cargo trusses. The pirates had left several containers untouched with their seals still intact.

"We checked the other sealed containers," Deborah reported. "Most of them were perishable goods. Spoiled. The pirates must've opened a few, seen the manifest, and left them. Not worth their time."

She jetted to an open container, its doors gaping like a wound. "But they made a mistake leaving this one behind."

Eli peered into the dark container, his suit light revealing something large and metallic, wrapped in what looked like heavy-duty padding. "What is it, then?"

"What's it look like?" she shot back. "We've got something that's not just salvage, but a real payday."

Leah's call crackled excitedly over the comms from the bridge of the Galilee. "I knew it! Y'all are just full of surprises! Oh, we could sell that for a fortune! Maybe the military would even give us a reward for it!"

"The military," Eli scoffed. "And what's that going to get us, Leah? A pat on the head and a fine for salvaging military hardware? It's more trouble than it's worth."

All of them were looking at Noah. He had remained silent since they left the bridge, his rage a cold, hard knot in his stomach. He was no longer a boy grieving. He was a man with a singular purpose, forged in the fiery crucible of vengeance.

He looked from Deborah, to the container, and finally to Eli.

"No," he said, his voice flat and hard. "We don't sell it."

He jetted closer to the container, his suit light illuminating the unmistakable shape of two massive, military-grade plasma cannons. The barrels were sleek and powerful, and they pulsed with a dark, dangerous energy. The same kind of energy that had ripped apart his childhood.

Noah looked directly at Eli, his eyes twin points of burning, resolute anger behind the helmet's visor.

"We're going to arm the Galilee!"

Chapter 19

The thrumming of the Babylon's engines was a constant, maddening beat against Josh's eardrums. He hadn't slept, not really. Every time he closed his eyes, he saw the hawk-faced Tactical Officer and the burly First Mate hunched over the plotting table, their voices echoing in his mind. *The Gomorrah... make short work of the bridge... he won't have time to beg.* The words were a brand on his soul.

He was back on watch at the navigation station, the cold blue light of the holographic display doing nothing to ease the frantic pulse in his temples. It had been a full day since he'd overheard the war council, and every passing hour felt like a countdown to an atrocity. His mind had become a prison, a maze of dead ends and impossible choices.

His first frantic thought was to send a direct warning. But how? He was on a pirate vessel, a ship designed to prevent such a thing. Every comms signal, every data packet, was logged and monitored. To send a warning would be a death sentence, not just for him but for the crew of the Gomorrah. Cain would intercept it, and his wrath would be a swift and brutal spectacle for the crew to witness.

What about escaping? The thought was a brief flare of light in the darkness. He could try to steal a shuttle from the docking bay, but the crew was always working down there, preparing for the assault. He was no Master Jair, but he had watched the way the man moved, all quiet menace and deadly grace. The moment Josh tried to get into a ship, Jair or one of his trainees would be on him like a hawk on a field mouse. And even if he succeeded, what then? The Babylon was armed. They'd fire on him without hesitation, a blip of fire against the blackness. A quick death, perhaps, but a pointless one.

Then he had another idea. He had been an idiot. A complete and total fool. Dr. Samuel had told him about the Dead Sea, that it was a pirate's paradise. A lawless port where criminals and smugglers did business with impunity. He should have realized something was wrong then.

He took a deep breath, his fingers dancing across the navigation console, a forced nonchalance in his movements. He brought up the holoscreen display, focusing on the transponder signal of the ship they were tracking. He had been told it was the Gomorrah, but he hadn't thought to check its registry. Now, with a few keystrokes, he ran a deep scan. The transponder was broadcasting a legitimate registry number and name. There was a legitimate ship named Gomorrah with a flight plan in this quadrant.

A cold, exhilarating jolt of realization ran through him. This wasn't an innocent freighter.

He went a step further, accessing the ship's comms logs. He searched for news feeds, specifically for reports of lost or hijacked cargo ships with similar cargo. He found it almost instantly: a news report detailing a recent attack on an unnamed freighter carrying a valuable cargo of refined stimulants. The ship and its crew were missing and presumed lost. He knew this was the cargo that was now onboard the Gomorrah.

The pieces of the puzzle clicked into place. Gomorrah. A pirate name. Captain Korach wasn't an innocent freighter captain; he was a rival pirate. The Gomorrah was a battle-hardened pirate ship carrying stolen goods, and Cain was hunting him down to take his ill-gotten gains.

A wave of relief, cold and overwhelming, washed over Josh. The gnawing dread in his gut receded, replaced by a cold, calculating resolve. The choice wasn't between being a witness to a murder and escaping to a cold death in space. It was about survival. A pirate-on-pirate war. Let them fight. The fewer pirates in the universe, the better.

And suddenly, the mission became an opportunity. If he had to help Cain, he would. He'd learn his tactics, his vulnerabilities, and maybe even get a chance to make his move when the two ships were engaged. He would learn valuable skills and gain Cain's trust, and when the moment was right, he would find a way to make his escape. He would save himself, and in doing so, he might just do some good in the universe after all. The moral dilemma was gone, replaced by a single-minded purpose. He had been an idiot, but he wouldn't be one any longer. The countdown had begun, and this time, he was ready for the fight.

Chapter 20

The Galilee's main galley, once a place of raucous family meals, felt different now. The mood was heavy, practical. Noah sat at the head of the table staring at a set of blueprints Eli had unrolled across the worn plastic surface. The plans were covered in Eli's spidery handwriting and a chaotic series of diagrams and calculations.

Eli, ever the showman, gestured to the drawings with a theatrical flourish. "Alright, then. Here's what I've cooked up." His thick Irish accent seemed to soften the harsh reality of their new mission. "We've got the two big fellas, the plasma cannons, and a pair of the wee sensor arrays. Now, ol' Gally was never meant for this sort of thing, so we'll be mounting the guns on the outside of the hull. They'll be hidden inside a pair of those standardized cargo containers, lashed to the forward section of the truss, one to port, one to starboard."

Leah leaned in, her bouffant red hair and huge glasses nearly touching the blueprints. "Lashed to the outside, you say? Honey, that seems right dangerous. What if they shake loose?" Her Southern accent was thick with concern.

"Not a chance, Aunt Leah," Noah said. "We'll be bolting them directly to the main structural members. They'll be as secure as if they were part of the hull itself."

"Right, the boy's got a point," Eli confirmed. "I've run the numbers. They'll hold. We'll rig up some hydraulic actuators to pop the container doors open when it's time to fire. The guns themselves are fixed, pointing straight ahead. To aim, we'll have to aim the whole ship, just like your father used to do with the tug arms."

He pointed to a different part of the diagram. "Now, the sensor arrays… they're the eyes of the beast. We'll mount one on the top, forward, port thruster pylon and the other on the bottom, forward, starboard pylon. That'll give us a wide field of view. We'll be running a lot of cable, mind you. A whole lot."

Deborah, who had been listening with her arms crossed, gave a terse nod. "And the problems, mate? I assume there are more than a few." Her crisp Australian accent cut through the room like a scalpel.

"There's the rub," Eli said, a hint of a smile on his face. "Gally's systems aren't designed for combat, you see. We've no fire control computer, so we'll have to jury-rig the sensor arrays' remote controls to a console on the bridge. It'll be a clumsy affair, so it will. More importantly, the power draw… these are thirsty lassies. We'll get a couple of shots, maybe three, before we risk a complete power failure. We'll have to bypass a few of the non-critical subsystems and reroute the power directly to the main guns. And finally, there's the heat, worse luck. No dedicated cooling. The cannons will have to radiate the heat into space through Gally's own heat sinks, which takes time. It's not a system for a drawn-out firefight, no. It's for a quick, decisive strike."

Noah nodded, absorbing it all. He stood up and looked at his crew. "Alright. We'll get started. Deb, you're on power. I need you to go over Eli's plan, check his numbers, and start prepping the bypasses and reroutes. Leah, you can get the crew quarters on the cargo deck prepped for storage. We'll need every spare inch for these new parts and whatever else we salvage. Jabez will be with me and Eli. We'll be working outside."

Deborah gave a short salute. "Right then, Captain."

The next three days were a blur of organized chaos. The Galilee drifted in the empty space of the derelict field, her running lights dimmed to conserve power. Outside, Noah, Eli, and Jabez worked in the frigid blackness, their spacesuits illuminated by their helmet lamps. They unlatched the plasma cannons from the Horeb's cargo frame and maneuvered them with a precision born of necessity. Jabez's powerful, articulated tool arms made quick work of the heavy lifting. He would hoist a cannon, his tank-like treads gripping the trusswork, while Noah and Eli secured the bulk containers to the Galilee's structure.

Inside the command pod, Deborah and Leah worked just as hard. Deb, with her sharp mind and even sharper demeanor, scrutinized Eli's power schematics, her Australian accent a constant, low murmur as she muttered calculations to herself. She moved with a purpose, stripping down panels and rerouting cables. In the galley, Leah, her face smudged with grease but her spirit undaunted, reorganized the stores with her characteristic hyperactive energy, humming a country tune to herself. The quiet camaraderie of shared purpose filled the ship.

The moment of truth arrived two days later. The Galilee had

moved away from the derelict field and was now hovering in empty space. The crew was on the bridge, the air thick with anticipation. On the main viewscreen, a small, unremarkable asteroid sat a few hundred kilometers away, a pale gray rock against the black.

"All systems are green," Eli reported, his fingers dancing over a secondary console. "Power is standing by."

Leah's hands trembled slightly as she gripped the remote controls for the sensor arrays, a pair of small, black boxes now strapped to her navigation station. She was focused, the usual energy replaced by a nervous determination. She nudged the ship, the Galilee groaning in response, lining up the guns with the asteroid.

"Targeting complete," she said, her voice a little higher than usual.

"Primary systems, secondary systems bypassed," Deborah reported, her stoicism a welcome anchor. "Power is stable, and holding."

Noah took a deep breath. He sat in his father's chair, the triggers for the cannons now taped to the armrests, a crude but effective modification. "Test shot one. Single Barrel. Low power."

He squeezed the trigger. There was a low hum, a surge of power, and then a beam of blue light lanced out from the forward truss. The shot sailed past the asteroid, a clean miss.

"Missed, honey," Leah said, her disappointment evident. "My apologies."

"Don't worry about it, Aunt Leah," Noah said calmly, his use of the informal nickname a small comfort to them both. "It's the first time. We'll get it right."

"Guns are warm, Noah," Eli warned. "Temps are starting

to climb."

"Test shot two. Single barrel. Low power." Noah adjusted his aim, making a micro-adjustment to the Galilee's thrusters. This time, the beam grazed the asteroid's edge, sending a shower of glowing rock into space.

"Graze, sweetie!" Leah called out, with a burst of cheer. "We're getting closer!"

"Temps are getting warm now," Eli said, tinged with concern. "She's pushing her limits."

"Test shot three. Low power. Single barrel," Noah ordered.

He fired again. This time, the beam struck true, a perfect hit. The asteroid glowed for a moment, and then a small chunk of it broke away and drifted into space.

A ripple of relief passed through the bridge. It worked. The cheers were cut short by a sudden surge in the ship's power grid. A faint smell of ozone filled the air.

"Temps are approaching the red, Noah," Eli announced. "We've got one shot left. One more, and then heat will melt the barrels and blow the system. It's now or never."

A chipper voice came from the cargo bay speaker. It was Jabez. "Statement: Endeavor not to detonate the vessel. Such an event would result in an abbreviated voyage."

Was that a note of gallows humor, Noah pondered. "Alright, everyone listen up," he commanded. "Full power. Both cannons. One last shot. Let's make it count."

Leah's excitement bubbled over. "Oh my stars, baby! This is it! You go get 'em!" She looked at the viewscreen with a fierce, almost motherly pride.

With a sigh of resignation, Eli flipped the final switch. The hum of the ship rose to a high-pitched whine. Power indicators on every console began to flash. The whole ship vibrated as if straining under an immense weight.

"All systems at maximum," Eli announced, his tone tight with tension.

Noah took a moment, his hands steady on the triggers. He took a deep breath, picturing Cain's sneering face. He was not a boy anymore. He was the captain of the Galilee.

"Firing," he said.

He squeezed both triggers. A massive, brilliant blue-white beam of pure energy erupted from both cannons. It was a twin fist of light, hitting the asteroid with a blinding flash. The rock didn't just break; it vaporized, a brilliant explosion of super-heated gas and dust that briefly outshone the distant stars.

Silence. The crew stared at the empty space where the asteroid had been. A low cheer erupted from the bridge. The Galilee had guns. And they worked.

Chapter 21

On the bridge of the Babylon, the usual quiet tension had been replaced by a bristling energy. Every station was manned, the crew moving with a focused, anticipatory urgency. Josh stood by the navigation console, the cool light of the holoscreen illuminating his face. Beside him, Ithamar nervously adjusted his spectacles, his eyes darting from the console to the figures on the bridge.

Cain, a cup of his customary green tea in hand, held court in the center of the bridge. He was a silent storm, his presence drawing all eyes without a single word. The burly First Mate Dathan, and the hawk-faced Tactical Officer, Delilah, flanked him, their competition for his approval a palpable, electric current.

"Captain," Delilah's words were crisp and efficient, "the fighter has confirmed. The Gomorrah is on the exact vector we predicted." A small, triumphant smirk played on her lips as she glanced at Dathan.

"My intel was sound," Mr. Dathan rumbled, puffing out his chest. "We'll be on top of them before they even know we're there."

Cain simply took a slow sip of his tea, his gaze moving between the two of them. His silence was its own form of praise, and it seemed to satisfy them both. He then turned his attention to navigation, his eyes locking on Josh. The boy felt a flicker of the old conflict—hatred mixed with a strange, dark pride.

"Navigation," Cain said, his resonance a powerful rumble. "We are less than a day out from the Dead Sea. The Gomorrah is a few hours ahead of us. They are expecting a leisurely transit through the nebula. Give me an attack profile that will give us the element of surprise. I want to be in striking range before they even get a sensor ping."

Ithamar's fingers flew across the console. "Sir, we…we can accelerate. A full burn. We get ahead of them, captain. The nebula…it will hide us…our approach. Gomorrah…she will not see us…not in time, sir. If we accelerate now, we can be there in…" he paused, a flurry of calculations playing on the screen. "…three hours, sir."

Cain's gaze remained fixed on Josh, ignoring Ithamar. "What do you see, Mr. Joshua?"

Josh took a deep breath, the cold resolve from the previous night firm in his mind. He wasn't the boy who dreamed of a life of peace anymore. He was a survivor. He accessed a different set of projections, the gravitational topography of the surrounding space. He pointed to a web of faint lines on the screen.

"Sir, Mr. Ithamar's plan is good," Josh said, his voice steady. "The Gomorrah is traveling on a direct course, but the nebula is bordered by the gravitational wells of the gas giant, Behemoth, and the asteroid clusters, Leviathan and Ziz. Instead of a direct burn, we can slingshot around them. It's less direct but would require far less power. The reduced energy signature combined with the nebula's interference would make us almost invisible to their long-range sensors until we are too close to be countered."

He looked up at Cain. "By using the wells, we'll build up more speed with less energy. We could be in position in two hours, sir."

Delilah and Dathan exchanged a look of surprise. Cain's expression remained unreadable, but a flicker of something—approval, perhaps, or a predatory satisfaction—danced in his eyes.

"Execute it," Cain commanded, his order sharp and clear. "Plot the course, Junior Navigator. I want the engines spooling up now."

Ithamar, wide-eyed, stared from Josh to Cain. He began to plot the coordinates, but it was Josh's plan, Josh's skill that was now in motion. The drone of the engines rose in pitch, a new, thrilling note of anticipation filling the bridge. The final countdown had begun.

For the next two hours, the bridge was a hive of quiet, focused activity. Josh remained at the navigation console, his fingers flying across the display, making minute corrections to their course as the ship wove through the gravitational wells of the gas giant Behemoth and a local asteroid cluster. The course was complex, but it was working. The Babylon was accelerating with a graceful, silent speed, its energy signature nearly nonexistent against the chaotic background of the nebula's interference.

"We're entering the final turn, Captain," Ithamar announced, his inflection tight with a mix of fear and excitement. "Closing on Gomorrah's position."

A cold, exhilarating jolt ran through Josh. He could feel

the proximity of the other ship, a faint ghost on the sensors, growing more solid by the minute. He had done his part. Now it was Cain's turn.

Cain rose from his command chair, his movements fluid and purposeful. He set his teacup down on a nearby console. The sound was soft, but on the otherwise silent bridge, it was a gunshot. He began issuing orders like a general on a battlefield, a steady current of command.

"Tactical Officer," he said. "Weapons and fighter status."

Delilah snapped to attention. "Main guns charged and ready, Captain. Point defenses are online. All systems are green. Our forward scout, Baal 01, is inbound for refueling, Captain. The two attack fighters, Moloch 01 and Moloch 02, are in the bay and hot-cocked. They have their orders: cripple their point defenses first, then any heavy batteries. The final fighter, Moloch 03, is prepped for launch in the bay, ready if needed."

Josh made a mental note of this. Four fighters. One was out scouting, two were about to depart, but one would remain in the bay, ready to launch. A ship prepped for launch… if he could just get off the bridge, maybe that was his chance for escape.

"First Mate," Cain's attention shifted. "Boarding parties."

Mr. Dathan puffed out his chest with a grunt of satisfaction. "Three shuttles are ready to launch, Captain. Twelve men in each. We'll be moving the moment their defenses are down. My shuttle will lead the breach of the port airlock. Master Jair will lead the second shuttle that breaches the hull in the engineering section. The third will wait for you and your men, Captain, and breach at the starboard airlock."

A glimmer of something like hope blossomed in Josh's

chest. Most of the crew would be off the ship during the boarding action. Cain himself would be leaving the ship. His opportunities for escape are not just a dream anymore; they are taking shape.

"Excellent," Cain said, his face a mask of satisfaction. "Navigation, what's our range?"

Ithamar stared at his console. "Five thousand kilometers, Captain! Launch window in ten seconds!"

"Launch the fighters!" Cain's order rang out across the bridge.

Chapter 22

The Galilee hummed a low, satisfied tune as it hung in the deep, silent blackness of Gethsemane's orbit. Docked at a massive, skeletal cargo port platform, the ship's running lights were a faint constellation against the sprawling network of gantries and conduits. On the bridge, the air was a familiar mix of recycled oxygen and the comforting aroma of roasted coffee.

Noah sat in the command chair, his gaze shifted from the main viewscreen, where the bright orange form of Jabez was visible, deftly maneuvering a massive container, to a secondary monitor displaying a cascading series of diagnostic reports. Every system was green. Eli's handiwork was, as always, flawless.

In the background, Leah's sweet, syrupy Southern accent was a steady stream of business and charm. "Well, bless your heart, honey, that's just a tragic price for such a lovely shipment," she cooed into the comms. "Now, what if we were to say… fifty percent? Just for us long-time partners."

The bridge doors whooshed open, and Deborah stepped through, her face a little flushed and a few strands of hair clinging to her forehead. Her gray coveralls were still perfectly neat, but the faint sheen of sweat suggested a hard day's work. She approached Noah, her posture ramrod straight.

"Captain," she said, her Australian accent a sharp command. "Offload is on schedule. We're a hundred percent in ten minutes. Jabez is just securing the final two containers."

Before Noah could reply, the doors opened again, and Eli shambled in, wiping grease from his hands with a dirty rag. "Aye, Noah, lad. Ran the final diagnostic on that power converter. Should be good as new." He gestured toward the monitor with a thumb. "What's the word? She holding?"

Noah gave him a simple nod and a thumbs-up. "All green, Eli. Perfect as always."

A broad grin split Eli's face, his weary eyes crinkling at the corners. "Then that's it! She's ready for the next run, Captain!"

Leah ended her call with a cheerful "Y'all have a wonderful day now!" She turned from her station, her face glowing with satisfaction. "And speaking of runs, we're a hit! We've made a tidy profit on this first go, and I've got a whole menu of new contracts waiting for us." She held up a data slate with a flourish. "The only question is, where do we go next?"

Noah stood up, a sense of relief and quiet pride washing over him. The bitterness that had filled him during the last voyage had softened, replaced by a simple sense of accomplishment. "I'll tell you what we're going to do. We're celebrating." He walked to the center of the bridge, his smile warm and genuine. "I've been told there's an Italian place in the port that's famous for their pasta. We're all going out for dinner. My treat."

A cheer went up from Eli. "Now that's what I'm talkin' about! Pasta, a glass of something nice… what a grand idea!"

Leah giggled, fluttering her eyelashes at Eli. "Oh, isn't he just the best, Eli? A gentleman and a captain. I do so love a man who knows how to treat a lady to a nice dinner."

Deborah, ever the professional, gave a curt nod. "Whatever you say, Captain. Just tell me what time we're moving out."

A tinny, synthesized voice crackled from the comms. "Affirmative, Captain. But you should know… no pasta for me. I'm afraid I'll never have a taste for the finer things in life."

The crew shared a laugh, the tension of the last few weeks melting away. The Galilee felt like a home again.

The restaurant, Capeo, was a stark contrast to the utilitarian world of a cargo port. Soft lighting cast a warm glow on white linen tablecloths, and the aroma of garlic and basil filled the air. A waiter in a crisp black suit and white shirt navigated the room with practiced ease, placing a dessert plate and coffee cup in front of each person. The tiramisu, a delicate mountain of cream and cocoa, looked as if it had been sculpted for a museum.

Even Jabez was with them. He had been rolled into a corner of the restaurant, his bright orange chassis a cheerful contrast to the muted decor. A small, neatly tied black bow tie was affixed to his frontal sensor array, a touch of humor that had been Eli's idea.

"Oh, Lordy, I don't think I can eat another bite," Leah groaned, patting her stomach over the explosion of color that was her puffy dress. "My mama always said a full belly is a happy one, but I'm about to burst right out of this here frock!"

"You're a disgrace to the entire spacer community, Leah,"

Deborah said, a hint of a smile on her lips as she adjusted the uncharacteristic bow in her tightly-pulled ponytail. "I've seen junior Loadmasters with more self-control."

Eli chuckled, digging into his tiramisu with gusto. He had traded his uniform coveralls for a cardigan and jeans, which were a touch rumpled, but he looked perfectly content. "Ah, what's a little bit of gluttony now and again, Deb? A spacer's got to enjoy the little things."

Noah took a slow sip of his coffee, letting the familiar warmth settle in his stomach. He was in slacks and a polo shirt, a simple and comfortable outfit. "It's a nice change of pace," he said, looking at his crew. "I'm glad we did this."

Once the plates were cleared and fresh coffee had been poured, the conversation turned to business.

"Right then, honey," Leah said, pulling out her data slate with a professional flourish. "I've got three options for our next contract." She projected a star map onto the table's surface. "First up, a simple run to Ur. It's a short hop, easy money, and we'll be back in port in no time." A small, bright icon blinked on the map. "Second, we have a longer, more lucrative contract with Chaldea. The route is a bit more remote, but it's a well-traveled lane, and the profits are great."

She paused, and the third option appeared on the map. The icon for their destination, Gehenna, pulsed with a foreboding red light. "And then there's this one. A high-risk, high-reward run to Gehenna. The cargo is invaluable, but the route is… tricky. It skirts the edge of the Dead Sea Nebula, and it's full of blind spots and celestial anomalies. Pirates have been known to operate in the sector, but it's not exactly a war zone. The money, however, is a game-changer. It would set us up for months."

Leah's eyes met Noah's. "Honey, it's a risk. A bigger one than the others."

A long silence settled over the table. Noah looked at the map, and a familiar cold feeling settled in his stomach. He remembered the last time his father had looked at a map with a similar red mark on it, a high-risk sector. But then, they had been a simple freighter, a family, not a ship bristling with plasma cannons. They had been defenseless. Now, they were not.

"We take the Gehenna contract," he determined, quiet but firm.

Eli's gaze snapped to his. The older man said nothing, but the look in his eyes said it all. *You're doing what your father did.*

Deborah, ever pragmatic, raised an eyebrow. "Are you sure, Captain? That route has a reputation."

"The money is worth the risk," Noah said, a lie he almost believed himself. He saw the doubt in their eyes and tried to justify it. "We're not just a freighter anymore. We've got the cannons now. We're ready for trouble. In fact… a part of me hopes they show up. It's time we put those guns to good use."

"Request: Please ensure my bow tie is properly stowed before engaging in combat," Jabez's synthesized vocalizer crackled from his small speaker. "This unit does not wish to be a casualty of fashion."

Noah was looking for justice, yes. But a part of him was looking for vengeance. He wanted to feel the jolt of the cannons firing, to see a pirate ship vaporized, to settle a score that had been festering in his heart. He saw the quiet understanding in Eli's eyes. Eli knew. He always knew.

Deborah gave a reluctant nod. "Very well, Captain. Your

call."

"Oh, it's not a death wish, honey!" Leah said, her intonation bright. "It's a new beginning! And we'll get through it together."

The crew paid the bill and headed back to the Galilee, a satisfied and eager group. They had survived their first cargo run and found a new rhythm.

Back aboard the Galilee, the rest of the crew had retired for the night and the ship felt like a tomb wrapped around two ghosts.

Noah stood alone on the bridge, the holographic star charts cycling slowly through their pre-programmed paths, the illuminated routes of Ur and Chaldea ignored in favor of the single, stark red line leading toward Gehenna.

The bridge door hissed open, and Eli stepped through, his gait heavier than usual. He didn't bother with the lights; the dim glow of the console was enough.

"They're all asleep," Eli said, his voice thick with worry. He walked to the main window and looked out at the lights of the spaceport, a thousand easy destinations winking in the void. "A grand dinner they had. They'll remember that fondly, those ones." Eli said, turning to face him. "I didn't want to be sayin' this in front of them. They're green, and a captain shouldn't have his decisions questioned by an engineer. But this ain't about respect, lad. This is about common sense and history. I think you should reconsider this Gehenna contract, I do now."

Noah braced his arms against the console edge. "The Gehenna contract pays nearly triple. We need the credits for upgrades, for better provisions, for spare parts that aren't salvaged junk. It's the smart economic choice."

"Ah, whisht! It's a fool's choice!" Eli snapped, the quiet ferocity of his tone cutting through the silence. "It's a route known for one thing: gettin' ships stripped and crews spaced. We could have taken Ur, safe and easy, and been back next month. We could have taken Chaldea, a decent payday with manageable risk. But you picked the one that's a magnet for every lowlife and blood-drunk pirate in the sector."

"And if they show their faces, we have something for them this time," Noah insisted, "We have the plasma cannons. We spent three days rigging them. Why? So we could crawl to Ur like a defenseless tug? We have firepower now. We should use it. We should take the riskier routes so others won't have to."

Eli stepped closer, the soft light casting deep shadows over his weary face. "Ah, the look of ye. The nobility. Just like your father."

He paused, letting the implication hang. "But you and I know the truth of it, don't we now, Captain?" The title was a sharp edge now. "This isn't about protecting other freighters. This isn't about somethings else."

Eli leaned in, his voice dropping to a harsh whisper. "This is about bait, sure it is. You chose Gehenna because it's the most likely place to run into Cain. You chose the highest risk because you want to finish the job he started. You want to use those jerry-rigged cannons to blow the Babylon out of the void."

Noah's face was a mask of furious denial, but his eyes betrayed him. They flickered with a raw, vengeful heat that was unmistakable. "That's not true. I'm thinking like a captain. I'm calculating the risk-reward ratio, and I'm factoring in our new capabilities."

"Your new capability is a thirst for vengeance that's going to get the rest of this crew killed, God help us!" Eli countered, throwing his hands up in exasperation. "You're lookin' for a fight, Noah! You're putting your trust in three quick shots and a green crew that's never seen combat! Just because we have weapons doesn't mean we should go looking for war!"

Noah pushed off the console and faced Eli fully, his young face etched with grim determination. "I saw what happens to defenseless ships, Eli. I'm not going back to hiding. We're taking the Gehenna route."

Eli stared at the boy, seeing not his young apprentice, but an angry young man—and the devastating path of the pirates who had ruined their lives. He took a slow, heavy breath, the argument spent. He had failed to reach him.

"Very well, Captain," Eli said, his voice flat with disappointment. "Then I'll be downstairs securing the engines and prayin' your cannons fire straight. But if you see that blaggard, I want you to remember your brother, not as a reason to fight, but as a reason to live, d'you hear me?"

The old engineer turned and walked out, leaving the young captain alone on the bridge with the quiet hum of the ship and the pulsing red line leading straight into danger.

Chapter 23

As Cain's order rang out across the bridge, two small, bug-like vessels, the Moloch 01 and the Moloch 02, launched from Babylon's docking bay. Twin blurs of silent menace, they streaked toward the unwitting Gomorrah.

The two fighters were like hornets leaving the hive, a pair of lethal insects against the massive bulk of the target. They emerged from the nebula's cloud and accelerated to full speed, closing the distance in a matter of seconds. As they approached, they spread their formation, each peeling off to a different side of the Gomorrah. Without a single warning, they began their strafing runs, a torrent of laser fire sizzling down the length of the larger ship. The Gomorrah's point-defense turrets erupted in a series of small, bright explosions, torn to shreds before they could even get a lock on their attackers.

The fighters zipped past Gomorrah's bow, then reversed their vectors with a grace that defied physics. They repeated the feat, roaring back down the length of the ship and obliterating the remaining point-defense guns. With the Gomorrah's smaller guns silenced, the Moloch 01 and Moloch 02 separated completely. One went high, arcing over the ship's primary hull, while the other went low, skimming along her underbelly. They launched their ship-to-ship missiles simultaneously, two streaks of brilliant fire that slammed directly into the Gomorrah's main gun batteries. The explosions were a furious blossom of light, and the Gomorrah shivered from the force of the blasts.

Just as the fighters finished their work, the Babylon emerged from the nebula, her massive form appearing like a ghost from the hazy light. The Gomorrah was crippled and helpless. On the bridge, a targeting beacon flared to life, acquiring the enemy ship in a matter of seconds. Cain watched, his face impassive, as the targeting system acquired its lock.

Josh watched the screens intently from his console. His stomach twisted, but his hands were steady. He was superb at plotting the approach; the execution was another thing entirely.

Cain's voice, sharp and commanding, cut across the bridge. "Ithamar, take the Conn for this engagement. Mr. Joshua, you've plotted us to the doorstep. Let's see how well you learn to open it."

Ithamar, his face pale and nervous, immediately bent over the controls. "Ye.., yes, Captain. Full lock acquired. Holding stable, *jee*, yes, holding stable."

Cain stepped lightly over to stand directly behind Josh, his presence radiating cold control.

"Look closely, Mr. Joshua. Observe the vector," Cain murmured, his voice low enough to be private, yet intense. "They are crippled, yes? But their escape vectors remain. A straight-on kill is too simple. A smart predator does not just destroy; he secures the prize."

Cain's hand brushed Josh's shoulder, a chilling, controlling touch. "I've ordered Ithamar to hit the drive first. Why?"

Josh, startled by the closeness and the question, stared at the crippled ship on the screen. "To stop them from escaping, sir. And to prevent them from firing a retaliatory strike."

"Simple, but incomplete," Cain corrected, his breath warm on Josh's neck. "The drive explosion provides a massive kinetic shockwave. That shockwave will destabilize their internal gravity field and vent the atmosphere from the engine room—making our boarding parties' job easier. Then, we hit the bridge to decapitate the snake."

Josh watched as the targeting system acquired its lock. The lesson was brutal, brilliant, and utterly terrifying. Cain was teaching him how to murder with efficiency.

"Fire," he commanded.

The Babylon's main cannons thundered, a pair of brilliant red bolts of energy lancing out into the void. The first slammed into the Gomorrah's primary drive, the explosion ripping away a large section of the ship's engine block. The second hit the bridge, turning the forward section of the vessel into a silent, burning ruin.

Josh watched it all from his navigation console, his eyes glued to the monitors. He felt a wave of conflicting emotions wash over him. A rush of exhilaration surged through his veins, the thrill of victory, the satisfying culmination of a clever plan. But it was quickly followed by a wave of nausea, a chilling sickness at the sight of the death and destruction he had just been a part of. He tried to rationalize it, to soothe the knot in his stomach by reminding himself that the crew of the Gomorrah were murdering pirates, just like Cain. They deserved this, he told himself.

Cain, unfazed by the carnage, simply turned to the First

Mate, Dathan.

"Launch the first two boarding parties," he ordered. "The ship is ours."

Dathan's face split into a wide, triumphant grin. "Aye, Captain." He moved quickly to the comms panel, bellowing as he relayed the order. The bridge buzzed with a tense energy as First Mate Dathan transmitted the commands over the comms, then bolted off the bridge to catch the lead shuttle himself.

On the main monitor, Josh watched the feed from Dathan's helmet cam. He saw flashes of laser fire and the blur of pirates moving through the halls. The First Mate's scarred face, a mask of grim satisfaction, filled a smaller window as he spoke. "Master Jair with team two reports Engineering is secured. There was no resistance. Team one and I are in the main crew section, mopping up."

"What about Captain Korach, Mr. Dathan?" Cain asked, his manner calm and precise. He was a surgeon now, his tone detached.

"He's with a few holdouts," Dathan replied. "They've barricaded themselves in the mess hall. We've got them pinned, but they won't surrender."

Cain's gaze drifted back to the monitor, his eyes narrowing on the chaos. He took a long, final sip of his tea and set the empty cup down with a soft click. "Excellent. I will deal with Captain Korach personally." He turned to the Tactical Officer, Delilah. "You have the Conn, Ms. Delilah."

Delilah's eyes gleamed, and she sat up straighter in the command chair, her expression a mask of satisfaction. "Aye, Captain."

Cain gave a nod to his men assembled at the aft of the bridge, and they moved as one, marching from the bridge with a quiet, deadly purpose. Josh watched them go, his heart pounding in his chest. His chance. It was now or never. Cain was leaving the bridge. Most of the crew were already off the ship in the boarding action. It was a long shot, but he had to try.

He turned to Ithamar, his face a grimace. "Ithamar… I'm not feeling well." He put a hand to his stomach. "All the… all the violence. It's too much."

Ithamar, his own face pale from watching the monitors, put a hand on Josh's shoulder. "I understand. I have navigation under control. You should go before you foul the deck."

"What is it, Mr. Joshua?" the Tactical Officer demanded, her tone sharp. She had already noticed the exchange.

Ithamar responded quickly. "The boy is feeling ill, Ma'am. The battle… he has no stomach for it."

A look of pure disgust crossed Delilah's face. "Go!" she snapped, pointing a finger toward the door. "Get it together and clean yourself up before you come back."

"Yes, Ma'am." Josh turned and walked calmly from the bridge, his steps quickening as soon as the door sealed behind him. He took a deep breath and began to run. His next chapter was about to begin.

Chapter 24

The bridge of the Galilee was a space of contained tension, a stark contrast to the celebratory dinner that had preceded this high-risk run. A star map, the vibrant, glowing heart of the bridge, occupied the center of the main tactical display. Streaks of light, representing the ship's course, were overlaid with a web of navigation data. Leah was at the helm, her hands a graceful blur over the console. Her fiery red hair, seemed to have an energy of its own, bouncing with every agitated movement.

"Well, bless my little heart, honey," she huffed into the quiet of the bridge, her Southern drawl stretched thin with frustration. "You know, my mama always said there was nothing sadder in the world than a dishonest man, but let me tell you, those folks at Gehenna are giving it a run for its money."

Noah, seated in the captain's chair, watched her with a calm he didn't quite feel. "At least you salvaged the deal, Leah. We got paid."

"Oh, we got paid, all right," she sniffed, her fingers dancing across the screen to calculate a new course. "But only after I had to threaten to publish their shady business practices all over the galactic trade-ways. And that's not even the half of it. I had three potential contracts for the return trip, and every single one of them just… vaporized. Poof! Gone."

A grim silence settled on the bridge. Eli's concerns had not come to pass…yet at least. But a light cargo load meant the profit for the return trip would be minimal, a disappointing anticlimax to the tense, uneventful journey to Gehenna.

"I tell you, Noah, a body just can't get a break." She shot a look at the console, a stormy expression on her face. "I am so glad we're getting out of this wretched system."

Suddenly, a buzz from the comms station. "Freighter FN-387, Galilee, your flight plan has been filed and accepted. You are cleared for departure. Proceed to Waypoint Alpha-Seven-Two-Niner. Good luck with the return trip. You'll probably need it." The tone was condescending, thick with a bored, lazy authority.

Deborah, who had been monitoring the comms, straightened her already ramrod-straight posture. "Orbital Traffic Control," she muttered. "They've been rude and unprofessional all day." She pressed a button on the console. "This is the Freighter FN-387, Galilee. Clearance acknowledged. We'll be on our way." Her response was crisp and polite, a model of professional decorum, but her expression was one of barely contained fury.

"Well, aren't they just a ray of sunshine?" Eli grumbled from his station, his brow furrowed as he checked a diagnostic report. He glanced over at Noah, a shared, weary look passing between them.

The ship, freed from the station's mooring, began to drift away from the port. Leah tapped a final command, and the ship's main drive flared to life, a silent plume of super-heated plasma that shoved them into the blackness of space.

"Don't you worry, sweetie," Leah said, her countenance a little brighter as they left the troublesome system behind. "Once we get back to Gethsemane, I'll go back to those other contracts. A little bit of Southern charm and a lot of business smarts, and we'll be loaded for bear."

Noah's gaze fixed on the viewscreen. The stars of the Gehenna system began to shrink behind them. A high-risk journey, a disappointing outcome. They had gotten out with their lives, but not the wealth they had hoped for. But, he should have been relieved, even grateful. They had crossed a well-known pirate haven and delivered their high-value cargo without a single incident. The new crew was safe. The jerry-rigged plasma cannons, thankfully, had remained silent. But instead of the easy calm of a successful run, a corrosive feeling of frustration settled over him. The safe passage was, perversely, a bitter disappointment. If he was honest with himself, he had chosen Gehenna because the statistics said it was a trap—and he had wanted to be the one to spring it. The fact that the trap had been empty felt like a personal failure. He hadn't been testing the ship; he had been hunting.

You should be thanking your lucky stars, Noah. The voice in his mind was Eli's, wise and weary.

Luck is just missed opportunity, the dark thought countered. *We were ready. We were armed.*

He pressed his fingers hard against the cool metal of the console. They had gotten out with their lives, but not the vengeance he craved. Hollow relief mixed with burning, unspent bloodlust. He had survived, but he hadn't achieved his goal.

The safe departure from Gehenna felt less like a victory and more like a simple delay...but the return leg was through the same space. Another risk, another chance.

Several days later, the Galilee was in the most dangerous part of the route back to Gethsemane. The stars were a thin scattering of diamonds against an inky blackness, and the thrum of the ship was the only sound in the dead of night. The crew was on high alert, their conversation minimal, their focus sharp. The threat of pirates, though unseen, hung in the air like a heavy mist.

Suddenly, a series of alarms blared from Leah's navigation console.

"What in the blazes?" Leah's hands flew across her controls, her eyes wide as she scanned her readouts. "We've got a massive energy burst on long-range sensors, honey. Big one, too. Looks like some kind of weapon discharge. It's on our starboard side, a few thousand kilometers out."

Before anyone could respond, Deborah, seated at the comms station, froze. Her face went pale as she pressed a finger to her earpiece. "Wait, I'm getting something. It's faint… just a blip. A distress signal." Her lilt filled with urgency. She worked her console, trying to amplify the signal, but it was gone as quickly as it had appeared. "It's gone," she reported, her frustration clear. "It was too weak to be sure, but it was there. Someone's in a spot of bother."

A collective dread fell over the bridge. There was no doubt in anyone's mind what had happened. A pirate attack. Another one.

Noah's face, which had been calm and stoic for the entire trip, went rigid. The familiar cold, vengeful feeling returned, stronger than ever. The memory of his family's last moments flooded his mind. It wasn't just a signal. It was a call to arms.

He stood up, his timbre firm. "Leah, plot an intercept course. Eli, get to engineering. Deb, get the power converters ready." He turned to face his crew, his gaze meeting each of their eyes in turn. "It's time we put those guns to use."

Eli simply nodded, his face a mask of grim determination. Despite the tension between them, he did not hesitate or question. Deborah gave a short, sharp nod of acknowledgment. Leah, who had already begun entering the new coordinates, stopped and looked at Noah. A wave of raw emotion passed over her face, and her tone, usually so melodic and gentle, came out as a fierce declaration.

"Let's do it," she said, trembling slightly. "Let's do it for my Becky."

The words hung in the air, a silent tribute to the woman they had all lost. It wasn't just about vengeance it was about family. The crew turned to their stations, a new purpose filling the air of the bridge. Brave or foolish, the Galilee, a freighter built for peace, was about to go to war.

The Galilee shuddered as its main drive roared to life, pushing the old freighter past its operational limits. G-forces pinned the crew to their seats as the ship accelerated with a force it had never been designed for. Noah, still standing, braced himself against his chair, his hands gripping the armrests. He saw the grim expressions on the faces of his crew. This was not the ship they knew. It was no longer a home, but a weapon.

"Leah, throttle to maximum. Eli, I want every ounce of power you can squeeze out of that engine."

He sat down, a flurry of new thoughts and instincts racing through his mind. He was no longer just Noah; he was

Captain Noah. And a captain had to be cunning. They couldn't go into a fight with there identity broadcast across the sector.

"Deborah," he commanded, his voice sharp and clear over the engine's rising whine. "Kill the transponder. Immediately."

Deborah's eyes widened for a fraction of a second, but she didn't hesitate. Her fingers flew across the comms console, and the transponder light, a constant beacon of their presence, winked out. The Galilee was now a ghost in the dark.

"I'm giving us a new callsign, just for this," he said. "From now on, on comms, we're the Archangel. And I'm Captain Gabriel."

Leah, her eyes still on her console, gave a tight smile. "I like it, sweetie. Got a certain ring to it."

"Weapons range in five minutes," Deborah reported tightly. "I'm picking up two distinct signatures. A standard cargo freighter and a second, smaller vessel with illegal power surges consistent with a pirate attack."

Noah's stomach tightened. This was it. The moment of truth. He took a deep breath. "Leah, put them on the main viewer."

The viewscreen flickered, then resolved into a chaotic scene. A trusswork freighter, a mirror image of the Galilee, was listing, its running lights winking out one by one. A much smaller, more agile pirate vessel was circling it like a shark, its weapons flashing with deadly intent.

Noah's heart hammered against his ribs. It was too close. Too familiar. The scene was a brutal echo of the day his world ended.

"Targeting sensors, Leah," he ordered, unwavering. "Bring

them online. Eli, you said we have a few shots before we're at risk?"

Eli, a grim set to his jaw, nodded. "Aye, lad. The heat and power limits haven't changed. We've got two, maybe three shots before we risk a catastrophic failure. A quick, decisive strike is the only way."

"We're in communications range," Deborah announced.

Noah grabbed the comms mike. He had to distract them. He had to draw their fire.

"This is the Archangel, to the unidentified vessel engaging a civilian freighter," Noah's resonance, now deeper and more authoritative, boomed across all frequencies. "Cease your attack immediately. We are a Port Authority patrol vessel. I repeat, cease and desist."

There was no response, but a moment later, the pirate ship broke off its attack. It turned, its thrusters flaring as it pushed to a high-g escape vector. For a moment, a wave of disappointment washed over Noah. He hadn't gotten his fight.

But then, he saw it. The pirate ship's acceleration wasn't quite enough. The two vessels were now on diverging paths, but for a brief window, they were within firing range.

"Leah, steer for an intercept course!" Noah yelled, the adrenaline surging through his veins. "Pull up the targeting sensors!"

Leah worked her controls, the Galilee groaning as she made a sharp, gut-wrenching turn. The pirate vessel, a sleek black needle, grew larger on the viewscreen. Noah gripped the triggers on his armrests, his heart a frantic drumbeat in his chest. He was going to fire. But not both guns. That would be foolish. He needed to be conservative so heat wouldn't melt them, and he would have no defense. He chose to fire only one, saving the other in case of a counter-attack.

He waited, a cold resolve settling over him. He held his breath, watching the targeting reticle line up on the fleeing vessel. He waited until the last possible second, when the two ships were at their closest point and the pirate was on the edge of his range.

Fwoooom!

A single, brilliant beam of blue energy lanced out from the Galilee's left-forward truss, a spear of vengeance that streaked across the void. The hit was a graze, a flash of blue light against the pirate ship's stern. The damage was light, but a piece of the outer hull ripped away, spiraling into space. A message had been sent.

The pirate ship didn't slow, but its thrusters flared in a desperate burst of acceleration, and it was gone.

"They're gone, Captain," Deborah said, her face filled with a mixture of relief and awe.

Noah watched the viewscreen, his hands still gripping the armrests, his knuckles white. The adrenaline faded, replaced by a bitter, sharp spike of fury. The graze was not enough; the message wasn't clear. "Cowards! They run when they see a challenge!" he muttered, the words escaping as a tight hiss before he choked the anger down. The satisfaction was there, but it was overshadowed by the deep, hollow frustration of a predator denied its kill.

"Abandon pursuit," he ordered, his voice hoarse. "Aunt Leah, turn us around. Let's go render aid."

Leah brought the Galilee around, her hands steady on the controls. The ship's powerful main drive, which had just pushed them on a warpath, now gently nudged them toward the damaged freighter. On the main viewer, the vessel, a standard trusswork cargo ship, was a battered, wounded bird, its running lights a dim, flickering testament to the recent fight.

As they drew closer, Noah saw the freighter's thrusters flare. It was under power and accelerating away from them as fast as possible. A wave of confusion washed over the bridge.

"They're running," Eli muttered, a puzzled look on his face.

"Deb, hail them," Noah commanded, grabbing the comms mike once more. "Open a wide channel." He kept the callsign of Archangel and his alias of Captain Gabriel.

"This is the Archangel, to the crew of the distressed vessel," Noah said, his tone now calm and reassuring. "We've driven off the pirates. We're here to render aid."

The channel was silent for a tense moment. Then, a tired, cautious voice crackled back. "This is Captain Esau of the freighter Canaan. I thank you for your... intervention." The words were laced with suspicion. "But we have no need of your assistance."

"Captain, your ship is damaged," Noah said, trying to hide the onset of frustration again. "We have a medic on board. We can offer medical assistance and our engineer can help with repairs."

"You are not Port Authority," Captain Esau replied, his tone hardening. "I can't see your transponder broadcast. And a commercial freighter does not carry plasma cannons." There was a long pause, and when he spoke again, his words were a cold accusation. "I have dealt with pirates before. I am in no mood to fall for their tricks a second time. My crew and

I will make repairs and get to port on our own. Stay away from my ship."

Noah tried to explain, to tell him that he was just a simple freighter like him, that he was only trying to help, but the captain of the Canaan had already closed the channel. The ship's thrusters flared once more, and it began to accelerate away at its maximum safe speed, a wounded but determined shadow in the dark.

A stunned silence fell over the Galilee's bridge. Leah, Eli, and Deborah exchanged bewildered glances. The elation from the battle had evaporated, replaced by a heavy disappointment. They had risked everything to save that crew, only to be accused of being the very thing they had fought against.

"Well," Eli said, breaking the silence with a sigh. "I suppose that's that, then."

Noah stood up, his shoulders slumped. The high from the successful shot was gone, leaving only the hollow ache of being misunderstood. "Weapons powered down," he ordered, the words came out as a broken sigh. "Leah, return us to our previous course. I'm heading to the galley for coffee. Does anyone else want a cup?"

One by one, they all answered yes, a tired chorus. Leah, with her usual hyperactive energy gone, looked exhausted. Deborah, the no-nonsense professional, seemed to have been deflated by the encounter.

Chapter 25

Cain and his escort marched through the ship's corridors. They were a grim, determined procession, their footsteps falling in a single, purposeful rhythm. They moved toward the main docking bay, their hands on their holstered weapons, checking the seals on their helmets and the charge on their sidearms.

Josh, a floor below, moved through a main corridor, his hand still clutched to his stomach. He paused, glancing down the empty hallway, the silence more unsettling than the noise of battle. He darted into a maintenance passage, the narrow space filled with the low buzz of power conduits. He was alone.

Aboard the third shuttle, Cain stood gripping an overhead handle, his gaze fixed on the cockpit. His men were strapped into their seats, their faces set in grim anticipation. The hatch sealed shut with a heavy clank. The pilot glanced back at Cain.

"Launch," Cain commanded, his tone a low, final whisper.

Josh crept through the mechanical labyrinth of the maintenance tunnels, his movements stealthy and precise. He could hear the ship's internal systems working all around him. He was a shadow, a ghost. He was so focused on being unseen that he forgot about the other problem: flying the fighter. He had flown the Galilee's shuttle pods and tugs, but a fighter? How much different could it be? Lost in thought, he failed to notice the hulking figure of Baruch, watching him from the shadows, a glint of cruel satisfaction in his eyes.

On the crippled Gomorrah, the First Mate Dathan and his team stood waiting at the airlock. The silence was broken by a dull thud, then the hiss of the airlock opening. Cain and his men stepped through the portal. Cain gave a single, curt nod to the First Mate. Without a word, the group set off for the mess hall, their grim purpose unwavering.

Josh reached the docking bay, a vast cavern bathed in the ship's low lighting. There it was—the Moloch 03, a sleek, silent bird of prey. He crept toward it, his heart hammering in his chest. A jeer, cruel and triumphant, cut through the quiet.

"What's the matter, Mr. Joshua? You need an airlock to vomit?"

Baruch stepped from the shadows, a wide grin on his face. He'd caught the little punk, and he was going to enjoy this. He saw his chance to settle the score and prove his worth to the captain.

Aboard the Gomorrah, Cain and his men arrived at the mess hall. Master Jair and his team stood guard at the door. Jair greeted Cain with a respectful nod. The door was barricaded, the sounds of survivors from inside muffled but defiant. Cain stepped forward. "Captain Korach!" he called out, his voice echoing in the corridor. "This is Captain Cain of the Babylon. I would ask you to do the civilized thing and surrender."

A bellow, defiant and enraged, screamed from inside. "Civilized! You call an unprovoked attack civilized. You can take your civility and stick it where the sun doesn't shine Cain! We'll die before we surrender!"

Josh was surprised, but Baruch's mistake was underestimating him. Master Jair's brutal training had taught him to react, not to think. Before Baruch could gloat further, Josh lashed out, a lightning-fast jab to the giant's solar plexus. The air whooshed from Baruch's lungs, his eyes wide in shock. Josh capitalized on his advantage, a swift pivot and a quick kick to the back of Baruch's knee bringing the brutish man to the ground. Josh grabbed a stray metal pipe, a small, heavy piece of scrap, and bludgeoned Baruch's head. The giant crumpled in a heap. Josh paused for a moment to ensure Baruch was down, then sprinted to the fighter and slammed the canopy shut.

A thunderous explosion rocked the mess hall as Cain's men blasted the door open. They stormed through the smoke, their guns blazing. A few moments later, the shooting stopped. "All clear!" a call announced. Cain stepped into the smoke-filled room.

Frantically, Josh began to study the fighter's controls. He was a pilot, but this was a war machine. The basics were the same, and a glance at the console confirmed his hope:

the pre-flight checklist was already done. All he needed was to fire the engines. He slammed the power up, the ship vibrating around him. He heard a loud *thud* against the canopy. Baruch, his head bleeding, had recovered. He was holding a sledgehammer and was beating it against the canopy, a look of pure, murderous rage on his face. The cockpit filled with the sound of metal against metal. Josh pushed the throttle forward. As the engines roared to life, the bay doors opened automatically, a safety protocol to vent the exhaust. Baruch, still hammering, was caught in the powerful torrent of the thrusters and was sucked out into the cold vacuum of space, his form a silent, tumbling speck in the void.

Cain marched toward Captain Korach, who sat amidst the smoking ruins of the mess hall. Korach, with his remaining strength, pulled a hidden pistol from the sleeve of his robe, pointing it directly at Cain. Cain did not break stride. With a blur of motion, he drew his sword and, in a single, brutal arc, cut Korach's hand clean off before he could fire. The hand and gun dropped to the ground with a soft thud. The two men locked eyes for a long moment, one filled with hate, the other with cold, ruthless purpose. Cain plunged his sword directly into Korach's heart.

Josh was in space. The massive gas giant Behemoth winked in the distance. He was free.

Chapter 26

The airlock hissed open with a familiar sound. Captain Esau, still visibly shaken, stepped out of the Port Authority shuttle onto the Canaan's bridge. His First Mate, a burly woman with a prosthetic eye, followed close behind. The two officers who had escorted them—a broad-shouldered man and his lean, hawk-faced partner in a rumpled suit—entered the ship and began their methodical, silent work. The Canaan's bridge was a mess of sparking consoles and broken screens, a grim tableau of a close call.

"Captain," the broad-shouldered officer said with calm detachment. "Officer Gideon, Port Authority. This is my partner, Agent Abner. We're here to take your statement and collect evidence related to the piracy attempt."

Esau flinched at the word "piracy." It felt too clean, too simple for the terror they had just lived through. He nodded toward Gideon, but his eyes were on Agent Abner, who was already meticulously sweeping a handheld device over the damaged consoles. The device squealed with a low whine.

"We just need you to walk us through it," Gideon continued. "One at a time. My partner will take your First Mate's statement in the galley. I'll take yours here."

Esau's heart pounded. He had been through this before, in

a different life. He wanted to get it over with, to move on. He took a seat in his command chair, the smell of burnt plastic and ozone filling the air.

"Let's start from the beginning, Captain," Gideon said, his datapad ready. "What was your first indication of a threat?"

"It was a pirate vessel," Esau began, his voice raspy and strained. "Came out of nowhere. No transponder. They were fast. They hailed us and demanded we surrender our cargo. They said they would leave us with enough life support to limp to the nearest port. I refused." He paused, a deep shudder running through him. "Then the attack started. Their cannons were brutal. We are an unarmed freighter. We had no way to defend ourselves." He clenched his fists, the memory still fresh and raw. "They spent an hour just picking us apart. It was a slow execution. The bridge took a hit. Our main thruster was vaporized, and our life support was failing. We were a sitting duck. That's when we sent the distress signal."

Gideon scribbled notes. "And the second vessel? The one that intervened?"

Esau's face soured. "That's the strange part. A bulk freighter. A big one, from the looks of it. No transponder. She hailed us using the alias 'Captain Gabriel of the Archangel.' It sounded like a kid's voice on the comms, but the orders were clear. 'Cease and desist.' She... she fired a warning shot."

On the bridge, Abner turned his attention to the comms logs. The log showed the hail from the unknown ship and the ensuing brief, one-sided conversation. He looked up at Esau, a single eyebrow raised. "A freighter? With weapons?"

"That's what I said!" Esau exclaimed. "Weapons. And good

ones, too. They fired a plasma cannon. It grazed their hull, but it took out a power conduit. Sent a clear message, but after that, the pirates were spooked. They fled."

Abner just grunted and went back to his work, but Gideon leaned forward. "This second vessel. The Archangel. Did you get a look at her?"

"Not a good one. It was all a blur. But their silhouette was wrong. It wasn't a standard freighter. The sensor data…" Esau trailed off, looking at Abner. "The officer can get it from the black box."

Gideon nodded and returned to his questioning. "And after the pirates fled? You said the Archangel tried to help?"

Esau's expression tightened. "Yes. The 'Captain' offered assistance. But there was something off about them. No transponder, weapons on a bulk freighter. It didn't add up. I told them to back off. Who helps a stranger and then doesn't want to be identified? It's not a normal response, not from a good Samaritan."

He looked at Gideon, then at Abner, a clear suspicion in his eyes. "I think they were pirates, too. Or some kind of vigilante group. Just another set of wolves."

The officers finished their interviews and meticulously documented the last details. Gideon's datapad buzzed as he cross-referenced the sensor data from the Canaan with known ships in the sector. The silhouette was odd, but the energy signature was more consistent with a commercial vessel's main drive, not a warship. The comms logs were a dead end.

"The Canaan's logs are clean, but the sensor data is strange," Gideon told Abner after they returned to their shuttle. "The energy signature is consistent with a bulk freighter, but the profile is all wrong. And the lack of a transponder is a big red flag."

Abner grunted in agreement. "A freighter with plasma cannons? Captain Esau's right to be suspicious. Could be a rival pirate gang or a vigilante."

"Either way," Gideon said, looking at the Canaan through the shuttle's viewport. "We've got a new player in the sector. Unidentified, armed, and dangerous."

The officers turned their attention to their datapads, the names of Captain Gabriel and the Archangel now officially logged into the system. The hunt for this new, mysterious vessel had begun.

Chapter 27

The cockpit of Moloch 03 was a cramped, utilitarian space, designed for combat, not comfort or long-range navigation. Josh, still strapped into the worn pilot's seat, felt the residual vibrations of the escape launch thrumming in his bones. Outside the reinforced canopy, the chaos of the nebula and the Babylon's lights faded to black. He was free, a fact that tasted like ash and triumph on his tongue.

But freedom, he was fast realizing, was just another kind of prison if you had nowhere to go.

The fighter, a squat, aggressive craft reminiscent of an ancient, twin-boomed atmospheric jet, wasn't built for interstellar travel. Its fuel reserves were already alarmingly low, designed for skirmishes, not daring escapes. Josh ran the diagnostics again, the numbers glowing an angry red on his console. Short. Too short.

His fingers danced across the navigational controls, a blur of practiced motion. He needed a port, a colony, anything. The system map slowly coalesced, highlighting the colossal, swirling grandeur of the gas giant Behemoth. *Behemoth.* He remembered Ithamar mentioning it, a landmark near the nebula, a place of resource extraction. A name appeared on his nav display: Ariel Station, a gas extraction colony in low planetary orbit. It was a long shot, dangerously far, but it was the only option within theoretical range.

Direct thrust was out. He didn't have the fuel.

A daring, almost suicidal plan began to form. He'd use Behemoth itself. Josh began plotting a course, his mind whirring through his mother's navigation lessons, superimposed with the tactical cunning he'd learned from Cain. He needed to execute a precise, terrifying dance with gravity – a slingshot maneuver around the gas giant. Too close, and Behemoth's immense gravitational pull would rip the fighter apart, crushing it in the unimaginable pressures of its deep atmosphere. Too far, and he'd miss his orbital window entirely, Moloch 03 becoming a tomb, drifting endlessly into the void.

Every calculation had to be perfect. Every micro-adjustment of the dying thrusters, precise. Sweat beaded on his brow as he fed the coordinates into the autopilot, his hands hovering over the manual override, ready to correct the slightest deviation. Moloch 03 shuddered, a faint groan from its over stressed frame as it began its perilous approach.

The view through the canopy became a breathtaking, terrifying panorama. Behemoth swelled, a canvas of churning oranges, deep reds, and swirling blues, its storm systems like gargantuan, furious eyes. The fighter dipped into its outer thermosphere, the heat shield glowing under the strain. Alarms chirped a nervous chorus, but Josh ignored them, his gaze fixed on the trajectory projections. His training with Jair, his escapes from Baruch, even Cain's cold lessons in resourcefulness—they all converged into this single, desperate act of will.

Then, just as the fuel indicator flickered on empty and the

gravitational forces threatened to pin him to his seat, he felt it – the subtle, life-saving nudge. The slingshot was working. He was being flung out, away from the giant, on a new vector, aimed, impossibly, toward Ariel Station.

Now, to get someone's attention. He cycled through the emergency frequencies, boosting the signal to maximum, pouring all his remaining power into a single, desperate distress call. "Mayday! Mayday! This is Moloch 03, solo fighter, severely fuel-depleted, trajectory to Ariel Station! Requesting immediate assistance!" He repeated the call, his voice hoarse, a tremor of exhaustion finally seeping through his steely resolve.

A moment of agonizing silence. Then, a crackle.

"Moloch 03, this is the Interstellar Patrol Corps vessel *Emmaus 7.* We copy your distress call. Hold your position. We have a lock on your signature. ETA five minutes. Do you require immediate medical assistance?" The words were calm, professional, and to Josh, it sounded like the sweetest music he had ever heard.

Relief washed over him, a physical wave that almost buckled his knees. "Negative medical, *Emmaus 7.* Just... a ride. " He allowed himself a small, shaky breath. He had done it.

Five minutes later, a sleek, utilitarian patrol ship, emblazoned with the Interstellar Patrol Corp's emblem, appeared out of the star-dusted black. Its docking clamps extended, and Josh, with the last vestiges of his strength, maneuvered the lifeless Moloch 03 into its embrace. The airlock hissed open, and the faint, recycled smell of a new life wafted in.

Chapter 28

The bridge of the Babylon was a study in controlled chaos. Outside the main viewport, the shattered remains of the pirate ship Gomorrah drifted in the blackness, a testament to Cain's ruthless efficiency. Flashing red warning lights still strobed across the command consoles, but a strange, tense silence had fallen over the bridge crew. Captain Cain stood at the central console, a porcelain teacup held in a perfect, unmoving hand. He sipped the pale green liquid, his gaze fixed on the wreckage. He appeared the picture of calm, a detached connoisseur admiring a work of art.

Delilah, the tactical officer, stood to his right, her flinty gaze locked on him. She shifted her weight nervously, trying to find the right moment to deliver her report. Before she could speak, First Officer Dathan strode onto the bridge, his posture a mixture of self-satisfaction and deference.

"Captain," Dathan said. "The boarding parties have returned with the spoils. A fine haul of refined stimulants, sir. They were good at hiding their treasures, but not good enough." He grinned, a brief flash of white in his scarred face. "No known survivors, Captain. We made sure of that. But if any of those vermin did survive, we sabotaged the comms. They'll be floating there for a thousand years without a way to call for help."

Cain nodded, a barely perceptible motion. He raised a hand, and Dathan's report ceased. "And the casualties?" he asked.

"Seven of the boarding party are wounded, sir. All non-critical. Samuel is tending to them now," Dathan reported.

Cain brought a hand to his comm bead. "Doctor Samuel. Report."

A moment passed before the doctor's strange, thick accent crackled over the comms. "Ve are fine. Just a few cuts und scrapes. Nothing dat my leetle sutures und antiseptics cannot fix. Your crew vill be vell und ready for de next fight, Captain."

"Excellent," Cain replied. He returned to his observation of the wreckage, then slowly turned to face the forward navigation pit. He had a specific purpose in mind. "Mr. Joshua," he called out, his tone carrying an air of expectation. "I have a new course for you to plot."

But his words fell on an empty seat. Ithamar, the navigation officer, was hunched over his console, a nervous, muttering mess. He fidgeted with his spectacles, casting quick, fearful glances at Cain.

Cain's gaze hardened, his eyes narrowing to an eagle-like intensity. He looked from the empty seat to the cowering Ithamar, and then finally to Delilah, who now had the captain's undivided attention.

"Tactical Officer Delilah," Cain said, the air on the bridge growing colder with each syllable. "Where is Mr. Joshua?"

Delilah visibly swallowed, her confidence shattering. "Sir… he… he feigned illness. He said he had to leave the bridge." She spoke in a rapid rush, her eyes darting away from him. "He snuck off to the docking bay. He stole a fighter, sir. He launched it and…we couldn't break off to pursue with your boarding party still on Gomorrah…the other fighters were already engaged…we…" Her voice trailed off.

Dathan let out a low chuckle, a triumphant glint in his eye. "Took off like a rat. A very clever rat, captain. Apparently, he had a last-minute visitor. One of my deckhands was ambushed."

Delilah flinched, and her inflection rose to a frantic pitch. "It's Ithamar's fault! He let him go!"

Ithamar whimpered, sinking lower in his seat, muttering to himself.

Cain was silent. His expression did not change. His gaze remained fixed on the tactical officer. Slowly, the silence stretched, growing heavier and more suffocating with each passing second. The teacup in his hand began to creak, a high-pitched sound of straining porcelain. The sound of a man-made object straining against a force too great for its design.

Suddenly, with a sharp, explosive crack, the cup shattered, the pieces falling to the deck with a tinkling rain of ceramic and green tea. In one fluid, devastating motion, Cain's hand moved to his side arm. He didn't look down. He didn't aim. His eyes remained locked on Delilah as he raised the weapon.

The pistol fired with a sharp *thump*, the plasma bolt a blinding flash. Delilah fell without a sound, a perfect, smoking hole between her eyes.

The bridge was plunged into a stunned silence. The crew froze, their hands hovering over consoles. No one moved.

Cain lowered his pistol and with a calm devoid of all emotion, "Mr. Dathan, have the deckhands clean this up. And find a new tactical officer." He then walked to the beverage dispenser and poured himself a new cup of tea. "Now," he said, taking a slow, deliberate sip. "Let's get back to work."

The bridge crew, with a shared, silent shudder, returned to their duties, the scene of the execution already a thing of the past.

Chapter 29

The airlock hissed shut behind Josh, the faint aroma of processed air a stark contrast to the acrid tang of exhaust in the fighter. Two stern-faced Interstellar Patrol Corps (IPC) officers, their uniforms crisp and bearing the stylized anchor and winged globe insignia, waited. They weren't overtly hostile, but their gazes were sharp, assessing.

"Joshua… that's your name, correct?" the lead officer asked, a woman with closely cropped gray hair and eyes that missed nothing. Her nameplate read Zipporah.

Josh nodded, his throat suddenly dry. "Yes, ma'am."

"And you claim to be a captive?" She gestured to the Moloch 03, now secured in the Emmaus 7's bay. "In a pirate fighter, originating from the vicinity of the Dead Sea nebula. That's a bold claim."

Josh took a steadying breath. "It's the truth. My family freighter, the Galilee, was attacked by Captain Cain and his pirates. They killed my parents, my brother, the whole crew, and he kidnapped me. I was held on their ship, the Babylon, for months. I just escaped during their attack on another pirate ship."

He was led from the Emmaus 7 directly into Ariel Station's security offices—a surprisingly bustling, if utilitarian, complex. The interrogation began almost immediately, a stark, windowless room replacing the vastness of space. For hours, Josh recounted his ordeal, details spilling out that he hadn't dared to speak aloud since his capture. He described the initial attack on the Galilee, the cold-blooded murder of his parents, the hazing by Baruch, the unsettling mentorship of Cain, the brutal training with Jair, and finally, his desperate flight.

He also provided everything he knew about Cain's operations: the rough location of the Dead Sea pirate haven within the nebula near the Behemoth gas giant, the pirate ship's name, Babylon, and even the approximate number and types of fighters it carried. He described the crude but effective way their weapons were rigged, the hierarchy of Cain's officers, and his own forced participation in the recent attack on the Gomorrah.

The officers listened, their faces impassive, taking meticulous notes. They asked follow-up questions, cross-referencing his statements with known pirate activity and sensor readings. "You mentioned they attacked another pirate ship. You were forced to plot the course?"

"Yes, ma'am. I was on the bridge. I saw it all," Josh said, the images of the ravaged ship still sharp in his mind. "It was… horrifying."

When the interrogation finally ended, Josh was led to a clean, albeit sparse, holding cell. It wasn't the brig of the Babylon, but it wasn't freedom either. He spent a day, then a second, in anxious solitude, the quiet of Ariel Station a constant reminder of his precarious position. He ate the surprisingly good nutrient paste they provided and tried to rest, but his mind raced. Would they believe him? Would they just lock him up like another pirate?

On the third morning, Zipporah entered his cell, her expression unreadable. She carried a datapad.

"We've made some preliminary inquiries, Joshua," she stated almost soothingly. "We've confirmed a pirate attack on the freighter Galilee at the time and location you reported. We also have scattered reports of increased pirate activity matching your descriptions of tactics. And your intelligence on the Dead Sea location… it aligns with some speculative data we've gathered." She paused, her eyes searching his. "Your story holds up."

Relief, potent and overwhelming, flooded Josh. He felt tears prick at his eyes, but he blinked them back, refusing to show weakness now.

"So, you believe me?" he asked just above a whisper.

Zipporah nodded slowly. "We do. You're not a pirate, Joshua. You're a survivor." She sat down on the edge of the cot. "What happens now, then? We can repatriate you, but it'll take time, bureaucracy…"

"I want to help," Josh leaned in, his words a low growl, his eyes burning with a fierce, unwavering resolve. "These pirates… Cain… they killed my family. They stole my life. I want to bring them down. I want justice."

Captain Zipporah studied him for a long moment, a flicker of something—compassion, recognition, perhaps even a shared fire—in her gaze. She saw the earnestness in his appeal, not just a boy seeking revenge, but a young man forged in trauma, determined to reclaim his future by fighting the darkness that had consumed his past.

She reached into a pouch on her belt and pulled out a small, sleek datapad. With a few taps, an official-looking form appeared on the screen.

"The Interstellar Patrol Corps has an academy," she said, her voice softer now. "It's a tough program, takes a year. We train our own. We need good people, Joshua. People who understand the risks, who know the enemy. People like you." She held out the datapad. "Think of us as the sheriffs of space. We do search and rescue, anti-smuggling, and anti-piracy. This is a way to get your justice, legally. A way to fight for a different kind of future."

Josh took the datapad, its cool surface a stark contrast to the burning intensity within him. The form was for enrollment. A new life. A new uniform. A new mission. It wasn't the Galilee, but it was a path. A way to hunt Cain, not as a desperate fugitive, but as an instrument of law. This was his chance.

Chapter 30

The Galilee was again in transit, the gentle thrum of the main drive a familiar blanket of sound. It was the kind of long-haul, uneventful journey that Noah used to dread, but now he welcomed the monotony. After the fiasco with the Canaan, the silence was a balm. Still, the memory of Captain Esau's accusations and the hollow feeling of being misunderstood gnawed at him. He sat in his father's chair on the bridge, the command console's glow washing over his face, lost in thought.

A gentle thud and the soft clinking of metal broke the quiet. Eli walked in, a hydro-spanner in one hand and a mug of what looked like steaming oil in the other. The old engineer set the mug on the console, the scent of over brewed coffee and an oily rag filling the air. The Canaan incident had given them both reason to reconsider their prior disagreement and a peace, perhaps an uneasy one, had settle between them.

"Ah, a grand day for it, so it is," Eli said, extending a verbal olive branch and a knowing look. "Yer twenty, lad. An' if I'm not mistaken, it would have been yer brother's birthday, too."

The words hit Noah like a physical blow. He had been so focused on his own journey he'd forgotten the anniversary of their birth, of the last time they were whole. A wave of sorrow and guilt washed over him.

Eli saw the shadow cross his face. "Come on now," he murmured as warmly as a hand on a shoulder. "Yer not sittin' alone on yer birthday. The galley's the heart o' the ship, and that's where ye should be."

Noah followed Eli to the galley. The space, normally a hub of activity, was quiet and bathed in the soft glow of the overhead lights. He immediately saw the photo of Isaac and Becky, younger and smiling in front of the half-built Galilee. Beside it, the picture of him and Josh as toddlers, laughing as they "flew" a toy spaceship through the mess hall, was a small, sharp stab to his heart.

Before he could get lost in the memories, the galley hatch slid open with a whoosh. Leah strode in, her bouffant red hair threatening to collide with the ceiling. She had shed the gray uniform coveralls and was wearing a flowing scarlet dress embroidered with glittering gold threads that shrieked against the utilitarian space. The scent of sweet jasmine and cinnamon followed her.

"Happy birthday, honey!" she chirped, her southern accent as thick as sorghum. Before Noah could react, she had him in a tight hug. "You look like you're attendin' a funeral, not a birthday party!" She pulled away and grabbed his cheeks. "You got two things to celebrate today, Noah. Your birth, and the fact that you're still alive to make a difference."

A familiar vocalization cut through the air. "Affirmative. Loadmaster Deborah has been preparing a celebratory meal. Loadmaster Jabez has been deployed for decorations and musical accompaniment."

Deb, a stern look on her face, entered the galley, holding a small plate with a single, neatly cut square of cake. Behind her, Jabez rolled in, a brightly colored party hat perched precariously on his head. A small, tinny rendition of "Happy Birthday" played from a speaker in his torso.

"The cake is a synthetic vanilla with bio-sweetened icing," Deb stated matter-of-factly. "Eli, you can have a slice once the captain has had his. Leah, please try not to get any glitter on the mess table."

Eli and Leah burst out laughing. Noah, for the first time in weeks, felt a genuine smile tug at his lips.

"Now sit still, honey," Leah said, placing a hand on his shoulder as she addressed Eli. "I swear he's a chip off the old block. My Becky used to get that same look when she was fixin' to worry herself sick. We were roommates in navigation school, you know. I was always the one gettin' us in trouble, and she was the one gettin' us out of it." She winked at Eli. "Kinda like me and you now, Eli." She leaned in and gave him a playful poke in the ribs. "Y'all are so serious, I swear."

Eli chuckled and shook his head, a wry grin on his face. "Aye, serious we are. But only 'cause the stakes are so high, so they are. I remember yer mam, Noah, a right brilliant lass. Taught you and your brother, Josh, everything she knew about the stars. When she wasn't teachin' she was chasin' after your da." He looked at Noah. "I remember when yer da, Isaac, got a little crazy with the thrusters. I warned him but he was havin' a grand ol' time. I saw him later, all red-faced, and he just shook his head and said, 'The boys were havin' so much fun, I couldn't stop myself!'"

Deb, standing sentinel with the cake, interjected. "I may not have known your family, Captain, but I know the man you are now. You had no desire to command, yet here you are. You had no desire to lead, yet here you are. You've used what you learned from Eli to make a new life, and you have us as a crew. You're doin' right by them, Captain."

Noah took a bite of the cake. It was surprisingly delicious. He looked from Deb's stoic but sincere face to Eli's kind eyes and Leah's tear-filled ones. He felt a profound sense of gratitude. They were not just his crew; they were becoming his family now. He had lost so much, but he had rebuilt something new, something strong. And his brother, what a team they would have made.

He swallowed a lump in his throat. "Thanks, everyone," he said, his voice thick with emotion.

Eli took the opportunity, a genuine smile on his face, and gestured at the cake. "It's a fine bit of baking, that is. But a Marine Loadmasters ? How did a tough Aussie Shelia like yourself learn to turn out a cake this good, then?"

Deb didn't smile, her expression remaining set, but she gave a slight, almost imperceptible shrug. "My mum ran a bakery back on Adelaide Station. Joined the Corps for the rations and the pay packet, you see. Didn't want to be covered in flour my whole life." She shifted her weight, brief and to the point. "Left the Corps after a bad deployment. Got sick of doing the brass's dirty work, to be honest. Needed honest work where I could look after meself."

"And that one?" Eli queried, pointing his chin at Jabez.

"Jabez and I crewed together on our last ship," Deb explained. "The captain retired and sold the ship, and he sold Jabez to a rental company. We were both out of work. That's when Ms. Leah found me, and I recommended Jabez as well, and here we are."

She spared a fond glance at the giant orange robot. "He's

been handling cargo on freighters for a century. Better 'n any bloke I've ever worked with, and he keeps quiet most of the time. That's a fair dinkum win-win in this Sheila's book."

"If he spoke more, I'll bet he'd have some stories to tell," Noah remarked, a note of curiosity in his tone.

Jabez, as if on cue, like a perfect waiter rolled forward and extended three tool arms with a coffee pot in one, cake in another, and spatula in another. He poured coffee into four mugs and served a slice of cake on four saucers, placing a slice and mug in front of each crew member. Eli, with a glint in his eye, raised his mug.

"To good ol' Gally," Eli said, he boomed. "She's home. She's family. She's future. And to Noah, her once and future captain."

Noah and the crew raised their mugs, clinking them together. The scent of coffee and camaraderie filled the mess, replacing the earlier grief with a quiet, shared hope. Noah looked at the family photos on the bulkhead, the old memories now feeling a little less painful. He was still angry, still driven by a desire for justice, but now, he knew he wasn't alone in his fight.

Chapter 31

The shuttle juddered as it settled onto the landing pad on Bethesda, its whine fading. Josh watched the main ramp extend, revealing a stark, gray-paved compound under the unforgiving light of a midday sun. This was the Interstellar Patrol Corps Academy, a place he was told would give him a new life. He clung to the hope, a small fire in his gut, but the sight that greeted him made it flicker.

Dozens of young men and women, clad in a mix of civilian clothes and ill-fitting hand-me-downs, stood packed shoulder-to-shoulder with him inside the shuttle. A cacophony of nervous chatter and coughs filled the cramped cabin. On the tarmac, a small group of senior cadets in crisp, dark blue uniforms stood waiting. They were a stark contrast to the new arrivals—poised, confident, and radiating an air of authority that chilled Josh to the bone.

The moment the shuttle doors hissed open, the air was shattered by a storm of shouts. "Move it, you maggots!" "Double time!" "Get on the line!" The senior cadets' taunts were a wall of sound, a chaotic blur of orders.

Disoriented, the new recruits stumbled out of the shuttle. Josh, gripping the strap of his small backpack, was swept up in the frantic tide of bodies. He ran, following the group until he found himself on a wide, blue-painted line on the tarmac. He placed his toes on the line as ordered, his heart pounding in his chest.

Immediately, a trio of senior cadets surrounded him. The one in front, a young man with a jaw set like granite, stepped forward until his nose was inches from Josh's. His eyes, the color of a winter sky, bore into him.

"Proclaim the Code!" the cadet bellowed, his a tidal wave of fury.

Before Josh could even draw a breath to respond, the other two cadets—one at each of his shoulders—began their assault. "You're a disgrace," one whispered, a slithering hiss in his ear. "Did your mommy dress you this morning, boy?" the other mocked low, taunting.

Josh took a deep breath, pushing down the twin onslaught of insults and the face in front of him. "I will not lie, cheat, or steal, nor tolerate those who do." He projected his voice as loudly as he could, trying to drown out the whispers.

The senior cadet's eyes narrowed. "Louder, noob! I can't hear you!"

"I WILL NOT LIE, CHEAT, OR STEAL, NOR TOLERATE THOSE WHO DO!" Josh shouted, the words ripping from his throat.

"You call that volume, recruit?" the cadet snarled, his eyes sweeping over Josh's face. "The rest of the code! Now!"

Josh continued, pushing through the verbal abuse. He knew the code, had memorized every word of it during the trip here. He recited it perfectly, his throat raw but unwavering. But the cadet in front of him simply shook his head, a flicker of something like disappointment in his eyes.

"That's a negative, recruit. Not at maximum volume. Now,

drop your gear and report to the parade grounds! Double time!" he yelled, punctuating the order with a sharp jerk of his head toward a large, open field.

Josh nodded and, without a second thought, turned and sprinted in what he thought was the right direction. He ran past the shuttle, his strides long and panicked. He was almost to a small, utilitarian building when a bark, clear as a bell and cutting through the chaos, stopped him dead in his tracks.

"Mr. Joshua!"

He spun around. The same senior cadet who had screamed at him was now pointing at him with an incredulous look on his face. "Mr. Joshua, that's the latrine! You're going the wrong way!"

A ripple of laughter, vicious and loud, spread through the senior cadets. He felt his face burn with shame. He wasn't on the Babylon anymore, but the familiar sting of mockery still burned just as hot. He took a deep breath, turned on his heel, and sprinted in the correct direction.

"That's right, Cadet Wrongway!" a shout from behind him, followed by more jeers and laughter. The name stuck, a new burden to carry. He ran harder, the desire to escape fueling his legs, the name "Cadet Wrongway" echoing in his ears as he made his way to the parade grounds.

Josh sprinted onto the wide, open parade grounds, the shouts of the senior cadets a cacophony behind him. He found himself amidst a sea of new cadets, all fumbling to get into some semblance of order. A senior cadet with a megaphone, his bellow echoing across the field, directed the chaos. "Form up! Four ranks! Squadrons of twenty! Move, move, move!"

Josh fell in with a group, his chest still heaving from the

sprint. They were a motley crew—a few in mismatched athletic gear, others in t-shirts and jeans. They all looked equally overwhelmed. As they jostled for position, a new roar cut through the noise, sharp and cold as a razor.

"Silence! I will not have my squadron looking like a herd of malnourished buffoons!"

A man emerged from the line of senior cadets. He was not tall, but his presence was immense. Perched atop his head was a perfectly creased "Smokey the Bear" hat, its ridged brim casting a permanent shadow over eyes that seemed to miss nothing. His face was a roadmap of hard-won experience, with a thick, gray mustache. His combat boots, spit-shined to a mirror gloss, reflected the harsh midday sun. He wore his crisp, blue uniform with an authority that bordered on the divine.

"My name is Staff Sergeant Caleb," he announced, his voice a bellow that held the promise of pain. "And I am your Drill Instructor. You belong to Squadron Seven. And as your DI, I am your mother, your father, your brother, your sister, your best friend, and your worst nightmare."

His eyes, cold and calculating, swept over the new recruits. He stopped at a skinny boy with big glasses and got right in his face. "What are you staring at, Cadet? Is my face too pretty for you?"

"N-no, sir!" the boy stammered.

The Drill Instructor's eyes narrowed dangerously. "So you're saying I'm ugly. Do you think I ugly recruit? " he barked in mock astonishment.

"N-no, sir!" the boy stammered even more desperately this time.

Staff Sergeant Caleb stepped back and pointed a finger at

the boy's chest. "You will not call me 'sir.' You will not address me as 'Mr. Caleb.' You will address me as 'Staff Sergeant.' Do you understand me?"

"Yes, sir!" the boy blurted, clearly terrified.

Caleb shook his head, a flicker of pure disgust in his eyes. He turned to the entire squadron. "Let's try this again. When you speak to me, you will address me as 'Staff Sergeant.' Not 'sir.' Not 'buddy.' Staff Sergeant. Is that understood?"

The recruits stood in stunned silence.

"I can't hear you, maggots! Is that understood?!" Caleb's words were a low, grinding rasp, a sound more menacing than a shout.

"Yes, Staff Sergeant!" The squadron finally bellowed in a ragged chorus.

"Again!"

"Yes, Staff Sergeant!"

"I still can't hear you! The dead in the dirt can't hear you! Again!"

"YES, STAFF SERGEANT!"

He moved on, his gaze now falling on a muscular young man who looked like a brawler. "And you, with the swagger. You think you're tough? I've seen tougher men break down crying for their mothers after five minutes with me."

Caleb's eyes finally landed on Josh. A flicker of recognition, a glint of cruel amusement, entered his gaze. "Well, well, well. If it isn't Cadet Wrongway. Word travels fast. You're already famous on your first day. Congratulations, Cadet."

Josh stood at attention, his face a mask of stone. He refused to show any reaction.

"From this moment forward, you will learn to think, move, and breathe as one. You will learn to walk as a unit, to turn as a unit, and to do exactly what I tell you, when I tell you."

The next few hours were a blur of shouted commands and frantic motion. "Left face! About face! Forward march!" Josh, a quick study, picked up the movements faster than most, but it didn't matter. The entire squadron was only as fast as its slowest member. They were made to repeat simple facing movements until their feet ached and their heads spun.

Then came the blur of the first day. The parade ground gave way to a series of sprints. They double-timed everywhere—to the barber shop where their heads were shorn of all but a regulation-length stubble. Josh's dark hair fell to the floor, a physical shedding of his past life. They double-timed to the quartermaster for their uniforms, identical sets of blue pants and shirts. They double-timed to the barracks, where they were shown their bunks and given four minutes to make them perfectly.

The only pause in the frantic pace was the chow hall. The drill instructors lined the recruits up, shouting "Four minutes to eat!" as they shoveled a bland, nutrient-rich paste onto trays. The meal was a frantic, silent affair. Josh ate quickly, his mind already calculating the quickest route back to the barracks to avoid being late. The chaos was a different kind from the Babylon's, but he understood the game. He had a job to do. He would take the insults and the exhaustion, and he would not break.

He was no longer a survivor running from his past; he was building a new future, brick by painful brick. The shame of his nickname still burned, but he compartmentalized it, pushing it down to a place deep inside. He was Cadet Wrongway. Fine. He would just have to be the best Cadet Wrongway the academy had ever seen. He didn't know what his new life would bring, but for the first time in a long time, he felt he was finally on his own path.

Chapter 32

Noah's fingers drummed a nervous rhythm on the armrest of the Captain's chair. He ran a hand over his chin, feeling the patchy, uneven stubble of his new beard. It wasn't much, but he hoped it gave him a gravitas he didn't yet possess. The Galilee was a familiar comfort around him, its low hum a constant companion. They were on a routine cargo run, a monotonous journey through a quiet sector.

Leah, her curly red hair an untamable cloud, leaned over her navigation console. "Got a blip, Noah. Looks like a standard Class-C freighter, 'The Hebron,' on the same lane, headed our way." She didn't sound concerned.

They continued their course, and the freighter on their screen grew steadily larger. Then Leah's brow furrowed. "Hold on, sugar. Picking up another blip. Much fainter." She tapped a few commands, her fingers a blur. "It's following that freighter. And it's slowly gaining on it. It's trying to hide its signature, but the energy emissions are too sporadic. It's could to be a pirate vessel."

The hum of the Galilee seemed to scream around them. Noah's gut didn't just clench; a spike of pure, raw anger shot through him. He didn't push the memory of his parents down; he harnessed it, letting it ignite the bloodlust he'd been struggling with. He slammed his hand flat on the console.

Eli was already looking at him, the old engineer's face set in a deep frown. "Captain, you'd want to be cautious here. Pirate activity is next to nil in this sector. It's suspicious, I grant you, but a rash move with these cannons could turn a suspicious blip into a bloody massacre. We could be making a bad mistake, we could." His gaze was stern, advising restraint.

Noah considered the counsel, seeing only a target. As much as he hated to admit it, Eli had a point. "Aunt Leah, turn off the transponder. Go dark. Eli, get a full charge on the plasma cannons and bring the targeting sensors online. We can intercept the pirate before they ever reach the freighter." He didn't care about saving the freighter as much as he cared about finding a worthy target for his weapons.

Lights dimmed on the bridge as the transponder went silent. The ship felt predatory now, and Noah savored it. On the main screen, the targeting reticle of their cannons locked onto the pirate vessel.

"Deb, open all the hailing channels. Wide broadcast. I want them to hear us. We need to confirm they're hostile." Noah felt the rush of the hunter. He *needed* them to fight.

Deborah's fingers danced across her console. "Channels open and waiting for your command, Captain."

Noah looked at the small, dark ship on his screen, his announcement filling the silent bridge and the cold vacuum of space beyond. "This is Captain Gabriel of the Archangel to the pirate vessel in pursuit of the freighter, registration number R-431-Hebron. Cease your pursuit and depart the sector. Failure to comply will be met with immediate and overwhelming force."

Leah's eyes widened. "Energy spike, darlin'! Their sensors

are focusing on us now. They've found us!"

A gruff, snarling answer over the comms channels. "Who dares challenge us? You've stumbled into the wrong quadrant, boy! This is Captain Barabbas of the 'Serpent.' You're about to have a very bad day. We're having you for salvage!"

Noah's mouth set in a thin, vicious line. He had his confirmation, the validation for the fight he desperately wanted. "Fire!" he commanded, the word a snarl.

The Galilee shuddered violently as the two cannons fired at full power and in unison, a brilliant flash of blue-white light streaking across space. The pirates, caught completely by surprise, were just beginning to bring their own weapons online.

The Galilee's shot, though powerful, was rushed. In his desire to fight Noah hadn't waited for Leah to get a proper target lock. It was a graze, ripping a massive, but non-critical gash along the Serpent's stern.

The pirate ship immediately retaliated. Their response was sloppy but fast. A flurry of auto-cannon fire peppered the Galilee's forward trusswork penetrating several cargo containers and severing power conduits. Warning indicators on Noah's console flickered violently, and a siren wailed briefly before Eli quickly silenced it.

"We're a target now, Captain!" Eli shouted, his Irish lilt strained. "We need an escape maneuver! This is a freighter, not a bloody fighter!"

Noah, driven by a need to annihilate, ignored the maneuver warning. "Eli, one more shot! Leah, get a lock on their engines!"

Leah, her hands shaking, tried to line up the lumbering Galilee for a second firing solution. "I can't bring her nose around, honey! We're too slow!"

Before she could lock on, the Serpent managed to fire its main weapon—a single, heavy energy bolt. It didn't hit the Galilee directly, but it slammed into the heart of the cargo trussworks, blasting loose more that a dozen containers in the forward section of the structure, missing the bridge by meters.

The impact was catastrophic as energy from the shot surge through busses and conduits. Alarms screamed. Sparks showered down from the ceiling, and the whole deck lurched sickeningly. Eli, who had been bracing against a console near the hatch, was thrown hard against the bulkhead. He slid to the floor, a dark patch of blood blossoming on the silver hair near his temple. He didn't move.

"Eli!" Noah screamed, his control shattering.

"Captain, they're maneuvering for another pass!" Deborah yelled, her voice breaking her usual stoicism.

Leah was sobbing, eyes wide with horror as she looked at Eli. "The cannons are overheating, Noah! We can't fire! We can't move fast enough!"

Noah saw the pirate ship's weapon system charging again. They were dead. They had lost. His thirst for vengeance had cost them everything.

But then, a raw, primal instinct took over. "Leah, full power to main thrusters! Straight burn!" he roared, throwing the manual controls forward. The Galilee, built for hauling, not fighting, lumbered forward like a wounded beast.

It was an insane move. The Captain Barabbas, seeing the freighter simply accelerate, must have assumed panic. He committed to his attack vector, banking to fire on the lumbering ship's flank.

It was pure, blind luck. Leah, interpreting the command for 'full burn,' overrode the dampeners. The sudden, uncontrolled surge of power caused the Galilee's loose cargo containers to buckle and then violently tear the mounting trusses. The sudden burst of escaping air and debris was like a shotgun blast.

The cloud of debris and pressurized gas slammed into the Serpent's nose just as it closed in. The pirate's ship was engulfed in the sudden chaos. One of the containers, laden with volatile mining explosives, lost its containment field when its power conduit was ripped off. It shattered against Serpent's hull in a massive explosion. Serpent's hull ruptured and her power core went critical. She was annihilated in a spectacular explosion that lit up the darkness.

Silence fell on the Galilee—a ringing, horrified silence. The ship drifted, now down a few tons of cargo, trusses, and cabling, but alive.

Deborah was the first to move, her Marine training kicking in despite her fear. "Leah, maintain thruster dampening! Jabez, medical bay prep! Captain, I'm taking Eli to the suite!" She rushed to the fallen engineer with surprising gentleness, Jabez rolling immediately to assist.

Leah, her face streaked with tears, stared at the now-empty viewscreen, then at Noah.

Noah looked down at his own shaking hands, then at the blood on the deck where Eli had fallen. The adrenaline was gone, replaced by a cold wave of sickening guilt. He had won, but not through skill, and the price was laid out on his bridge floor. He had been reckless, angry, and blind. He had almost killed them all.

The Galilee's medical suite was small, sterile, and blindingly lit. The smell of antiseptic synth-gel hung in the air. Eli was stretched out on the narrow cot, a thick bandage wrapped around his head.

Deborah was meticulously dressing a burn on his left shoulder, her movements precise and economical. She wore a tight, focused frown, looking every inch the former Marine medic.

The hatch hissed open and Noah stepped in. He looked ravaged. His shirt was clinging to his skin, his face pale green with nausea and guilt, and his eyes were wide and red from shock and unshed tears.

"How is he?" Noah asked, his voice barely a croak, eyes locked on the still, pale figure of his mentor.

Deborah didn't look up, her Australian accent clipped and businesslike. "He's right as rain, Captain. Tough old bloke, this one is. Knocked him out cold, though. That's a decent concussion; gives you an idea of how thick his skull is, considering he hit the bulkhead at *that* velocity. The power surge singed his shoulder, a second-degree burn, but nothing a bit of synth-skin and some rest won't fix. He needs a couple of days horizontal, then he'll be back in the engine room, whingeing about oil levels."

She finished with a decisive pat to the bandage, collected her supplies, and gave Noah a look that was both accusatory and professional. "I'm setting the chronometer for monitoring. Don't wake him for a proper chat, Captain. He needs the sleep." She gave a curt nod and slipped out, leaving Noah alone with Eli.

Noah approached the cot, the nausea twisting in his stomach. The bright lights only magnified the dark bruise blooming under Eli's eye. For a terrible, freezing moment, when Eli had crumpled, Noah thought he had lost the only family he had left. The victory over the Serpent felt less than meaningless; it felt like a disaster.

As Noah reached out a trembling hand toward his mentor, Eli's eyes fluttered open. He blinked slowly, his brow furrowed in confusion, before a flicker of concern sharpened his gaze.

"Gally?" Eli's voice was rough, his Irish accent thick and weak. "Is she sound? The crew?"

" Gally's fine, Eli," Noah whispered, swallowing hard. "Everyone's fine. We… we won."

Tears welled in Noah's eyes, hot and immediate. He sank onto the stool beside the cot, burying his face in his hands.

"I was so scared. I thought I'd lost you. I thought I killed you, Eli," Noah choked out, the admission tearing from him. "I'm so sorry. I was wrong. You were right. I… I let vengeance take over. I didn't maneuver. I just wanted to see them burn."

Eli's injured hand reached up slowly and patted Noah's back, a touch that was surprisingly firm.

"Ah, whisht now, lad. None of that," Eli murmured. "Don't be blamin' yourself for everything. Look at me, Noah."

Noah lifted his head, tears streaming down his cheeks.

"It's an easy thing to get justice and vengeance all jumbled up in your head when you've had a hurt like yours," Eli said, his voice soft but clear. "The anger, it's a powerful engine, sure it is. But it's a dirty one, and it'll tear up your insides."

He paused, resting his hand on Noah's arm. "Your Da and yer Mam, they wouldn't want you vengeful. But they would want you to seek justice. They'd want you to use that ship and those fool cannons to fight for the defenseless and to protect the innocent."

"You did the right thing today, Noah. You saved that freighter. But you did it the rash way," Eli continued, his eyes full of gentle wisdom. "It's not wrong to want to do the right thing, but it's important to do the right thing the wise way. We won today out of blind luck, and I'm payin' the price for your recklessness. Message received, I'd say."

Noah nodded, wiping his eyes with the back of his hand. His body was still shaking, but the guilt was momentarily tempered by his mentor's forgiveness and clarity.

"You're right," Noah said, his voice firming up with a renewed purpose. "We need to be smarter. We need a plan to do this the wise way."

Eli smiled, a small, tired grin that barely moved his bruised face. "That's the man I know. Now, go run your ship, Captain."

Thousands of miles away, the freighter Hebron was back on its course. Its captain, an older man with a weary face, sat on his bridge, a data-slate in his hand. His comms had picked up the bold broadcast from a vessel calling itself the Archangel, and his sensors had detected the brilliant, violent flash of the Serpent's demise. He replayed the audio file, listening to the young voice, filled with an authority it hadn't yet earned, but backed by a terrifying power.

"Captain Gabriel of the Archangel," he muttered to himself. He had no idea who they were, but they had just saved his life without him even knowing. The galactic authorities, however, were already taking notice. A new, powerful player was operating in the sector, and their actions were as mysterious as they were lethal.

Chapter 33

Cain sat in the high-backed leather chair of his command cabin, the only light coming from the faint glow of a datapad on the polished mahogany table before him. Outside the viewports, the swirling crimson of the nebula gave his fortress-like cabin a perpetual, bloody twilight. He was a man accustomed to control, to seeing his plans unfold with the elegant precision of a master tactician, and Josh's escape was a needle in his gut. A brilliant, vexing needle.

The boy had potential. Cain saw a spark in him—the same cold, determined fire he recognized in himself. He had planned to forge Joshua into a ruthless tool, a weapon to be wielded against the very systems that had created them both. He had taught him, tested him, molded him. And the boy had fled, not with the panicked flight of a coward, but with the ruthless cunning of a survivor. The brazenness of it infuriated him. More than that, it was a breach. A security breach that could bring the full weight of the Interstellar Patrol Corps down on the Dead Sea. The thought made his knuckles ache with suppressed rage.

He remembered a day long ago, back on the opulent estate of his family. He was a boy, no older than Joshua, mocked and dismissed by his elder brother, who would one day inherit the family's vast financial empire. The boy's sole purpose was to act as a decoy during a hunt for a beast that had been terrorizing their lands. His brother had handed him a broken hunting rifle.

The beast was a Goliath wolf-cat, all muscle and fury, with teeth like daggers and eyes that gleamed with feral intelligence. It stalked him, a living shadow, its low growl a constant threat. His brother and his hunting party watched from a safe distance, convinced he was a dead man. Cain ducked behind a gnarled tree, his heart pounding, the weight of his useless rifle a mockery in his hands. He could hear his brother's jeers echoing through the forest. He could have run, but he saw the beast as more than an animal; he saw his brother's mockery given physical form. He felt a cold fury, a resolve to turn the tables. He wouldn't just survive; he would conquer.

He used the land as a weapon, the forest floor his battlefield. He dodged, weaved, and scrambled, luring the beast into a dense thicket of thorns. He taunted it, drawing its focus away from a deep, boggy ravine he had spotted earlier. The wolf-cat, enraged, charged, but it didn't see the treacherous ground. It was in that moment of triumph that Cain lunged, not for the throat, but for the side, plunging his hunting knife into the beast's flank. The beast roared, thrashing wildly as it sank into the muddy ravine. When he emerged, caked in mud and blood, he carried the beast's severed head, a grim trophy of his victory. The family praised his "luck" and "bravery," but in his heart, he knew the truth. It wasn't luck. It was the heady thrill of the hunt—the rush of outwitting a stronger foe. And in that moment, he vowed he would never again be the weaker party. He would have power—the kind that broke and remade worlds.

The pub on the Dead Sea was a maelstrom of noise and sweat. The pirate captains were already drinking, a rough-hewn collection of cutthroats and opportunists. Cain and his first mate, Dathan, entered the room, and though the sound didn't die completely, a palpable shift occurred. Heads turned, and whispers followed the "Gentleman Pirate," immaculate in a clean uniform, as he took a seat at a large, round table. It was a table of equals, or so it appeared.

Around the table sat Captain Abimelech, a scarred brute with a booming laugh; Captain Samson, a quiet, one-eyed man who rarely spoke but always listened; and Captain Jezebel, a shrewd woman with a flinty gaze and a mind for numbers. Cain started the conversation with a nod to each of them, a show of respect. "Gentlemen. Captain Jezebel. A moment of your time, if you'll spare it."

He began by discussing the recent raid on the Gomorrah, the pirate ship they had destroyed. "Korach, may he rot in the void, was a fool. A glutton. I tried to reason with him after he betrayed the last truce, but his greed was insatiable." He watched their faces carefully, testing the waters. "He refused to honor the division of a cache, and worse, he had a spy in our own port master's office. The fool was so drunk on his own power he didn't realize he was a ticking time bomb for all of us."

Cain knew this was a lie, a fabrication built to justify his vengeance on Korach and to hide the true source of the security leak—Joshua's escape. He saw the doubt in the eyes of Samson and Jezebel, but he pressed on, planting a seed of fear.

"Korach's carelessness led to his demise, but it also painted a target on all of our backs," Cain bent closer, his whisper barely cutting through the silence. "His greed made him reckless in his methods, and it has garnered unwanted attention from the eyes of those who seek to destroy us. There can be no doubt they are searching for this place."

"What are you saying, Cain?" Abimelech growled, his hand resting on the hilt of his cutlass. "Are you saying the IPC knows about us?"

Cain didn't answer directly. Instead, he simply took a sip of his tea. The silence stretched, and the other captains began to get nervous. Abimelech grumbled, "The IPC can't find us in this nebula."

Cain smiled, a wolf's grin. "No, they can't. Not yet. But Korach left a trail so they have the data. It's a matter of time. We need to move before its too late."

"And go where?" Jezebel asked, her gaze fixed on him.

Cain offered a few options, each with a subtle flaw he was quick to point out. "There's the Veil, but it's too exposed. Or the Labyrinth, but its twisting passages are a nightmare for our larger vessels." He let them chew on the options, watching as they began to squabble amongst themselves. He had them now, a group of desperate men and women who, for all their power, lacked a leader.

He finally stood, drawing all eyes to him. "There is one other place. It's a personal holding, a remote rock I inherited from my family. It's small and inconspicuous, and I've kept it quiet." He paused, letting the words sink in. "But it is perfectly hidden. I'm willing to open it up to all of you. It's a place where we can rebuild without the fear of a surprise attack."

He was giving them a common enemy and solution while also

making himself their new king. The gentleman pirate had just made himself king of a new pirate empire.

"It is a charitable act on my part. We must stand together, not against one another. We must unite or we will fall, one by one, to the IPC."

He watched the captains whisper and nod. They saw the logic in his words, the elegant solution to a problem they were only just beginning to grasp. They would follow him, not because he was the biggest or the strongest, but because he had the most cunning.

Chapter 34

The IPC patrol vessel, designated IPC-734, drifted silently through a graveyard of shattered metal and charred hull fragments. Officer Zipporah, her breath a plume of vapor inside her helmet, guided her thrusters through the debris field, her partner floating in her wake. They were following the coordinates provided by their newest and most promising informant, Cadet Joshua. He'd given them the location of a recent battle, a place where the pirate ship Gomorrah had met its end.

Zipporah's helmet comm crackled. "Confirmed, ma'am. The size, the structural integrity… this is definitely what's left of the Gomorrah."

They secured a magnetic line to a piece of wreckage and began their spacewalk. The interior was a blasted ruin. Bulkheads were torn open, scorched by plasma fire, and a haunting silence filled the space where a crew once lived and died. They found what they were looking for: a pirate flag, half-burned, plastered to a wall, and a series of illegal modifications to the ship's weapons systems. It was all the proof they needed.

Zipporah's partner, a young officer named Malachi, spoke up. "We've got some data fragments on the bridge, but the logs are gone. Too much damage."

"It's a long shot, but maybe the fragments can be pieced together," Zipporah replied. She paused, looking at the sheer scale of the destruction. "One thing is certain: this wasn't a quick raid. This was a professional hit. The kind of damage you see when one warship takes down another." The wreckage of the Gomorrah was the clearest sign yet that a power play was underway in the pirate underworld.

Back on Ariel Station, Zipporah sat in front of a monitor, a comms call blinking. On the other side of the connection were two Port Authority officers from Jericho: Gideon, a broad-shouldered man with a professional demeanor, and Abner, a lean, hawk-faced man with a detective's gaze.

"Officer Zipporah, IPC," she began, getting straight to the point. "I'm investigating a recent surge in pirate activity, and I believe I've tied the attack on the freighter Galilee to a subsequent attack on a pirate vessel, the Gomorrah."

Gideon and Abner exchanged a look of surprise. "We were just about to file a report on another attack," Abner said, his eyes narrowing. "It was on a freighter called the Canaan. The pirates were routed by a third party. Its captain called himself 'Captain Gabriel of the Archangel.'"

"And that's not all," Gideon added, bringing up a new file. "We just received a report from the captain of the Hebron. They were also attacked by pirates, but the same 'Captain Gabriel' intervened."

"The captain of the Hebron provided a recording of the hail from the Archangel," Abner said, playing the file.

The recording played, revealing a young voice, filled with authority. "This is Captain Gabriel of the Archangel to the pirate vessel in pursuit of the freighter, registration number R-431-Hebron. Cease your pursuit and depart the sector. Failure to comply will be met with immediate and overwhelming force."

"The captain also provided sensor logs," Abner added, showing the data. "They show a massive energy burst consistent with weapons fire, and the pirate vessel, identified as the Serpent, was completely vaporized."

The room was silent as the data flickered. Zipporah rubbed her chin, a dozen possibilities running through her mind. This was no longer just a turf war. Who was this Captain Gabriel? A rival to Cain, equally intelligent and manipulative? Or a vigilante operating on his own? The information from Josh was solid; Cain's ship, the Babylon, had destroyed the Gomorrah. Yet here was evidence that a second, unknown player was also hunting down and destroying pirates. The void was getting more crowded and more dangerous. There were more questions than answers, and Zipporah ended the call, knowing she had stumbled onto something much bigger than a simple pirate investigation.

Chapter 35

Bethesda's sun became a daily antagonist, a blinding spotlight for a relentless, year-long performance of pain and discipline. The name "Cadet Wrongway" wasn't a taunt anymore. It was a call sign, a legend earned on the very first day. Joshua wore it like a badge of honor, a public acknowledgment of a rookie mistake, and a silent promise to himself that he wouldn't make another one. He ran until his lungs felt like fire, sprinted up hills until his legs turned to lead, and did push-ups until his arms trembled with a deep, bone-weary exhaustion. Staff Sergeant Caleb, a permanent scowl etched on his face, was a shadow of discipline, his orders a constant bellow. He never offered praise, only the absence of a shouted correction, and that was enough.

One morning, during a round of punitive push-ups, a cadet collapsed from exhaustion. Caleb stomped over, his spit-shined boots thudding on the tarmac. He loomed over the whimpering cadet, his tone a low, menacing growl. "What is your major malfunction, cadet?!" he bellowed. "Get your backside up and finish your set or I'll put my boot so far up your stern the water on my knee will quench your thirst!" The rest of the squadron, despite their own pain, struggled to suppress their laughter, knowing the slightest twitch would earn them more misery.

In the classroom, in stark contrast to the physical torment, Joshua's mind worked with the quiet precision of a chronometer. He was a different kind of weapon here. The officers teaching celestial mechanics and astrogation would present a problem on the holoscreen—a dense web of gravity wells, asteroid fields, and solar winds. While other cadets struggled with the math, Joshua saw a three-dimensional ballet, an elegant path through the chaos. The lessons from his mother and the brutal training under Cain had given him an intuitive understanding that went beyond theory. When he was called to the front to solve a problem, he would simply walk up and, with a few confident touches, trace a perfect, logical route that astonished his instructors.

This intellectual dominance extended to the ship simulators, which were built to mimic the bridge of an IPC patrol cutter. During a tactical exercise, a simulated pirate vessel, with its superior speed and firepower, had outmaneuvered every cadet who came before him. Josh, however, saw a weakness. He ignored the textbook evasive maneuvers. Instead, he steered his vessel directly into the path of a simulated plasma flare from a nearby star. The computer shrieked warnings of a fatal course, but Josh held steady, using the flare's chaotic discharge as a temporary screen. The pirate ship, unable to follow the erratic path, lost its lock. It was a counter-intuitive tactic that should have been suicide but was, in his hands, a stroke of genius. The simulator officer, a man with a row of medals on his chest, shook his head in quiet disbelief. "That boy's a natural," he muttered to a colleague after the exercise. "He thinks like a captain, not a cadet."

The same unnerving talent extended to hand-to-hand

combat. Under the unforgiving eye of Staff Sergeant Caleb, Josh moved with a fluid, lethal efficiency. Master Jair's lessons had forged a fighting style born of necessity. While others relied on brute force, Josh used his opponent's momentum against them, a calculated dance of feints and counter-attacks. During a sparring session, he disarmed a larger opponent with such speed and grace that the other cadets stopped to watch. Caleb saw it all. "What's wrong, Wrongway?" he'd growl, the name now a veiled nod of respect. "Your opponent isn't fighting back?" The hint of a smirk on Caleb's face was the highest praise Josh could ever hope to receive.

Between the main events, the daily ritual of military life continued. Uniforms were starched, boots polished to a mirror shine, and barracks were immaculate, their bunks made with the precision of a master builder. On the firing range, Josh had a steady hand and a solid fundamental understanding of the pistol, a result of his time with Master Jair. He wasn't a perfect shot, but he was a good one, and that was enough. A year passed in this blur of pain and progress, and with each passing day, the soft edges of the boy who ran away were filed down into the sharp, steely resolve of a man. The memory of the Galilee was now a fuel for his ambition, not a weight of grief. He was no longer just a survivor; he was a machine of justice being built, brick by painful brick, for a future he was finally beginning to control. He was Cadet Wrongway, and he was ready. His journey to find justice, and maybe something else, was just about to begin.

Chapter 36

The mess hall of the Galilee, normally a place of warm light and easy camaraderie, felt heavy and vast. Noah stood by the wall, absently stroking the new growth of his beard as he stared at the old family photos. He saw his parents, Rebecca and Isaac, smiling wide, their arms around his and Joshua's younger selves. The memories felt both precious and impossibly distant. He was still lost in them when the last of the crew arrived, the quiet clatter of coffee mugs a somber punctuation to the silence.

Deborah, ever the pragmatist, broke the ice. Crisp and devoid of emotion as usual, "All present, Captain. Let's get to it."

Noah turned, taking a deep breath. "Thank you all for coming." He looked from Eli to Aunt Leah, to Deborah and the silent robot, Jabez. "When we found those cannons, I saw them as a way to defend ourselves, but also as a path to revenge. Then, as we've taken every chance we could to deal with the pirates… I've come to realize something. I've been reckless, seeking vengeance, and in doing so I've put us all in danger. All I can feel now is the weight of what we did." He paused, his gaze dropping to the floor. "I can't bear the thought of losing another family. This crew… you're my family now. And I can't stand by and watch you come to harm." He looked up, his eyes meeting theirs. "So, I've made a decision. At the next port, you can leave. We have enough in our accounts to hire a replacement crew and give you each a decent severance. I'll carry on the family business on my own, but I won't put you in danger again. I'm sorry for my reckless actions, and thank you for everything you've done. You've helped me rebuild my parent's dream."

Before Noah could say another word, a fully recovered Eli slammed his mug down on the table, the loud clack echoing in the room. "Don't ye dare, lad. Your family was my family, and this ship is my home. We've been through too much together to just walk away." The old engineer's Irish brogue was uncharacteristically firm. "If ye think I'm gonna let ye go off fightin' pirates without me to patch yer ship, ye've another think comin'. We're in this together, lad."

Tears streamed down Leah's face, her bouffant red hair quivering. "Oh, Noah," she said, her deep Southern accent thick with emotion. "My Becky loved you so much, and so did your daddy. They would be so proud of the man you've become. We can't leave you now. My place is here, on this ship, with this family. I'm stayin' right here where I belong."

Deborah stepped forward. Her body language was a clear statement. "Right then, Captain," she said, her tone brooking no disagreement. "This isn't happening. I was a Marine back in the Zion military. Fought plenty of despots and terrorists, I have. I came to this ship looking for honest work, but when you made the decision to defend that freighter, I realized I was right where I needed to be. I'm bloody sick of the blokes that prey on the innocent and hide in the shadows. So you can forget about hiring a new Loadmaster, because I'm not going anywhere."

Just then, Jabez, who had been sitting motionless against the wall, whirred to life. "Input: Crew Emotional State is registering as 'Volatile Loyalty.' Output: Processing indicates current Cohesion Level has increased by 47%. Caution: Disassembly of this unit is non-optimal." The tension broke as the crew looked at the orange, boxy robot, its painted-on smile unchanging. A wave of shared laughter rippled through the galley, clearing the air and solidifying their resolve.

The shared laughter at Jabez's declaration melted the last of the tension, replaced by a renewed sense of purpose. Noah's shoulders, which had been slumped with the weight of his guilt, straightened. He looked at each of them, his eyes glistening with unshed tears.

"Thank you," he said, his voice thick with emotion. "All of you. Thank you." He took a deep breath, collecting himself. "But Eli's right. We can't be naive. We've been lucky. So far, the pirates we've faced have been unprepared. That won't last. They know about the Archangel now, and the next time we cross paths, they'll be ready for us. She can't withstand sustained fire, and she's a freight hauler, not a warship. They could disable her and get a boarding party over here. We need to be ready for the worst."

A determined silence fell over the crew, a moment of shared resolve. Then, the practical minds took over.

"With our recent profits, we can afford more than just basic repairs," Eli said, his eyes gleaming with a newfound purpose. "We can upgrade the old girl. I can get some industrial-grade heat sinks for the cannons. That'll let us get off a few more shots before they overtemp. I can also do some serious work on her powerplant and the main drive. Give us more power and more speed to get out of trouble." He grinned, a roguish glint in his eyes. "And I can set up some lovely little surprises for any unwanted guests. Nothin' says 'welcome aboard' like a booby-trapped passageway."

Deborah's Marine training was on full display. "My top priority is the crew. I can teach you some basic close-quarters combat techniques. How to use a spanner as a weapon. How to break a choke hold." Her eyes scanned the room, assessing each of them. "As Gally's medic I'll make sure the med-bay is fully stocked and that everyone knows basic first aid and buddy care. We can even get some surplus firearms and set up a firing range in one of the empty cargo containers."

Jabez, who had been listening with his head tilted, whirred softly. "Captain's authorization required. Awaiting confirmation to begin up load protocol application for security function." His tone was still chipper, but it was clear he was ready to get to work. "Upon authorization, I will install a mobile security program. Note: lethal force is a negative variable. My systems are configured for non-lethal sonic blast and the use of manipulator arms for threat neutralization."

The others looked to Leah. She'd been quiet, her hands clasped on the table. A soft smile touched her lips, and she looked at Eli. "Well now, Eli, bless your heart, you just think of everything, don't you?" she said, her Southern accent as warm and sweet as honey. She looked back at Noah. "Honey, I may not be able to fix a ship, or fight, or be a robot," she said. "But I can feed a crew. I'll take care of the cooking. A well-fed crew is a happy crew, and a happy crew fights harder. And I'll be here to tend to your wounds and put a patch on your clothes. Lord knows these drab gray coveralls could use a splash of color. I'll make sure this ship is always a home to come back to, no matter what happens."

The plans poured out, a torrent of ideas born from a shared passion for their new purpose. The fear and sadness of the past few days were gone, replaced by a sense of unity and fierce determination. They were a family, not by blood but by choice, and they would do whatever it took to keep their home in the stars safe.

Chapter 37

The air on the parade grounds of the Interstellar Patrol Corps Academy was thick with the weight of expectation. A thousand young men and women stood at rigid attention, their dress uniforms crisp and spotless in the morning light. For Joshua, the world had narrowed to the space between his ears. The sound of the assembly was a drone of distant anticipation that he had long ago learned to tune out.

He remembered the chaos of his first day, the barrage of insults and physical drills, and the biting nickname Staff Sergeant Caleb had branded him with: "Cadet Wrongway." Now, a year later, that name felt less like a taunt and more like a badge of honor, a testament to how far he had come.

The ceremony began. A six-person Honor Guard, their movements a perfect ballet of discipline, marched onto the field. They carried the colors: the golden IPC flag and the standard of their class. As they passed, the murmur of the crowd subsided, replaced by the sharp, metallic click of a thousand heels.

From the podium, the Senior Cadet pronounced the command with an ear splitting shout, "Class 427, prepare to Proclaim the Code!"

Joshua's mind snapped back to the present. He stood a little straighter, his chest swelling with a shared sense of purpose.

"PROCLAIM THE CODE!"

In a single, deafening wave of sound, a thousand voices rose as one, a storm of unified resolve.

"I WILL NOT LIE, CHEAT, OR STEAL, NOR TOLERATE THOSE WHO DO!" they roared. "I WILL DEFEND THE INNOCENT, AND CHALLENGE THE TYRANT! I WILL UPHOLD THE LAW OF THE VOID, AND SERVE MY FELLOW CREW!"

The words filled him with an unexpected sense of awe. This was the vow he was making. It was a promise to live and die by a purpose larger than himself. He thought of his parents, and Noah and how he wished they could see him now. He thought of their deaths at Cain's hands, and the rage that had once consumed him. The code wasn't about vengeance. It was about justice. The rage hadn't vanished, but it had been contained, forged into a new, cleaner purpose.

The speech from the Commandant, Rear Admiral Josiah, was a blur. It was a canned address about sacrifice and honor, a forgettable stream of platitudes he had heard a hundred times. Josh's mind drifted back to the past, to Cain and the dark, manipulative intelligence that had both tortured him and taught him. He thought of the Dead Sea, the lawless pirate port where he knew his enemy now held sway. Going after Cain wasn't just a mission; it was a personal debt. He owed it to his family, and to the boy he once was.

Finally, the drone of the Commandant's speech ended. "PUBLISH THE ORDERS!" Rear Admiral Josiah bellowed, his voice carrying the authority of a fleet.

Another officer, a senior captain, took the podium and began to read from a large, official-looking document.

"On this day, the third of Octavius, twenty-five thousand forty-seven, Class 427 has completed all training requirements. Their conduct and diligence have distinguished them in the finest tradition of the Interstellar Patrol Corps, and they are, by my order, hereby graduated and promoted to the rank of Ensign, signed, Director Uriel, Director of the Interstellar Patrol Corps."

A slow, steady march began. One by one, the cadets broke from formation, walking in a single file line toward the stage. Each name was read aloud, and Josh watched as his classmates, now fellow officers, crossed the stage, accepted their diplomas, and were pinned with their new gold bars.

"Cadet Joshua," the speaker called out.

Josh took a deep breath. His turn. He marched forward, his movements precise, a mirror image of the discipline he had just witnessed. He mounted the steps, coming to attention directly in front of Rear Admiral Josiah. His mind flashed back to his first day, to the snarling senior cadet whose face had been inches from his, and the two other cadets at his shoulders who had mercilessly ridiculed him. Now, here he was, with the academy's Commandant in front of him and two senior officers at either shoulder. But this time, their presence was one of honor, not torment.

He shook the Commandant's hand, his grip firm. He took his diploma, and saluted, the crisp snap of his arm a silent exclamation of pride. The gold bars were pinned to his shoulders by the two officers. He turned to face the crowd, and heard his assignment announced.

"Ensign Joshua is assigned to the IPCS Bethel, a patrol cutter where he will serve as Navigator."

He fought to suppress a smile. *Navigator.* His mother's

dream for him, and now his own. The name of the ship, Bethel, "the house of God," seemed a perfect omen. He couldn't keep a quick, involuntary smile from crossing his face as he marched to the end of the stage.

He was stopped by a final, familiar presence. Staff Sergeant Caleb, the man who had pushed him to his limits, stood waiting. Caleb's expression was a mixture of pride and a silent, hard-won respect. The gruff drill sergeant, a man who had never smiled once in his entire career, gave him a perfect, unflinching salute.

"Congratulations, Ensign," Caleb said, his tone softer than Josh had ever heard it. "It's been an honor, sir."

The words hit Joshua like a physical blow. The "sir" was a formality, of course, but the emotion behind it was real. For the first time, he hadn't been called "Wrongway." He was just Joshua, a newly minted officer. In that moment, he felt a lump form in his throat, and the pride he felt for himself was dwarfed by his respect for the man who had molded him. He returned the salute, a powerful, unspoken goodbye.

He returned to the formation, a new man with a new purpose. The last cadet made their way across the stage. Then the senior cadet, now an Ensign, marched to the podium one last time.

"Class 427!" he bellowed. "DISMISSED!"

The cheer that followed was a joyous explosion. The white caps of the cadets' hats flew into the air, spinning like a flock of birds, as cheers and thunderous applause erupted. Joshua beamed, a wide, true smile, his chest alight with a happiness he hadn't felt since before the attack. He had done it. The path to justice was clear now, and he had a new ship, a new purpose, a new life.

Chapter 38

The days and weeks that followed their pact were a blur of hard work and renewed purpose. The Galilee became a training ground, a warship in disguise. Time passed in a series of vignettes, each a small lesson in their new, dangerous life.

In the thrumming heart of the engineering section, Noah worked with Eli, their movements a silent, practiced ballet. For a time, he was an apprentice again, not a captain, and the work was a solace he hadn't realized he'd missed. Sparks flew from Eli's welder as he fused an industrial-grade heat sink onto the main cannon power conduit. "She'll take more a' the fire now, lad," Eli said. "Gally's built for it." Noah's hands moved with confidence, tightening a plasma regulator, the work feeling both familiar and sacred. It was here, amidst the grease and the drone of the ship's engines, that he felt most connected to his old life, to his father, and to the boy who had been so fascinated by the inner workings of the ship. The stress of command melted away, replaced by the simple, satisfying rhythm of a job well done.

In the largest of the empty cargo holds, Deborah ran their close-quarters combat training. The space was cold, echoing, and unforgiving. "This isn't about strength, ya drongos," she barked in her Aussie drawl. "It's about knowing how to use your body, not just your grunt. How to turn a threat's momentum against them." She demonstrated a basic wrist lock, fluid and deadly. Noah, Eli, and even Leah struggled at first, their movements clumsy and uncoordinated.

"Alright, you two," Deborah snapped, pointing a finger at Leah and Eli. "Go again. This time, I want you to make contact and give it some bloody welly."

Eli, with a theatrical sigh, squared up against Leah. "Mind ye be gentle, darlin'," he said with a wink.

"Oh, Eli," Leah purred, her eyes glinting behind her enormous glasses. "I'll be as gentle as a possum in a hen house."

The next moment was a whirlwind of unexpected grace. Eli moved to disarm her, but Leah, with a surprising burst of speed, sidestepped and wrapped her arm around his neck. Eli was unprepared for the sudden move, and the next thing he knew, he was on his back, staring up at the ceiling. Leah was on top of him, her hair a wild halo of curls. She leaned in, a sly smile on her face. "Looks like I finally caught me a man," she said, before helping him to his feet. A chorus of laughter filled the bay, even from Deborah.

After their training sessions, Jabez was put to the test. A human-sized target was set up in the cargo bay, and the robot, now programmed for security, moved with blinding speed. "Per Captain's authorization … Deploying Sonic Disabler." its mechanical voice announced. A high-pitched, piercing shriek filled the space, and the crew immediately covered their ears. The target crumpled, and a human-sized dummy was knocked to the ground. "Security Protocol … Successful." Jabez announced with a whirring flourish, its painted smile unchanging.

But the most important part of their training happened in the galley. Leah, with a flurry of pots and pans, took command. She would spend hours cooking, filling the ship with the aroma of home. One evening, after a long day of drills and repairs, the crew gathered for a meal of fried chicken, mashed potatoes, and collard greens. They sat around the table in the cozy mess hall, a warm and comforting light spilling from the lamps. The conversation was easy, not about vengeance or pirates, but about their lives, their pasts, and their hopes for the future.

"Deborah, that was an impressive throw you showed us today," Leah said, passing a bowl of potatoes. "Where'd a tiny little thing like you learn to do that?"

Deborah snorted. "Size doesn't matter, Leah. It's leverage. And a lot of practice." She pointed her fork at Noah. "Captain, your form is still terrible, but your determination is a sight to see."

Noah grinned, a genuine, relaxed smile. "I'll get there. Eventually."

Eli shook his head. "Well, I can tell ye this. After that fall, I'm glad we've got a medic on board." He winked at Leah. "Almost dislocated me pride, ya did."

As Noah looked around at his crew—the grumpy engineer, the fierce Loadmasters, the hilarious navigator, and the silent robot—he knew they weren't just a crew. They were a team, they were a family working toward a future.

Chapter 39

The cold, sterile air of the starport was a stark contrast to the humid air of the academy. Josh, in his crisp new Ensign's uniform, felt a thrill of anticipation as he approached the IPCS Bethel. She was a beauty, a sleek, purposeful vessel designed not for hauling cargo but for hunting pirates. Her hull was a deep, official gray, and her lines were clean and modern, evoking a sense of swift, no-nonsense authority. Visible armaments—plasma cannon turrets and missile launchers—were nestled in her streamlined form, a promise of the force she was capable of.

He walked up the gangway, his footsteps echoing on the metal ramp. The sound was a cadence of purpose, a drumbeat for his new life. At the top, a Marine Private stood ramrod straight beside a pedestrian gate, his posture a testament to the discipline of the Patrol Corps. Josh stopped a few feet from the gate, snapped to attention, and gave a crisp, formal report.

"Ensign Joshua, reporting for duty. Request permission to come aboard."

The Marine's eyes, as sharp as a laser beam, flicked down to a datapad on a nearby stand, checking his roster. Finding the name, his demeanor shifted instantly. He came to attention, his movements a single, fluid motion, and his hand shot up in a perfect salute. Josh returned it with a snap, the gesture feeling earned and deeply satisfying.

"Permission granted, welcome to the Bethel, sir."

Josh felt a silent wave of triumph wash over him as he stepped across a painted yellow stripe on the deck, a symbolic line that marked the formal entrance to the ship. He was officially aboard.

"Stand by, sir," the Marine said, dropping to a businesslike tone as he tapped a few keys on a datapad. A moment later, he looked back at Josh. "Your escort is proceeding directly, sir."

The Marine's words were barely out when a new Ensign rounded the corner, his footsteps quick and purposeful. He was a black man with a shaved head, thin and not particularly tall, but his face was dominated by a big, friendly grin. He moved with a happy-go-lucky energy that was almost contagious. The sight of him, an engineer's badge over his left breast pocket, brought a pang of remembrance to Josh. He saw the easygoing nature, the enthusiasm for the ship's inner workings. It reminded him so much of Noah. The memory, once a source of pain, now filled him with a quiet sense of affection.

The Ensign extended a hand with a vigorous handshake. "Jambo!" he said with a deep Kenyan accent. "My name is Ensign Adriel, and I am to be your escort. It is a pleasure to meet you." His wide smile was infectious. "Welcome to the Bethel or "Ms. Beth" as us crew dogs like to call her! She is the finest ship in the fleet, a true beauty, and a pleasure to serve on. I am quite sure you will love it here."

Josh returned the handshake, a genuine smile on his face. "Thank you, Ensign. The pleasure is mine."

"Please, call me Adriel. So, my orders are simple," Adriel explained, his movements as animated as his words. "First, I will show you to your quarters so you can get settled. Then we'll do a quick tour of the vital areas, and I will get you to your appointment with the Executive Officer, the XO. We should have you settled and ready to go in no time."

Adriel's infectious energy and positive attitude were a stark contrast to the brutal, structured world Josh had just left. He knew, with a certainty that was both comforting and surprising, that they were going to be fast friends.

"Here we are, your new home!" Adriel announced, pushing open a hatch.

It was a small cabin, functional and clean, with two narrow bunks built into the wall. A single duffel bag sat on one bed. Without a word, Josh walked over to the other bunk and dropped his massive duffel with a heavy thud that made the entire frame shudder. Adriel chuckled.

"My sincerest apologies. My gear is already stowed," he said with a grin. "Shall we continue?"

The tour was a whirlwind. Adriel led him through the ship with the energy of a man who loved his work. He showed Josh the compact, efficient heads and the crew lounge where off-duty sailors could relax. In Main Engineering, the air was thick with the smell of ozone and hot metal, a complex maze of conduits and power generators. Adriel's face lit up as he described the intricacies of the drive system, speaking with a technician's love for his craft. They moved on to the Combat Information Center (CIC), a dark room filled with the soft glow of data screens where the crew monitored all of the ship's vital systems. Adriel proudly pointed out the battle-hardened consoles and the crewmen on duty, their faces illuminated by the green light of the displays.

Finally, they arrived at the Officer's Mess, a cozy galley where the smell of spiced meat filled the air. They grabbed plates and found an empty table.

"So, the XO," Adriel said, his tone turning serious as he scooped a helping of vegetables. "Commander Uzziel. He's fair, but he's all business. He'll want to get a measure of you, see what you're made of. He'll test your technical knowledge and ask about your background. Just be honest, direct, and show him you're a professional. You'll be fine."

After lunch, they took a lift to the bridge. The buzz of consoles and the murmur of quiet conversation filled the air. The bridge of the Bethel was a place of quiet command and concentrated authority. Adriel led him to the Navigation station, a sleek console with multiple screens and a command chair. Josh's heart skipped a beat as he looked at the station, the one his mother had taught him to love, the one he had mastered as a boy. It seemed like a lifetime had passed since then.

"Ensign Joshua," Adriel announced to a man at a nearby command station. "Reporting as ordered."

The officer turned from his console. He was a tall, stern-looking man with a neatly trimmed beard, his face calm and focused. "Lieutenant Obadiah, Navigator First Class," he said, extending a hand in a firm, professional grip. "Welcome to the Bethel, Ensign. I trust Ensign Adriel gave you a good tour."

"Yes, sir. He was very thorough," Josh replied.

"Good. You are my new navigator, and I expect you to be ready. You will be on duty soon enough." The Lieutenant turned back to his console, a clear signal of his focus on the task at hand.

With a nod, Adriel began to lead Josh toward the aft of the bridge. "Right then. Now for the last stop," he said with a playful grin.

They arrived at the XO's office, a polished wooden door that stood in stark contrast to the utilitarian steel of the ship's corridors. The door was closed. Adriel stopped a few feet away, his cheerful demeanor giving way to a more formal expression.

"This is it, my friend," Adriel said. "I'll wait out here for you."

Adriel's presence was a comfort, but the closed door felt like a final wall. The friendly tour, the conversations, the sense of belonging—all of it faded, replaced by the weight of the moment. Josh stood alone, a raw recruit in a new uniform, about to face the second-in-command. The easy camaraderie was over. The test had begun. A nervous knot tightened in his stomach as he raised his hand to knock.

Josh took a deep, steadying breath, his hand still raised to the door. He let it fall in a single, confident knock.

"Enter," a deep voice commanded from within.

He pushed the door open, stepped inside, and came to a rigid attention in front of the commander's large, polished desk. The man behind it, Commander Uzziel, was a figure of quiet authority. His dark hair was streaked with gray, and his eyes were focused on a datapad. He didn't look up, not even when Josh gave a sharp, formal salute.

"Ensign Joshua, reporting as ordered," Josh stated, his intonation clear and professional.

"At ease, Mr. Joshua," the commander replied with a calm counterpoint to the tense air in the room. He still hadn't looked up from the datapad. "I'm reviewing your records from the academy. You marks are excellent, particularly in navigation and hand-to-hand combat, I see. Very impressive." He finally looked up, his gaze intense. "I demand high standards aboard the Bethel, but it appears you are up to the task. Keep performing like this aboard and you'll do very well."

He leaned back in his chair. "So, tell me, Ensign. With a resume like yours, you could have gone anywhere. Why did you choose to serve in the Patrol Corps?"

Josh stood taller, choosing his words carefully. "Pirates took my family, sir. I needed a new one. And this organization provides justice, not just for me, but for all those who are preyed upon by criminals."

Commander Uzziel nodded slowly, his expression shifting to one of respect and empathy. "I'm sorry for your loss, Ensign. Your resolve is impressive. The Bethel, Ms. Beth is the right ship for you." He leaned forward, tapping a few notes on his console. "There are a few administrative details to cover. You'll be assigned some work details; all junior crewmembers get them. Ensign Adriel will get you up to speed. You'll also have professional military education coursework to complete. And your training under Lieutenant Obadiah will begin with the second watch tomorrow."

He stood, signaling the end of their conversation. "I know you've had a long day, Ensign, and you probably want to hit your bunk, but there is some additional business to attend to." He hit a button on his desk. "You may come in now."

To Josh's complete shock, the woman who entered was Special Agent Zipporah. She was just as he remembered her from his interrogation, her eyes sharp and intelligent.

"Hello, Mr. Joshua," she said, a small smile on her face.

Commander Uzziel turned back to Josh, a hint of something unreadable in his gaze. "Ensign, your reputation precedes you."

Chapter 40

The pirate flotilla arrived at Gehinnom not as a unified fleet, but as a staggered, chaotic procession of rust-flecked ships limping into orbit. A failed colony sprawled across the surface of a dry, dusty, red planet below, its lifeless domes and skeletal towers mocking the very idea of a new beginning. Orbiting the planet was a dilapidated space station—a skeletal wreck of a place with empty docking bays and a haphazard network of catwalks and external braces. The station was the heart of Cain's new pirate empire.

Aboard the Babylon, the tension was a physical presence. The tactical officer, a slender, pinched face man named Malkiel, meticulously scanned the incoming ships. He was competent but not exceptional, and the only reason he had his new post was because Dathan, the First Mate, had put in a good word. Dathan, now more arrogant than ever, stood behind him, his presence a constant reminder of Malkiel's debt.

"Micromanaging again, are we, Malkiel?" Dathan sneered, leaning over the tactical console. "You can thank me later for this view. From now on, every ship that enters this port will be a tribute to Captain Cain."

Malkiel ignored the jibe, his fingers tapping on the console as he confirmed each ship's ID and assigned it a docking bay. "All ships have been accounted for, Mr. Dathan. They're a mess, but they're here."

Cain entered the bridge, his presence a study in calm. His uniform was impeccable, and he carried his customary cup of steaming green tea. He moved to the bridge window, looking out at the new pirate haven. He didn't see a mess; he saw a foundation.

"Contact the entire flotilla," Cain ordered. "Open a channel to every bridge."

Malkiel nodded, sending a wide-band signal across the fleet.

"Captains," Cain began, his voice amplified and broadcast to every ship. "Welcome to Gehinnom. I know the journey was difficult, and I thank you for your faith. I assure you that this desolate rock and this humble station will provide us with the security and solitude we need to thrive."

His tone was like a balm on the weary pirates' nerves. He spoke not as a cutthroat but as a statesman, the gentleman pirate welcoming his guests. He detailed the patrol routes, the resource allocation, and the new rules of engagement. He spoke of unity and purpose, but his words carried a subtle threat—a promise of retribution for anyone who would threaten the new order. He concluded his speech by toasting the new empire, his teacup a solitary chalice raised against the backdrop of the dusty red planet.

"We have stood at the edge of the abyss and refused to fall into it," Cain continued, his gaze still fixed on the station. "Our enemies, the Interstellar Patrol Corps, believe they have the advantage. But they are wrong. They do not have our cunning, our courage, or our will. Here, in the heart of

Gehinnom, we will forge a new empire."

A moment of silence passed, the other captains responding with murmurs of agreement and the low rumble of engines. But the unity was shattered by a sharp, feminine screech that cut through the open channel.

"Speak for yourself, Cain!" the woman spat. "This place is a dump, and I'm not in this business to play soldier and build empires. I'm here to get rich." It was Captain Jezebel, her face a mask of scorn on the Babylon's comms screen. She saw only a squalid end to her career, not a new beginning.

Cain's expression didn't change, but his eyes narrowed imperceptibly. He raised a hand in a silent, fluid gesture. Dathan and Malkiel, who had been trained by Cain for exactly this kind of situation, moved as one, their fingers flying over the tactical board. With a series of silent gestures and pointed looks, Cain directed his bridge crew: weapons systems were armed, targeting solutions locked.

"Any of you who agree with me are welcome to join me," Jezebel continued, emboldened by her defiance. "I'm leaving this graveyard now."

As her ship's engines began to whine, readying for a jump to hyperspace, Cain spoke, his tone quiet but cold.

"Fire."

A single, unified volley from the Babylon's cannons ripped across the void, turning Jezebel's ship into a cloud of expanding vapor and debris. The explosion was a brilliant, silent flash against the darkness of space.

Cain got back on the comms with a smooth, apologetic murmur. "My sincerest apologies for that tragic incident, Captains. It is a sad thing when one of our own falls prey to a lack of vision. Captain Jezebel, in her haste and misguided desire for personal gain, clearly did not have the spirit of unity we all share. The risk that she would give away the location of our new base was simply too high. There was nothing else I could have done."

On the bridge of the Babylon, Dathan and Malkiel watched in silent awe. The other captains, now his vassals, responded with whoops and cheers. The chaotic arrival was a fitting metaphor for the pirate world itself—messy and disorganized, but now, for the first time, under the quiet and ruthless control of a single, powerful mind.

Chapter 41

Ensign Joshua stood in stunned silence, his carefully constructed composure threatening to shatter. Special Agent Zipporah's presence was the last thing he expected. She moved with a quiet, confident grace, her gaze meeting his with the same piercing intensity he remembered.

"Agent Zipporah," he managed to recover. "I... didn't expect to see you here."

Zipporah's smile was a small, knowing thing. "I'm not assigned to the Bethel, Ensign. But Commander Uzziel was kind enough to grant me a few minutes of his time." She looked from Josh to the commander. "We have what we need for the project, sir. I was hoping we could take this conversation down to the Combat Information Center."

Commander Uzziel, a man of few words, nodded and stood. "Ensign Joshua, you will join us. This is a unique opportunity to witness tactical intelligence analysis in action."

Josh followed them, his mind reeling. He had given Zipporah information a year ago, but she hadn't said they had what they needed then. He had always assumed his information had been insufficient. The CIC was a hive of controlled chaos, filled with the soft hum of consoles and the low murmur of officers at work. The trio moved to a secure tactical console dominated by a large holomap.

Zipporah gestured to the holomap, which displayed a star chart with a nebula glowing ominously in the center. "For years, we've searched for the pirate haven known as the Dead Sea. We've had dozens of sightings from victims, but never a precise location." She turned to Josh. "Your account, however, gave us the exact coordinates of the battle between the pirate ships Babylon and Gomorrah. We recovered some fragmented nav data from Gomorrah's wreckage, and my team at the Port Authority has been cross-referencing it with your story."

Josh watched, a knot forming in his stomach, as she began to overlay data on the holomap. "We now have three key pieces of information. First, we have the course the Babylon was on, based on your intel. Second, my team has analyzed Gomorrah's nav logs. Third, and most importantly, we have a detailed gravitational map of this sector, including the local nebula."

She stepped back, a challenge in her gaze. "Ensign, based on your knowledge of Babylon's course and the battle itself, show us how you found Gomorrah and show us the path of Babylon."

Josh's old training kicked in, pushing his anxiety aside. He approached the console and inputted a few commands. He selected Babylon's icon and plotted a winding course that twisted through the nebula. The course was a work of art, a path only a true navigator could have envisioned, designed to use the gravitational ebb and flow to mask their approach and to throw off pursuers.

"The Babylon used gravitational topography to accelerate along this path without needing a large burst from the engines," he explained, gaining confidence as he continued. "Then, Captain Cain ordered me to take her through this nebula, to use the radiation field to jam Gomorrah's long-range sensors."

As he worked, he added small details from his memory: a specific engine burn, a subtle course correction, the moments where he had used the gravitational landscape to gain a tactical advantage. He drew the projected path of the Gomorrah, showing where the two ships converged.

"The battle occurred here," he said, pointing to a specific point on the map. "The Gomorrah's drive was destroyed and her wreckage was adrift after the battle." He entered the drift calculations, the holographic wreckage spreading slowly away from the point of impact. "She would have drifted along this specific gravity path."

"That's exactly where we found her," Zipporah confirmed. "So now we have precise data on the gravitational currents and topography, partial information on Gomorrah's original course, and Ensign Joshua's recollection of the Babylon's movements. Ensign, please bring it all together," she instructed.

Zipporah and Uzziel watched in silence as the data came together, with Josh's insights bringing the abstract numbers to life. The lines on the holomap converged on a single point: a dwarf planet hidden deep within an asteroid field inside the nebula. As he finished his analysis, an icon labeled "The Dead Sea" materialized on the holomap.

Zipporah let out a low whistle. "It was hiding in plain sight. It took all the pieces of the puzzle to find it."

Commander Uzziel stared at the image, his face a mask of quiet shock. He turned to Zipporah, then back to Josh, an unreadable expression on his face. He shook his head slowly, a hint of awe in his eyes.

"We'd better get the Captain down here to see this," he said.

A moment later, the double doors of the CIC slid open, and a new figure entered. He was a broad-shouldered man with the confident bearing of a seasoned commander. His neatly trimmed beard and calm, authoritative gaze marked him as Captain Zechariah of the IPC Bethel. His eyes swept across the room, acknowledging Zipporah and his XO. He paused for a moment on Josh, a question in his eyes before turning to his second-in-command.

"Commander, you said you had something to show me?" he asked, his tone ringing with authority.

Uzziel led him to the tactical console where the holographic map of the nebula still hung in the air, a glowing web of data. "Captain, we believe we have located the Dead Sea." He gave a quick, concise summary of the process: the recovered nav data from the pirate ship Gomorrah, the gravitational map of the sector, and the missing piece of the puzzle that Josh had provided. "We've been able to pinpoint its exact location, a dwarf planet hidden inside an asteroid field within the nebula."

Captain Zechariah studied the holomap intently. The intricate dance of lines and vectors made perfect sense to him. He was a tactician, and he understood the brilliance behind the analysis. He finally looked up, his gaze finding Josh.

"How in the heavens did you piece all this together?" he asked.

Uzziel motioned to Josh. "With the help of Ensign Joshua,

sir. His knowledge of the Babylon's course and the battle's tactical layout was the key. He was able to use the gravitational data to extrapolate Gomorrah's drift and pinpoint the dwarf planet."

Zechariah looked Josh over, a flicker of professional respect in his eyes. "Well done, Ensign. That's a level of tactical analysis I've rarely seen from an officer of your rank. It's a privilege to have you aboard."

He then turned to Zipporah, his expression turning serious. "Agent, you've been working on this for a year, haven't you? You're telling me this information is old news, that it could be compromised?"

"It's over a year old, Captain," Zipporah confirmed. "It's possible that it is too late."

Uzziel stepped forward, his resolve clear. "Nonetheless, sir, this is the best opportunity we've had in years. We have to take advantage of it."

Zechariah's silence was brief but heavy. He looked from his XO to Zipporah, then back to the holomap. He understood the risks, but the reward was too great to ignore. He nodded once, a firm decision made. He reached for a comms panel on the console and keyed in a secure channel.

"This is Captain Zechariah of the IPCS Bethel to Central Command. I'm requesting full authorization for Task Force Gideon. We have a target. I repeat, we have a confirmed target. The Dead Sea has been located." He paused, listening to the confirmation. "Understood. Task Force Gideon is a go. Assemble the fleet."

He turned to his XO, filled with a new, urgent energy. "Commander, assemble the fleet. And Ensign Joshua," he said, turning back to Josh, "you just earned yourself a spot on the first watch. I want you to be the one to plot our course."

Chapter 42

Captain Cain stood at the viewport of his office, a stark, functional space bathed in the cold light of a dying sun. Below him, the rusting lattice of the station, Gehinnom, clung to the failed colony of the same name. It was an old holding of his family, a forgotten piece of property that now served as the anchor of his new pirate empire. The view was a testament to his power: two pirate ships were berthed at the docks, their hauls being offloaded. He could see the flash of shackles, a few dozen men in chains who would be put to work on the dilapidated berths. The pirate captains, normally as independent as any asteroid drifter, had fallen in line under his authority and the promise of security and intelligence he could provide.

The door hissed open, and Dathan entered, his scarred face grim. "The captains of the Kedar and Ishmael have filed their manifests, sir. Their crews are offloading the take and the new prisoners now."

Cain turned from the window, a small, knowing smile on his face. He sipped his green tea, a quiet counterpoint to the controlled chaos unfolding below. "And what of the Dead Sea, Dathan? Have our beacons reported any activity?"

"The beacons remain silent, Captain," Dathan reported, a

hint of nervous energy in his stance. "We've had nothing from the remote sensors, and all the charges are still in standby, just as you ordered."

Cain's smile faltered, replaced by a subtle flicker of disappointment. It had been over a year since Mr. Joshua's escape. The boy was so clever, so resourceful. Cain had seen in him a kindred spirit, someone he could have forged into an amazing weapon. Joshua had so much more potential than this dullard Dathan. He would have been Cain's tool, his weapon, eventually his partner, and even one day, his successor. Surely, he would have given the Port Authority or the IPC everything he knew.

Yet, there was nothing. No significant change in patrol routes, no increased scrutiny, no raid on the Dead Sea. The silence was baffling. Cain had left behind a web of sensors and traps, expecting a response, anticipating the inevitable hunt. But all he heard was silence.

Perhaps, he thought, a faint sense of regret touching his cold heart, Mr. Joshua did not survive his escape attempt after all.

Chapter 43

The bridge of the IPC cutter Bethel, fondly known as Ms. Beth by her crew, was a study in controlled tension. The crew moved with a quiet, focused energy, the only sounds the soft hum of consoles and the clipped reports of officers. Captain Zechariah sat in the command chair, his gaze fixed on the main viewscreen, which showed nothing but the swirling, ionized dust of the Dead Sea nebula—the perfect place to hide a dwarf planet and a pirate haven.

"Commander," Zechariah said calmly, cutting through the silence. "Bring Task Force Gideon to General Quarters."

"Aye, Captain," Commander Uzziel replied. A tone, high-pitched and urgent, cut through the air, signaling the crew to battle stations.

The bridge immediately shifted. Ensign Adriel, the cheerful engineer, disappeared into his station, his face now a mask of concentration. Lieutenant Obadiah, the senior navigator, took his place at the nav console.

Joshua, assisting Obadiah, ran a final diagnostic on the nav controls. He hunched over his screen, his brow furrowed. "Lieutenant," he murmured, his voice tight with apology. "My approach was off a few degrees. We've arrived with a one hundred klick deviation from the target waypoint. We're slightly off the mark, sir."

Obadiah, a stern man with a professional calm, glanced at the numbers and gave a slight, almost imperceptible shake of his head. "A hundred klicks, Mr. Joshua? After navigating through that much rock and gravitational anomalies? I think you're splitting frog hairs. We're well within operational parameters. Don't sweat it, Ensign." He gave Josh a slightly amused look, recognizing the young man's genius and his accompanying perfectionism.

It was surreal; the same course he had plotted for Cain was now the path he was plotting for the very people hunting him.

"All stations report ready, Captain."

A beat passed, and then a comms officer spoke up. "The ship is at General Quarters, sir. All ships in Task Force Gideon are reporting ready as well."

"Good." Zechariah took a deep breath, his eyes surveying the bridge. "All ships assume Phalanx formation." He nodded to the flight control officer. "Launch the Viper Flight and have them scout ahead on the primary approach. We proceed on their clearance. I don't doubt the pirates have a welcome planned for us."

A small display near the viewscreen showed four sleek IPC fighters detaching from their carrier vessels and streaking silently toward the nebula's thickest regions.

The wait was agonizing. Then, Debriefing:

"Captain, Viper Flight reports contact!" the comms officer announced. "They've encountered multiple armed sensor drones. Lightly armored, pirate tech. Vipers are engaging."

A flurry of comm chatter followed, quickly muted on the bridge's main speaker, but visible in the comms officer's focused stance.

Moments later, the report came back. "Viper Flight reports target neutralized. Four armed drones destroyed. All systems nominal, Captain. Path is clear."

A collective sigh of tension seemed to ease from the bridge crew.

Zechariah allowed himself a curt, satisfied nod. "As expected. They put a tripwire out, and we cut it. Very well. The threat is now neutralized. Proceed on my mark." He waited a moment, his hand on the comms button. "Mark."

With a subtle lurch, the Bethel and her sister ships eased into the nebula. The viewscreen went from a simple starfield to a chaotic maelstrom of color and light. Particles and cosmic dust swirled past the windows. The nebula's interference was immediate and thick, distorting sensor readings and drowning out long-range comms. The ships were blind and deaf, relying only on short-range scanners and the crew's keen eyes.

Every shadow, every cluster of rock, felt like a potential threat. The ships moved at a crawl, their thrusters barely whispering. The tension in the air was so thick it felt like it could be cut with a knife. Zechariah's face was a stone mask, his focus absolute. He knew this was not a traditional battle. It was a hunt, a slow and methodical search for predators who knew how to hide. Joshua, hunched over his own console, watched the data streams, every nerve ending screaming. He knew their enemy. He just had to find them before the enemy's true welcome found Task Force Gideon

Captain Cain sat in his command chair, below him, the organized bustle of Gehinnom continued, a testament to his authority. But his calm facade was about to be broken. The door to his office hissed open, and Dathan burst in, his normally grim face alight with a frantic, eager energy.

"Captain, the beacons at the Dead Sea! They're active! We have contacts, multiple of them!" he blurted out, a hint of genuine excitement in his voice.

Cain did not so much as flinch. He simply raised a hand, a silent command for Dathan to compose himself. He took a slow, deliberate sip of his tea, placed the cup on his desk, and with a single touch, the monitor came to life. The sensor readings confirmed it: the telltale energy signatures of several IPC vessels, entering the nebula just as he had predicted.

The moment he had been preparing for had finally arrived. For a year, he had waited, a hunter patiently watching his trap. Now, the prey had taken the bait. A cold, sly smile spread across his face, a stark contrast to the quiet rage he felt in his heart.

He looked up at Dathan and issued a chilling command. "Ready the Babylon for combat. Inform all available captains that they are to do the same. And arm the charges. This is the moment we've all been waiting for."

Cain pulled up a navigational chart on the main screen, highlighting a single red point in the void between two stars. "This is a La Grange point between the two stars of a binary system. The stellar flares make sensors nearly useless, and the offsetting gravitational fields mean we won't need to burn any fuel to hold station. It is the perfect place to set an ambush."

He paused, a glint of cruel genius in his eyes. "The IPC fleet will have to pass nearby on their return trip, and when they do, we'll be waiting. All ships are to rendezvous here in 20 hours. Any no-shows will be charged double for their berths on the station, and I am putting a one million credit bounty on each cutter in the IPC fleet."

"Aye, Captain!" Dathan replied, his countenance filled with a hungry eagerness. He saluted and turned to leave.

Cain watched him go, a faint expression of disdain on his face. He turned back to his desk, finished off his tea, and took a deep breath, his eyes closed. His moment was at hand. The game had begun, and he was ready. He stood and, with a renewed sense of purpose, marched off to the Babylon.

The IPC Task Force Gideon had made it to the dwarf planet. The long, slow journey through the nebula was over, but the tension on the bridge of the Bethel remained. The crew had made it this far without contact, but they knew the pirates' home turf was full of secrets and hidden dangers.

A voice cut through the tense quiet on the bridge, a report from the surface. "Commander, the marine teams have confirmed the station is abandoned. No sign of personnel, just the remains of a few fires and scattered equipment. They've found a few terminals and are downloading what they can."

Frustration rippled through the crew. For all their careful planning, for all the risk, they had arrived at an empty house. Josh, in particular, felt a crushing disappointment. He had given them the perfect location, but it had been for nothing. The pirates had slipped away, and Cain was still out there, free.

Ensign Adriel, the engineer, clapped a hand on Josh's shoulder. "Hey, do not worry. Sometimes, a hunt ends in a good story, even if you do not catch the prey." His deep

Kenyan accent was a small comfort, but Josh just nodded, his gaze fixed on the empty dwarf planet on the viewscreen.

The marine commander's final report came in, dry and clinical. "Sir, we have secured a few encrypted files and some salvageable equipment, but the site is a bust. We are preparing for extraction."

Captain Zechariah, his jaw tight, addressed the fleet over the comms. "All ships prepare to return to base. We've done all we can here."

The fleet, in a solemn, frustrated ballet, began to break orbit and form up. The IPC cutters, their engines now rumbling with a sense of defeat, set their exit course and began to accelerate out of the nebula.

Just as they began to pick up speed, the void around them erupted. A series of small asteroids, seemingly innocuous just moments before, exploded in a cacophony of white light and shrapnel. The concussive blasts slammed into the hulls of the ships. Alarms blared across the bridge of the Bethel, replacing the tense quiet with a jarring, urgent symphony of chaos. The ambush had been sprung.

Chapter 44

The jarring clang of alarms was gone, replaced by a high pitched ringing in Josh's ears. He was on the deck, a sharp pain radiating from his temple. The air was thick with smoke, and the lights of the bridge flickered erratically, casting long, dancing shadows.

"Josh! Wake up!"

A hand slapped his cheek, and Josh's eyes fluttered open to see the worried face of Adriel. He was bleeding from a cut on his brow, but his eyes were wide with a fierce, urgent focus.

"Adriel? Why are you here? You need to go fix the power…" Josh mumbled, his mind still clouded by the concussive blast.

"There's nothing to fix here," Adriel said in a frantic whisper. "The ship's spinning. We need a navigator, not another engineer. We're going to crash."

Josh's gaze shot to the Navigation console, and he saw it. The body of Lieutenant Obadiah, his trainer, lay sprawled across the deck plates in an impossible, broken angle. The sight of it, more than the pain or the smoke, jolted him to full, terrifying clarity. The adrenaline hit, and in an instant, he was on his feet.

"I got this," he said, his tone sharp and confident. "Go fix stuff, Adriel."

He sprinted to the Navigation console. The panel was dark and smoking, the display cracked and useless. Just like in the sims. He slapped his hip, and his datapad was miraculously still there. He pulled up his emergency checklist, his fingers flying across the screen. Cut the main power to nav. Switch to internal battery backup. Power up the limited backup mode. The console shuddered to life, a vibration of power returning. He ran a quick diagnostic, saw the ship's dangerous tumble through space, and began to issue commands.

"Helm! Who's on the helm?" he yelled over the crackle of a blown comms panel.

"Helm present," an anonymous helmsman responded, her voice strained. "She's not answering to port or to pitch, sir!"

"Engineering, status report!" Josh barked.

"Almost there, sir, just a few more seconds!" Adriel replied.

Josh glanced around the bridge, his eyes searching for his commanders. Captain Zechariah lay face down at the rear of the bridge, motionless. A medic was tending to Commander Uzziel, who was slumped in his command chair, conscious but dazed. It was up to him.

"Got it, auxiliary flight control is now online!" Adriel's declaration was a welcome lifeline.

"Helm, put one hundred-eighty degrees of pitch on the ventral thrusters! Now, a hundred and ten degrees to starboard, full burn!" Josh ordered.

The ship lurched, the deck beneath Josh's feet groaning as the thrusters fought against the tumbling momentum. Slowly, painfully, the deck stabilized, and the ship came to a standstill.

A new tactical display bloomed to life. The crew, battered and bruised, stumbled toward the viewscreen. The carnage of the task force was laid bare. Two ships, reduced to debris clouds. Another, a smoking hulk with a disabled main drive. The remaining vessels, including their own, were heavily damaged. An audible gasp filled the smoke-filled air as the crew stared in horrified disbelief. They were alone, wounded, and in enemy territory.

Josh looked around, his heart pounding in his chest. Adriel and he were the only officers on the bridge. The enlisted personnel, their faces streaked with grime and blood, looked to him for orders. It was a heavy, terrifying burden.

"We need to find out who's still with us. Communications," Josh ordered. "Patch me through on the emergency fleet frequency."

A Chief Petty Officer at the comms station, a grizzled woman with more years of service in her expression than Josh had in his life, nodded. Her quick, professional movement was a small, steady anchor in the chaos. "Open and secure, sir."

Josh took a deep breath, the taste of ozone and fear on his tongue. He had to say something. He had to be in command.

"All vessels of Task Force Gideon," he began, his voice still shaky but gaining strength with each word. "This is Bethel. We have sustained heavy damage and numerous casualties but are under power and control. Please report your status to the fleet… by the numbers."

The silence on the comms was excruciating. Then, one by one, the responses began to filter through.

"IPC Cutter Shiloh reporting. Heavy damage to aft thrusters and port side batteries. Main drive is offline."

"IPC Cutter Adullam reporting. We're in a similar state to the Bethel, heavy damage, but under power and control.

Casualties are moderate."

"IPC Cutter Tabor reporting. We have sustained heavy damage but are under power and control."

Josh's heart sank at the grim accounting. Two vessels completely destroyed, and the remaining ones, including their own, were all severely crippled. A new, authoritative voice cut through the comms.

"This is Captain Abijah of the IPC Cutter Tabor." The name, one Josh had only heard in mission briefings, brought a wave of relief. He wasn't alone. "Is Captain Zechariah available, Bethel?"

Josh hesitated. The words stuck in his throat, a final, painful acknowledgment of the scale of their loss. "Negative, sir. Captain Zechariah is among the dead. Commander Uzziel is incapacitated."

A pregnant pause hung over the comms channel. The unspoken gravity of the situation was a tangible weight. Josh held his breath.

"Understood," Captain Abijah said, his tone firm and resolved. "I assume command of Task Force Gideon. All vessels, maintain your positions and assess damage. We will begin search and rescue operations immediately."

Josh let out a small, silent exhale of relief. The burden of command, for now, had been lifted. He looked around the bridge, the chaos still palpable but now with a clear sense of purpose. He wasn't in charge of the fleet, but there was still plenty he could do. He had a job, and he had to do it.

Twenty-four hours later, the space around the Dead Sea was a graveyard. The fleet had reassembled, a grim parade of battered and broken ships. The Tabor towed the powerless

Shiloh with her primary tractor beam, its hull scarred and dented. On the Bethel, the air still smelled of burnt metal and blood. The med bays were overflowing, forcing the crew to convert cargo bays into makeshift hospitals. In the ships' morgue, bodies lay in cold storage.

Josh hadn't felt this devastated since the day the Galilee was attacked. But that was a grief of loss; this was a grief poisoned by guilt. *It was my intelligence,* a voice screamed in his head, *my reckless desire for vengeance.* He had been so eager to finally go after Cain, so focused on the target that he had been careless in his debrief. He should have been more cautious. He should have anticipated Cain's traps. His own burning desire for justice had clouded his judgment, and it had cost them all dearly. He had practically strong armed the Captain into this decision. The faces of the wounded and the silent forms of the dead—they were on him. The flood of memories—his parents, the crew, the senseless violence—now brought a fresh wave of self-loathing. This had to be Cain's doing. His rage, cold and bitter, began to boil, now aimed as much at himself as at the pirate. He saw his own, long-dormant desire for vengeance reflected in the eyes of his fellow crewmates.

"He did this," Josh said, his jaw clenched, the words barely masking his inner turmoil. "He used us. He just wanted to hurt us."

Adriel, who had been working tirelessly on repairs, put a hand on Josh's shoulder. "My friend, you are not wrong to be angry. But do not let it consume you. That is what he wants. We are IPC. We do not do what he does. We bring justice."

A new figure, a severe-looking woman, Bethel's senior tactical officer, entered the bridge. It was Lieutenant Commander Barak, the acting captain until Uzziel recovered. She had moved her from the Combat Information Center to the bridge, a clear signal that the ship's immediate survival was her priority.

She walked to the command chair, her face a mask of resolute focus. "Captain Abijah has ordered a return to base at Bethesda." she said, her voice betraying no emotion. "We will set a slow and deliberate course. I want all crews on watch and every sensor on full. We will not be surprised again."

Josh looked out at the broken ships around them. They had suffered a terrible loss. But they were still a fleet, damaged and grieving, but unbroken. With a final, shared glance with Adriel, he watched as the three remaining cutters and their support vessels turned as one, leaving the nebula behind. Their long journey home had begun.

Chapter 45

The Galilee cut a clean path through the blackness of deep space en route to New Canaan. On the observation deck, a small sparring ring was set up. It was a hive of activity. Jabez whirred softly, a soft clicking noise as his optics followed the movements of the crew. In the ring, Leah, with a dancer's grace, feinted and weaved around Jabez. She ducked under his massive arm, and then, with a fluid movement, her hand gently tapped the robot on the back. "Got you, sugar!" she said, a mischievous grin on her face.

Noah and Deb watched, a quiet respect in their eyes. "She's a natural," Noah said, shaking his head in disbelief.

Deb, her expression unreadable, simply nodded. "Fluidity of motion, Captain. It's a key advantage."

The two of them stepped into the ring. Noah's form was all raw power and aggression, while Deb was a study in efficient, precise movements. They moved around each other, a dance of feints and dodges. Noah lunged forward, his fist shooting out in a direct, powerful strike. Deb, to his surprise, didn't block it. She let it come, her body suddenly going limp. Noah's fist connected, but his momentum carried him forward, and Deb, with a quick reversal, used it to send him tumbling to the deck.

He landed on his back with a soft thud, and Deb knelt over him, their faces mere inches apart. In that moment, surrounded by the hum of the ship and the gentle glow of the observation deck, there was a spark, a brief flicker of attraction that hung in the air between them.

Jabez's synthesized voice boomed, an interruption that broke the moment. "Attack Protocol Failed. Defensive Countermeasures Engaged."

The moment was gone. Deb stood up, a small flush on her cheeks, and helped Noah to his feet.

Later, in the engine room, the plasma cannons and upgraded engines performed better than any of them could have dreamed. During a test fire, the newly reinforced plasma cannons sliced clean through an asteroid, the energy bolts a blinding flash against the void. Temperatures held stable; the new heat sinks were working perfectly. The engines pushed the Galilee to speeds they had only ever seen in a simulation, the deck vibrating with an exhilarating thrum of power.

Eli grinned as a holographic map of the Galilee's corridors flashed on his datapad. He tapped a few commands, and on the security cameras, a section of the hallway ahead of Jabez erupted in a burst of white foam. The hulking robot, its treads whirring, rolled to a stop just short of the bubbly mess. "Obstruction detected," Jabez announced in its happy, mechanical voice. A moment later, Noah appeared on another camera feed, testing a pressure plate. As his boot hit the floor, a piercing shriek echoed down the hall, followed by a blinding strobe light from a repurposed maintenance panel. "Well," Noah said, a hand over his eyes, "it's certainly effective. A little disorienting, but effective."

"Alright, team," Noah said, grinning widely. "Let's get this thing back on track. We've got a delivery to make."

The mission was a simple one: transport medical supplies and hydroponic equipment to a small, remote colony called New Canaan. As the Galilee entered the system on course to the colony's orbital platform, the simple run immediately turned complicated.

"Honey, I'm reading unusual traffic," Leah called from navigation, her deep Southern accent tight. "Two blips. A stationary contact, that'll be the station. And a fast-moving, unannounced vessel. Looks like a heavily modified transport."

Noah's grin vanished. "Visuals, Aunt Leah."

The main screen snapped into focus, showing the peaceful, garden-like habitat of New Canaan under a pale yellow sun. But looming nearby was a dark, menacing ship—a pirate corvette—its weapons systems openly charging and focused on the station's main airlock. The colonists, a friendly and peaceful group, were clearly being harassed and cornered.

"Pirates. Trying to board the station," Deb stated flatly from her communications console, her eyes already scanning for damage indicators.

Noah felt the familiar spike of adrenaline, but this time, it was colder, sharper, and tempered by Eli's recent counsel. *The wise way.*

"Eli, transfer full power to the main thrusters, and prep the weapons, but monitor heat levels closely. Leah, lay in a wide intercept course, and start tracking a firing solution on their main drive."

He took a steadying breath, the image of his family's

wreckage far away. "And Deb, tight-band channel direct to the pirates vessel. Time for a reintroduction."

Noah's voice, clear and steady, filled the bridge. "This is Captain Gabriel of the Archangel to the vessel harassing the New Canaan station. You have ten seconds to disengage and clear the sector, or we will open fire. We are armed, and we are not a threat you want to engage."

The pirates didn't bother with a reply, their systems simply went to full charge.

"They're accelerating toward the airlock, Noah!" Leah shouted. "Trying to force a breach before we can get into position!"

"They're underestimating us," Noah said, a grim focus settling over him.

"Leah, NOW! Hard turn to starboard, full lateral thrust!"

The Galilee lurched, not with the agonizing slowness of the last fight, but with a trained, powerful sweep. Leah, anticipating the pivot, compensated to maintain the firing solution.

"Targeting lock confirmed, honey. I have a clean solution on their main thruster array," Leah reported, her tone unusually professional despite the underlying tension.

"Eli, half power to the cannons! Limits to Max safe heat!" Noah commanded.

"Heat is nominal, lad, and holding!" Eli called back immediately.

"Fire!" Noah commanded, slamming the firing stud.

Fwoooom!

A pair of, brilliant, blue beams of energy lanced out. This time, the aim was perfect. The shot—judiciously set to half power—slammed into the pirate corvette's rear section. It didn't explode the vessel, but it tore through the main power conduit for the port thrusters. The pirate ship immediately lost cohesion, its nose dipping sharply as one side of its propulsion system failed.

"We got 'em! Pirate vessel is on partial power!" Leah exclaimed, her shock turning to elation.

The pirate ship, now crippled and spinning, executed a desperate, chaotic turn, its guns blazing. Its shots peppered the Galilee as it was attempting to flee.

"Damage report, Deb!" Noah demanded, wrestling the old urge to destroy.

"Superficial scorch marks, Captain. No structural damage. Their shots were wild," Deb confirmed.

Noah fought the urge to line up a second shot. *Justice, not vengeance.* He exhaled slowly.

"Stand down. Abandon pursuit," he ordered, the words tight but final. "Aunt Leah, turn us back to the New Canaan station. Let's finish this delivery."

Later, in the colony's small, warm mess hall, the colonists were effusive with gratitude. Noah and the crew sat at a small table, having just offloaded their full cargo.

"You came out of nowhere, Captain Gabriel," the colony director said, pushing a plate heaped with fresh-baked bread and synth-meat towards Noah. "You saved us from a total disaster. They were minutes away from breaking the airlock. That meal is on us, and every meal after, for as long as you stop here."

The crew laughed, the tension finally dissolving into tired relief. They had faced a threat, fought wisely, and won without disaster. Noah looked at his crew—Eli, sipping his coffee; Leah, still buzzing with energy; Deb, eating methodically; and Jabez, quietly monitoring the room. He felt no guilt, only the quiet, profound satisfaction of a captain who had led his crew well.

As they ate, the communal holoscreen flickered to life with an emergency broadcast from the IPC. The announcer's mood was grim, the words cutting through the easy conversation and laughter.

"...we have sustained heavy casualties during an operation in the Dead Sea nebula," the IPC official reported. "Several vessels are confirmed lost, with others in a state of critical damage. Task Force Gideon has officially been declared..."

The news cut out just as quickly as it had begun, replaced by the colony's regular programming. A heavy silence fell over the room. Noah and his crew looked at each other, their faces suddenly drained of all color. The joyous mood was gone, replaced by a cold, numbing fear. Their quiet, safe lives had just been shattered by a single news flash, and Noah couldn't shake the terrible feeling that the storm was finally upon them.

Chapter 46

The journey home was a grim procession. The small, battered fleet limped through the vast emptiness of space, its pace dictated by the crippled Shiloh, which was being towed by the Tabor. On board the Bethel, the air was thick with the silent exhaustion of a crew pushed to its limits. The ship herself groaned with every shudder, her damaged hull and jury-rigged systems a constant reminder of their defeat.

Lieutenant Commander Barak was the unyielding core of the ship. Her presence was a pillar of strength, a study in quiet, steely resolve. Since she was the acting captain, she rarely left the command chair, delegating the CIC to her second, a quiet, sharp tactical lieutenant who had become a mirror of Barak's tireless work ethic.

In the engineering section, the relentless buzz and grind of damaged systems was a symphony of chaos. Here, Ensign Adriel, Josh's friend and roommate, seemed to thrive. His Kenyan accent, normally a source of cheer, now carried a frantic, determined energy. He darted between sparking conduits and hissing vents, his shaved head a blur of motion. While the rest of the crew was worn to the bone, Adriel was the sole source of optimism. He seemed to relish the impossible challenge, his deep joy in problem-solving a defiant contrast to the collective misery. He split his time between a station on the bridge, offering immediate engineering support, and the ship's cramped engineering compartments, where he assisted his immediate supervisor, the chief engineer. If Barak was Ms. Beth's brain, Adriel was her beating heart.

On the bridge, the weight of the fleet's survival rested squarely on Joshua's shoulders. As the only remaining navigator, the long and painful journey was his responsibility. He stood alone at the navigation console, a ghost of the ambitious ensign he had once been. The holographic star charts glowed before him, but his mind was on the faces of the crew members they had lost. His guilt and rage mixed to form a cold, hard knot in his gut. Every course correction, every fuel calculation, was a step closer to the inevitable, and with each one, the ghost of Cain's face seemed to flicker in the dark void outside the viewport. He was the one who had gotten them into this mess, and he was the one who was going to get them out. The knowledge was a heavy burden, but also a source of grim determination.

In the cold, chaotic emptiness of the Lagrange point, the pirate fleet sat in silent, disciplined formation. On the bridge of the Babylon, the only sound was the ship's systems and the faint clink of porcelain as Captain Cain raised his cup to his lips. He sipped his green tea, his gaze fixed on the main viewscreen, which showed only the swirling, angry hues of the binary stars and the shimmering haze of solar flares.

Dathan, a hulking mass of scars and muscle, stood beside him, a coiled spring of impatience.

"Captain," Dathan rumbled "All ships report ready. But

they're getting restless. We've been holding position for over a day."

Cain simply raised a hand without looking at him, a silent command for patience. He took a slow, deliberate sip of his tea, the picture of perfect stillness amidst the suppressed tension of his crew.

A new voice cut through the quiet. Malkiel, the Tactical Officer whom Dathan had promoted, hunched over his sensor console. He was a slender man, his face a constant mask of nervous energy.

"Captain," Malkiel said in a tense whisper. "I'm getting something. Sensor contacts. The flares are making the readings unclear, but the energy signatures that I can see match what we're looking for. It's likely the task force."

A predatory smile, cold and knowing, spread across Cain's face. "The bait has been taken," he murmured, more to himself than to his crew. He set his cup down with a soft, final sound.

"Dathan, inform the fleet to go to battle stations. All hands to their posts," he commanded, his inflection now a low, chilling purr. He turned to Malkiel. "Launch fighters. Moloch one, two, and three are to proceed at flank speed. Tell them not to engage. They are to confirm the contact, and then return. No engagements without my direct order."

"Yes, Captain," Malkiel replied, his fingers flying across the console.

Cain's gaze flickered to the side, where Malkiel and Dathan exchanged a quick, furtive glance. Dathan's smirk was clear. The tactical officer was a pawn, but a useful one.

Malkiel echoed through the comms. "All ships, launch your fighters. The Babylon will send three."

On cue, three separate sections of the Babylon's hull

opened, revealing the sleek, black shapes of the Moloch fighters. Simultaneously, from the two other pirate ships in the fleet, twin hatches hissed open, each releasing a pair of their own fighters. In all, seven small ships, silent and deadly, detached from their motherships and streaked away, swallowed by the stellar haze.

Cain watched them go, a glint of cruel genius in his eyes. The trap had been set. The jaws were about to snap shut. He was ready.

Adriel, having just completed a repair on a flickering comms panel, noticed the deep lines of exhaustion on his friend's face. He knew words wouldn't help. He slipped away for a moment and returned with a steaming mug, placing it gently on the console next to Josh. "We don't need you falling asleep and getting us lost, my friend," he said, a tired smile crinkling the corners of his eyes.

Josh looked up, surprised, a faint smile touching his lips. He took a long, grateful sip of the dark brew. It was warm, bitter, and a small, comforting moment of peace in a world of pain and chaos. "Thanks, man," he murmured, his voice tight with emotion. "I swear, I think I see them laughing in the stars sometimes."

Adriel put a hand on his shoulder. "They are not laughing, my friend. They are watching. Watching you, watching all of us. You have their lessons in your heart. You are using them to bring us home. That is all that matters." He squeezed Josh's shoulder once more, then turned and headed back to the engineering deck.

As the door hissed shut, leaving him alone once more, Joshua took another sip of his coffee. He was about to set the cup down when his eyes caught a flicker on a secondary sensor display. It was an anomaly—a brief, faint energy signature that should not have been there. He put the mug down, its warmth forgotten, dialed in the instruments. He ran a diagnostic, tracing the signal. It was a faint but distinct signature, and there was a pattern to it. A pattern he recognized.

The quiet of Babylon's bridge was shattered by the frantic report from Malkiel. The three Moloch fighters, now returned to the fleet, had delivered their report.

"Confirmed, Captain! It's the IPC fleet! Four cutters," Malkiel tensed with nervous excitement. "They're in a slow formation, with one of their ships being towed. Its main drive is offline!"

A fierce, brutal joy lit Cain's face. He stood, his posture instantly changing from relaxed command to coiled fury. He was no longer the man sipping tea; he was a predator, a hunter who had cornered his prey.

"Dathan, you have your orders," Cain snarled. "Fighters will screen us until we are properly engaged. Then they will focus their fire on the crippled cutter. Target its life support. Take out the heart of their formation first."

He pivoted toward Ithamar, the nervous, muttering navigation officer, his presence alone enough to make the man jump. "Mr. Ithamar! Plot an intercept course. I want us on their port flank in three minutes. Give us a full burn. And inform the fleet, all ahead full! The hunt is on!"

Ithamar, his spectacles fogged from perspiration, fumbled with his console, his muttering now a frantic prayer. Dathan's answer "Aye, Captain!" was a hungry roar. The silence of the

Babylon was gone, replaced by the deep, shuddering vibration of a ship coming to life. The viewscreen, once a window to the serene void, now filled with the angry flare of engine exhaust as the entire pirate fleet surged forward, a pack of wolves closing in on their wounded prey.

The quiet of Bethel's bridge was shattered by Joshua's declaration. "Acting Captain, I have a contact! Multiple brief signatures, fast-moving, and coming from the direction of the binary system."

Lieutenant Commander Barak, her face a mask of stone, was already moving. "General Quarters! All hands, battle stations!" Her voice, a shout of authority, cut through the sudden frantic movement on the bridge. She turned to the CPO at the comms console. "Inform the Tabor. Possible hostile contacts hiding in the interference of the binary system on our starboard flank. Advise they prepare for attack."

The message was sent in a heartbeat, but it was already too late. On the tactical display, the faint blips resolved into seven distinct signatures, moving with terrifying speed. "They're fighters," Josh breathed, his eyes wide with a horrifying familiarity. "And they're on an attack vector!"

"Lets show those blaggards that Ms. Beth still has some fight left in her! Evasive maneuvers!" Barak yelled over the blare of the klaxons. "Bring the main cannons to bear!"

Suddenly, a call crackled through the comms. "Bethel, this is Tabor! They're here! They've identified us as the flagship and are concentrating fire! We're taking heavy damage!" Captain Abijah's tone was strained, filled with the raw chaos of combat.

On the main viewscreen, a flash of brilliant white light bloomed. A direct hit. The Tabor's tractor beam, a solid line of blue energy, flickered and died. The Shiloh, a dead weight without its tether, began to drift helplessly toward the Adullam.

"Collision alert!" came a warning from the helm. Too late. The two ships, unable to maneuver in time, slammed into one another with a sickening crunch of tortured metal.

Barak, seeing the unfolding disaster, knew what had to be done. "Helm, get us between the Tabor and those fighters! We'll run interference!" She was a shield, a bulwark against the coming storm. "Launch operational fighters. Launch now!"

In the hangar, Bethel's remaining fighters launched, a small squadron of hornets. On the bridge, lasers and plasma bolts lit up the viewscreen, and the ship shuddered with each impact. Then, a direct hit to the bridge section. The world turned into a chaotic maelstrom of screaming alarms and sparking consoles.

When the chaos subsided, Joshua was on his feet again. The air smelled of burnt ozone and blood. A medic was tending to Adriel, who was slumped over his console, a deep cut on his forehead and his arm at a grotesque angle. He was alive, but barely. And Lieutenant Commander Barak lay motionless by the command chair, a piece of shrapnel embedded in her chest.

Josh's eyes darted to the main viewscreen. The Tabor, their last hope, had been overwhelmed by the pirate fleet. Her hull was pocked with explosions. A final barrage of fire tore through her bridge, and with a silent, agonizing gasp of exploding atmosphere, the flagship was no more. The Bethel and Adullam were alone, two wounded prey now the sole focus of the hunt.

And then, he saw it. The lead pirate vessel, a familiar, predatory silhouette against the fiery chaos of the binary stars. The Babylon. Cain's ship. The killer of his family, the man who had enslaved him and now injured his friend. A cold, bitter rage filled him, a familiar feeling from a long-lost past. For a moment, he saw nothing but red. He wanted to scream, to lash out, to charge headlong into the coming fight.

But he couldn't.

A chilling voice, a ghost of a memory, echoed in his mind. *"Your mind is a tool, Mr. Joshua."* It was a lesson from that same cruel mentor who was trying to kill him now.

Josh took a deep, shuddering breath, his hands clenched into fists. He had to keep his head. He had to use everything he knew. He was a navigator, and he needed to navigate. He began to work.

His fingers danced across the console, his mind a blur of calculations. He used the shifting gravitational fields of the two stars, the very thing Cain had used to hide, as a weapon. He plotted a course that skirted the edge of a solar flare, using its chaotic energy to mask his approach. He executed a full burn, knowing it would tax their already strained engines. He would fly them through a cloud of debris, the scattered remains of their own destroyed fleet, using the wreckage as a shield.

He was no longer a victim. He was a hunter.

"Helm! Full power to ventral thrusters! Plot a course for that debris field!" Josh barked, a cold, clear command. "And tell the gunnery crews to prepare to fire on my mark!"

He held the coffee cup, now cold and forgotten, and then

threw it aside. It clattered to the deck. His focus was absolute. He saw his opening, a single, fleeting chance to turn the tables. He waited, his eyes fixed on the display, and then he gave the command to fire.

A powerful salvo of plasma bolts shot from the Bethel, a desperate last stand. They didn't hit Babylon. They hit the smaller pirate ship next to her. The resulting blast, a brilliant white flash of pure energy, was more than enough to obliterate the ship, sending a wave of fiery shrapnel toward Babylon's side. The pirate flagship shuddered, its hull taking a direct hit. Cain, on his bridge, would feel the blow. He would know that someone had dared to defy him.

Josh watched the pirate fleet scatter, their formation broken. He had lost, but in his defeat, he had won a small victory. They were hurt, and they would remember the name of the ship that had done it. They would remember the Bethel.

Chapter 47

The diner, for all its chrome and plastic glory, was a warm and welcome sight. It was a greasy spoon in the truest sense, a neon beacon in the pre-dawn gray of the spaceport. Inside, the air was thick with the scent of fried bacon and eggs. Noah slid into a red vinyl booth, his gaze drifting across the menu. He was still half-asleep.

Eli sat across from him, already nursing a cup of coffee the color of crude oil. "Tis about time we had a proper breakfast," he grumbled, his Irish accent thick with satisfaction. He gestured to the waitress, a weary-looking woman with tired eyes. "Four of them 'all-day breakfasts' for the table, darlin'. And keep the coffee comin'."

Leah and Deborah joined them, sliding into the booth on the other side. "I'm certainly glad to have someone else cook for a change," Leah said, her bouffant red hair threatening to topple her huge glasses. "I've been going over our import permits, honey. Everything's in order."

"I'd rather have no surprises," Noah muttered, his eyes on the holoscreen above the counter. It was tuned to a local news station, currently running a report on the new agricultural contracts on the Outer Rim. The footage was grainy, but it showed a field of crops with a soft, green glow. It was a stark contrast to the dark, violent life that Noah now led. He was a cargo hauler by day, a vigilante by night, and the two lives felt so different that he sometimes forgot which was the real one.

Deborah's sharp voice cut through his thoughts. "The cargo's squared away, Captain. Jabez and I ran a final check on the manifests. Everything is secured." Her no-nonsense tone always brought a sense of order to the chaos of their lives.

Just then, the screen above the counter flickered. The cheerful music of the agricultural report was replaced by a shrill emergency alert tone. An anchor's face, grim and unsmiling, filled the screen.

"We interrupt this program with a breaking news update," the anchor began, his voice laced with an urgent gravity. "The Interstellar Patrol Corps has released a preliminary report on the deadly attack on Task Force Gideon. The IPC fleet, which survived an apparent minefield trap in the Dead Sea nebula, was subsequently ambushed by a pirate fleet while limping back to its home station. Initial reports are at least three vessels have been confirmed lost, with others in a state of critical damage."

A shiver of dread ran down Noah's spine. He and the crew had heard the news about the initial ambush before, but this was different. This was a follow-up attack. The news was raw, immediate, and grim.

The anchor continued, "Video footage recovered from a surviving IPC vessel shows the ferocity of the pirate assault. Casualties are believed to be high on both sides…"

The screen flashed to a chaotic montage of video clips. It was a shaky, low-resolution mess of starships and explosions.

One clip, perhaps only a second or two long, showed a damaged IPC cutter, its hull on fire. Another showed a massive vessel cloaked in shadows, its thrusters flaring with menace, a smear of crimson markings on its hull. The dread in Noah's stomach turned to ice. He knew that ship. He had seen it in his nightmares. It was the Babylon.

His hand, holding a coffee cup, shook violently. The hot coffee sloshed over the rim and spilled across the table, a dark stain spreading across the white plastic surface.

"Noah, what's wrong?" Leah asked, her tone filled with concern.

He pointed a trembling finger at the screen. "That ship," he choked out a strangled whisper. "I know that ship. It's... it's Cain."

Eli glanced at the screen, his face hardening as he took in the image of the pirate vessel. The grim reality of their war was now on a public news screen. He reached across the table and placed a hand over Noah's, his grip firm and steady. "Son, calm yourself," he said, his brogue quiet but authoritative. "We'll deal with this. But right now, we need to breathe."

Noah took a deep, shuddering breath. The air, thick with the smell of fried food, now felt heavy and suffocating. The news report was an ugly, inescapable truth. Their war was a real one, a war that killed people and destroyed lives. It was bloody and real, and Cain, the man who had taken everything from him, was a part of it. The storm was here.

Chapter 48

The air in Cain's office was heavy with the smell of sweat, and unbridled discontent. From his perch high in the central spire of the pirate haven, Gehinnom, he had a perfect view of the docks below. The sight was a sobering one: the familiar, crimson-streaked hull of the Babylon was scarred and pocked, its main thruster array a twisted wreck of metal and fused circuits. Beside it, the damage to the other pirate vessels was just as bad, if not worse. They were husks, stripped of their fighters, their gun emplacements silent.

A dozen pirate captains sat before him, slumped in chairs. Gone was the jovial camaraderie of the Dead Sea. This was a command meeting, and Cain was holding court. Their usual pints of ale were noticeably absent, replaced by somber mugs of black tea. The mood was a thunderhead of bitter complaints, with each captain recounting their grievances and the damage to their ships.

"We walked right into it, Cain," grumbled one captain. "All my fighters are gone. They took my best man, too."

"My ship is a sitting duck," another chimed in. "We lost our main cannons in the retreat. How are we supposed to make any money now?"

Captain Abimelech, a brute with a booming laugh, was

silent for once, his face a mask of grim frustration. Captain Samson, a quiet, one-eyed man, merely watched Cain, his one good eye narrowed, waiting.

Cain, ever the gentleman, sat calmly behind his large mahogany desk, sipping his green tea. He let the complaints wash over him like so many insignificant ripples. When the silence finally settled, he placed his cup on the desk with a soft click and leaned forward, his voice a low, soothing counterpoint to their anger.

"You're right," he began, his voice calm and reasonable. "We took a beating. Three of our best ships are now scrap. Most of your fighters are gone. We lost good people. But tell me something, my friends." He paused, his gaze sweeping across the faces of the captains. "When has a pirate fleet ever inflicted such a wound on the IPC? When have you ever seen a major IPC task force so thoroughly broken and mauled?"

He stood and walked to the window, gesturing to the crippled ships below. "Look at them. Six cutters, and only two made it back to port. And those two are damaged. Do you know what that means? It means they are crippled. Their patrol routes are now nearly empty. Their anti-piracy operations are at a standstill. Their remaining forces will be spread so thin they will not be able to challenge us any longer. We didn't just win a battle for a sector, my friends, we just bought ourselves the entire quadrant."

The mood in the room began to shift. The captains straightened in their chairs, a few of them exchanging glances. A flicker of hope and greed lit their eyes.

"This is not the time to lay low," Cain declared, his chest rising in confidence. "This is the time to seize the advantage! Our ships need repairs, yes, but more importantly, our pockets need to be filled. There's a fortune waiting for us out there, ripe for the taking. And if we happen to bring back more than we need… Well, that's what pirates do."

He walked back to his desk, pulling a datapad from a drawer. "I have a list here of the crews who weren't in port for the battle. Their ships are fully operational. They have already received their marching orders." He then scrolled down. "Repairs on Captain Ishmael's vessel are nearly complete. He'll be ready to launch in a day. The Nineveh and the Sodom can both be underway within a few days."

He looked up. "One last thing. Captain Adonijah of the Goliath was killed in the battle. A great loss." He paused for a moment before looking at Dathan, his first mate, who stood just to the side of Cain's desk. "But his ship and his crew live on. As of now, Dathan, you are Captain of the Goliath. Take what's left of her crew and make them your own."

Dathan's scarred face broke into a rare smile, and he nodded, a fierce loyalty in his eyes.

Cain then reached into a small safe behind his desk, pulling out two thick wads of credit chits. He tossed one to Captain Abimelech. "One million credits, as promised. For each of the IPC cutters you destroyed." He tossed the second wad to Captain Samson. "And for you, a thank you for your… quiet competence. You earned it, Captain."

Abimelech's booming laugh returned, and he and Samson began counting their earnings with wide smiles. The tension in the room had evaporated, replaced by the giddy buzz of money and a new sense of purpose.

"Now," Cain said, gesturing to the corner of the room. "Let's pour some proper drinks and toast to our victory, and to the future of our trade. To us, my friends!"

Pints of beer were passed around, and a chorus of toasts erupted in the room, their drunken cheers echoing off the walls. Cain simply watched them, a satisfied smirk on his face. The pirates thought they had a victory. What they didn't know was that they had just traded a few wrecked ships for a blank check to rebuild his power. He had lost a battle, but he had won the war.

Chapter 49

The conference room was a study in sterile efficiency. The air was cool and smelled faintly of wood polish and leather. At one end of a long, polished table sat the surviving officers of the Bethel and the Adullam, their faces etched with the strain of the battle. At the other end, a panel of senior officers, their expressions unreadable, sat in judgment. At the center of the table, a three-dimensional tactical projection pulsed with the grim data of the ambush.

Admiral Zephaniah, an imposing figure, cleanly shaven, salt and pepper hair and an air of quiet authority, presided over the panel. Flanking him were two unnamed ship captains, a master tactical officer with the rank of Commander, and an intelligence officer with the rank of Lieutenant Commander.

The tactical officer, a woman with a no-nonsense bun and a severe expression, gestured to the projection hovering above the table. Her cadence, though precise, carried a slight German accent. "At this point," she began, crisp and dispassionate, "the IPC fleet is in full retreat. The pirates have the advantage in numbers and maneuverability. Their flagship, the Babylon, is leading the pursuit. They are focused on taking down the Bethel and the Adullam."

She looked directly at Josh. "The initial hit on Bethel's

bridge was devastating, but Lieutenant Commander Barak was able to order a launch of the remaining fighters before she fell. The Tabor and Adullam followed suit, and the fighters were able to engage and eliminate all seven pirate fighters. The IPC fighters then focused their fire on one of the pirate vessels, destroying it, while the Tabor and Adullam destroyed another. It was then that the Tabor was overwhelmed. At this point, the Bethel sustained a second, direct hit, and Lieutenant Commander Barak was killed. As the only remaining officer on the bridge, Ensign Joshua found himself in command, again. Ensign Joshua, would you please brief the panel on what transpired next."

Joshua straightened in his chair, his posture a testament to his academy training, though his hands were clenched in his lap beneath the table. He took a deep breath, the memories of the chaotic maelstrom of screaming alarms and sparking consoles still fresh in his mind. He recalled the silent, agonizing gasp of the disabled vessels' destruction, the sight of the Babylon, and the familiar silhouette of the ship that killed his family.

He spoke with confidence, clear and steady. "The Tabor was destroyed, leaving Bethel and the Adullam as the sole targets. The Babylon was in a position of overwhelming advantage. I realized that a conventional defense would be futile. I needed to do something… unconventional."

His mind went back to that moment on the bridge, the cold, bitter rage that had threatened to consume him, and the ghost of Cain's voice echoing in his head: *Your mind is a tool, Mr. Joshua.*

He continued, his gaze fixed on the tactical display. "I used the gravitational fields of the binary stars to gain an advantage. I plotted a course that skirted the edge of a solar flare to mask our approach, then ordered a full burn to take us through the debris field of our destroyed fleet. We used the wreckage as a shield."

He paused, a flicker of that desperate focus from the battle returning to his eyes. "I saw my opportunity, a single, fleeting chance. We fired a full salvo of plasma bolts, not at the Babylon, but at the smaller pirate vessel next to it. The resulting blast was enough to obliterate the ship, sending a wave of shrapnel into Babylon's flank. It crippled their momentum and caused significant damage."

The tactical officer nodded slowly, her expression now one of grudging respect.

"The pirates were momentarily scattered," Josh concluded. "They broke formation and retreated. We were able to make a series of evasive maneuvers to lose them. We then located the survivors of the disabled vessels and transferred them to the Adullam." He paused, a weight of grief settling on his shoulders. "We were able to recover all the IPC fighter pilots, as well as the skeleton crew from the Shiloh, but the Bethel and the Adullam were too damaged to tow her remains. We left her adrift."

The silence that followed his statement was heavy with unspoken questions. The panel looked at him, their expressions still unreadable. Admiral Zephaniah finally broke the silence, his voice low and thoughtful.

"Your tactical decisions, while unorthodox, saved two-thirds of your crew, Ensign. They also inflicted a significant blow to the pirate flagship."

The debriefing concluded with a quiet efficiency that belied the chaos of the battle. When the final officer had given their testimony, Admiral Zephaniah stood. His gaze, calm and measured, settled on Joshua.

"Ensign," he said, his tone carrying the authority of his rank. "Report to my office at 1500 hours."

Josh's heart pounded. He saluted, a crisp and precise motion he had practiced countless times, and exited the conference room, leaving the others to their murmured postmortems. He found the door he was looking for at the end of the long corridor. A polished brass plate on the door read "Director, Fleet Operations." He straightened his uniform and knocked once.

Inside, a secretary sat behind a large, neat desk, her back ramrod straight. She looked up. "Ensign Joshua?" she asked, her tone flat. "The Admiral is expecting you. You can go right in."

Josh moved past her, his boots making no sound on the plush carpeting. The Admiral's office was a spartan space, but the large window behind his desk offered a sweeping view of the dry docks below. He could see the skeletal forms of ships in various states of disrepair, the damaged hulls of the Bethel and the Adullam visible among them.

"Ensign Joshua reporting as ordered, sir," he said, snapping to attention and delivering a sharp salute.

Admiral Zephaniah, seated at his desk, gestured to a chair. "At ease, Ensign. Please, have a seat."

Josh sat, his back straight, his eyes scanning the office. He noticed a nameplate on the desk that read "Big Z," a small detail that felt oddly out of place in the formal space. The Admiral's gaze was direct, unwavering.

"Ensign," the Admiral began, "we've taken a serious blow.

The pirates know this. They're emboldened. This is a time for extraordinary measures, not desperate ones." He paused, his expression serious. "We've lost several good captains and a number of ships are out of action. The patrol routes are thin. We need to fill the gaps, and we need to do it now."

He then slid a small, black box across the desk. It was simple and unmarked. Josh's eyes fell to the box, and he slowly reached out and opened it. Inside, resting on a bed of black velvet, was a set of silver double-bars—the rank insignia of a Lieutenant.

"Congratulations, Lieutenant," the Admiral said with a note of pride.

Joshua stared at the insignia, his mind racing. He looked up, his confusion plain on his face, but his voice was tight with the weight of his thoughts. "Sir, I… I don't understand. I'm too young. I'm not ready for this. And… I shouldn't be promoted. This mission… it was my fault. My intelligence. My eagerness to find Cain. I should have known about the traps in the Dead Sea. I should have known he'd follow up with an ambush. I know him, sir. I should have anticipated it all. I failed. And on the Bethel… I was in command… too many lives were lost under my watch." The words tumbled out, a confession heavy with self-reproach.

The Admiral leaned forward, his elbows on the desk, his expression softening slightly. "Your actions tell a different story, Lieutenant. And your guilt, while understandable, is misplaced." He held up a hand. "First, let's be clear: you did not make the decision to raid the Dead Sea, Lieutenant. I did. That burden is mine, and mine alone. Furthermore, you escaped Cain's clutches on the Babylon long before it ever reached the Dead Sea. How could you possibly be expected to know what awaited us there? Speculation is one thing; actionable intelligence is another. You gave us the best data you had at the time."

He continued, his voice firm but reassuring. "As for the ambush, you were not alone on that bridge, Josh. The Bethel was not the only ship in the fleet. There were many other higher-ranking and more experienced officers on all those bridges—officers who knew the risks, who were making decisions alongside you. To shoulder all that blame, to claim sole responsibility for such a complex disaster, is simply inaccurate. There is nothing for you to feel guilty about, son. You performed admirably in impossible circumstances."

"Your mother taught you skills most officers don't learn until they're in the academy," the Admiral continued, returning to his initial point. "And while a captive on the Babylon, you honed your combat and tactical skills. Your experience as a captive gives you unique intelligence into pirate operations and into the mind of Cain himself. Your actions in the Dead Sea nebula demonstrate a level of skill and leadership that is, frankly, astounding for an officer of your rank. We don't have time for a formal promotion ceremony, Lieutenant. We're in a war. And you just proved to us that you're one of our best weapons."

The admiral's words had barely sunk in when he delivered another shock. "The Bethel will be out of dry dock in a week. When she is, you will be her acting captain."

Josh shot to his feet, protesting. "Sir, I can't. I've only just graduated from the academy. I don't know how to manage a ship or a crew."

"You already have," the admiral said, cutting him off with a firm hand gesture. "Twice now. Under the most challenging of circumstances. We need ships on the patrol routes, Lieutenant. We need them now."

He saw the fear in Josh's eyes and softened his tone. "You won't be alone. I'll assign you to a sector adjacent to more experienced captains. If you need to engage, advice and support are nearby. And I'll be assigning you a civilian administrative assistant to handle the paperwork and logistics you haven't been trained for. You will not have to worry about administrivia. And if need be, you will have a direct line to me." He tapped his nameplate with a finger. "To Big Z."

The Admiral's final words were not a request but a command, and Josh knew there was no room for debate. He had a new rank and a new, daunting responsibility.

Chapter 50

The Galilee cut through the void on a route with high-risk and a long, bloody history. The pay was excellent, but Noah and his crew were no longer motivated by credits. For them, every high-risk run was a silent vow to protect the defenseless. They took these jobs to leave the safer routes to the defenseless freighters who had no means to fight back.

Noah sat in the command chair, the quiet confidence of a battle-tested captain settling over him. He wasn't the boy who had salvaged his ship from scrap; he was a leader reforged in fire. Eli sat nearby, monitoring the engine systems, a grumpy but endearing presence that grounded them all.

"Well, now, honey," Leah drawled from the navigation station, her glasses perched on her nose. "My passive scan is pickin' up somethin' mighty odd." She looked over at him with a frown. "A mining station in orbit around a large asteroid. Its transponder's bein' mighty rude, dropin' offline and then comin' back, and I'm hearin' what sounds like some awfully distorted distress calls."

Noah's jaw tightened. "Deborah, run a full scan. What's the station's designation?"

"Designation's Gilboa, Captain," Deborah's crisp Australian accent replied. "Mineral processing facility. Seems to be a major source of rare earths in this sector. Looks like the blokes are in a bit of trouble."

Noah was already leaning forward, his gaze fixed on the screen. Rare Earth minerals would be a lucrative score. The pirate raid was unmistakable. The small station's automated defense systems were offline, and several small ships were latched onto its hull.

Noah, became cold and resolute, "There are people down there. We're goin' in."

He took a deep breath, slipping into the alias that felt more real to him with every battle. "Deactivate the transponder. Bring the plasma cannons to full power. Open hailing channel."

Deborah acknowledged. "Transponder off. Weapons online. Channel open."

"Attention all vessels," Noah's announcement boomed over the open channel, his words crisp and clear. "This is Captain Gabriel of the Archangel. To the pirate vessel currently engaging Gilboa station, this is your only warning: disengage and withdraw immediately."

The pirate ship, a sleek, black vessel, was an unfamiliar model. A jagged, blood-red mark was painted on its hull, a grotesque reminder of Cain's brutal empire. Noah knew he had to act fast. They had learned the hard way the Galilee wasn't good in a maneuvering fight. He had to exploit the element of surprise and seize the initiative immediately. If they could score a decisive hit the fight would be over before it began, but if not a pitched battle would be a close run thing. He brought the Galilee around, positioning her to get a clean shot without hitting the station. The ship groaned in protest as he pushed her harder than ever before, the sound a low, desperate whine.

"I've got a target lock! Bring our sweet Gally a little more to port Noah and we'll have 'em right where we want 'em!" Leah declared

"Hold on, everyone!" Noah yelled as he initiated a tight turn. "We've got one shot!"

He fired a single plasma bolt, a lance of white-hot energy that tore across the black. The low-power hit struck the pirate vessel's main weapons array with a flash of light. The pirate ship, the Aram, reeled from the impact. A moment later, their main cannons fired in a desperate reply. Noah, already committed to his evasive maneuver, watched as the shot streaked past the Galilee's stern, missing by a matter of meters.

On the pirate bridge, the attack was a complete surprise. Captain Samson, an imposing figure with a single, dark eye, stared at the damage report on his tactical display. The hit had overloaded his weapon systems, and now his ship was a sitting duck. He needed to get out of the fight and make repairs.

"All hands, sever all tethers!" Samson roared. "Break contact with the station! Get us out of here!"

He abandoned several of his crew to their fate on the station, as his ship turned and fled.

Noah watched the pirate vessel accelerate away, its thrusters flaring with menace. His hand clenched on the control stick, a part of him aching to give chase, to hunt the ship down and tear into it. He knew it was one of Cain's, a piece of the puzzle, and a direct line to his vengeance. But as his eyes flicked to the station's flickering lights, a different impulse took hold—the needs of the inhabitants were more immediate, more real than his long-held thirst for revenge. For a fleeting, agonizing moment, the two competing instincts battled in his gut.

A few minutes later, the Galilee was docked with the station, her docking clamps thrumming. The station was a ghost town, its halls silent save for the hiss of environmental systems and the rhythmic stomp of boots. Noah, Deborah, and Jabez had suited up and entered the station, leaving Eli and Leah to monitor the ship.

Their intelligence was sound. Sensor readings and comms traffic confirmed the station's small crew had barricaded themselves in the central control room. Their pursuers—three pirates—were a few corridors away, attempting to breach the fortified door.

The massive orange chassis of Jabez, his treads moving nearly silently on the polished floor, took point. His two forward sensors whirred, and the graffiti smile painted on his head seemed to grin with anticipation. Deborah and Noah followed, their weapons ready.

They rounded a corner and came upon the pirates. They were fully engaged with the locked-down door, their backs to the approaching team. They never saw it coming.

Jabez was a blur of motion. His movements were fluid and precise. A retractable arm shot out, a pulse of energy lancing out and hitting one pirate's helmet, causing his lights to flicker and his body to go limp. A second pirate felt a high-frequency sonic burst incapacitate his suit's motion controls, sending him sprawling to the ground. The third pirate's weapon was instantly disabled by a targeted magnetic pulse from Jabez's other arm. All three fell, their bodies twitching for a moment before they went still.

Jabez turned to his captain, a faint, red glow coming from his optical sensor. "Threat neutralized. 1.4 seconds. Optimal."

Noah and Deborah simply stared, dumbfounded. Noah's jaw was agape, his words catching in his throat. "Wow," was all he could manage. He knew Jabez was capable, but he had never seen the full extent of the robot's capabilities in person.

Deborah lowered her rifle, a hint of disappointment in her voice. "That's it? I was looking forward to handing out some beat-downs."

Calming his nerves, Noah privately shared Deb's sentiments. He would have gotten a perverse pleasure doing violence upon these lowlifes. Yet, he was relieved. If he'd had to engage the pirates, it would have been all to easy to keep pulling the trigger. Jabez may have saved him from doing something regrettable, or saved him from getting killed. Either way, this was a better outcome.

Just then, the heavy, armored door to the control center hissed and slid open. A crew of five stood in the doorway, three of them armed, their guns raised. On the floor behind them, two pirates lay unconscious and tied up.

Stunned silence fell over the corridor, broken only by the hiss of the station's air handlers. Noah slowly raised his hands in a gesture of peace, a nervous laugh escaping his lips. "Uh, hi," he said. "I'm Captain Gabriel. Do you have any coffee?"

A few minutes later, Noah sat in the control center, a cup of bitter, but welcome, station-brewed coffee in his hand. He was making small talk with a couple of the station's crew while Deborah, in full medic mode, was expertly bandaging some minor cuts and scrapes. The mood was a mix of exhausted relief and cautious curiosity.

Suddenly, a crackle came over their comms. It was Leah. "We have another ship approaching, honey! High speed! Energy signature is huge, like she's powered up for a real fight!"

Noah's head snapped up. He, Deborah, and Jabez took off at a dead run, their footsteps echoing down the corridor. As they raced toward the docking bay, Noah gave the order. "Eli, power up the guns! Get ready!"

On the bridge of the Goliath, Dathan felt the familiar thrum of the ship's massive engines. The report from Samson had been a bitter pill—a full-scale assault thwarted by a single freighter. The shame of it was an acid burn in his gut. But beneath the humiliation, a raw, burning ambition took hold. This "Captain Gabriel" had made a fool of one of Cain's men. Now was Dathan's chance to show his master that he was worthy of command, to earn the respect Cain had withheld. He would not just defeat this interloper; he would humiliate him.

Aboard the Galilee, Eli grimaced at his console. "The big fella's still too far out, lad. But I can buy us some time, so I can." He aimed a low-power shot directly at the inbound vessel, the blast a mere flash of light in the vast distance. The shot was never meant to hit, but it forced the Goliath to take a series of evasive maneuvers, slowing her approach.

Noah, Deborah, and Jabez burst onto the bridge, still in their bulky space suits. Noah pulled his helmet off, shaking his head. "Aunt Leah, give me the rundown," he said, taking his command chair.

"She's a big brute, Captain, bearing 120 point 035, closing on our position at 100K" Leah, her voice tight with concern. "Massive energy signature, huge power plant. My readings say we're not a match for her, not by a long shot."

A green light flashed on Eli's console as he fired again. The Goliath was forced to swerve. "Heat sinks are workin', gun temps are nominal, power's stable," Eli reported, a hint of pride in his Irish accent. "We haven't used full power yet, no, but we're gettin' there."

Noah's gaze was fixed on the tactical display. The Goliath was turning, her guns beginning to point inward toward them. He took a deep breath, his mind running through the grim options. There was no escape. They couldn't outrun a ship built for a fight. There was only one option.

"Aunt Leah," Noah said, his tone dropping to an icy calm. "Set a course straight at her. Engines to 75%."

From the Goliath, a hail filled with taunts and threats filled the bridge. "You're a brave fool, Captain Gabriel! But you're no match for the Goliath! Surrender now, and I'll spare your lives!"

Deborah shot a worried glance at Noah. "Captain, we're heading directly at them! They'll tear us to shreds!"

"That's the plan," Noah replied. "We can't outrun them, and we can't hide. By heading straight at them, we present the smallest target silhouette, and our superstructure protects the most vital areas—the powerplant and the main drive."

On the Goliath's bridge, a crewman pointed at the tactical display. "Sir, they're engaging! They're on a direct intercept course!"

"Good," Dathan said, a grim smile on his face. "Maintain course, and accelerate. Fire at will!"

On the Galilee's bridge, the ship shook as the Goliath's first shots streaked past them. "They're firing!" Deborah reported, her eyes glued to her console. "Shots are going wide, but they're bracketing us! They'll get a hit soon!"

Noah was a pillar of calm. "Eli, increase power and rate of fire. Get 'em if you can." He turned to Leah. "Aunt Leah, set collision course, maximum acceleration now. Let's put those engine upgrades to the test!" He then looked to Deborah. "Deb, you and Jabez get ready for damage control. We may take some hits or overload some power circuits."

The crew, knowing full well that their captain was playing a mad game of chicken, went about their duties with cold grit and determination.

"Sir, they're accelerating! I believe they mean to ram us!" a crewman from the Goliath's bridge shouted.

"Continue and keep firing!" Dathan roared, his fists clenched. "Hit! That! ship!"

"Sir, she's not presenting a big enough target! She's accelerating too quickly!"

Just then, one of Eli's shots, now at full power, streaked by the Goliath's bridge, a brilliant flash of plasma that shocked the crew.

Leah's fingers flew across her controls. "Impact in sixty seconds, Noah!!"

The Goliath's return fire began to hit its mark. Plasma

blasts grazed the sides of the Galilee, and several cargo containers were vaporized off their trusses.

"Fifty seconds!" Leah called out.

The Goliath's navigator was sweating, his eyes wide as the Galilee grew larger and larger on his screen. "Twenty seconds, Captain! Collision imminent!"

Dathan's face was a mask of rage and disbelief. He had never imagined a ship would be so bold. "Hard to port!" he roared in a mix of fury and fear. "Hard to port!"

The massive Goliath shuddered, her broadside turning toward the Galilee. It was the perfect moment. "Fire now Eli!" Noah yelled.

Eli unleashed a full-power volley from both cannons. The blast hit the Goliath's exposed side, a blinding flash of plasma that tore the ship in half. The main drive, still at full power, went spinning off into the void, a small sun of roaring engines, while the forward section drifted, dark and silent except for the occasional electrical discharge.

Leah let out a shuddering breath. "We did it!" she said. Just as she was about to cheer, a new contact blipped on her console. "Uh oh, new contact. IPCS Cutter."

A broadcast crackled over the open channel. "Unidentified Vessel, this is the IPCS Cutter Sheba. You are engaged in illegal activities. Power down, heave to, and prepare to be boarded."

Noah checked his console. Leah had already programmed an escape route. The Galilee was at max power and still accelerating fast. The Cutter couldn't possibly catch them now.

"Aunt Leah," Noah said, a grin on his face. "Let's get out of here."

Aboard the wreckage of the Goliath, Dathan had survived the blast, his emergency evac suit's integrity holding against the vacuum. He had made his way to a shuttle bay. Another pirate was already in the cockpit of a small escape shuttle, his eyes wide with fear. Dathan pulled his sidearm, shot him once in the head, and pulled his limp body from the seat. He took the controls, launched into the void, and set a new, vengeful course.

Chapter 51

The bridge of the IPCS Bethel was a place of quiet, rhythmic efficiency. The soft vibration of the engines, the glow of consoles, and the easy banter of the crew created a professional calm that belied the recent, brutal events. Acting Captain Joshua, a steaming mug of coffee warm in his hands, felt a moment of peace. He'd barely slept since his promotion, the weight of command settling into his bones. His new administrative assistant, a woman named Tamar, was a starkly professional presence at his side. She was a no-nonsense, retired IPC veteran, a Black woman with a Canadian accent and an air of unflappable competence.

Tamar slid a datapad across his console. "The performance reviews for the senior enlisted are ready for your signature, Captain," she said. Her tone precise, "I've highlighted the key points for your review, eh? All you need to do is verify and sign, Sir."

Josh glanced at the pad. The reports were impeccably organized, with neat summaries and spaces for his signature. It was an overwhelming task he hadn't even had time to consider, and she had already handled it. He felt a wave of gratitude. "Tamar, thank you. You have no idea how much this helps."

She gave a small, professional nod, her gaze fixed on the main viewscreen as if anticipating his next command.

Just then, the Chief Petty Officer at the communications station spoke up. "Captain, incoming encrypted message from Fleet. Priority One."

Josh's posture immediately shifted from relaxed to alert. The quiet on the bridge deepened as all eyes turned to him.

Tamar, with an almost imperceptible nod to the CPO, moved toward the bridge's tactical station, leaving him to address the message privately. She had a sixth sense for when to step back, a quiet guardian of the captain's attention.

"Put it on the secure channel," Josh ordered.

A new transmission blinked onto the main viewscreen. The IPC Fleet symbol was replaced by a tactical animation of a recent skirmish. The scene unfolded with the brutal, dispassionate logic of a computer simulation. A pirate ship, the Aram, was shown attacking a mining station. Then, a new contact appeared on the screen, a lone trusswork freighter with a familiar, lattice-like fuselage but also two cannons that blazed with lethal precision. The animation showed the freighter engaging the Aram, which promptly retreated. Just as the freighter's crew began to assist the station's survivors, a second, larger pirate ship, the Goliath, arrived. A tense standoff ensued, followed by the freighter destroying the Goliath in a single, audacious shot.

The accompanying text message scrolled beneath the animation. It was a formal after-action report from the IPC cutter Sheba, which had arrived on the scene just as the battle ended. The report noted the mysterious vessel was named Archangel by its captain, Gabriel. The intelligence analysis was starkly uncertain about its motives, classifying the ship as either a new, dangerously effective pirate vessel or a vigilante operation. The orders were clear and unyielding: the Archangel was to be considered a threat. If encountered, it was to be either captured or destroyed.

Josh felt a cold knot form in his stomach. The animation of the trusswork freighter was a punch to the gut. The familiar grid of the hull, the forward command pod with its two "eyes"—it was a ghost from his past, a stark reminder of his family's ship and the violence that had ended their lives. The sight filled him with a painful mixture of nostalgia for the home he had lost and the chilling memory of the day it was destroyed.

The communications officer piped up again. "Captain, Fleet intel included the Archangel's last known trajectory, logged just after the engagement with the Goliath. Analyzing the vector, sir, it appears to be heading directly into our sector."

The confirmation snapped Josh into action. He strode to the tactical console, pulling up the deep-space charts and projecting the Archangel's vector against the known gravity wells and patrol lanes. "If they're trying to resupply or lay low, they'd be heading for the old Caesarea asteroid belt's shadow," Josh murmured, tracing a path with his finger. "It offers the best cover and the clearest route to jump-point access outside our main patrols." He had a new target and a specific plan.

"Open a secure channel to Captain Jethro of the Zion," Josh ordered, recalling the Admiral's instruction to consult with the senior captain in the adjacent sector.

When Jethro's face appeared on a tactical monitor, Josh was direct. "Captain, we have a firm trajectory for the Archangel leading into my sector. I've charted an intercept course at the Caesarea belt shadow. It's the most logical point for them to hide or jump. I'm requesting you rendezvous with the Bethel at those coordinates for a joint operation."

Jethro, a veteran with a thick, gray beard, nodded after studying the data Josh sent. "Understood, Lieutenant. Your analysis is sound. I concur with the rendezvous point. We'll meet you there. If you spot the Archangel on your way, you may pursue and track, but you are not to engage until the Zion arrives. Is that clear, Captain?"

Josh stood a little taller, a blend of trepidation and resolve in his eyes. "Perfectly clear, sir. Bethel out." He turned to his helmsman. "Set a course for the Caesarea belt shadow. Maximum velocity. We're going to intercept."

A voice cut through his thoughts, bringing him back to the present. "Well, isn't this going to be fun?"

Ensign Adriel, Josh's friend and the Bethel's cheerful engineer, stood beside him, his arm still in a sling from the ambush. His typically happy-go-lucky demeanor was still there, but a touch of seriousness lingered in his eyes.

"We just finished a war with pirates," Adriel continued, his Kenyan accent thick. "Now we get to start a new one with a guy who destroys them for us. It seems like a strange way to fight a war. And a trusswork freighter? That's an odd choice for a pirate ship. They're usually big and slow, and pretty much unarmed."

Chapter 52

The air in the Gehinnom's central spire was stale and cold. For Dathan, it was the chill of a tomb. He stood before Cain's large mahogany desk, his neatly tied ponytail askew, his scarred face a mask of nervous terror. The scent of green tea filled the room, but Cain wasn't sipping it. He wasn't doing anything. He was just watching, a silent, unnerving presence.

Dathan had survived the destruction of the Goliath, but he was certain he would not survive this meeting. He had been on the bridge of the Babylon when Delilah, the tactical officer, reported Joshua's escape. Cain had executed her with the effortless finality of swatting a fly. Dathan had just lost an entire warship. He felt a tremor in his knees and began to speak, his tale a frantic spill of half-truths and grand exaggerations.

"It was a trap, Captain," Dathan stammered, his professionalism evaporated by terror. "The freighter—the Archangel— it was like nothing I've ever seen. Fast, sir. Faster than any freighter has a right to be. And the weapons… they were enormous. Military-grade plasma cannons. We barely got a shot off before she was on us. It was a tactical retreat, Captain, I swear it."

He continued to embellish, painting a picture of a ferocious, heavily-armed dreadnought and a crew of hardened veterans. He described the captain, "Gabriel," as a legend in the making, a ghost of a man who moved with impossible skill. Anything to make the defeat seem less like a personal failure and more like an unavoidable disaster.

Cain remained perfectly still, his dark eyes unblinking, his face a neutral mask that gave Dathan no clue as to his thoughts. The silence stretched on for what felt like an eternity after Dathan finished. He was certain this was it. He would be lucky if Cain simply shot him.

But Cain wasn't angry. A cold curiosity had pushed the anger aside. The details of the battle—the trusswork freighter, the audacious gamble, the name "Archangel"—they all pointed to an unusual opponent. An opponent who could take a ship that was nothing more than a giant storage rack and turn it into a predator. Cain felt a jolt of exhilaration. Just as he had neutralized the IPC, a new adversary had emerged. He had hoped for time to luxuriate in his success, but he loved a new challenge even more.

His mind reeled, sifting through possibilities. Who was this "Gabriel"? And why was a trusswork freighter his ship of choice? Cain had a memory of a family freighter, the Galilee, a ship that resembled the description. The family that had owned it was long dead. Or were they?

He looked up, a hint of a smirk on his face as he realized Dathan was still standing there, quivering. Cain waved a dismissive hand. "Go. Take command of the Moab. She's small, but she needs a captain."

Dathan's shoulders slumped in relief. He was alive. He was a captain. "Yes, sir!" he said, his face thick with gratitude.

He spun on his heels and left quickly, unable to believe his luck. The Moab was a battered vessel, but it was better than a grave. What Dathan didn't know was that a death sentence could come in many forms. The Moab was slow and poorly armed, a tempting target for a vigilante with an ax to grind.

As the door closed, Cain's smirk faded. He opened a private comm channel on his desk. "Mr. Ithamar," he said, his voice low and serious. "I need you to scour every transmission, every port log, every scrap of data. I want to know everything about a vessel named the Archangel and its captain, Gabriel. Leave no stone unturned." He paused, his eyes fixed on the empty space where Dathan had just stood. "It seems we have a new game to play."

Chapter 53

The bridge of the Bethel was a study in focused silence, the only sound the low hum of the active sensor array. They had arrived at the Caesarea asteroid field, a graveyard of ice and rock, and were now patrolling the most probable exit points.

"Helm, maintain current speed and course," Joshua ordered, his voice low and tight. "Sensors, increase active sweep energy by twenty percent. I want every shadow in this cluster lit up."

"Captain," the sensor officer reported, his voice cutting through the quiet. "Contact. Bearing zero-one-eight, mark seven. Faint, but definitely a vessel. Matching the profile of the target freighter. Trusswork hull, lattice construction. The contact is running silent, hugging the shadow of a Class-Gamma asteroid."

Josh's pulse spiked. The Archangel. "Confirmed target acquisition. Helmsman, set an intercept course. Tactical, lets get Ms. Beth ready to fight. Warm the railguns. Not a shot fired until the Zion is here, but be ready."

The Bethel angled into the asteroid field, her superior engine power allowing for rapid, precise maneuvers. Josh leaned over the tactical display, his focus absolute. The guilt he carried now manifested as a burning need for control, for perfect execution. *I will not be careless again.*

Aboard the bridge of the Galilee the atmosphere was thick with anxiety. The recent destruction of the Goliath meant they were now the most wanted vessel in the sector. The escape route Leah programmed when they ran from the Sheba had brought them here to the Caesarea asteroid field. It seemed like an excellent place to lay low for a while, but maybe not.

"Dear me, an IPC cutter, highly advanced sensor array," called Leah from the helm, her voice strained. "They're pinging the whole sector like church bells falling down stairs. They've detected us, sweetie. They're closing fast, real fast!"

Noah gripped the arms of his chair, the familiar controls of the ship a lifeline in the chaos. "A cutter, that fast? They're hunting us. Status report, Deb."

Deborah focused at her console. "Her transponder IDs her as IPC Cutter Bethel. She is currently plotting a maneuver to flank our position. It appears their intent is to force us out of cover." Her voice was calm and deliberate as ever.

"They think they know which rock we're hiding behind," Noah muttered, wiping sweat from his brow. He pointed at the tactical display. "Leah, put us on a micro-burn toward that asteroid. Keep us tight in the shadow. We're running silent and deep. The cargo containers should help mask our heat signature too. We want them to commit to their trap."

The Archangel lumbered slowly into a new position.

Josh stared at the flickering sensor shadow on his display. It had to be the largest asteroid in the cluster. The freighter would be using its mass as a shield.

"They're trying to draw us in, Captain," the sensor officer cautioned.

"They're trying to disappear," Josh corrected, already plotting the move. "Helmsman, adjust course to circle that asteroid wide. Weapons, prepare to fire two low-yield sensor decoys on the port-side trajectory. Give them a wide berth— we're not going to chase. We're going to trap them."

Josh's plan was aggressive: he would use the Bethel's superior speed to perform a wide circle around the asteroid. The decoys would simulate the Bethel's initial trajectory, forcing the Archangel to believe its escape route was blocked. As the Archangel tried to break cover on the opposite side, the Bethel would be waiting, guns hot, with the entire escape path cordoned off.

"Executing flanking maneuver now, Captain," the helmsman confirmed.

The Bethel executed the fast, wide maneuver perfectly, sweeping around the massive asteroid. Josh's hands were braced on the console, his heart hammering in his chest.

"Tactical!" he snapped. "Where are they?"

The sensor officer's voice cracked with surprise. "Negative contact, Captain. The shadow is empty. They're not there!"

Josh felt a sickening lurch in his stomach. He'd guessed wrong. The shadow was empty, and now the Bethel was fully exposed on the opposite side of the asteroid, facing open space. He had not only failed to spring the trap, but he had given away his position and sacrificed his tactical advantage.

The Galilee sat in the shadow of a much smaller asteroid, exactly where Josh had assumed no large ship would hide. The ship was silent, the crew holding their breath.

"The cutter is executing a wide flanking maneuver," Leah whispered. "They missed us."

Noah let out a slow, careful breath. "Now we wait. They have to slow down to search the cluster they just cleared."

Suddenly, Jabez's chipper voice broke the silence, his eyes sensors fixed on the retreating Bethel on the tactical display. "Captain, opportunity. Their flanking maneuver has taken Bethel out of a viable pursuit curve. Recommend: maximum acceleration in T-minus three-point-five seconds, heading one seven five. IPC Bethel will be unable to come about and match our escape vector in adequate time to continue pursuit."

Noah stared at the display. It was a bold, terrifying dash across open space, but Jabez's geometry was impeccable. The Bethel was committed to the wrong maneuver, and the error was a game changer.

"Leah, you heard the 'bot. Give me one-seven-five. All ahead full, now!" Noah commanded. "Eli, we need everything Gally can give us!"

"Aye lad, I'm overriding the safeties now! The mods we made can take 'er. Just not fer too long." Eli replied, his voice tense as his fingers manipulated the engineer's console

The main engines fired at max power, shaking the entire ship as the massive freighter began its urgent, desperate dash.

"Sir, they've broken cover! Bearing one-seven-five! They're at full acceleration!" the sensor officer announced.

Josh slammed his fist on the console. "Turn us around! Full power to thrusters! Get us on that vector!"

The Bethel began to turn, but the inertia of the failed flanking maneuver was a dead weight. Every second the cutter spent correcting its mistake was a hundred kilometers the Archangel gained. Josh watched the distance between them expand, his heart sinking. He was too slow. He had failed.

Just as the Archangel was a speck on the viewscreen, a new, massive jump-signature bloomed on the tactical display.

"Captain, IPCS Zion has just arrived!"

The Zion was perfectly positioned to block the escape route—a minute too late. Captain Jethro's angry voice blared over the comms. "Bethel! What in the blazes was that? You let him slip right past me!"

Josh could only watch the Archangel disappear into the darkness. The wave of frustration and self-loathing hit him like a physical blow.

Aboard the Galilee, the roar of the engines was the sound of salvation. The second IPC cutter, the Zion, was visible behind them, but the gap was now insurmountable.

Noah and Leah sagged in their seats, their faces shining with sweat and relief.

"We… we made it," Noah breathed.

"Crikey Jabez!" I never knew you had tactical programming too." Exclaimed Deborah. "That was brilliant!"

Jabez in his typical chipper robotic tones, "Observation; simple geometry problems are well within my capability to calculate."

"The Bethel's tactical error was critical. They can't chase us down now." Noah acknowledged as his shoulders slumped in relief. "Aunt Leah, reset course to our destination, we still have a shipment to deliver."

"I'm on it, honey. I tell you that was closer than two rabbits in thimble!" the relief evident in Leah"s drawl.

"I've restored all safeties and systems to normal, Cap'n. No harm done." Came Eli's input. "Now if ya don't mind, I think this ol man needs a wee respite from all the shenanigans. I'll be in the mess if I be needed."

They shared an exhausted, collective sigh of relief. The danger was gone, for now, thanks to the quick thinking and a tiny mistake of a green IPC captain.

Chapter 54

The air in Cain's command center was thick with the scent of green tea and the drone of consoles. Cain stood before a holotable displaying a star chart, his senior officers gathered around him like vultures awaiting a kill. His first mate, Malkiel, hovered over his shoulder, while Captain Abimelech, the scarred brute with a booming laugh, rubbed his hands together in anticipation. The pirate fleet was back to its fighting weight, their ships repaired, their crews eager for plunder.

"Gentlemen," Cain began, his intonation commanding absolute attention. "Our latest efforts have left the IPC crippled and the sector open. But a new pest has emerged." He gestured to a small, isolated point on the star chart. "The Shechem, a medical frigate. It is unarmed, carries no cargo, and is crewed by doctors and nurses. It will be traveling through a nearby system in two cycles."

Malkiel tilted his head. "Sir, why a medical frigate? There's no profit in it."

Cain's lips curled into a thin smile. "Exactly. This is not about profit. This is about a test. Our intelligence suggests a vigilante has been operating in this area, preying on our vessels. He calls himself 'Gabriel of the Archangel.' It was he who destroyed the Goliath, and a foolish rumor has it that he is a man of conscience."

He leaned in closer to the holotable. "He won't respond to a direct challenge, not with the IPC and every bounty hunter in the sector looking for him. So we will give him a different kind of challenge. We will go after something so innocent, so defenseless, that it will be an affront to his sensibilities. He'll have to show himself."

Cain then turned to his navigation officer, Mr. Ithamar. "Mr. Ithamar, your research has been invaluable. You believe the Archangel is one and the same as the Galilee, do you not?"

Ithamar, a small, nervous man, fidgeted with his spectacles. "The probability is high, sir. Both vessels are trusswork freighters and frequent the same high-risk routes. It is an unusual coincidence."

"A coincidence I mean to end," Cain said, his gaze returning to the star chart. "So here is the plan."

He laid out his strategy. His flagship, the Babylon, would lead a small, effective force to ambush the Shechem. The ambush would be brutal and swift. They wouldn't just take the ship; they would make it a public display of power.

"While we are doing that," Cain continued, "we will have our operatives at every major port and station that are Archangel's most likely ports of call. They will be tasked with spreading a little rumor—just a whisper. A rumor about a planned capture of the medical frigate Shechem. We will let the 'rumor mill' do the work for us."

He looked at his captains, his eyes glinting with a cunning fire. This was more than a simple raid. This was a psychological operation, a game of chess against an opponent he hadn't even met. He was fascinated by the unknown, by this captain who had seemingly appeared from nowhere to challenge his authority. He wanted to look into his eyes and see the man who had become such a problem.

"Let's see if this 'Captain Gabriel' truly is the savior they say he is," Cain said, a slow, malevolent smirk spreading across his face. "Or just another ghost looking for a fight."

Chapter 55

The activity of the space dock was a constant bustle against the soles of Deborah's boots. After the close run with the Goliath and the Bethel, is was good to be laying low in port for a while, she mused. She stood in the port office, the air crisp and sterile, her datapad clutched to her chest. Through the large viewport, the vast, empty grid of the Galilee's trusswork was visible. Below, on the cargo platform, the last of their haul was being meticulously stacked by a small fleet of cargo bots. Amongst them, a bright orange streak moved with purpose—Jabez, the "Job" series material handling robot, was indeed on the job.

A barrel-chested longshoreman leaned against the opposite counter, tapping a stylus against a datapad. "Right then, that's everything," he said, his voice a rumbling bass. "Another smooth run. Your captain knows how to run a tight ship. No mucking about, no fuss."

A rare, almost-smile touched Deborah's lips. "We don't have time for mucking about, mate. A job's a job, and we do it right the first time."

The longshoreman chuckled. "Fair enough. But it's a dangerous business out here these days, with Cain makin' a name for himself. They say he's gotten a real taste for blood since he put that lashing on the IPC fleet. Not good for anyone." He paused, lowering his voice conspiratorially. "But there's a new player in town, too. Heard a few whispers down the line about a ship they call the Archangel. Folks are saying she's the one who took out the Goliath. Big story."

Deborah's posture stiffened. She was suddenly all business. "That's just a rumor, mate."

"Maybe so," the longshoreman said, looking around as if the very walls had ears. "But there's another rumor, a nastier one, tied to it. The talk is that Cain is so miffed about the Goliath, he's going to make innocents suffer until the Archangel comes out and fights proper. He's made an open threat against a medical frigate, the Shechem, sailing out of the port of Corinth."

The casual tone of the conversation was an effective mask for the sinister implications of the news. Deborah's grip tightened on her datapad. "Has the Interstellar Patrol Corps been notified?" she asked, her Australian accent more pronounced with her rising anxiety.

The man shrugged. "Probably. But they're still licking their wounds from the last fight, aren't they? Don't have many ships out this far. Reckon they're more focused on keeping their core worlds safe. Means it's up to us smaller operators to look out for each other." He squinted at her, his brow furrowed with concern. "Just thought you'd want to know, seeing as your lot run the same kind of routes. Best to keep clear of that Corinth run for a bit."

Deborah didn't answer. She turned and moved with a sudden urgency toward the airlock, the longshoreman's surprised expression visible in her periphery. She had to get back to the ship. She had to tell the crew. The Archangel was being called out. And she knew in her gut that Captain Gabriel, and the man he truly was, would be unable to resist.

The airlock hissed shut behind Deborah, the familiar pressure change a welcome return to the confines of the Galilee. She strode onto the bridge, her boots ringing on the deck plating. The comforting hum of the ship's systems filled the space, a stark contrast to the buzzing anxiety in her mind. Noah sat in the captain's chair, hunched over a holotable displaying their current cargo manifest, while Eli leaned against the co-pilot's console.

"Captain," Deborah said, in her clipped manner, cutting through the quiet. "I need to report something."

Noah looked up, his brow furrowed. "What is it, Deb? Everything all right with the transfer?"

"The cargo is all set, no worries there," she said, her hands moving restlessly over her datapad. "It's what I heard at the port." She recounted the conversation with the longshoreman, her usual measured tones replaced by a hurried, almost breathless pace. She described the rumors of Cain's rising power and the open threat against the medical frigate, the Shechem. "He's making a trap for us. He wants to draw out the Archangel."

A heavy silence fell over the bridge. Eli pushed off the console, his expression grim. "The man's a coward. Preying on the helpless to get a fight."

Just then, the main airlock cycled open, and Leah, their hyperactive navigator and purser, burst onto the bridge, her red bouffant hair a whirlwind of curls. Her huge glasses were perched on her nose, and her usually cheerful face was tight with worry. "Y'all! Y'all are not gonna believe what I just heard!" she exclaimed, her Southern accent a rapid-fire series of stressed syllables. "I was talkin' with the port authority on the way back, and they're all in a tizzy! Said there's a rumor Cain's put out a threat, against a medical ship, the Shechem! Said he's usin' it as bait to draw out that Gabriel fellow!"

She stopped, her chest heaving as she took in the grave expressions on her crewmates' faces. "Oh," she said, her expression dropping. "Y'all heard it too, then."

Noah stood from the captain's chair, walking to the main viewport. The vast, starry canvas was a beautiful but impersonal backdrop for the ugly decision he now faced. The logic was clear. Cain's actions were a direct challenge to the very idea of justice Noah and his crew had been fighting for. Ignoring this would be a betrayal of his new purpose and his family's memory. It would also be a cold, pragmatic business decision. But Noah wasn't a businessman anymore, not really.

He turned back to his crew, his face a mask of resolute fury. "Aunt Leah, get us a course. Corinth sector. I want us there in two cycles, full burn."

"Noah, lad, you sure about this?" Eli asked, letting his concern show. "It's a trap, plain and simple. We'd be flying right into a lion's den."

"It doesn't matter," Noah, firm as durasteel replied. "We can't run and hide like cowards while he kills innocent people. We're the only ones who can stop him."

Leah's fingers flew across her console, her worry morphing into a nervous energy that fueled her work. "Course set, Cap'n!" she chirped.

Deborah stepped forward, her drill-sergeant-like demeanor returning with a vengeance. "Then we'll get ready," she declared. "I'll go through the internal defense systems and check the med bay. A trap is only a problem if you walk into it unprepared."

"Eli," Noah said, turning to the grizzled engineer. "I want a full systems check. Cannons, drive core. Every single diagnostic you have. I want us in top fighting condition."

Eli nodded, his grumpy expression now replaced by one of grim determination. "Aye, lad. On it."

Noah looked from one crew member to the next. Eli, a grumpy but loyal mentor. Leah, a source of light and unyielding support. Deborah, a pillar of professional calm in the face of chaos. They weren't just a crew anymore; they were a family. And he knew, with a certainty that settled deep in his bones, that a family protects its own.

"Get to it," he said, his voice resonating with a quiet authority that his father would have been proud of. "We have a medical frigate to save."

The command deck of the Bethel was a space of quiet, controlled efficiency, but for Acting Captain Joshua, the calm was an illusion. He sat in the command chair, the holographic display of a star chart a cool blue glow on his face. He was reviewing fleet logistics and the slow, arduous process of rebuilding after Cain's devastating ambush, but his mind kept looping back to Caesarea. The failure to corner the Archangel—that wily trusswork freighter that just happened to look like his old family ship—was a raw wound.

If I hadn't made that mistake, if I had just trapped him, Josh thought. If he had captured the Archangel, he would have one less hostile player to worry about, and he could have focused the fleet entirely on Cain. The memory of Jethro's disappointed voice, stoked his frustration into cold, bitter resolve. He needed a win, not just for the IPC, but for his own sense of competence.

A chime sounded, and the CPO at the comms station looked up from his console. "Acting Captain, priority one alert from Port Authority Corinth. It's encrypted with IPC Intel protocols."

Joshua's stomach clenched. A priority alert meant something was happening right now. "Patch it through."

A woman's voice, tight with fear, filled the bridge. "This is Captain Ruth of the medical frigate Shechem! We've received a threat from an unknown source. Multiple pirate ships, believed to be Cain's fleet. They've given us a two-cycle ultimatum: surrender or be destroyed. They're doing this as bait, they said, for a vigilante ship called the Archangel. We are unarmed! We request immediate IPC intervention! Our destination is Corinth." The transmission ended with a crackle of static, leaving a tense silence in its wake.

The calm on the bridge evaporated. Joshua's mind raced, a whirlwind of rage and dread. Cain. It was always Cain. The man who had murdered his parents, crippled the IPC fleet, and now used innocent people as pawns in his twisted game. The audacity of it, the sheer depravity, sent a cold fury through him.

He looked at the star chart. Corinth was too far away for the adjacent sector captains to get there in time. Admiral Zephaniah's orders were to avoid direct engagement without support, to be cautious and rebuild. But caution would mean the Shechem and everyone on board would die. Josh knew, with a certainty that was both chilling and liberating, that he could not wait. This was a chance not just to save lives, but to finally deal a decisive blow. If he could reach the Shechem in time, he could tackle Cain and, if the Archangel showed up, capture that vigilante menace as well.

"Lieutenant," Joshua said, turning to his tactical officer, a lanky man with a neatly trimmed mustache and a heavy Texan drawl. "What's our ETA at max burn?"

"Sir, with all due respect, that's a direct violation of standing orders from Admiral Z" Lieutenant Nathaniel, his acting XO, replied, his brow furrowed. "Corinth is well outside our patrol zone, and we'd be movin' into a hostile sector without backup. Ms. Beth is repaired, but she's not a battleship, Captain."

"I am aware of the risk, Lieutenant," Joshua replied, his gaze unyielding, his voice hardening with conviction. "And I am tired of reacting to Cain's cruelty. He only has the audacity to pull a stunt like this because he knows we're reeling. We will not be cautious, not when lives are on the line. We will not let him use the Shechem as bait, and we will not give the Archangel a chance to slip through our fingers again." He turned to face his crew. "This is a rescue mission. We have a duty to protect those who cannot protect themselves."

He moved to the navigation console and began to enter the new coordinates himself, his fingers flying across the controls with the instinct of a born navigator. "Course laid in. Get us to maximum velocity."

Just then, from the engineering station, a sound with a deep Kenyan accent rang out. "Whoop whoop!" Ensign Adriel gave a triumphant fist pump, his infectious enthusiasm a welcome jolt of energy on the tense bridge. "We are ready, Captain! Full burn it is! Let's show dem pirates what Ms. Beth can do!"

Joshua returned to the comms station. "CPO, send an alert message to all local IPC captains and Admiral Zephaniah. It's a SITREP, not a request for permission."

The CPO nodded, his face set with grim resolve as he tapped at his console. The message appeared on the main screen, concise and to the point.

> PRIORITY ONE ALERT: Intelligence received. Pirate attack imminent. Target, Medical Frigate Shechem, Corinth. IPCS Bethel proceeding at maximum velocity to engage. Request reinforcements ASAP. Bethel out.

With the message sent, Joshua looked at the crew. He was done with guilt and hesitation. It wasn't just about his desperate need for justice, now there were innocent lives on the line. He had been a victim once, but now, he was fighting back on his own terms.

The medical frigate, Shechem was a vessel of mercy and peace. Unarmed and stately, she cut a slow, predictable path through the void toward the Corinth system. On her bridge, Captain Ruth, a woman with kind eyes and a face etched with the weariness of a thousand rescue missions, watched the star chart with a growing sense of dread. Four blips had appeared on her long-range sensors, and their vectors were anything but peaceful. They were closing fast.

"Captain, they're not responding to our hails," her comms officer reported, a nervous tremor in his voice. "They've locked our drive signature."

"All stop," Ruth ordered, her voice clear and precise with a proud British accent, despite the hammering of her heart. "Raise our diplomatic transponder. Broadcast our mission and medical status on all open channels. No cargo. No weapons. Just doctors , nurses and patients."

Her words were met with a low, menacing chuckle that echoed across the bridge's comms console. A face appeared on the main viewscreen, framed by a neatly trimmed beard and a roguish smile. Captain Cain. The news reports had not done him justice; he exuded a chilling, cunning charisma.

"Captain Ruth, a pleasure to make your acquaintance," Cain

said with a smooth, silken purr. "I'm afraid your medical status is a matter of complete indifference to me. We are here on a matter of principle, not profit."

"This is an act of war against a neutral vessel," Ruth protested, her inflection gaining a sharp edge of defiance. "We are a humanitarian ship, protected under galactic law! The IPC will not stand for this!"

Cain's smile widened, showing a flash of white, even teeth. "Oh, I'm counting on it. I'm afraid your humanitarian efforts have become quite the problem, and a public example must be made. Now, you have a choice. You can surrender your vessel and we'll take it off your hands, or we can make this more… *interesting*."

The Shechem's bridge fell into a panicked silence. It was a choice between a slow, horrifying death and a quick, terrifying one.

Ruth's defiance, however, was not so easily broken. "We will not surrender to pirates! Not ever!" she declared, her hand already moving to the helm controls. "Helm, full reverse! Let's get us out of here!"

But it was a futile effort. The Shechem, built for stability and patient care, was as nimble as a brick. The pirate ships—the Babylon, the Moab commanded by Dathan, the scarred Aram captained by Samson, and a burly freighter named the Tyre, commanded by Abimelech—began to dance around the helpless frigate. They were not aiming to destroy her, just to torment her. The Moab zipped past, its jury-rigged weapon-mounts spitting bursts of plasma that grazed the Shechem's hull, leaving scorch marks but doing little structural damage. The Aram and the Tyre flanked her, their bulk intimidating, their maneuvering precise and practiced.

"They're herding us!" a crew member shouted.

"They're just playing with their food," another said, his voice trembling.

All the while, Ruth issued repeated, frantic distress calls. "This is the Shechem! We are under attack by Cain's fleet! We request immediate IPC intervention! Our destination is Corinth! Please, someone, anyone, help us!"

On the Babylon's bridge, Cain stood before a holotable, watching the spectacle with a satisfied smirk. He had no intention of ending this quickly. He wanted to draw out the agony, to make it a public display of his power, to ensure the Archangel would hear the cries for help and, unable to resist, would fly directly into his beautifully crafted web.

The Galilee's deck shook with a bone-deep vibration, the protest of a freighter pushed far beyond her limits. The main drive screamed behind them, its steady roar a constant companion on their desperate flight. On the bridge, Noah stood over a holotable, its display a swirling vortex of star charts and tactical readouts. Eli, hunched over his engineering console, watched the engine diagnostics with the practiced eye of a worried parent.

"Full burn, Captain," Eli muttered, his Irish brogue thick with concern. "She's not built to sustain it like this, lad. We keep this up, somethin's gonna pop, and we'll be dead in the void."

"We don't have a choice, lives are in danger." Noah said, his gaze fixed on the glowing blue sphere representing their destination. "But, we can't just go in guns blazing. We're one ship against a fleet. We need a plan."

Deborah strode onto the bridge, her datapad held tight against her chest. "I've been going over the cargo manifest," she said. "We've got a number of containers still on the trusses." She tapped a few keys, and a detailed list appeared on the holotable. "One of them, manifest number G-47, is a shipment of deep-space comms satellites. Fitted with radar and high-gain sensors. Not military grade, but they're powerful."

Noah's eyes lit up. "A distraction," he breathed. "A flare in a cave. We launch them, make 'em go active, and flood the sector with so much junk data it'll blind their sensors. It might give us an opening, let us get in close enough to…"

"To do what, lad?" Eli grumbled. "To get our heads blown off? That's not a plan, that's a prayer."

"It's all we've got," Noah retorted, turning back to the holotable. "Aunt Leah, what's our ETA to the Shechem's last known position?"

Leah's words, tinged with a nervous tremor, rang out. "We're closin' on their position, honey. We'll be in sensor range in 'bout thirty minutes."

Noah's mind worked furiously. "Half an hour. That's all the time we have." He turned to Eli. "Get out there, Eli. I need you and Jabez to rig those satellites for immediate deployment from the trusswork. Set them to go active as soon as they're clear of the ship. I want them scattering in every direction, screaming as loud as they can."

Eli's grumbling stopped. He understood the desperate gamble. "Aye, lad. On it." He moved toward the main access hatch, the urgency in his movements a clear sign of his grudging acceptance.

"Deb," Noah said, turning to his Loadmasters, "get the

boarding tubes ready. We might need to get in close."

Deborah nodded, her demeanor as grim as his own. "On it, Captain."

Noah then turned to Leah. "Aunt Leah, set a course tangential to the Shechem. Don't approach directly. I want to come in from the side. Once we're within a few thousand kilometers, cut all engines. We'll coast in, running as silent as we can."

Leah punched the commands into the navigation console, her face a mask of nervous concentration. "Course set, Captain. Cuttin' engines in… ten… nine…"

The deck settled into an eerie stillness as the roar of the main drive died. All that remained was the low, steady thrum of the ship's internal systems. The silence felt deafening, a prelude to the storm they were about to enter. They had mere minutes to rig a cargo of satellites into a desperate weapon. The fate of the Shechem now hung in the balance, resting on a prayer and the hope of a distraction.

On the bridge of the Babylon, the mood was one of casual cruelty. Cain sat in his command chair, his customary steaming cup of green tea cradled in one hand, his gaze fixed on the Shechem on the main viewscreen. The medical frigate was being expertly harassed by his ships, a terrified bird in a cage. He took a slow sip of his tea, a faint smile on his lips.

He was a patient predator, and he whispered to himself, a low, intimate sound lost in the drone of the ship's systems. "Where are you, Captain Gabriel? Show yourself."

Silent minutes stretched into an agonizing eternity for the Shechem crew, but for Cain, it was a moment of perfect anticipation. He was waiting.

Suddenly, the silence was shattered. Malkiel, his nervous first mate, broke the quiet. "Sensor contact! Sir, we have contact!"

Cain's smile widened into a sly grin. "There you are," he whispered with a note of triumph. He stood, setting his teacup down with a sharp click, and took charge of the bridge. "Where's the contact, Mr. Malkiel? Is it a single vessel?"

Malkiel's hands flew across his console, his brow beaded with sweat. "Sir... it's... it's *everywhere!*"

On the tactical display, dozens of new contacts flared to life, not as distinct ships but as a massive, confusing cloud of sensor returns. The raw data was a cacophony of electromagnetic noise, a thousand conflicting signals that drowned out everything else.

Cain's eyes narrowed, but there was a flicker of admiration in their depths. "Clever," he murmured. "He's cloaked his approach with a swarm of drones. He's brought other angels with him."

"We cannot get a solid lock, Captain," Malkiel stammered. "The jamming is too effective!"

"Mr. Ithamar" Cain commanded with icy calm, "Isolate the source, if you please. I want a location."

Ithamar, the nervous navigation officer, hunched over his console, his fingers a blur. "Working on it, sir... I am getting general locations... three possible sources, all moving at high velocity." He muttered to himself in his thick Indian accent as he worked. "Ah, the numbers, they are a mess... a beautiful mess, but a mess nonetheless."

Cain turned to his officers, his voice laced with cold fury. He toggled his comms. "Moab! Turn about and engage contact one. Search and destroy. Aram, you will take your vessel and intercept the third contact. I will take the Babylon and engage the central contact, it is mostly likely to be our prey. Abimelech, you will screen my approach with the Tyre. Mr. Ithamar, plot the intercept courses!"

Ithamar obeyed, and the pirate fleet's ships repositioned on the holotable. Cain returned to his chair, a cruel glint in his eye. He had been looking for a challenge, a worthy adversary. Now, he had him.

On the bridge of the Galilee, a tense silence reigned, broken only by the soft whir of the life support and Leah's low murmurs as she monitored the nearly-blind sensor display. The main viewscreen showed nothing but the inky blackness of space, occasionally punctuated by the distant, faint glow of stars. Eli and Jabez had returned, their faces grim, but the successful launch of the satellites had bought them crucial time.

"It's working," Deborah breathed a hushed whisper, as she watched the tactical display. They had programmed the satellites' broadcasts with a frequency notch which allowed their own sensors some limited capability. The faint energy signatures of Cain's pirate fleet were beginning to split and move away, chasing the phantom signals of the decoy satellites. "They're falling for it, Captain. They're chasing our ghosts."

Noah nodded, his eyes fixed on the display. The Galilee was now a silent, massive ghost herself, coasting quickly along a vector that would slice a path directly between the Shechem and the receding pirate ships. The very interference they had created, however, was now a double-edged sword.

"Honey, our sensors will be blind as a bat as we close in"

Leah murmured, her brow furrowed. "I can barely track anything with all this interference."

"And if we power up the plasma cannons, it'll be like lighting a beacon in the dark," Eli added. "They'd know exactly where we are."

Noah chewed on his lip, the internal debate clear on his face. He had a brief window, a moment where they were effectively invisible. He could attempt a risky, blind shot at the fleeing pirate vessels, but the chances of hitting anything were slim, and the power signature would immediately give them away. Or he could stick to the plan.

Suddenly, an idea struck him. "Eli," he said, "can a tight-beam comm transmission get through all this noise?"

Eli thought for a moment. "Maybe, lad. Maybe. If we're close enough. Gally's tight-beam transmitter isn't very powerful."

Noah nodded, a new resolve hardening his features. "We'll take it. Deb, open a comm channel to the Shechem, tight-beam transmission only."

Deborah's fingers flew across her console. "Channel open, Captain."

Noah leaned into the comms console, he spoke with authority and calm. "This is Captain Gabriel of the Archangel. We are here to help. Captain Ruth, would you be so kind as to share your last known vectors for the pirate vessels, and a live feed from your sensor array? We might be able to find a way to make this work."

On the other end, Captain Ruth's reply was filled with a desperate, hopeful relief. "This is the Shechem! Yes, Captain Gabriel! I'll patch it through now!"

The Galilee's bridge lights flickered as the data stream from the Shechem poured in. Leah worked frantically, integrating the information with their own limited sensor returns. "The vectors are a mess, Noah, but with our own data and what she's sending… I think I can make a triangulation work!"

A few tense seconds later, a series of glowing red blobs appeared on the tactical display. They weren't sharp, distinct ship signatures, but they were solid enough. Four of them, in a rough formation.

"Bingo," Noah said, a grim smile on his face. "Eli, get ready to power up the cannons. We have a firing solution."

On the bridge of the Babylon, Cain sat forward in his chair, a silent observer of the chaos he had created. On the comms channel, Captain Abimelech's bluster was a steady stream of complaints. "Cain, we're not picking up nothin' but static! This is a waste of fuel and time! We're chasing ghosts, I tell ya!"

Cain listened with a thin-lipped smile, his fingers drumming a patient rhythm on the arm of his chair. "Patience, Captain Abimelech," he said, his tone calm and patronizing. "A hunt is a delicate thing. The Archangel can't hide forever. Maintain your course and keep your scanners wide." He didn't wait for a response, simply closed the channel.

He took a slow sip of his tea, a moment of tranquil contemplation in the heart of the storm. He was in command, he had the advantage, and the game was playing out exactly as he'd planned.

A moment later, Malkiel, now a terrified shriek shattering the calm. "Captain! We have another contact! It's—it's behind us, sir! Between us and the Shechem!"

The teacup in Cain's hand was suddenly a fragile, useless

thing. In an uncharacteristic moment of pure, unadulterated rage, he hurled it against the command deck's viewport. The ceramic exploded in a shower of tiny, glittering shards, the green tea a dark, viscous stain spreading across the polished floor.

He was not angry at Captain Gabriel. He was furious at himself. He, the master tactician, the grand manipulator, had been outsmarted by a simple, elegant ruse. He had been so focused on the distractions, the faked contacts, that he had never once considered the real threat was moving in silent and unseen.

A slow, chilling smirk returned to his face, a mask of cold admiration that replaced the flash of fury. "Well played, Captain Gabriel" he murmured to the shattered remains of his teacup. "Well played."

"Sir! Massive energy spike!" Malkiel screamed again, his voice on the verge of breaking. "She's firing!"

On the bridge of the Galilee, the calm was shattered by the high-pitched whine of the salvaged plasma cannons powering up. The ship's internal lights dimmed as the massive weapons drew from the drive core, their energy signature a silent beacon in the void.

"No solid lock, lad!" Eli yelled from his station, his hands a blur over the targeting console. "Just that big ol' mess of a sensor blob!"

"Fire a warning shot." Noah ordered, his eyes glued to the display. "Low power, Eli. Try to bracket it."

A low thrum vibrated through the deck plates as the starboard cannon discharged. On the main viewscreen, a flash of brilliant white light lanced out into the darkness, a silent, deadly beam streaking toward one of the red blurs on their tactical display. It missed its mark, flying wide of the target.

"Blast it all!" Eli grumbled, preparing for another low-power shot.

But then, a new data point appeared on the tactical display. The pirate vessel, a burly freighter, reacted to the near miss. It made an evasive maneuver, a sudden, panicked lurch to starboard.

It was a mistake.

The movement, a clear, solid action within the mess of false signals, gave the Galilee's targeting sensors something to bite into. The computer's algorithms instantly filtered out the static and latched onto the unmistakable silhouette of a single ship.

"I got it!" Eli bellowed, a triumphant grin spreading across his grimy face. "Solid lock! Full power, Captain?"

Noah didn't hesitate. "Full power, Eli! Let 'em have it!"

The Galilee shuddered as the weapons systems went to maximum. A blinding beam of pure plasma erupted from the cannons, a star-bright column of light that tore through the void. It struck the burly pirate vessel amidships, and the ship, a modified freighter, had no chance. It buckled under the impossible heat and force, its hull glowing a furious red-hot before it disintegrated in a spectacular, silent explosion.

On the bridge of the Babylon, a moment of stunned silence hung in the air. The crew had braced for their own destruction, but the blinding flash of plasma had struck the Tyre instead. The bulky but powerful freighter simply evaporated in a silent, violent spectacle.

Then, a second later, the concussion hit.

The bridge lurched as the energy wave from the exploding freighter washed over them, a shockwave of twisted metal and raw energy. Alarms shrieked, consoles flared with warning lights, and Cain's crew was thrown about the deck.

Cain was the first to recover. He gripped the arms of his command chair, his eyes fixed on the viewscreen where the silent, expanding cloud of debris now marked the Tyre's grave. He had expected a diversion, perhaps a few potshots. He had not expected this kind of decisive, surgical strike.

"Mr. Ithamar!" Cain's roar cutting through the klaxons. "Stabilize us now! Get a solid lock on that vessel!"

The panicked crew scrambled to obey. The shaking slowly subsided as the Babylon's engines compensated.

A cruel, knowing grin spread across Cain's face. He knew who he was dealing with now. This wasn't some foolhardy vigilante. This was a man who understood tactics, who used the environment as a weapon.

"So, he has more tricks," Cain growled dangerously. "But he's given himself away, and he's out numbered."

He toggled his comms, his voice now a smooth, chilling purr that belied his fury. "Moab, turn about and engage the contact. It's the Archangel. Time for you to get your revenge, Mr. Dathan."

"On it, sir!" Dathan's responded with a frantic mix of bloodlust and terror.

Cain leaned back in his chair, his eyes glinting with a predatory fire. He had been playing a game of chess. But now, his opponent had flipped the board. It was time for a bludgeon. It was time to show this Captain Gabriel the difference between a skirmish and a real war.

On the bridge of the Galilee, the moment of triumph was short-lived. The tactical display showed the triumphant result of their first strike: a silent, expanding cloud of debris that had once been the pirate ship Tyre. Leah's tone, now high-pitched frantic, broke the tense quiet.

"Oh, goodness! Captain, that little ship, the Moab? She's broken off from the others. She's comin' right at us!"

Noah moved to her station, his face a mask of grim determination. He watched the glowing red dot accelerate on the display, its vector a straight line toward them. He had a choice to make, and he had seconds to make it. He couldn't leave the Shechem undefended, not when the other pirate vessels were still out there.

"Leah, can you get a lock on her?" Noah asked.

She shook her head, her face a grim mask. "Too small, and she's still in the middle of all that satellite noise. The sensors can't get a clean read, honey."

Noah couldn't fire blind. He'd miss, and they'd lose valuable time and cause heat build up in his weapons. He looked back at the Shechem's position on the tactical display. The medical frigate was a tiny, defenseless speck.

"I have an idea, Captain," Deborah said, her pronouncement a sharp and decisive cut through the tension. She gestured toward the external cargo manifest. "The containers. We can jettison them. Give them blokes something else to shoot at"

Noah's eyes widened as the idea clicked into place. "A shield. We leave a section of cargo behind the Shechem."

"It won't be much," Deborah said, "but it'll be something. Better than nothing, anyway."

Noah didn't hesitate. "Do it, Deb! Jettison all aft containers! Tell Captain Ruth to stay within the cluster of debris and containers we're about to create!"

Deborah's fingers tapped the keys of her console. A series of deep thuds resonated through the hull as the magnetic clamps holding the external containers disengaged. One hundred massive, metal cargo boxes were released into the void, a swirling, tumbling mass of improvised cover.

"Full power, Aunt Leah!" Noah ordered, his chest filled with furious resolve. "Set an intercept course for that inbound ship! Eli, get the cannons ready for close-quarters combat! We are going to meet this fight head-on!"

"Course set, Captain!" Leah said, as she laid in the new heading.

The Galilee shuddered as the main drive roared to life again, its flight path now a direct line toward the oncoming Moab. They had provided a temporary shield for the Shechem and had decided to take the fight to the enemy. Now, it was just a matter of who would be the faster gun.

The Moab wasn't a fast ship, not normally, but Dathan was pushing the engines well passed red-line and climbing. Power conduits were heating up. Permanent damage would set in soon, but he did not care. He'd burn the Moab to ciders if he had to. Just as long as he took out Archangel in the process. Dathan watched as the massive, silent form of the Archangel turned to face him. The trusswork freighter, which moments ago had been a ghost, was now a roaring, accelerating force.

"She's comin' right at us!" one of his crew members shouted.

Dathan's hand was already on the firing controls. His face, scarred from a hundred pirate brawls, was a mask of cold fury. This wasn't just a job; it was personal. He had been there, on the Goliath, when the Archangel had charged their ship. He remembered his last-second, desperate evasive maneuver to avoid a collision, a move that had exposed his ship's broadside. He remembered the blinding flash of the plasma cannons, the sickening silence as the Goliath was blasted in two, and the quiet, almost disappointed look on Captain Cain's face.

This time would be different. He would not flinch.

"Fire at will!" he bellowed, his voice raw with a desperate need for revenge.

The Moab's jury-rigged weapons spat out a volley of plasma bolts. They were fast, but the Archangel was accelerating hard, her massive engines screaming with a fury Dathan had never seen in a freighter before.

It was like déjà vu. The two ships were closing in a game of chicken, a tiny, fast predator against a massive, lumbering beast. The distance between them shrank with terrifying speed. Dathan squeezed the trigger, his heart pounding a furious rhythm against his ribs. He felt a moment of absolute, panicked certainty. He had to fire. He had to hit his target. He could not, would not flinch again.

On the bridge of the Galilee, the calm gave way to a fevered pitch of controlled chaos.

"Fire at will, Eli!" Noah's voice was a sharp command. "Let's see if we can get a hit!"

Eli's face was a mask of grim concentration as the weapons discharged, but the shots were wild. The Moab, smaller and faster, danced through the void, its own weapons now finding their mark. Sparks flew from the Galilee's massive hull as plasma bolts grazed the trusswork, the minor impacts a grim prelude of what was to come.

It was a horrifying replay of the battle with Goliath. Two ships, one a relentless hunter and the other a lumbering beast, closing on an inevitable collision. Noah could almost feel the phantom crunch of metal from the Goliath's death.

A cold, determined calm settled over him. "Eli, forget the cannons! Leah, set a collision course! Bracing for impact!"

Leah's eyes widened, her Southern accent gone, replaced by a simple, terrified number. "On it, Noah. Twenty seconds to impact."

Noah's gaze was fixed on the tactical monitor, the two converging dots a digital representation of his impending doom. He was betting everything on the pirate's bloodlust.

"Deb, prep the port-side containers for jettison!" he ordered. "Get ready to hit the release the moment I give the word!"

The proximity alarms began to blare, a shrill, insistent wail that pierced the tension on the bridge.

On the main comms screen, a furious roar came from the Moab. "I'll kill you, Gabriel!" Dathan's cry was filled with a maniacal rage. It was also exactly what Noah needed to hear.

With strained gasps, Leah counted down. "Four seconds to impact, Noah!"

"Jettison cargo now!"

A series of sharp thuds echoed through the hull as the container clamps released. A massive wall of metal boxes was launched from the Galilee's port side, a chaotic cloud of debris set adrift in the void.

"Two seconds to impact!"

It was now or never.

Noah took a deep breath. "Thrusters, hard to starboard!"

The Galilee flinched, just as Dathan had done on the

Goliath. The Galilee shuddered violently as its maneuvering thrusters fired, pushing the enormous ship just enough to the side to avoid the head-on collision. The Moab, however, was too committed. It flew straight, its speed a deadly, unstoppable force.

The pirate ship, moving at thousands of miles per hour, slammed into the cloud of metal containers. The collision wasn't a single impact but a rapid, cacophonous series of brutal blows. The Moab was shredded, torn to pieces as the cargo containers, now transformed into deadly kinetic projectiles, ripped through its hull. The ship disintegrated in a gruesome, silent ballet of light and twisted metal, leaving nothing but a second cloud of debris in the blackness.

On the bridge of Babylon, the shock of the Moab's destruction was quickly replaced by a cold, calculating fury. Cain, his famous gentleman's composure, a thin veneer over his mounting frustration, watched the tactical display. He had already ordered Captain Samson to break off his search and circle the Aram around and approach the Archangel from the rear. He had a new plan, one born from a place of simmering rage.

He was without his beloved green tea, the shattered cup a testament to his rare moment of lost control. The one silver lining, he mused, was the unexpected death of the dullard Dathan. A minor victory, but a victory nonetheless.

"Set an intercept course for the Shechem," Cain commanded. He watched his crew work, the ship moving with a tactical precision. "Commence firing. 50% power on the guns, slow rate of fire. I want to wound her, not destroy her. She's still the bait in this trap."

The Babylon shuddered as its main cannons began to fire, a series of deliberate, precise strikes aimed at the helpless medical frigate. Cain watched as the Shechem's hull was peppered with plasma bolts.

He then had his comms officer open a channel, a wide-band transmission he knew the Archangel would hear. A satisfied smirk spread across his face as he stared into the void.

"Captain Gabriel," he began, his voice a smooth taunt. "I must congratulate you. A most clever ruse. I must confess, for a moment, you had me fooled. A very impressive display." He paused, letting the silence hang heavy, broken only by the crackle of plasma fire. "But now the game is over. Your cleverness, I'm afraid, has a cost. And I'm afraid your humanitarian principles will not save your new friends. I will show you the difference between a clever gambit and true power."

He watched the viewscreen, expecting to see the Shechem writhe in agony. Instead, he saw his shots, muffled and scattered, harmlessly impacting a field of floating debris. The cloud of cargo containers the Archangel had jettisoned was now serving its purpose, a makeshift shield protecting the medical frigate.

Cain's jaw tightened. His gentlemanly composure was gone. He slammed his hand on the arm of his chair. Such a simple, clever solution. Gabriel had outwitted him, again.

On the bridge of the Galilee, a red dot on the display, larger than the others, began moving toward the Shechem. Its targeting indicators flared, a tell-tale sign of weapons fire.

Noah's eyes narrowed, his gaze fixed on the display. His hand shot out, his finger jabbing at the display. "That's him," he said, his tone pure, cold fury. "Eli, new target! Babylon! Full power!"

Eli nodded, "Aye, Captain," he said, his face a grim mask of recognition. He worked at his console, the high-pitched whine of the plasma cannons building again. He noticed the heat sinks were working, a testament to his handiwork. But the temperatures were climbing fast. The Galilee's power grid was not meant for sustained high-power output like this.

The main viewscreen showed the distant, impotent flashes of the Babylon's cannons firing on the Shechem. Noah watched as a few shots got through but the debris field of cargo containers was holding…for now. He knew it was a temporary reprieve at best. The pirates' heavier guns would tear through it in a matter of minutes.

He made a quick decision. "Leah, set a new intercept course. Direct for the Babylon."

"We're going to do this again, sweetie?" Leah's projected a note of weary dread as she looked from Noah to the monitor.

Just then, Jabez, the orange material handling robot, rolled forward from his station. He had been a silent observer, but now the audio of his synthesized vocalizations filled the air. "Practice makes perfect. The third time is a charm."

Noah nodded, a grim smile touching his lips. He was done with distractions. He was done with hiding. He was going to face Cain directly. He was going to put Gally, his family's ship, on a course with vengeance.

Chapter 57

The Galilee came about and screamed through the void, her main drive again at maximum burn on a direct intercept course with the Babylon.

On Cain's flagship, the pirate crew had turned their attention to the helpless Shechem, their weapons deliberately wounding the medical frigate in an attempt to draw Archangel into the fight. But it was also a tactical error and the break Noah needed. By turning to engage the Shechem, Babylon had exposed her broadside. Eli had a clear shot.

"I have a lock!" Leah cried

"Yes!" Noah pumped his fist. "Eli, full power on the cannons and fire!"

"Aye, lad," Eli said, a glint in his eye as he took the firing solution. "Let's give 'em a good howyadoin'!" The high-pitched whine of the plasma cannons built to a fever pitch. A blinding two beams of pure energy lanced out from the Galilee, silent, deadly bolts of lightning in the void.

Cain, in a flash of horrified clarity, realized his mistake. His frustration had clouded his judgment, leading to a fundamental tactical error. "Hard to starboard! Engage the Archangel directly!" he roared, but his command came too late.

The plasma bolt struck the Babylon with a concussive blast. The ship shuddered violently. Alarms shrieked, and sparks erupted from consoles as the bridge lights flickered and died, leaving the deck in the eerie glow of emergency red. Crew members were thrown from their stations.

"Damage report!" Cain bellowed, gripping the arms of his chair.

A report came from the smoke-filled engineering access. "Main power's down, Captain!" another crewman yelled. "Engines are offline! We have only thruster propulsion!"

Cain's composure, though brittle, returned. "Small batteries, engage the Archangel! Engineers, get the main guns and engines back online immediately!"

On the bridge of the Galilee, a cheer erupted. "We got him, Captain! His main guns and drives are offline!" Eli yelled, a triumphant grin on his face.

But the excitement died as quickly as it had come. A red warning light flashed on Eli's console. "Blast it!" he cursed. "The power relays are shot! The cannons are down, Captain!" The heavy use had overloaded the old systems, and the ship's main weapons had shut down to prevent a catastrophic meltdown.

"Get them back online, Eli!" Noah snapped, his gaze fixed on the enemy ship.

As Eli frantically worked, the Galilee drifted into Babylon's small-arms range. Laser bolts began to pepper the ship. A series of explosive impacts rocked the bridge, and alarms blared.

"Captain, we're taking fire!" Deborah's voice cut through

the noise, her face grim. "Small caliber, but they're getting through!"

"Damage to the maneuvering thrusters!" Leah cried out with panic.

Jabez, the orange material handling robot, rolled swiftly to Eli's side, a panel in his chest opening to reveal an array of diagnostic tools. He began to assist in repairing the overloaded systems.

"Leah, set a course to get us back to the Shechem!" Noah commanded. "We need to get back to providing cover for her." He then added, "Slow us down! She's a crippled duck, and we'll conserve power. We'll need better control with these thrusters damaged."

Aboard the Babylon, Malkiel's tension was so tight his words became a nervous squeak. "Sir, the Archangel is slowing down and changing her course! She's moving away from us!"

Cain's face was a mask of furious contemplation. "And engineering reports?"

"Main engines are coming back online, sir! But no main guns yet."

Cain's eyes, filled with a cold, contained rage, fixed on the retreating form of the Archangel. He had been outmaneuvered. He had been tricked. He was through with games. He was going to give Gabriel a taste of his own medicine.

"Give me manual control!" he growled. "Full acceleration! Collision course!"

On the Galilee, the calm turned to terror. The tactical display showed the Babylon, a massive, crippled warship, suddenly accelerating at maximum velocity. Its course was a straight line—a line that would intersect with theirs in a matter of seconds.

"She's coming for us!" Leah cried out, her Southern drawl back, laced with pure panic. "We can't outrun her, Noah! Not with our thrusters like this!"

Noah felt a cold dread settle in his stomach. Even with their engine upgrades, Gally was too big, too slow, and with the damaged thrusters, too clumsy to get clear in time.

"Oh, he's angry now, he is." Eli muttered, watching the ship on the display. The Babylon charged forward, her small guns blazing, the bolts sparking against the Galilee's thick hull.

At the last second, a small burst of light erupted from Babylon's side. "What's he doing?" Leah shrieked. It was a final, desperate thrust, a maneuver designed to shift the point of impact just enough. It worked.

The two ships collided with a shuddering, metallic shriek that reverberated through the their hulls. It wasn't a head-on impact, but a brutal, grinding sideswipe. The belly of the Babylon smashed into the trusswork of the Galilee's external cargo lattice. The ships, locked together in a death grip of twisted metal and grinding plastic, began to tumble slowly through the endless blackness of space.

Chapter 58

The bridge of the Aram was a hive of quiet tension. Captain Samson, a lean man with a scar that bisected his left eyebrow, watched the tactical display with narrowed eyes. His orders were simple: circle around the primary engagement and hit the Archangel from the rear. It was a flanking maneuver, a simple, effective tactic taught to every rookie pilot. He was in a perfect attack position now, all he had to do was engage.

Then the impossible happened.

The Archangel, a civilian transport, charged head-on into the pirate warship. A blinding bolts of plasma lanced out, striking the Babylon with a concussive blast that even at this distance was a sight to behold. The Babylon reeled, her main gun emplacements going dark, her engine cluster dimming to nothing more than pinpricks. The Archangel then drifted, taking small-arms fire. Then Samson saw the Babylon come to life, her main engines fired again. She charged forward directly at Archangel, then her thrusters flared briefly followed by the sight of the two ships, a freight hauler and a pirate warship, smashing into each other in a cacophony of twisting metal. The collision sent them tumbling, a single, lifeless wreck.

Samson raised a hand to the comm officer. "Secure main

engines. Full stop."

He leaned back in his command chair, the shock giving way to a slow, creeping realization. This wasn't a battle. It was a mutual suicide. Cain, the mighty pirate lord, was dead. Or if he wasn't, he was in a deathtrap, locked inside a tumbling hull.

His gaze flickered to the tactical display, to the two dead ships, then to his own. The Aram, in full battle readiness, her guns hot and her crew primed. The plan had been to attack the Archangel, but with both ships helpless, he could do something far more profitable.

I am Samson, destroyer of Archangel. The title sang to him. *And Cain's successor.*

A slow, wolfish grin spread across his face. "Raise a comm link. Priority One, to the Babylon."

A moment later, the comm officer shook his head. "No response, Captain. All her comms are offline."

"Of course they are," Samson said, his tone a low growl of satisfaction. "Crew, we have a new objective. Engage the wreckage." He leaned forward, his grin widening. "Full power to all weapons. We're going to pick through this carcass and make sure nothing stirs."

He watched the energy readouts on his console as the ship's massive laser cannons began to thrum, power building, waiting for his command. He wouldn't risk getting close. The Aram could easily destroy the crippled ships from a distance. One pass wouldn't be enough, not for two such big ships. But he would keep firing until every last piece of the wreckage was nothing more than a fine mist of debris.

Chapter 59

The command deck of the IPCS Bethel rumbled with a bone-deep vibration, the protest of a ship pushed well past its designed limits. Ensign Adriel, his eyes alight with a mix of engineering pride and boyish glee, gave a low whoop. "Ms. Beth is singing, Captain! I didn't know the old girl had this much fire in her."

Acting Captain Joshua, however, remained a still and focused presence in the command chair, his gaze fixed on the main holoscreen. On the display, the battlefield was a cruel, silent ballet. The two massive ships, the Babylon and the Archangel, were locked in a death grip, tumbling slowly through the void. The live data stream from their long-range military-grade sensors had been monitoring the situation for minutes now. They'd seen the shift in the pirate fleet's maneuvers, watched the plasma bolt rip into the Babylon, and finally, witnessed the violent, grinding collision.

"Well, that's a bit of a pickle," Lieutenant Nathaniel, his Texan drawl as calm as ever, said from his tactical station. "Look at the Aram. She's not movin' on the Shechem or the wreckage. She's just… sittin' there."

A low murmur of confusion rippled through the bridge crew. It was a strange maneuver. The Aram was a predator, and there was fresh meat on the table.

Tamar, standing at Josh's side, her eyes fixed on the display, had a sudden, terrible realization. "Captain," she said, her voice quiet but sharp. "He's not waiting for orders, eh? He's waiting for an opportunity. He thinks Cain's gone."

Joshua's eyes narrowed, his mind racing. "You're right. He's not here to rescue his boss. He has his eye on the throne." A cold fury, familiar and deep, settled in his bones. He knew this kind of greed. It was the same kind that had driven Cain to destroy his family.

"General quarters!" he commanded, his orders ringing with authority. "Sound the alarm! All hands to battle stations!"

The ship was instantly plunged into a maelstrom of blaring alarms and a flurry of activity. Josh cut through the chaos, clear and unyielding. "Lieutenant Nathaniel, prepare for immediate engagement! Our target is the Aram! Our objective is to stop her before he can destroy those ships." He paused, his gaze fixed on the entangled vessels. "Once the Aram is dealt with, we will board the wreckage. I want teams ready to go. We must confirm if either Cain or Gabriel are dead or alive and if alive, take them into custody."

Moments later, a calm professionalism settled over the bridge as each station reported readiness. "Weapons online, Captain," the weapons officer reported. "Sensors ready," the CPO confirmed. "Main drive at maximum velocity," Adriel announced, his boyish grin back.

Joshua moved to the navigation console, his fingers flying over the controls with practiced ease. The holoscreen before him shifted, a new intercept course plotting itself with chilling precision. He glanced at the timer counting down the distance to the Aram.

Twenty seconds.

On the comms, a voice, filled with a pirate's rapacious glee, crackled on their open channel. "Babylon, do you require assistance? Aram is standing by to assist." The comms officer looked at Josh. "No reply, Captain. Babylon's comms are completely offline."

Josh only nodded, his face a grim mask. He didn't need a reply to know what was happening.

Five seconds.

On the bridge of the Aram, Captain Samson watched the timer on his holoscreen, the number dropping steadily toward zero. The ship droned with the building power of its laser cannons, ready to fire on his command. He was close now. He could almost feel the cold, satisfying finality of his plan. He had betrayed Cain, he had seen his opportunity, and now, he was going to take it all.

Just then, his comms officer cried out, his face shown with a mix of shock and dread. "Captain! New contact, bearing two-four-seven mark one-one-zero… Sir! It's the IPC! It's the Bethel!"

"No!" Samson roared, a surprised, choked sound. He slammed his hand on the firing controls.

On the bridge of the Bethel, the weapons officers cut through the tense silence. "Captain! The Aram is firing!"

"Fire, all batteries!" Joshua commanded with a thunderous roar. "Take her down!"

The Bethel shuddered as its military-grade weapons unleashed a massive, overwhelming barrage. Beams of pure energy and a storm of kinetic projectiles lanced out, a coordinated attack that dwarfed anything the pirates had thrown. The Aram, her forward armor designed for single combat, had no defense against the full might of the IPC warship. She was struck by dozens of simultaneous blasts. Her hull, a moment before a proud pirate vessel, was reduced to a spray of shrapnel and a brilliant, expanding ball of fire that briefly illuminated the entangled wreckage of the Babylon and Archangel. The Aram simply ceased to exist.

Chapter 60

The void was a silent, unforgiving witness as Captain Cain, clad in a sleek black vac-suit, led a boarding party of his remaining able-bodied crew across the twisted, groaning hull of the Babylon. Their destination was the entangled Archangel, a monstrous, impossible fusion of two ships. As they traversed the scarred metal, Cain's boot scraped over a section of the hull that had been peeled back by the collision. Beneath, a massive, hand-painted letters revealed her true name on the side of the hull: Galilee.

A brief, vindicated sneer twisted Cain's lips beneath his helmet. He was right.

Just then, a brilliant, silent flash of light erupted in the distance. The flash was far too small for them to make out what it was; it simply appeared and was gone. Cain barely registered it. He was too focused, too consumed by the burning need to confront Gabriel. "Move!" he barked into his comm, urging his crew forward.

They reached an airlock on the crew and command section of the ship. The breach was swift, a practiced explosion of shaped charges, and the thick metal door buckled inward. Inside, the pirates shed their vac-suits, revealing their worn combat fatigues and an array of salvaged weapons. Cain gripped his plasma rifle, the familiar weight a comfort in his hands. He took a deep breath, the stale recycled air of the Galilee filling his lungs.

This walk, he thought, the memory a ghost in his mind. *I've made this walk before.* He remembered the day he had led his men onto the Galilee, the day he had killed her crew. He had a brief, flash of a woman's face—a memory from the past. He remembered a boy, young Joshua, pulling a weapon from the floor and wounding his gunner, Baruch, a shot that had earned him his life. Joshua had been a child then; a boy. Who was this new Captain Gabriel? This was no boy; this was a man who understood tactics, a man who had fought him to a standstill. He was angry.

On the bridge of the Galilee, the emergency lights cast long, dancing shadows. Despite the chaos of the collision, the ship's core systems remained operational. The Babylon had indeed hit the trusswork section amidship, a resilient lattice of steel tubing, conduits, and a few remaining cargo containers. Nothing vital in the forward command and crew sections had been compromised or the aft power and engine sections, though the structural integrity alarms still blared intermittently.

Noah, Eli, Leah, and Deborah watched the internal security feeds with grim anticipation. The pirates, fifteen strong, were making their way through the corridors, clearly intending to reach the bridge.

"Alright, Deb," Noah said, his voice calm, almost detached. "Time to welcome our guests."

Deborah nodded, her fingers dancing across the console. "Activating 'Strobe Surprise' in Gamma-9. A blinding, disorienting strobe light flared from repurposed maintenance panels down the corridor, forcing the pirates to shield their eyes. Confused, they turned and headed toward the closest open area. The Deb set off the foam jets from the fire suppression system. She sequenced the jets, steering the pirates right where she wanted them to go: the mess hall.

But the Galilee crew wasn't watching from the bridge anymore. They were waiting. They had taken up a defensive position in the dimly lit mess hall, using the tables as barricades. As the first group of pirates stumbled through the door, blinded and disoriented by the strobes, they were met with a fusillade of laser fire.

"Ambush!" Cain roared, his countenance thick with fury. "Get down!"

The pirates returned fire, but they were still disoriented, and their shots went wide. Eli, a grin of pure, animalistic joy on his face, sprang from behind a makeshift barricade, a heavy pipe in his hands. He swung it in a wide arc, catching one pirate across the knees and sending him sprawling. As another pirate raised his weapon, Leah, with a dancer's grace, sidestepped and wrapped her arm around his neck, putting him in a wrist lock and disarming him. The grueling training sessions Deborah had put them through were paying off now.

A massive, orange blur of motion hurtled from behind a pillar. It was Jabez, its metallic voice booming almost joyfully. "Security Protocol: Engaged!" A pirate spun to face the robot, but a retractable arm shot out, a pulse of energy lancing out and hitting his helmet, causing his body to go limp.

The mess hall had become a chaotic blur of motion. The pirates were better armed, but the Galilee's crew had home-field advantage and a fierce, primal will to survive. They fought with a desperate, ferocity, disarming and trading blows with the pirates. The air filled with the sounds of grunts, the clang of metal against armor, and the sharp hiss of plasma. A pirate, a large, hulking man, lunged at Deborah, but she went limp, using his own momentum to send him tumbling over her shoulder. He landed with a heavy thud, his head smacking against a table.

But there were too many of them. Cain, his own movements a study in ruthless efficiency, fought his way to the front. He watched in cold fury as his men fell, defeated not by superior numbers, but by the sheer, unexpected grit of the civilians.

"Enough!" he roared, a chilling command that echoed over the melee. He fired a plasma round, not at a person, but at a support beam in the mess hall. The beam shuddered, and a low groaning sound filled the air.

Noah looked up, his eyes meeting Cain's. He knew what the pirate lord was doing. He was going to bring the ceiling down on them.

"To the cold storage!" Noah yelled, his voice strained. "Run!"

Battered and bruised, the crew scrambled for the heavy blast door that led to the cold storage bay. They were a mess of cuts and bruises, blood stains and plasma burns spotted their gray coveralls, but they were alive. They had fought and won a small victory.

With a final heave, they slammed the door shut, locking the thick metal with a heavy clang. They collapsed against it, panting, the adrenaline wearing thin. They had survived, but they were trapped.

On the other side of the door, Cain's cold rage was absolute.

He kicked a fallen table out of his way, his eyes fixed on the blast door. He had lost six men to a bunch of civilians and an ancient robot. He took a deep, shuddering breath, a practiced motion that smoothed his expression into a calm, gentlemanly mask.

"Ithiel, you and Adonijah get to work," he said, his tone even. "Get this door open."

He turned away from the door and walked over to the mess hall's galley. With unhurried, deliberate movements, he found a cup and a packet of green tea. He activated the water dispenser and waited patiently for the steaming liquid to fill his mug. He would not rush this. He had them now. He would wait. He would enjoy every moment of their fear.

Chapter 61

The void was silent as the Bethel's boarding pods detached and settled against the hull of the Archangel. Joshua, his face a grim mask of determination, followed his squad of IPC marines with practiced efficiency. Their breach of the auxiliary airlock on the crew and command section was a silent affair, the shaped charges a whisper against the metal hull.

Inside the sterile corridor, the marines moved with the quiet, professional grace of highly trained soldiers. They systematically cleared each section of the ship as they made their way toward the bridge. Every corner was checked, every access panel secured. They were met with little resistance. The alarms from a much earlier, more violent breach still blared in the distance, a loud distraction that worked to their advantage.

Reaching the bridge, Joshua's team quickly secured the room. The consoles glowed with emergency lights, but the room was empty. "Clear!" a marine reported, his rifle sweeping the final corner.

Joshua moved to the main security display. The ship's internal sensors showed a concentrated cluster of movement in the mess hall. He could hear muffled shouts and the distinct sounds of a brutal, close-quarters fight echoing faintly through the ship's internal comms. He pulled up the live security feed for the mess hall, his stomach clenching.

What he saw was not what he expected. The pirate lord had indeed found his target, but they weren't being slaughtered. They were fighting back. He watched in grim fascination as the pirates clashed with a group of civilians in gray coveralls, the standard uniform of freighter crews everywhere. The battle was chaotic, but the civilians—battered, bruised, but fiercely determined—used the environment to their advantage. He saw a flash of orange take down a pirate with a single, precise pulse.

He watched as the civilians were slowly beaten back. They were good, surprisingly so, but they were no match for the superior numbers of the pirates. He saw a man, their leader by the looks of him, call out an order. He must be Gabriel, but the video was too grainy, the scene too chaotic to make out his features. The civilians scrambled, exhausted, and retreated to a large, reinforced door on the far side of the room.

The blast door slammed shut, sealing them inside.

Then, Joshua's eyes settled on the pirate commander, a chillingly familiar form. There was no mistaking who this was. It was Cain. He watched as the pirate captain kicked a fallen table out of the way, then composed himself. With unhurried, deliberate movements, Cain walked over to the mess hall's galley, found a cup and a packet of green tea. He activated the water dispenser and waited patiently for the steaming liquid to fill his mug.

"Cain" Joshua whispered, the sight of Cain's casual sadism more terrifying than any battle cry. The man was a monster.

He wasn't even frustrated anymore; he was simply waiting to enjoy the kill.

Joshua's calm, professional demeanor shattered. "Marines! Avoid engaging the civilians in the gray uniforms unless they engage you first. We'll deal with them later. The pirates are the priority, that one is the leader." He said stabbing a finger at Cain's image on the monitor. "Move! Double-time to the mess hall! Now!"

His marines, sensing the urgency, complied without question. They dropped their caution and sprinted through the ship's corridors, moving at a dead run.

Meanwhile, in the cold storage bay, the chilling air was heavy with the scent of recycled air and fear. Outside, a muffled symphony of chaos erupted. The sounds were different this time—not the disorganized rage of the pirates, but a rhythmic clang of boots, the sharp, authoritative bark of a new voice. Then came the retort of plasma fire and the wet thud of bodies. The Galilee crew, exhausted and bruised, huddled together, listening.

"They're fighting," Eli said in a hoarse whisper. "Someone's fighting the pirates."

The sounds of the battle were a chaotic mix. It was a vicious, up-close melee, not a long-distance firefight. They could hear the shouts of the pirates, wild and frustrated, clashing against the sharp, disciplined commands of the newcomers. The fight was a toss-up, a desperate, grinding clash in the cramped mess hall. It sounded like a brutal struggle, and for a moment, the crew simply listened, their own breath ragged.

Noah looked at his crew, their faces streaked with grime and blood. He could see the fear, but he could also see something else—a flicker of resolution. They had already faced down Cain and his men. They wouldn't hide now.

"They're the good guys," Leah said, her voice shaking but firm. "We can't just… leave them to it."

A new series of thuds and shouts, closer this time, punctuated her words. Noah looked from her to Eli, to Deborah, to Jabez standing in silent readiness. He saw his own conviction reflected in their eyes.

"She's right," Noah said. He took a deep, shuddering breath. "We help them. We break their backs."

With a sudden burst of renewed energy, they shoved the heavy blast door open and charged out. They were a small, battered force, but their entry was a shock to both sides. The pirates, already struggling, were now fighting a two-front war.

The tide turned instantly.

The Galilee crew, knowing every choke point and hiding place, fought with a desperate, wild fury. Eli charged another pirate, a wordless scream of vengeance on his lips. Leah, with a cry of defiance, joined the melee. Deb, seeing a pirate about to get the drop on one of the newcomers, quickly dispatched the pirate with a precision strike to the back of his neck. Their small, brave rebellion was the straw that broke the camel's back. The pirate line fractured, their will to fight dissolving under the new, unexpected pressure.

Cain, saw it happen. He saw the professionals from the IPC and the wild, bloodied civilians fighting side-by-side. He knew an untenable situation when he saw one. He disengaged from his fight and began to retreat, heading for a maintenance shaft that led to the ship's engine room. He knew he was the only one who could escape now.

Just as he turned, he saw a black-armored marine break free from a melee of his own. The marine saw him too.

Noah, still fighting, saw it all as well. He saw Cain's retreat, and he saw the black-armored marine, a stranger who had saved them, chasing after him. Noah's own heart was hammering in his chest. He couldn't let the fight end without him. He dropped his weapon and ran, his legs burning, following them both into the darkness of the ship.

Chapter 62

The chase was a brutal, silent sprint through the broken intestines of the Galilee. Cain, his breath a ragged gasp in his chest, pounded through the corridors, his boots slipping on spilled oil and coolant. He was fast, a lifetime of running and fighting making him a blur of motion. But just behind him, a dark, armored figure was gaining ground, its footsteps an ominous, methodical beat. The figure was a ghost, impossibly fast, and with a shock of fear, Cain realized why. The marine had shed his heavy armor, the tactical plates and helmet abandoned for pure speed. It was a calculated risk that spoke of a deep, personal hatred.

As Cain burst through the final hatch, he found himself in the main shuttle bay. A single shuttle, still attached to its re-fueling umbilical, sat silent and waiting. Salvation. He sprinted for it, his hand outstretched. But a shadow fell over him. He spun, his body ready for a fight, and was met with a fist to his jaw. He staggered back, shaking his head.

Before him stood, not a Marine, but Mr. Joshua. His face was bruised, his nose bloody from his earlier fights, but his eyes burned with a cold, clear fury. The two men stood in the middle of the docking bay, the metallic hum of equipment the only sound. The air was charged, thick with a history of violence and betrayal.

Cain took a slow, deliberate breath, a thin wisp of steam escaping his lips. A slow smile spread across his face, a mask of predatory calm. "Well, Mr. Joshua," he said, his voice mocking. "It seems my lessons have paid off."

The fight was a brutal, graceful dance, an eerie echo of their sparring sessions on the Babylon. Josh moved with a fluid, precise rhythm, a testament to Master Jair's relentless training, but also the added tactics he'd learned from Caleb at the academy. He parried Cain's strikes with a practiced ease, delivering sharp, clean counters that landed with bruising force. He was an equal, a match for the man who had murdered his family, and he knew it. He wasn't just fighting; he was winning.

But Cain wasn't just fighting. He was playing his old games.

"Look at you," Cain said, with twisted pride. "So strong. So fast. You think you did this yourself? I made you. Every blow you land, every move you make, is a testament to my mentorship." He dodged a strike and countered with a blindingly fast kick to Josh's ribs. "You could have had so much more, you know. An empire. My right hand. The heir to my legacy."

He moved, a blur of motion, forcing Josh to retreat.

"And now…" Cain's eyes narrowed, a cold, regretful fire burning in them. "I regret saving your worthless life, Mr. Joshua."

A brief flash of doubt, a momentary hesitation, crossed Josh's face. He knew the truth in Cain's words. He was who he was now because of Cain's training. But his parents… his brother… they had made him too. And Cain had killed them all. He was not Cain's tool! The thought solidified his resolve and fueled a raw, unthinking rage. He lunged forward, not with a plan, but with a blind, desperate need for vengeance.

The move was too late. Cain had seen the hesitation, the flicker of doubt in his eyes. He anticipated the coming charge. He shifted his weight, ever so slightly, and used Josh's momentum, not to fight it, but to propel it. He pivoted, a cruel smile on his face, and with a single, sharp shove, sent Josh flying. He slammed into the wall with a sickening thud and slid to the floor, unconscious.

Meanwhile, Noah arrived. He sprinted into the docking bay, spotting a cargo tug and ducked behind it, his heart hammering in his chest. He saw the fighting, the two figures a blur of motion in the dimly lit bay. He watched, helpless, for an opening. He heard the muffled conversation, Cain's chillingly familiar voice. *I made you... I regret saving your life.*

He saved him? Noah's mind reeled. *This marine... he knew Cain, too?*

His thoughts were shattered when he heard Cain speak, a sickeningly intimate murmur: "Mr. Joshua." Noah's blood ran cold. The marine was young. *Josh... could it be?*

Suddenly, the marine went down. Cain didn't hesitate. He grabbed a crowbar from a workbench and used it to pop open the shuttle's hatch. He yanked the hatch open, his eyes on the prize. He began to climb in.

But as he did, the crowbar he'd just used was yanked back, and with it, he was pulled from the shuttle and sent sprawling to the floor. Cain lay there, dazed, and his vision cleared. Staring down at him was another Joshua, but not quite the same. Cain's face twisted in confusion. "Mr. Joshua?"

"No," Noah said, his voice a low, vengeful growl. "I am

Gabriel."

He raised the crowbar and brought it down on Cain's head with a sickening crack. The pirate lord went limp.

Noah took a moment to catch his breath. He looked at his brother, then back at Cain. He dragged Josh's unconscious body out of the docking bay, his arms burning with effort, and sealed the door behind him. He looked through a staging area's small porthole and saw Cain stirring, a faint moan escaping his lips as he struggled to get back on his feet.

Noah's eyes met his, and for a split second, Cain knew. He knew who he was, and he knew what was coming. Noah's expression was deadpan.

Noah hit the manual override. With a shriek of groaning metal and a hiss of venting air, the massive outer bay doors slid open. A powerful gale of escaping atmosphere pulled Cain from his feet. He was sucked into the vacuum of space, a small, insignificant mote of dust in the vast, unforgiving darkness.

Chapter 63

Josh's eyes fluttered open to the sterile white ceiling of a medical suite. The air smelled of antiseptic and a faint, comforting warmth. A low, rhythmic beeping was the only sound. A face, belonging to a woman with kind eyes and a severely tight ponytail, was bent over him. She was carefully bandaging a deep gash on his forehead.

"You're awake," she said, her tone uncharacteristically soft and efficient.

Josh winced, a wave of pain rippling through his head. "Yeah," he rasped. "Where… where am I? Are you a doctor?"

"No," she replied, her hands steady as she finished the bandage. "I'm a Loadmasters. And you're in Gally's medical bay."

He looked around the small room, his gaze catching on a small, framed photo on a side table. His heart stopped. It was a picture of his family. His parents, Noah, and himself, all smiling and happy. The sight was a punch to the gut. *The Gally…*

"You're back on Gally, Josh."

The voice came from the doorway, a sound so familiar, so laden with years of buried memory, that it brought tears to his eyes before he even turned. Noah. He stood there, bruised but whole, his face a mix of disbelief and overwhelming relief.

Josh's breath hitched. "Noah?" he whispered, his voice cracking.

Noah simply nodded, a single tear tracing a path through the grime on his cheek. "I thought you were dead," he choked out.

"I thought you were dead too," Josh sobbed, struggling to sit up.

Noah rushed to his side. They met in a desperate, tearful embrace, Noah's arms wrapping tightly around his brother, holding him as if to prove he was real. They held on for a long, quiet moment, the years of pain and loss finally giving way to the impossible joy of being together again.

"Cain," Josh asked, pulling back slightly, his face a question of fear and vengeance. "What about Cain?"

Noah's expression grew cold. "Cain won't hurt anyone anymore."

"Well ain't yee a sight for sore eyes, lad?" he boomed from the doorway.

It was Eli, his frame filling the entrance. His face was streaked with tears as he rushed forward, his arms wide. He engulfed Josh in a bear hug so fierce it nearly crushed the air out of him. "Josh! Josh! You're alive, lad, you're alive! The saints be praised!"

Eli's embrace was followed by a woman with a smile so wide and a Southern accent so thick it was almost a physical presence. It was Leah. Noah, wiping a tear from his eye, grinned. "Leah, this is my brother Josh." He turned to Josh. "Josh, this is Leah. She was Mom's friend, and now she's our Navigator. We all call her Aunt Leah."

Leah's eyes filled with fresh tears as she hugged Josh fiercely, her expression overflowing with over-the-top emotional joy. "Look at you! Just look at you! Thank goodness, thank goodness, my sweet nephew!"

From the doorway, a low, mechanical whirring sound caught their attention. It was Jabez, its chassis still dented from the fight. "Statement: Galilee requires a crew. Crew complement is now complete."

The moment was perfect. Josh, overwhelmed by the warmth and emotion, smiled for the first time in what felt like a lifetime. "Can I get a cup of coffee?" he asked, his voice still hoarse.

A chorus of laughter erupted from the crew. "He asks for coffee!" Eli bellowed, a fresh wave of tears in his eyes.

Just then, the door opened again. It was Tamar and the Bethel's XO, Lieutenant Nathaniel. Tamar's professional, composed demeanor contrasted sharply with the emotional chaos in the room. She held a datapad in her hand.

"Captain," the XO said, a note of deference in his tone. "Just wanted to check on ya, sir."

The Galilee's crew looked at each other, their eyebrows raised in unison. Noah's mouth was a silent question. *Captain?*

"Acting Captain," Josh quickly corrected, his cheeks flushing. "Just filling in."

Lieutenant Nathaniel, his Texas accent a calm drawl, nodded. "Two more IPC cutters have arrived. Reckon they're too late to join in the fun, but they'll be here to escort the Shechem back to Corinth and tow the Galilee to a dry dock. The Admiral will be mighty pleased to hear Cain and his pirates have been dealt with," he said, and then, with a knowing wink at Noah, "Though he might not be so happy to hear that

Gabriel and the Archangel got away."

A soft, private smile passed between Noah and the XO.

Tamar stepped forward, handing the datapad to Josh. "I've already drafted your after-action report, sir. All you have to do is proofread and sign. And given your injuries, I've also taken the liberty of putting in your request for convalescent leave. Thirty days of recovery time before you have to report to Big Z at Fleet Ops."

Josh looked at the datapad, then at Tamar, and finally, his gaze settled on Noah, Eli, and Leah. He looked at the family photo on the side table. A gentle, peaceful smile spread across his face.

"I think I'll spend my leave at home," he said, his voice quiet but firm. "Here, on Gally."

Eli let out a roar of approval, Leah clapped her hands with joy, and even Tamar's stern expression softened. A moment later, a mug of steaming black coffee appeared in Josh's hand.

Epilogue

A month had passed, and the quiet bustle of New Jerusalem's dry docks had replaced the silent void. From the wide windows of their temporary high-rise apartment, the crew of the Galilee had a perfect view of their home. She was berthed below, surrounded by the skeletal arms of cranes and the swarm of repair crews, a testament to the brutal collision and the battles that followed.

Inside, the air was warm with the rich smell of a home-cooked meal and the easy chatter of family. Leah, in full Southern Aunt mode, was in her element. A huge meal was spread across the table, a feast of comfort food designed to put a smile on everyone's face. Bowls of creamy macaroni and cheese sat next to a platter of crispy fried chicken, and a heaping pile of collard greens steamed invitingly. It was a going-away dinner, a bittersweet celebration for Josh's departure.

"Ah, look at that," Eli grumbled, gesturing toward a team of dry dock engineers through the window. "Look at those clowns. Probably gonna put the stabilizer fins on backward. They'll have a heckuva time gettin' home if they mess with me Gally."

A wave of laughter passed around the room. It was easy to laugh now. The financial sting of their ordeal had been softened by the rewards and bounties they had claimed for taking down Cain and his ships. Between the insurance settlement for the "unfortunate pirate incident" and their new status as pirate-hunting heroes, they were in good shape.

Leah smiled, a sly look in her eye. "Oh, hush, Eli. You know I've used every trick in the book to keep our insurance premiums from going up." She leaned in with a conspiratorial whisper. "I even got 'em to give us a discount for Jabez as ship security. They figured a robot was a sound investment, bless their hearts."

The thought of Leah haggling for a discount from the stern-faced underwriters was too much for Noah, who laughed until his ribs ached. After the last of the food was cleared away, Leah brought out a pot of freshly brewed coffee. They all settled back, sipping their mugs and talking long into the night.

Josh still had to finish out a year of his IPC commitment. But Big Z, the Fleet Admiral, had authorized his request to go on inactive reserve for the remainder of his four-year tour after the year was up. The crew was sad to see him go, but the plan was solid. Josh would be back between patrols, and if all went according to plan, he would be ready to serve full-time again just as Gally was ready to re-enter space.

"Just a few more months," Leah said, her voice turning soft as she looked out at the ship. "And we'll all be back where we belong."

The crew grew quiet, a shared understanding passing between them. They had almost lost their ship and their lives, but in the process, they had found each other.

"Statement: The crew of Gally is family," Jabez's vocalizer said from the corner of the room, cutting through the silence. "They are home."

The crew looked from their ship to one another, a fierce love burning in their eyes. They embraced, a group hug full of laughter and a few quiet tears.

The next morning, as Josh slung a duffel bag over his shoulder, he stood by the front door. Noah walked with him, a hand on his shoulder.

"You'll be back," Noah said. It wasn't a question.

"I'll be back," Josh confirmed. He gave Noah a final hug, then opened the door.

Deborah was standing outside, leaning against the hallway wall. She watched him leave, a small smile on her face. As Josh walked away, she turned to Noah, a playful glint in her eyes.

"You know," she said with a teasing grin. "Your brother's kind of cute."

A Note from the Author

To the Readers of *Galilee Rising*,

If you are reading this, it means you've reached the final pages of Noah and Joshua's journey—at least for now.

As a new and independent author, I can't tell you how much it means to me that you chose to spend your time in this corner of the galaxy. I know that with thousands of books just a click away, taking a chance on a first novel from an unknown writer is a genuine risk. I am deeply honored that you took that risk with me.

Writing this story was a labor of love, born out of a passion for space opera and the complex bonds of family. My goal was to provide an adventure that was as clean as it was thrilling, and seeing it in your hands (or on your screens) is the greatest reward I could ask for.

Because I don't have a big publishing house behind me, I rely entirely on the support of readers like you. If you enjoyed the voyage of the *Archangel*, there are two ways you could help me keep this work going:

1. **Leave a Review:** Even a single sentence on Amazon helps more than you know. It tells the "algorithm" that this book is worth showing to others.
2. **Spread the Word:** If you have a friend who loves a good space adventure without the grit of modern sci-fi, please

let them know about Noah and Joshua.

Thank you again for your time, your trust, and for letting me share this story with you.
Safe travels through the stars,

Allan Grandgenett

Leave a review for Galilee Rising here!

Follow me on Amazon here: https://www.amazon.com/author/algrandgenett

Follow Me Here!

Sneak Peek: Valley of Shadow

Departure

10...9... I gripped the yoke, my knuckles white. The Co's hand was on the throttle, poised. *5...4...* I could hear Samuel take a sharp, nervous breath over the intercom. *3...* I glanced at my crew one last time, a silent exchange of trust. *2...1...* The Launch Officer's final, emotionless call: *"Launch."*

An immense, jarring force shoved the dropship forward. The g-forces compressed us into our seats, a physical assault on our bodies. This was no gentle departure. It was a violent, brutal kick into space meant to get us out of the tube and away from the carrier as fast as possible. My vision blurred as the launch tube's lights streamed past like tracers. The sheer kinetic power of catapult made me feel helpless. It felt like being fired from a cosmic cannon.

The g-forces abated as we cleared the launch tube, and the darkness of space rushed back to fill the view port. "We are out," the Co said, her voice strained but steady. "Primary systems are still green."

The tactical display lit up as the other dropships in our formation, Juda 22, 23, and 24, appeared as green icons. I gave the command. *"Juda 20 flight, cleared to rejoin in-trail."*

With practiced precision, the other three Samsons fell in

behind us, a perfectly aligned chain in the void. We were a single entity now, four dropships with one purpose. "Nav, update on our escorts."

"Creature 10 flight approaching from our starboard," the Nav reported instantly. "ETA 20 seconds. Bulls two-seven-zero by two-zero-five at 5-Kay-Kay."

We held our position as two squat, angular shapes appeared on our screen, their main engines glowing red. The A-21 Cherub fighters were affectionately called "Warthogs" by the fleet, and for good reason—they were all gun and armor, built for punishing ground attacks. Two smaller, leaner AX-21 drones flew in close formation with each manned fighter.

"Creature 10 flight, this is Juda 20 lead, we are joined." I said over the secure comms.

"Copy, Juda 20," the lead pilot's voice came back. *"Creature 10 flight is joined."*

With our escort in place, I gave the final command. *"Juda 20 flight and Creature 10 flight, go radio silent. Maintain listening watch."*

We drifted in orbit, the dropship quiet for a few precious minutes before the chaos resumed. All of us gazed out at the void—stars twinkling, the blue-green curve of Sidon filling half the windscreen. For a moment, our thoughts were our own.

Samuel, the secondary Loadmaster, broke the silence over the intercom. "Any of you ever seen one of them—the enemy?"

"No one's ever seen one outside that black armor they wear," the navigator replied. "They always incinerate themselves before capture or death. Just—poof! Up in smoke. Nothing left but ash."

The copilot, usually reserved, joined in. Her voice was low, almost hesitant. "They seem to be like us. Humanoid—two arms, two legs, about our size. Even their tech matches ours." She paused, a shadow passing over her features. "Some call them the Fallen. I don't know why. There's something… wrong about them. Like they're a reflection twisted in the dark."

"But where did they come from? They just seem to pop up out of nowhere," Samuel pressed, his battle nerves making him chatty.

The navigator answered, "No one knows for sure. They just appeared one day, out of the unexplored regions beyond this system. Speculation abounds. Some say we bumped into unfriendly, territorial galactic neighbors. Others claim they come from the fringes of the galaxy—those ancient, uncharted parts. Places where the stars themselves seem afraid to shine."

Talk of the enemy made acid stir in my gut. I glanced at the console and saw we were rapidly approaching our de-orbit point. It was time to get the crew back on task.

"All I know is, they're the enemy. All they seem to want is to kill, steal, and destroy—and we're here to put a stop to it," I said, hoping my voice carried enough resolve. "All right, crew. Back on task."

The cockpit became eerily silent save for the low thrum of the engines. We maintained a listening watch as we began our slow, gravitational descent toward the planet below. I looked at the clock. Barely two hours had passed since I had knelt in the chapel, yet it felt like a lifetime.

Then, a faint crackle broke the silence on the listening channel. It was the next dropship formation. "*Salem Tower,*

Reuben 30 flight, requesting launch."

The universe seemed to hold its breath. Seconds later, a new set of icons appeared on our tactical display, fresh meat for the grinder. I felt a surge of cold dread for them, a premonition of the terror to come. I sent up a quick, silent prayer. A low, growing hiss began to shake the ship as the air molecules of the atmosphere began to press against our hull. It was time.

"Nav, initiate de-orbit checklist."

"Copy. De-orbit checklist" Caleb was back to business as usual, "De-orbit burn in 5…4…3…2…1"

There was a brief nudge and the Samson nose dipped below the curve of Sidon's horizon.

"Hull integrity" he continued.

"Heat shield integrity at 95%," the Eng's voice reported, calm but with an undercurrent of strain.

"Atmospheric entry confirmed," the Nav snapped. "We're going in."

Suddenly, a sound! It was a deep, powerful boom that shook the entire dropship. One. Then another. The sound of the naval artillery fire from the *Salem*, a thunderous crackle ripping through the thin atmosphere to provide cover. The dropship shuddered violently under the assault of the explosions. The ride was getting rough. Very rough.

Descent

After what seemed like an eternity, the ship's shuddering subsided, and the ride smoothed out. The cabin's low rumble returned, a comforting counterpoint to the thunder of our re-entry. I felt the physical tension drain from my body, a fleeting moment of relief. We'd survived the passage.

The Eng's solid voice cut through my thoughts. "Heat shield integrity at 80% and beginning to recover, all systems still green."

The Nav piped up next, a familiar edge of efficiency in his voice. "We're on course, on speed, on descent profile. We're one-minute-thirty ahead of our Time-On-Target, Pilot. We'll lose the slop in the low-level."

I nodded, even though he couldn't see it. *Slop* was a military term for excess time, and Caleb would make sure we hit our drop zone right on the second.

From my right, the Co confirmed, "All Juda and Creature ships are still in formation. Signals report green across the board. Nothing from Salem Actual on the D-link."

My turn. My hand reached for the checklist binder. Now the real mission began. "Very good. Combat Entry Checklist."

"Combat Entry Checklist Acknowledged, Eng," Noah's voice replied, the familiar sing-song of our well-practiced procedure carrying on. We were a well-oiled machine, transitioning from one state of being to the next without pause. The checklist was our bridge from the tranquility of space to the chaos of combat.

"Cargo locks" the Eng called.

"Set and secure," came Samuel's quavering voice from the back. The airman was still a bit shaken by the reentry.

"Defensive Systems."

"Armed, Semi Auto, Program 2" the Co confirmed.

"Sensors."

"Sweeping, clear," the Nav snapped.

"Fuel status…"

The checklist continued, a litany of checks and confirmations that prepared us for the coming engagement. Moments later, the Eng called the checklist complete, and the cockpit's quiet professionalism was shattered by the scream of ground-based anti-air fire. The fight was on.

The cockpit erupted in noise. Klaxons shrieked a high-pitched, incessant wail. Our tactical display, a moment ago a clean picture of our formation, was now a chaotic mess of symbols and vectors. The ground below, still a distant blur of clouds and continents, was a hive of red icons. "Missile launch!" the Nav's voice cut through the alarm, sharp as a whip. "Two inbound! At our twelve o'clock!" My eyes flicked to the display. Two glowing red lines streaked toward us from the planet's surface.

"Creature 10, Juda 20 lead, two inbound, advise!" I yelled into the comms.

"Copy Juda!" Creature 11's voice was calm, almost bored. *"Creature 12, send out the dogs. Juda flight, maintain formation."*

"Roger that!" Then we saw Creature 12 responded immediately. The Co and Nav both confirmed his command on our console, a flash of shared, unspoken understanding. In my peripheral vision, I saw the two tiny icons representing Creature 12's AX-21 drones detach from his wing. They streaked out, twin streaks of blue fire against the blackness of space.

The klaxons continued their deafening cry. A moment later, two small yellow explosions appeared on the display as the drones shot down the incoming missiles, detonating them harmlessly far from our formation.

"Good hits!" Creature 12 said. Then, a touch of grimness entered his voice. *"One drone lost. Creature 11, I'm joining up on the remaining drone to engage the SAM site."*

"Copy Creature 12. Go get 'em. Creature 11 is staying with the dropships."

The conversation was a blur of efficiency, a testament to the seamless coordination that came from years of flying together. Just as the missiles were neutralized, a new threat appeared on our scopes.

"Triple-A!" the Nav yelled, his voice strained. "We're painted! Heavy fire ahead!"

The dropship shuddered. Not from a close explosion, but from the combined force of a hundred automated cannons on the ground, all trying to zero in on our flight path. It felt like we were flying through a hailstorm of hot lead.

"MAYDAY! MAYDAY!" Creature 12's voice broke in over the comms, a gut-wrenching scream. *"I'm hit! I'm hit! Lost flight controls! I'm going down!"*

The display showed Creature 12's icon blinking red before vanishing entirely. My stomach turned to ice.

"Creature 12 is gone!" the Co snapped, her voice breaking just for a second. *"Creature 11, we have a man down!"*

"I see it," Creature 11's voice was ice cold, void of all emotion. *"Creature 10 flight will break formation and gain separation from the dropships. We are now running attack and over-watch."*

I knew what that meant. He needed space to maneuver and deal with the threat and so did we. The Cherub's icon peeled away, his engines screaming as he tore off toward the ground with drones in tow.

With our escorts gone, the responsibility fell to me alone. The Triple-A fire was getting heavier, tearing through our protective screen of atmosphere. *"Juda 20 flight"* I ordered. *"Cleared fluid trail! Go defensive as required and countermeasures at your discretion, but keep clear of each other!"*

An audible boom came from our right side followed by the tight voice of Juda 24's pilot. *"Juda 24 has taken damage! Right wing is hit! Lost number 4 engine!"*

"Juda 24, Lead. You are cleared to abort and return to Salem. Godspeed, Judah 24!"

The icon for Juda 24 peeled away, a sad green tear in the tactical display. The rest of the formation was maneuvering defensively, popping chaff and flares while their electronic countermeasure sent our noise. Our once-perfect line scattering into a chaotic trail, each dropship fending for itself.

I squeezed the trigger on my yoke, sending a shimmering cloud of countermeasures into the atmosphere, a futile hope to confuse the fire below.

A moment later, the screaming of the Triple-A fire began to quiet as we descended into the mountainous low-level route. The shadows of the peaks gave us cover, a brief moment of respite.

Over the comms, Creature 11's voice returned. He was all business. *"Juda 20, we've got our hands full down here but will maintain over-watch for hostile fighters. We will rejoin with you after the drop. Good hunting."*

I didn't answer. With palms sweating I just pushed the yoke forward, driving the C-260 deeper into the valleys. This was getting real, too real.

A Valley of Shadow

We dropped into a mountain valley, pressing down to less than a hundred meters off the floor. Down low it was dark; the shadows of the mountains kept the valley in night while dawn broke on the rest of the planet. I flew at a height that followed the contours of the surface and kept us well below the mountain peaks. The formation maintained fluid trail, which gave each ship freedom to maneuver and also complicated the targeting solution of any hostiles on the ground. The threat warning systems went quiet, my ears relaxed. My crew was quiet, focused. The only sounds were the thrum of the engines and the rush of air past our fuselage as we raced across the planet's surface. I was in the zone, my eyes focused through the Heads Up Display, picking my path through valleys, my hands moving the controls by second nature. I loved this part.

The Nav interrupted the moment. "Five klicks to waypoint Whiskey Alpha One. That's our breakup point. We are TOT minus 27 seconds."

"Co, send it over the D-link," I ordered.

"Copy. D-link message sent, Juda 20 flight clear off at Whiskey Alpha One as briefed, single ship run-ins, TOT as fragged," my Copilot announced in her no-nonsense tone.

"Pilot," Caleb piped up again, "Turn now heading two-seven-five, for 53 klicks. Next is our Initial Point for the run-in to the DZ."

As the instrument showed us passing the waypoint, I turned westbound. At the same time, our remaining two wingmen split up to take their own random routes to the Drop Zone. We would each run-in to the DZ from a different direction to keep the enemy guessing. Our drops would be 15 seconds apart to prevent a midair conflict with each other. Perfect timing was key, or this could go very bad, very fast. I was now driving to the Initial Point, or IP, where the run-in leg officially began. Time to get back to business. "Crew, Run-in Checklist."

"Run-in Checklist Acknowledged, Co," "Nav," "Eng," "Load," each crew position sounded off. Their voices grew more intense as we rapidly approached the objective area.

The Copilot ran this checklist. "Computed Air Release Point—CARP, Checks Copilot."

"Checks Pilot."

"Checks Nav."

"Drop altitude 130 meters. Checks Copilot."

"Checks Pilot."

"Pressurization."

"Depress."

"Altimeter setting, Checked Copilot."

"Checks Pilot."

"Red Light."

"On."

As I made the next turn, the Nav took over. "We are now IP inbound. Four minutes to drop, two minutes to slow down (SD)." He adjusted his display. "Your Point of Impact—PI, is the hot cargo pad at the northeast corner of the airfield."

On the horizon, I could just begin to see the outlying parts of the city ahead and the vague location of our target airfield. It struck me for a moment how peaceful the scene was, a quiet town in the predawn light set in a snow-covered valley. That was all about to change.

The next event would be the slow down. Attempting to drop at our current airspeed would tear the troopers and bundles apart. But slowing down made us more vulnerable to ground fire. We would press in at speed until the last possible second, slow as aggressively as the Samson could, make the drop, then accelerate out as fast as possible.

"SD in 30 seconds!" the Nav barked. Then exactly 30

seconds later, "Slow Down, Slow Down Now!"

At his command, I ripped all four throttles to flight idle. My body lurched as the thrust driving us forward abruptly died off. I pulled back gently on the stick, climbing slightly to our drop altitude and leveling there. "Flaps, 50." There was a momentary floating feeling as Ruth lowered the flap lever. I pushed the throttle forward part way to capture our drop airspeed.

As we closed in on the drop zone and the enemy position something strange happened. I felt cold soaked to my bones and for a moment a wave of apathy ran through me, almost like a voice. *"What's the point of all this? Just go home."* It seemed to say.A cue, flashing insistently on my Heads Up Display indicating 3 minutes to the drop broke me out of the momentary fog. The Nav had missed the time call too. Apparently I wasn't the only one affected.

"Nav! Time! " I demanded.

"Sorry Pilot, I spaced out for a moment there. Not sure..." Caleb snapped out of his moment of stupor. "Inside three minutes to drop!" he barked.

"On altitude and airspeed," the Co confirmed, shaking her head like she was trying to clear water from her ears.

I looked back at the Eng, he was rubbing his hands together vigorously. Whether he was warming them or trying to relieve some nervous tension, I didn't know.

Something had rattled us, but I wasn't sure what or how. Its was strange and visceral. I touch the cross on my neck and pushed the thought aside. Now was not the time to dwell on it. "Its game time crew. Stay focused!" I said to re-cage myself as much as the rest.

"Pilot, I show you 24 right, correcting left, on the bar," the

Nav continued to, now back in the game.He was guiding me to the drop, his tone only slightly more calm now.

It was time to open up. "Clear to open ramp and door," I advised the Loadmasters in the back. Moments later, I heard the roar of air rush and felt the rumble as our cargo ramp and drop opened the entire aft of the aircraft like a cave in the sky.

"Jumpers are standing, minimum maneuvering," the Loadmaster informed us. We were now at our most vulnerable. Low and slow, and any aggressive defensive maneuvers would toss jumpers and equipment all over the cargo compartment and possibly out of the ship.

The Drop

It was exactly then when Satan himself decided to join the party. The air defense around the base spotted us, and the tranquil sky lit up with fire and flak. "In coming!" Ruth shouted. At the same time, our Radar Warning Receiver began screaming warnings.

I began some gentle S-turns in an attempt to muddle the aim of the gunners on the ground. It was the best I could do with jumpers standing in the back. "Counter! Counter! Counter!" I commanded. The pickle button was depressed, and several powerful thumps of countermeasure stores jettisoning from our Samson could be heard and felt. The flak was going wide, and the missiles were biting off on the decoys. It was working, for now. It wouldn't last long.

"30 Seconds to drop! Pilot, you're 100 left, track left, correct back to the right," the Nav cried, his voice not quite panic, but close.

My S-turns had gotten me off the run-in course. I only had a few seconds to get us back on track. I eased to the right, just enough to get us on the CARP at the last second. Thunderous explosions were all around us; the shock waves rocked our craft, rattling us like rocks in a can. With white knuckles, I fought the controls to keep her steady. It was worse than flying through a hurricane. I wanted to offer up a quick prayer for deliverance but didn't have the presence of mind left to do it.

"Back on altitude and airspeed," the Co confirmed again, somehow still stoic and professional despite the chaos.

Her calm seemed to infect the Nav as well. Business was back in his tone. "Pilot, you're back on the bar, nice job! 10 seconds to drop…5…4…3…2… GREEN LIGHT!"

The Copilot flipped the drop light switch from red to green and hit the release button. Immediately, an extraction parachute fired out the tail of the Samson. The roar of the floor rollers was deafening as the chute inflated and dragged the pallet out of the cargo compartment and into the open air. I pushed forward on the stick, fighting to keep the nose level as the huge weight transferred aft, then suddenly was gone. An instant later, dozens of jumpers marched off the ramp to the shouts of the Jumpmasters, "Go! Go! Go!" I could hear and almost feel their boots stomp the floor as they practically ran off the ramp and into the sky.

"Load clear!" the Loadmaster declared.

Escape

The moment we heard "Load clear," the Nav called "Red Light." Ruth switched the drop light back to red, announced "On," and then I took over again. "Flaps, Up. Clear to close Ramp and Door. Run Completion of Drop checklist." The Copilot raised the flap lever while the Loadmasters closed up the back end. I smashed the throttle full forward and began an aggressive acceleration. The Eng was running the checklist this time. Noah reported, "Flaps Up, Ramp and Door closed and locked."

Free to maneuver again, I immediately banked into a hard left turn to break away from the enemy fire. I gave another "Counter, Counter, Counter" command, and stores pickled off with more thumps. From the Nav, "Pilot, your escape heading is 195." I turned in the indicated direction and dropped down low again, using the slight descent to both accelerate and mask us behind terrain. I chanced a glance over my shoulder out the left-aft window. The airbursts from the flak were falling behind. They hadn't kept up with my turn, and we were quickly getting beyond their range. Even better, I saw Juda 22 making their run-in, but with defenses still focused on us, our wingman was in the clear for the moment. The random approach tactic was working.

"Pilot, Nav. Escape point is 70 klicks ahead. I have programmed in a holding pattern. Right turns, legs 10 klicks."

"Very good," I breathed, releasing some of the tension. "We'll hold until the rest of the formation can rejoin, and we will Return to Base—RTB—together. Co, check in with Creature 10, advise him of our status."

Ruth got on the radio. *"Creature 10, Juda 20 Lead, checking in as fragged. We're holding as designated awaiting two to rejoin."*

"Copy Juda 20, this is Creature. I have words from Salem Actual that Juda 22 and 23 have dropped successfully and are inbound to your position as fragged. I will join up Tail-End-Charlie and escort you back to Salem as planned. Be advised, it was a bit hairy up here. I'm down to one drone." He still sounded almost bored. Fighter pilots. Go figure.

"Copy that Creature, you're an angel. See you momentarily," the Co signed off.

Our holding point was a random fix far from any populated areas or defenses. Enemy fighters would be the only threat here, and we could detect them coming from hundreds of clicks away. By the time we had completed our first orbit, Juda 22 had arrived, and another turn after that, Juda 23 made it, albeit with a few holes. Creature 11 was indeed just in trail of Juda 23. *"Juda 20 flight cleared to rejoin, and report status."*

"Lead, Juda 22, no alibis, status Alpha 1."

"Lead, Juda 23, one alibi, injured jumper with minor shrapnel injury. Status Alpha 2 for booster hydraulic system leak due to battle damage. No assistance required. We can stick with you."

Alibi was brevity for any jumper or cargo that wasn't dropped. Alpha status was a report of any mechanical issues with their ship. Alpha 1 meant nothing was wrong, Alpha 2 was minor malfunctions, and Alpha 3 a severe problem. I took over the radio for a moment just to reassure my wingmen that the Mike Charlie was paying attention. *"Juda 20 Lead copies all. Juda 23, will you need medical response upon landing?"*

"Negative Lead, jumper is ambulatory and stable. Minor cuts and bruises only."

"Very well, Juda 20 flight close to wedge formation and we will commence ascent. Break, Break. Creature 10, we're going when

you give us the all clear."

"Juda 20, Creature 10. Picture is clear. I am in position, Tail-End-Charlie, and will cover your ascent."

"Copy Creature. Juda 20 flight commencing ascent now. All ships maintain radio silence until reaching orbit." Then I directed the Co, "Get on the D-link. Advise Salem we are on ascent to orbit and relay our status."

The Nav, his tone back to that of a human calculator, "Pilot, next heading is 115, commence ascent in 80 klicks, ascent path plus 35."

"Thanks Caleb." I switched to using first names, hoping dropping formality would help relax the crew. "Ruth, you wanna fly the approach?"

"No thanks, Sir." She held her hand out palm down. Her face was calm and professional as always, but her hand was shaking like a leaf in the wind.

"Yeah, me too," I replied with total understanding. I kicked on the autopilot and settled into my seat as the Samson pitched up and began its crawl back to orbit.

Ascent

Our ascent back to orbit began smooth. We were beyond range of ground-based defenses, and no hostile fighters were in the area. If it stayed that way, it would be a routine trip back to the carrier. I took the lull in the action to offer up a quick, prayer that we had made it through the drop. I prayed for the troops on the ground and the fate of Creature 12, finally for the safety of Reuben and Levi flights. I kept it silent of course, a prayer wasn't something my crew would understand.

Perhaps my prayer was too little, too late, because just then Ruth perked up. "Pilot, we just got a new D-link message from Salem Actual. Ground troops are encountering heavier than expected resistance from the enemy. Reuben and Levi flights report battle damage and numerous alibis. They had to waive off due to concentrated enemy fire. The ground commander is requesting close air support."

This was bad news. I glanced at our tactical display. Creature was still Tail-End-Charlie. Our flight path was currently clear. If it remained so, we didn't need him back there. I broke radio silence and reached out. *"Creature 10, Juda Lead, you copy that last D-link from Salem Actual?"*

"I did indeed, Juda. Whatcha thinkin'?"

"I see no threats on the board for us. If you have ordnance, you have more important things to do back dirt side."

"I concur, Juda. Picture remains clear. I have a few rounds and rockets left, as does my wing drone. I'm sure those Marines could use 'em."

"Roger that, Creature, you are cleared off. Good Hunting."

And just like that, Creature's icon on the tactical display dropped back and disappeared. We continued to climb, passing through the middle layers of atmosphere.

I.F.E

The ascent was broken by a high-pitched, insistent *chirp* from the Flight Engineer's panel, followed instantly by a dull, red light flashing on the central warning display.

"Warning light, Utility Hydraulic Pressure, Eng!" the Co snapped, the tension instantly returning to the cockpit.

"I see it," Noah replied, his voice a tight thread of concentration. "Pressure is fluctuating… dropping rapidly. Pilot, you're losing Utility System boost!"

There was a "ding" indicated the autopilot had given up. I grabbed the yoke and immediately felt the change in controls. The *Samson* was becoming a stubborn, half-dead beast. In the thinner air, the utility system provided half the power to our thrust vectoring vanes. Without it, the subtle adjustments that kept us climbing cleanly were gone. I had to wrench the yoke to effect a small change in our climb angle.

"I've got it," I grunted, fighting the yoke. "Controls are sluggish. Eng, check for obvious leaks, run the Utility Hydraulic Failure Checklist. Nav, get me an updated time to orbit and a damage assessment estimate for Salem."

Noah's voice became the steady, rapid singsong of procedure. "Utility Hydraulic Failure Checklist acknowledged. Reservoir quantity check… it's zero. We have complete system loss, Pilot. Pump failure likely due to battle damage. Shutting off power to the pumps before we have a fire!"

"Urrgh" I grunted, struggling with controls. "Must have been some flak hit near the tail. A slow bleeder."

"Pilot," the Eng continued, "we've successfully bypassed the system for the ascent, but we're going to have significant problems on landing. We have lost half our control boost for the atmospheric phase, and the landing gear is Utility System dependent as well."

The Co leaned forward, her composure tested. "The manual gear extension requires the Eng and Loadmaster, sir. They have to crank the main gear down with wrenches."

"I know the drill, Co," I replied. "Noah, get the Loadmasters on the line. I want you two and Mary in the cargo bay as soon as we level out in orbit. Samuel will need to be the intercom relay." I took a deep breath. "This is going to be a hard day for the maintenance chief. We're coming back with a problem."

For the next few minutes, the cabin was filled with the heavy grunts and strained commands as I wrestled the dropship into orbit using raw strength, compensating for the dead controls. Once we leveled out, I kicked the autopilot on for the cruise phase. It could handle straight and level for a few minutes. The immediate struggle was over, but the final, deadly challenge loomed.

"Pilot," the Eng called over the intercom. "We're making the run-through now. Mary is on the hydraulic pump handle. I'm on the visual."

I pictured the cramped, manual process: the two of them working in the loud, dark recesses of the cargo bay, using hand tools to force two massive landing gear into place.

A few agonizing minutes later, a heavy *thunk* vibrated through the hull. "Pilot, we've got the right main gear down and locked! Good green indicator! We're proceeding to the left."

Then, the strain in the Eng's voice was clear. "Pilot, Loadmaster and I are putting full torque on the handle. It's not moving. The gear bay door must be jammed. We can't get the left main to drop."

I gripped the yoke, a wave of cold dread hitting me. *This is it.* "Copy, Eng. Attempt the manual blow down and then abort. Do not injure yourselves. We are landing with two main gears down and locked, and the left main up. Prepare the cargo bay for an emergency, one-sided landing. Loadmasters, clear the cargo deck."

The Eng's voice was professional but weary. "Copy that, Pilot. Preparing for emergency landing."

I looked at the Nav. "Caleb, relay the full status to Salem Actual. Declare an In Flight Emergency - IFE. I need a clear approach path and a dedicated emergency response team on the landing deck. We're coming in hot, heavy, and sideways." I looked at the Co, Captain Ruth. Her shaking hand was now resting, palm-down, on the center console, but her eyes met mine, absolutely steady. "Co, strap in. Time to earn our pay."

Final Approach

The slow, steady burn back to the *Salem* was agonizing. The cockpit's usual working hum had been replaced by the quiet anxiety of three people pretending everything was routine. Above it all, a frantic Eng and his Loadmaster relay were working desperately in the back, but the left gear remained stubbornly stuck in the half-open bay.

I was flying the approach profile manually, and the *Samson* was a brute. Without utility hydraulic boost, the large vectoring vanes felt like they were set in concrete. Even minute course corrections required a heavy-handed, counter-intuitive shove on the yoke, and the resulting response was always delayed, heavy, and excessive. I was constantly over-controlling, wrenching the stick to one side only to realize the ship was overshooting, forcing me to haul it back the other way.

"Pilot, Nav," Caleb's voice was strained as he watched the intercept vector on his screen. "We are approaching the critical intercept gate. Current velocity is plus five. Adjusting intercept path seven degrees right, now."

I pushed the yoke right, fighting the resistance. It felt like trying to steer a barge with a wooden plank. The

Samson responded a full second later, slowly pitching over. I corrected instantly, but the ship overshot the new line.

I broke radio silence to address the other ships. *"Juda 20 flight, this is Juda 21. We have just become Alpha 3 for hydraulic failure and are declaring an in flight emergency. Juda 22, you take the lead for Juda 20 flight. Proceed to contingency holding point Bravo and contact Salem Approach Control. Good luck."*

"Copy, Juda 21. Juda 22 has the Lead, proceeding to Bravo. Godspeed, Juda 21."

Just like that, the three dropships that had flown the mission as one were split, leaving us completely isolated.

"Pilot, you're right drifting further right on your intercept path," the Nav warned. "Need a hard correction left. Now."

The consequences of being off—bouncing off the *Salem's* hull or missing the carrier entirely—flashed through my mind. I applied heavy pressure left, using my shoulder and arm strength.

"Hold that input, hold it!" the Co commanded, her eyes fixed on the attitude indicator, ignoring the sweat beading on my forehead. The maneuver finally brought us back onto the line but the loss of control was terrifying. We were relearning how to fly this ship in real time.

"Nav, confirm we are on the course and on climb path."

"Pilot, you are on the bar and on the ball. Holding steady. Beginning final deceleration in 5 … 4 … 3 … 2 …slow down, slow down now." he chanted, this time with complete calm. The braking thruster fired and we all lurched forward in our seats.

Ruth reached for the comms. *"Salem Tower, Juda 21 Emergency. Single-ship, on final approach.Two green, one red. Full stop."*

"Juda 21, Salem Tower copies. We have your status. Carrier will maintain course and station-keeping. Bay three is cleared and foam-down is complete. You are cleared for landing. Emergency crews are standing by."

The Eng, now back in his seat began the last checklist, the litany a calming anchor in the mounting chaos. "Before Landing Checklist."

"Acknowledged, Co."

"Seat belts and shoulder harnesses. Fastened, Unlocked"

"Pilot," "Copilot" "Nav," "Eng," "Primary Load," "Secondary Load"

"Landing Gear."

"Two green, one red and locked up. Checked Pilot."

"Checked Copilot"

"Retro-thruster Check."

"All attitude control thrusters armed and responsive. Retro-burn sequence nominal."

"Cargo, secure, Loadmaster"

"Before Landing Checklist complete…"

The *Samson* drifted into the final approach zone, her massive nose looming over the docking bay. The zero-g environment magnified the difficulty; I had to continually fire the main thrusters and adjust the vectoring to maintain relative position with the *Salem*. The carrier deck was massive, but it felt as small as a postage stamp.

"Pilot, final descent rate is critical," the Nav warned, his voice a low, urgent murmur. "Remember the high gear. You're coming down heavy on the right."

I could see the deck now, a grid of lights rushing up to meet us. I focused entirely on the nose of the ship. The goal wasn't just landing—it was *touching down* with zero lateral movement and absolute minimal downward velocity, then keeping the damaged left wing from smashing into the deck.

I triggered the final retro-burn, throttling down the main power. The *Samson* hung suspended just over the deck, the airlock lights blazing. I fought the heavy controls one last time, gently nudging the nose right to compensate for the single deployed gear.

"Ten meters… five… three…" the Co called out the altitude, her voice now a prayer of its own.

I eased the last bit of thrust. The right side of the *Samson* connected with the deck with a metallic *shhhhk*, followed by a shuddering groan. It held. The right struts took the full weight. For a terrifying second, the ship listed hard to port, the wing dipping toward the deck. If it settled too fast, the hull would buckle.

With a final, desperate shove on the yoke and a burst from the remaining functioning thrusters, I managed to keep the heavy wing airborne just long enough for the emergency magnetic clamps on the carrier deck to fire and bite deep into the hull. The *Samson's* list was arrested as the clamp slammed into place, and locked down.

The ship stopped shaking. The klaxons stopped.
Silence.

The Co was the first to speak, her voice completely calm, as if she'd just landed a simulator. *"Salem Tower, Juda 21 secure on deck. We made it."*

I leaned my forehead against the dash, the breath I didn't know I was holding finally escaping my lungs. *Thank you.* The prayer had found its way out after all.

The battle for Sidon is joined but the battle for humanity

has just begun!

VALLEY OF SHADOW, *A Christian Military Space Opera*
Coming Spring 2026

If you enjoyed this journey, please **Follow Allan Grandgenett on Amazon** to receive an automatic notification the moment *Valley of Shadow* is released.

Thank you for reading.

About the Author

Allan Grandgenett is a twenty-year veteran of the US Air Force. He served first as a maintainer and then as a pilot—a background that provides the technical "bones" for the starships and tactics in his novels. Today, he continues to serve the Air Force as a civil servant in the field of Flight Simulation, ensuring the next generation of aviators is ready for the cockpit.

Originally from an Iowa farm, Allan now calls the natural beauty of Arkansas home. When he isn't at the flight simulator or the writing desk, he is likely enjoying the Arkansas outdoors or spending time with his wife and family.

For Allan, the "Military" in Military Sci-Fi isn't just about the hardware; it's about the heart. Having lived the life of an aviator, he understands that the most intense battles often happen in the quiet moments between sorties—in the cockpit of the soul where faith and fear collide. His writing aims to capture that authentic military experience, honoring the camaraderie, the weight of command, and the quiet resilience required of those who serve.

Allan is a lifelong devotee of the Sci-Fi "greats," but as an author, he has a specific mission: clean science fiction. He is dedicated to writing "High-Octane, Low-Grit" adventures—stories that deliver the adrenaline of a space dogfight and the depth of military life without the profanity or graphic content of modern sci-fi. By focusing on family bonds, the strength of faith, and the resilience of the human spirit, Allan writes stories that can be shared across generations.

He believes that a good story should offer more than an escape; it should offer an anchor. By weaving timeless spiritual truths into the fabric of a futuristic universe, he hopes to leave his readers with a sense of hope that remains long after the engines of the *Galilee* have cooled.

Galilee Rising is his debut novel. Allan's mission to bring light to the deep reaches of space. He is currently at work on his next project, *Valley of Shadow* which continues to explore the intersection of technology and the human heart.

You can connect with me on:

🌐 https://www.amazon.com/author/algrandgenett